A TALE OF STORMS

TALES OF FAIRY | BOOK THREE

ANN DAYLEVIEW

Onyx Fire Press, LLC

ISBN: 978-1-7363705-5-1

Printed in the United States of America

Design by Graphics by Geka

Dedication

For the angry ones,

Who are angry, grieving, and carry quiet hope that this broken world can heal. May these pages remind you that even in the darkest times, there is power in your voice and magic in refusing to look away.

DEDICATION

CHAPTER I
Freddie

Gray fog rolled into Freddie's mind. Screaming, cold, blood, death... Her stomach twisted as she shook her head, trying to rid it of the nightmarish memories from just a few months ago. The bookshop's scent of old paper and cat slowly brought her back to the present. She crouched on the ground, rickety shelves loomed on either side of her. Among their contents were faded tomes with pages that had been yellow for at least a couple of decades, some even centuries. Beside her, Pelrin's long blond hair curtained his face as he poured over a book, oblivious to the thoughts that had ripped her away from this moment.

Taking a deep breath, Freddie returned to the book she was supposed to be reading. The dissociative episodes, as her therapist called them, were getting less frequent with every month, but they still left her feeling chilled as though some bit of Winter was permanently embedded in her skin. Usually, she'd go to Amanda, or even Raul, for comfort when she was dealing with feelings too big for her body. But now, that wasn't possible, and it was all her fault. Getting them away from Elessea was no easy feat, but bringing them here would be nearly impossible for Pelrin to accomplish on his own. She sucked in a breath to disguise the sob that was threatening to pull itself from her body. They weren't safe as long as they were in Fairy, and if something happened to their sleeping bodies... She pressed her trembling lips together and forced herself to squint at the tiny text on the page.

Hobs have the power to brew potent sleeping drafts by mixing unicorn tears with one of their own eyelashes. The result is far more powerful than herbal remedies and will leave the drinker refreshed and energized when they wake.

Useless. Every book she found was utterly useless. And with the police all but giving up on their case, she was her friends' only hope of returning home. The images of Raul's mother doubled over, her body trembling in the arms of his sister, and Amanda's brother shouting at the police flashed in her mind. Freddie gasped. No, she had to save them—no one else even knew where to look.

"Fred, you okay?" Pelrin tucked his hair behind his pointed ear and cocked his head in her direction.

"I'm—I'm fine." The words were a lie, but they seemed to put others at ease. She hadn't been okay in months, but now she was past the period when not okay was acceptable.

"Did you find something? You gasped..."

She shook her head and closed the book with a huff of dust. Plucking another from their pile titled *All Fae Curse*, she feigned an avid interest in the introduction, which outlined the different types of fae. Brown and red fae, according to the book, were barely magical, not much more remarkable than humans. Freddie scowled. Funny how half the fae realms had been conquered by such unremarkable fae. Flipping the book over, she spied the author's name and punched it into her phone. A black and white image of a wizened dryad appeared at the top of the search results—of course, he was a green fae.

Pelrin's forces were clinging to Summer by the barest thread after losing the capital to those "unremarkable fae". If the author of this book were still alive, he would probably go mad with shock at the state of the war.

Freddie skimmed past the fanciful descriptions of green and gold fae. On the next page, was a hand-drawn map of the fae realms. She was about to read more when Pelrin nudged her.

"This one talks about a sleeping curse put upon a human royal by an enraged fairy. It says here: when the human princess fell asleep, so did her kingdom." Excitement tinged his voice as he flipped through the next few pages. Freddie closed her book over her finger and moved closer to lean over his broad shoulder.

"They must have found some way to break it. There aren't any kingdoms of sleeping people now." The story sounded familiar, like something she might have read for AP Euro, then promptly forgotten after the exam last year.

"Uh, well, I think I know how that one was solved. It's a common tale we learn about in school, but it's not helpful."

"What?" Hope hovered in her chest, fragile as a naga's egg.

"It's just...true love's kiss broke it."

She blinked. "What did the curse say? Maybe there's another way to interpret it?"

Pelrin shook his head and pointed to a line of text. *The kiss of true love is the only way to lift the curse and awaken her.* "But how are we going to know who to kiss? How would we even begin to find their true love?" Pelrin lifted the book as though to throw it at the opposite shelf, but a low growl made him freeze. An orange tabby poked its head around the corner and pinned him with its yellow glare. Lowering the book slowly, Pelrin placed it in their done pile and avoided the cat's eyes. It let out a warning chirp before continuing on its patrol of the shop.

Freddie twisted, cracking her back, and went back to reading. The pages were so thin, it was like turning over winter leaves. With each moment, she feared the page might tear. Still, she skimmed for any hint of curses. The next few pages were an overview of the fae realms. She frowned. Wasn't this book supposed to be all about curses? Drawing her finger down a page outlining Autumn, she paused.

Each object gifted to the gold fae rulers was imbued with the power of the realm's magic. However, the transitional realms contain not only the powers of their elements but also their season. In the case of Autumn, the Staff of Wind holds the power of change. It was most famously used during the formation of the Treaty of Realms. Fae used its powers to break a curse that turned a prominent human ally into a bird to prevent them from arguing on behalf of the magical community.

She froze, her hands trembling on the page. It broke a curse. If this staff did that, did that mean the ring could too? Freddie flipped through the pages to find a note on Spring, but it only said that the object gifted to Spring remained a mystery and its powers were unknown. She twisted the band around her finger, then pulled it off and shoved it in her pocket where it would stay. Aiden's amber eyes burning with betrayal, still haunted her dreams. She didn't need to look at a constant reminder of him. Still, she didn't dare abandon the protection it offered her.

"Hey, Pel. What about this?" She flipped back to the page with the staff, and Pelrin glanced over.

"Sure, a magical wishing stick would be great. Do you know where it is?"

"Wishing stick?"

He grunted as he shifted to the side, tucking his wings closer to his body to prevent them from knocking over any books. "Those tines on the staff, each one holds a wish. Once all of them are gone, it's just as useful as all of the other objects. But no one has seen it in centuries, so who knows how many—if any—are left."

Freddie's shoulders slouched. "Right. I guess this is pointless, too."

"Keep reading, maybe there's a clue about where the staff is located." The pity in Pelrin's voice was nearly palpable. She supposed he might be right, after all, the staff was the only thing that *might* be able to break the curse. Unlike everything else, they definitely knew that would not.

"I have to go, it's getting late, and I'm not supposed to stay out past four." Ever since she'd snuck out to rescue Pelrin, her mom had all but air-tagged her. Freddie pulled out her phone and stared at the Uber app on her phone. Her name, "Wyn", was written at the top, a not-so-subtle reminder that her parents had control of her account. While she was fine taking public transit, her parents had insisted on Ubers. They were "safer", aka trackable.

"I should be getting back too. I'll know if something big happens, but my uncle shouldn't have to handle things on his own for too long."

They looked at each other for an uncomfortable minute. Pelrin's stare seemed to want more emotions than she was ready to give. Freddie could barely deal with her feelings; his were far too much for her to handle. Especially not after Aiden. Her heart thudded painfully, and she stood, clutching the shelf for support.

Pelrin was on his feet beside her in moments as though he feared she was too weak to stand. She shot him a glare, and he grinned back sheepishly. If she'd thought he was overprotective before, now that she'd nearly died in Fairy, he acted as though she was made of glass. All she wanted to do was disappear into herself, but she knew she couldn't. Maybe once she freed Amanda, Raul, and Jefferson, but she couldn't give in to her own desires before that.

"Are you getting that one?" Pelrin asked, gesturing to the fragile book in her hands.

Freddie glanced at the red sticker indicating the price in the three digits and shook her head. "It's way too expensive."

"I've got it."

"Are you sure?" She shifted. Usually, she made it clear she wanted nothing to do with Pelrin's gifts. It was a slippery slope from that to indulging in his late-night company and going on dates. Just because she and Aiden weren't together anymore didn't mean she'd run to Pelrin. But this wasn't about her. This was for her friends, and they were as much his friends as they were hers...

"Yeah, it's not that pricey." He grinned, flashing his disgustingly dazzling smile. If the dictionary had pictures, his image would be next to "storybook prince". He was your typical white, blond boy, with blue eyes, but his fae magic made everything about him more beautiful. From the perfect smoothness of his skin to the brilliant glow of his eyes, Pelrin was *perfect*. At least on the outside. No matter how gorgeous he was, it couldn't make her forget the devastation that had come with his admission of cheating on her. She'd forgiven him, but that and getting back together were two completely different things.

The orange tabby rounded the corner again and eyed the book in her hand as she passed it to Pelrin. It seemed to say, "Don't you even think about stealing that". Freddie made an exaggerated show of walking to the counter, but still, the creature followed them and leapt into the arms of a grizzled, human woman eating peanuts.

She snapped one in half as she looked from Pelrin's wings to the book in his hands. "We have glamour detectors." Her fingers drummed on a finger-sized iron brick, and Pelrin recoiled. He put on a brave front, but Freddie saw past the bravado. The iron crown

Mab had forced him to wear had left scars, even though the burns had healed.

Pelrin ducked his head and fumbled in his pocket to pull out a thick black credit card. She snatched it out of his hand and punched the number into a dated machine. Making a note in her book, the woman nodded as the machine beeped, and he returned his card to his pocket. "Good day," he rasped and nearly stumbled out of the shop.

Freddie followed him, the heat of the afternoon sun pressing down on her and the humidity making her suck in a breath. Summer in DC was nearly unbearable. Perhaps there was a reason it was so awful here; the politicians were practically demons after all.

"Call me if you need *anything*." Pelrin pulled her into a one-armed hug.

She hunched into his side and nodded. "Just take care of them, Pel."

"Of course, they're safe in Verbena. Oberon won't waste forces attacking us where we're strong. That louse would rather pick us off on the mainland until we're cornered."

Freddie bit her lip. How long would it be until the island off the Summer coast was no longer a stronghold and Oberon could attack? There was a tightness around Pelrin's eyes and forced smile. No doubt, he too was worried. With his mother still trapped in the capital, all the responsibility of what to do next fell to him. Would he truly prioritize their friends?

An Uber pulled up in front of the store, and Freddie checked her phone to ensure it was the one she'd ordered. "I'll keep reading. Who knows, maybe I'll find something." There was scarcely any optimism in her voice, and from the half-hearted shrug Pelrin gave her, he seemed to feel similarly.

They said their goodbyes, and she slid into the car. Freddie breathed out as she leaned against the seats and stared out the windows. The city slipped into more residential streets, and the car came to a stop in front of a brownstone. She got out and waved to the driver as they pulled away.

The place she was supposed to call home summoned an instinctual scowl across her features. It didn't feel like home, and she doubted it ever would. Her true home, the place she'd grown up in and the place where her parents had abandoned her, was back in Pennsylvania. This was the location the Fallus's decided to keep them like caged birds. She let out a breath. By the end of the summer, she'd be eighteen and free to find her own place near school...if she could afford it.

The scents of mashed potatoes and Costco rotisserie chicken washed over her as she stepped inside. Her father sat in the living room, eyes closed, as the news played on the TV. In the open space, Freddie could see directly into the dining room where the table was set. Blessedly, there were only three plates, which meant none of her father's disgusting colleagues would be over to ruin the meal.

Her mother's back was to her at the stove, and a marble island separated her from the rest of the house. Freddie slung her bag over the railing to the top floors and kicked off her shoes.

"Perfect timing," her mother called over the newscaster. "I'm just about done here. Can you take the silverware to the table?"

Freddie didn't respond but crossed the living room to the island and set the forks and knives on the folded pieces of paper towel her mom had laid out. Steam from the mashed potatoes wafted up to her, teasing her with their buttery aroma.

"Earl?" Her mother clapped loudly, and her father jerked awake.

"Sorry, is it ready?"

"Come sit." She glided over to her seat at the table's right—Freddie took the spot on the left while her father sat in the middle.

Silence settled over them as Freddie picked at her food. It wasn't unusual; ever since she'd returned, it'd been hard to speak with them. After all, they had moved while she'd been held captive in Fairy. Her father had chosen his job over her, and her mother had followed. The guilt was clear in the way they acted around her, rarely saying no to any request. It was only when it came to the obsessive safety measures that they overruled her.

"I have some good news," her father said.

Freddie jerked. Her father rarely spoke, preferring to express himself in grunts and expressions. To break a silence and start a conversation was purely her mother's territory.

Like her father typically did, her mother didn't respond. However, she beamed as though struggling to hold back words.

"I'm going to Europe next week for the rest of the summer. We have some business in London."

Freddie had long learned that asking her father about his job would only make her angry. Still, she couldn't help but roll her eyes at his mention of London being in Europe. Hadn't they just fought to be free of their *fae-loving* brethren on the mainland? "Have fun."

"It should be. Not just for me, but we thought this would be a great opportunity to get you out and about too."

"There's a lot more to do and see over there," her mother said. "I know it's been hard since Amanda was lost, but you can't just stop living because of it. She'd want this for you."

Freddie glared. Her mother had purposefully only brought up her human friend, even though she knew Freddie and Raul had been just as close. Not to mention Amanda's vampire boyfriend had been part of their friend group too. All of her friends had been ripped away from her. Except Pelrin, which was little consolation. "They're not dead. They're in Fairy, not that anyone is doing anything about it."

"The borders have been closed since the war began. Not even the police are allowed over."

"And the FIDs? They can't do anything? Isn't that the entire point of the *Fae* investigative department? It's not even that bad over there, I—"

"London is just the kind of experience you need. Besides, you'll even have a friend going. That girl from your class is interning with us. That one you hung out with when you briefly returned to us between *escapades*." The disgust in her father's voice was more than apparent, and a cold shiver of realization shot through her.

Her fork clattered to her plate. "Mallory? You expect me to spend the entire summer dragged off to a foreign country with *Mallory*? I'm good at home." Anything would be better than spending extra time with the girl who'd publicly called her crazy after the first time she'd returned from Fairy. The word frenemy was too kind for their relationship; downright enemies would be a better description.

"If you expect us to pay for summer school, then you *will* accompany your father on this trip, young lady." Her mother tightened her grip on her utensils and made a show of sawing at her chicken.

"You would let all the work I busted my butt over to graduate go to waste?" Tears pricked the corners of her eyes. They couldn't seriously be doing this to her. She was so close to being free.

Her father grunted. "I was hoping you'd be excited and would consider it an early birthday gift, but the decision has been made. We're leaving next week."

CHAPTER 2
Aiden

Aiden tensed as the smell of burnt flesh and spicy raw magic rose in a black cloud from the other side of the grassy hill. Twisted limbs and weapon shards stretched up like grim flowers amid the haze of spent spells. Sucking in a breath, he clenched his fingers as he stared out at the silent battlefield.

Freezing frosts. It was over—far too late to make a difference. If Mare had just roused him earlier, he could've made it. Even with his magic only half recovered from Oberon's draining, he could've done something. Now, bodies of brown and green fae alike lay in mangled heaps. It would have been impossible to determine the battle's victor if not for the lack of fairy soldiers on patrol and magical barriers around the field. If the green fae had won, they would've ensured they held the land they'd fought so hard for. This smoking pit could only mean one thing: Oberon had won, but barely. At least that was some relief.

A shadow beside him stretched and solidified into the form of a young, dark-skinned woman. "Are we too late? Who won?" Mare's black eyes widened as she stared past him to the horror beyond. "Curses, we *are* late."

Aiden shrugged. "We won, and that's all that matters."

"But Oberon isn't going to be happy that we lost so many soldiers. He might— "

"There's nothing he can do that he hasn't already."

It hadn't been too long ago when the threat of their Majesties' punishment was enough to spike his fear. But ever since Mare's mom had devoured his despair, the anxiety had lessened. It also helped that Mab, the more *creative* of the two, was dead. The thought sank in his stomach like a stone.

Before her death, Oberon would at least leave him with enough energy to stumble back to his rooms. Now, each night the king would drain him until blackness eclipsed his vision—a punishment for killing her, regardless of the intent.

"I'm just looking out for you. Oberon has been less than thrilled with you of late."

"You think I haven't noticed? I murdered his wife." Though technically Wyn had killed her, he'd just been her weapon. Wyn's betrayal still burned like a picked scab. He tried to shove such thoughts to the back of his mind, but even the slightest reminder seared.

"You lost him Winter. He probably mourns that loss more than Mab." Aiden opened his mouth to cut her off, but she held up a hand. "Though really that human girl was to blame."

Aiden's jaw tightened, and he forced his features into the mask he adopted any time someone mentioned Wyn. "It was a lot of things that led to Winter's fall. I doubt a human would have been successful without the prince."

"All I know is I wouldn't want to be her. Oberon might see hunting her down as a waste of resources now, but after the war, he'll surely want revenge."

Aiden swallowed hard. The thought of Wyn dead pained him nearly as much as that of her betrayal. He couldn't get lost in such distractions. Not now. "Let's just figure out what happened here. The human doesn't matter."

Mare nodded, and they moved in opposite directions across the field, looking for clues as to how the green fae managed to hold out for so long. Aiden massaged his temples and stepped around a goblin with vines sprouting from his mouth and eyes. Why did Mare have to bring up Wyn after he tried to put all his energy into forgetting her?

What she'd done had made sense. He could even see how she might have thought killing Mab had been helping him. But couldn't she have at least given him some hint as to her plans? It was bad enough Oberon used him for his magic, but having Wyn do the same broke something in him. He'd loved her, and against all reason, he *still* loved her, but she'd used him. How was he supposed to rationalize that? Perhaps it didn't matter. After all, Oberon didn't give him the freedom he'd once used to visit her, and even if he did, getting caught would mean a horrible death for them both. It wasn't worth it.

Aiden crouched to study a mark in the blackened ground. It was deep and tinged with ash. An ifrit wouldn't have the power to do this, it was the work of a gold fae. His fingers curled into fists as the image of the Summer Prince—his arms wrapped around Wyn—shoved to the front of his mind. While he might not put *her* in danger, it'd cause him no pain to end the prince. It was *his* fault after all Aiden was in this mess in the first place.

He ran a finger through the artful twists in the blackened earth. Whoever this warrior had been, he knew more of their magic than brute force. Aiden let out a huff. It was probably not made by the prince but by his uncle. He flexed his fingers before rubbing them off on his pants. The general had been the kindest of the Summer royals when he'd been forced into their court after their king had murdered his parents. Still, mercy wasn't something Aiden was ready to spare the man should he confront him again. He'd still refused to acknowledge the brutal torments Aiden had faced at the hands of the prince. Perhaps he was not much better than the rest, only with a different facade.

He rose and followed more marks indicating the general's presence until he saw Mare's form ahead, kneeling in a patch of glittering dirt.

"We're getting close to the Nightmare Plains; there's sand in the earth." She stood and gestured around her.

"Are you saying they crossed from Winter through the Plains?"

"Of course not, that'd be suicide. They probably went through troll territory."

"And that's less suicidal?"

Mare rolled her eyes. "You faced a nightmare, *and* my mom. Do you really think a troll is their equal?"

Aiden huffed a humorless laugh and stepped forward to examine the ground. It could have been heat from the general's magic, but that wouldn't explain why it was so dark. He scooped some up and let the cool bits fall through his fingers. It was soft as ash. A blast of flame wouldn't cause this.

"They must be using something besides the crown. I've never seen anything like this, have you?" He straightened and brushed the remaining dust off his pants.

"It looks like magical residue from some sort of creature...What is that?"

Aiden followed where she pointed and stooped to pick up what appeared to be a feather glinting like a blade in the hazy sunlight. It was stiff and far too heavy to be from an ordinary bird. He turned it over and then stifled a yelp, dropping it to the ground in a soft huff of dust.

"Are you okay?"

"Fine." Silver blood leaked from a thin line on his finger. His magic would heal the cut quickly, though it was still painful.

"We need to get back. Take that. Oberon will be wanting answers."

Tucking the feather into the pocket of his black leather jerkin, Aiden looked to Mare, then pulled on his magic to wend back to the Autumn stronghold. The world blurred, then solidified before a high-tiered building in a clearing surrounded by flame-colored trees. The air around them was earthy with a crisp bite that chilled his cheeks. It would've been pleasant if not for the foreboding dread building in the pit of his stomach.

It was so different from the palace in Winter. Where there'd been sharp edges of glittering ice, their place in Autumn was made of wood, painted in red and gold to mimic the forest around them. Each of its tiers was made from interlocking pieces carved in delicate curls. The Winter Palace, it seemed, had been built to intimidate, while the Meditation Center was inviting, almost.

Mare appeared by his side, and they walked up the wooden steps. The eyes of the brown fae who guarded the stronghold followed them inside, but none dared speak. It was a change from Winter where they'd been emboldened to call him "dog" and other such foul names, which seemed to amuse Mab. Now she was dead, by his hand as far as they knew, the other soldiers were less inclined to push their luck.

They stepped into a large, open room. It'd once been used for communal meditation, allowing the Autumn fae to connect their minds to one another. They'd been so practiced in the art of peace, it'd been far too easy to defeat them. Aiden swallowed hard at the memory of their screams and the acrid stench of the smoke from each ransacked village.

Now, soldiers sparred in the open space. They stepped aside as he and Mare walked past and followed the stairs to the top level. Each step seemed to chill the blood in his veins until he stood trembling before the door to Oberon's chambers.

"Aiden?" Mare nudged him.

He straightened and tried to look relaxed. "I'm fine, let's just get this over with."

She looked like she wanted to say something else, but sighed and knocked three times. There was a shuffling, as though someone was moving piles of paper. Footsteps, deliberate but hard, sounded from the other side.

"Enter," came Oberon's voice. Mare pushed open the door to reveal a man leaning casually against a plain wooden desk. He appeared to be in his late thirties with sweeping brown hair and dark, twinkling eyes. He'd almost look kindly, if not for the sinister expression marring his handsome features. "I expect you have good news for me?"

Flicking a nervous glance at Aiden, Mare stepped forward. "We arrived after the battle had concluded. It seemed to have been short-lived, and our side defeated the Summer forces."

"And what did the patrol soldiers say happened? I hardly think Summer would allow us an easy victory."

She fidgeted with the end of her braid but responded in an unfazed tone. "There were none. They were all dead, both sides."

"Are you telling me all the soldiers I sent to protect the pass are dead? That is no small loss, and you have nothing to show for it." He snarled, pushing off from the desk and advancing towards them.

"We studied the battle. It seemed the Summer general led the attack, but the prince had yet to show himself. And there was one more thing." Aiden pulled the feather gingerly from his pocket and showed it to Oberon. "We found this amongst a pile of black ash."

Oberon stepped closer to inspect their findings. "No wonder." He huffed a laugh. "A stymphalian."

Aiden looked at Mare, who wrinkled her brow. It appeared she'd never heard of that creature either. Although when it came to Fairy, their education at Mab and Oberon's side was severely lacking.

Oberon seemed to notice their confusion and scoffed. "I suppose it is my fault for failing so much in your teachings. Stymphalians are rare creatures that can boost the power of those with fae blood by taking it from others. Those fools in Summer must've thought that only applied to those who could use magic; however, our forces would've gotten a boost too. No wonder it was over so fast. Keep it, maybe it could give you the power to *win* me a battle for once."

Aiden tucked the feather back into his jerkin, and they watched as Oberon turned and stared at the desk, lost in thought. The minutes ticked by as Aiden stood stiffly, hoping Oberon would forget he was there. His fate was inevitable; whether or not Oberon was pleased meant little. The rebel king would still rip out Aiden's magic as he had every night in the eight years he'd lived with them. Somehow, without Mab sharing in the magic, Oberon's greed had intensified, making the process even more miserable. Perhaps it was just Oberon capitalizing on the increase in magic, or maybe he was overcompensating for his ever-aging human body.

"You're dismissed," Oberon snapped.

Mare jerked her head at the door and looked at Aiden. He didn't move; the dismissal hadn't been meant for him. After a moment's hesitation, she took a step towards the door and paused.

"It was my fault we were late. I took too long to get ready and slowed Aiden down."

"I'll keep that in mind. Don't let it happen again." Oberon folded his arms across his chest. "Now go."

Mare hurried to the door, and with one last look at Aiden, she left him alone with Oberon. Silence fell over the room, as Oberon returned to his desk. He twirled the feather between his fingers, then looked up at Aiden.

"This war needs to end. We're so close." He sagged into his chair and reached for the box containing his crystal wand.

Aiden's limbs turned to stone, his eyes trained on the wand. *You've survived this before. It's not so bad.* Though the thoughts did little to comfort him against something his body knew so well.

"Nothing to add? Do you want this war to continue indefinitely?"

"I-uh..." He'd been used to Oberon's statements being rhetorical. "Of course not."

"I suppose I'll have little use for you after the war has ended. My wand has stored enough of your magic to ensure I live to a ripe old fae age."

Aiden's jaw fell open. He'd been drained every night since child-hood, and that was all for Oberon to stockpile his magic? What was the point in continuing to take it now? "You—you don't need me?"

The king let out a hah. "I never needed you. Now, though, it might give you more motivation to realize just how disposable you really are. You didn't truly think I was surviving day to day while being foolish enough to send you into *mortal* peril, did you?" He withdrew the glittering instrument, marveling at the way the light from the gas lamp shone through it.

Aiden opened and closed his mouth, but words failed to find their way to his lips. With a shuddering breath, he bowed his head. "You intend to kill me? Now?"

"Find me a way to quickly end this war, and I'll consider letting you keep your wretched existence once it's over." Oberon strode closer, tapping the wand against his palm. "Come, let's be done with this."

Aiden forced himself forward, his rationality telling him to step back, but the life debt forced him to obey. Kneeling before Oberon, he fixed his gaze upon a spot on the wood floor. Why did the man continue to do this to him when he had more than enough? Tears pricked at his eyes, not from sorrow, but for the first time in many years, from the frustration of not being able to fight back.

The wand touched his forehead, and the world exploded into white-hot pain. He struggled to maintain consciousness, but like every night recently, he failed.

Aiden woke to someone dragging him by the legs down the hall. He squinted up at one of the flickering sconces to see Mare's slim form at his ankles.

"I can help." A voice sounded from behind him. Aiden wanted to turn, but it took all his strength just to half open his eyes.

"We're almost there, Tati. I need you to get the door," Mare said. Tatiana sidestepped him and inched her curvy figure along the wall to haul open a plain door.

Knots in the wood floor bumped against Aiden's back as they dragged him inside and rolled him onto a soft mattress. He groaned, closing his eyes to savor the comfort. Usually, he slept with the other soldiers on a pallet in one of the training rooms. Though he missed the privacy of his own space, it was some comfort to be surrounded by others. Images of endless hours alone in Mab's dungeon flashed through his mind, and he shuddered. *It's over.*

"Aiden, are you awake?" Tatiana hovered over him, the tip of her dirty blonde braid brushing his cheek.

"Let him rest. He needs it."

Aiden fluttered his eyelids, struggling to keep them open. The mere thought of replying to Tatiana nearly sapped him of energy.

"Stop trying to stay awake and heal," Mare snapped.

He couldn't even give her a scornful look before sleep claimed him again.

When he woke next, it was to the giggling of Mare and Tatiana. Well, Tatiana, Mare didn't so much giggle as hum her amusement at whatever they were looking at. Slowly, he pushed himself up onto his elbows. The two were hunched over something in Tatiana's hands, so enthralled they hadn't noticed him.

"What's that?" His voice was weak, but speaking hardly pained him now.

Tatiana jumped, her eyes going wide and then softening. "It's a manga about the Autumn nobility before the fall—a romance." Mare's lip quirked, and she looked sidelong at the other girl.

"Autumn didn't have nobility before we took it. A council of representatives from the towns governed them."

"This book takes place before the first fall when gold fae ruled." Mare leaned back and draped an arm casually over her knee.

"The author is supposed to be some sort of long-lost Autumn princess!"

"Citizen." Mare rolled her eyes. "She's not a gold fae. And she's a Human Realm historian turned writer."

"Manga artist." Tatiana nudged Mare in the ribs. For a moment, they stared hard at one another as though to argue, but then turned away, blushing.

Something struggled in Aiden's chest as though tethered to his heart. He and Wyn had shared moments like that, but now... Now it was hard to think of her without remembering she'd hurt him, and yet still he ached to be with her. Why couldn't he have one thing in his life that was easy?

Tatiana scooted across the floor to where Aiden sat and held the manga out to him. She flipped to a random page where there were a plethora of images of a human woman, dressed in a flowing gown and adorned with jewels, and a fae man dressed in ancient-style robes. Aiden frowned and took the book, trying to make sense of the words.

"I must still be too tired to understand this. It's like reading backwards." He passed the book back to Tatiana, but she didn't take it.

"You have to read it right to left and top to bottom."

"Of course I do…" He pulled the book back towards him and let his mind try to parse through the new pattern of reading. It took a few minutes before he was fully comfortable flipping through the pages.

Typically, he wouldn't be interested in romance—just the premise dragged back thoughts of Wyn, but there was something about the Autumn fairy… He paused on a page that featured him in a throne room, holding an elegant staff. It was slim and had a emerald star at the top, surrounded by seven tines. Aiden flipped the page. The human broke off one of the tines, and some sort of light seemed to come from where she broke it.

There was a word bubble that read "I wish we could always be together". The relatable wish pained his heart. But on the next page, the human was drinking from one of the famous chalices from which the gold fae could share their power. She transformed into a fairy, and the two shared a kiss—a happy ending that would forever be out of his own reach.

"I've never heard of someone wishing to become fae, and it be granted. It's a stretch for something that's supposedly written by a historian."

Tatiana wrinkled her nose. "Well, it's fiction, but the staff is supposedly real. The Staff of Wind was said to be the most powerful of the four objects since anyone could use it."

"Are you sure? I thought only gold fae—"

"Yes, typically only gold fae can use the objects, but the staff has those little stick thingies around it, and when broken, they can grant anyone's wish. So, yeah, the hurricanes and powerful winds are for gold fae only, but the wishes..."

Aiden flexed his jaw. Not for the first time did he envy Tatiana's education, but he pushed the thought aside and stared back at the staff. "And you're sure it's true?"

"Yes! We learned about it in school."

He breathed out, then flipped through the end. The happy couple was kissing, but a few pages back a fairy who appeared to be a royal held the staff and wended. "So, this whole time there's been this object we could use to just wish the war would end?" How would that even work?

"Well, it was lost for a reason; we can't have that kind of power," Tatiana said.

"But what if we could?"

"We'd have to find the staff first," Mare said. "And we have no place to look."

"We could ask the author." Tatiana flipped through the pages of the book, and Aiden leaned over her shoulder, heart pounding. Perhaps it was the exhaustion or his strong desire to put as much distance between himself and Oberon as possible, but finding this wishing staff was starting to feel like a possibility. She passed the book to him, opened to a page in the back which showed a drawing of a dark-haired woman standing before a large clock tower.

"Do you know how to find her?" It wasn't as though he could merely wend to the author; he had to know at least something of her location. And the Human Realm was so vast, finding one person in it, even with a vague location, would be near impossible.

"I'm not sure where she lives. There's a link to her site, but we don't have internet." Tatiana sucked the bottom of her braid.

"Isn't that building in the picture pretty famous? I swear I've seen it before." Mare pointed a sharpened black nail at the image of the author.

Tatiana shrugged. "That's Big Ben, but this photo doesn't necessarily mean she lives there. It could be from her vacation. Oh wait!" She flipped to the front of the book. "Her publisher is also in London, I bet they know where she lives."

"Great. Where can I find this publisher?" Hope rekindled in Aiden's chest. London was a real place he could find, and if this publisher had an address, maybe finding this mystical wishing staff wasn't such a far-fetched opportunity.

"It doesn't say where it's located, but I'd bet any manga shop owner in the city could tell you. It was a pretty close-knit community back home—I mean, back when I was at school." The ghost of sadness flashed across Tatiana's features. Aiden couldn't help remembering the sorrow of her teachers when they saw she was leaving. It was cruel of Oberon to force her to stay here, though perhaps he was only doing so because he had no easy way of sending her back.

Mare folded her arms. "This is so stupid. What will Oberon say when he finds out you are chasing a mythical object you read about in a romance book?"

"He'd be intrigued that I was hunting down a lost artifact that could end the war."

Mare rolled her eyes. But it didn't perturb him, or Tatiana for that matter. She giddily paced the room, clutching the book to her chest.

"Don't worry, Aiden, I'll give you all the information I can find."

He nodded. "Thank you, I'm glad you're willing to help me."

"Why wouldn't I?"

"Mab, she…"

The brightness in Tatiana's expression darkened. "It wasn't your fault. That girl, that *human*, she tricked us. Once this war is over, I hope my father hunts her down. She used me just as much as she used you."

Aiden turned away. Tatiana was right to hate Wyn, so why couldn't he let himself feel the same? Letting out a long breath, he pushed himself into a fully sitting position. "Forget the human. The more days that pass, the stronger Summer will become. If we can find the staff and use it to wish Summer defeated, the war could be over."

"IF." Mare shook her head. "If that thing even exists."

Aiden bit his lip. It had to exist—it was his best chance of ending the war and pleasing Oberon. If he succeeded, maybe the man would set him free. After all, he didn't need him anymore.

CHAPTER 3
Freddie

So many people back home had romanticized London. Freddie had seen glamorous photos of Big Ben, the Eye, and of course the royal residence at St. James's Palace, whose staunchly human architecture served as a reminder of the imperial might of humans against the fae. Even the royals themselves, though little more than figureheads, prided themselves on their carefully curated bloodline to ensure their "dedication to the Human Realm". She scowled as they passed the red-brick building. The soldiers stared hard at the street before them. Unlike the ones back home, not a single one had any brightness in their eyes—no fae. Something about this city held an unexpected ugliness that made her throat tighten.

"Isn't it lovely?" Mallory pressed her pert nose to the window.

The black town car they'd piled into circled through yet another dizzying roundabout. Freddie scowled as she scanned the people rushing about past cafes and shops. Shimmering gold trim, marble statues of men and women so realistic they might have been frozen in place, and opalescent domes reflecting the gray sky all hinted at fae design.

"It's something," she muttered.

They'd learned the city's brutal history in school. Before the separation of Fairy and their realm, fourteenth century London had been a hub of fae commerce. That is, until humans had grown envious of the fae's wealth and turned on them. It'd been the start of the Seven

Year War in which fae were hunted and burned at the stake. While the city seemed harmonious enough now, the fae here had never recovered all they'd lost.

"Everything is just so much more sophisticated than New Wall."

Freddie grit her teeth. At least on the plane, she'd been able to shove her headphones in and block Mallory out. But now her battery was dead, and the redhead was taking full advantage of Freddie's forced attention. Skimming the streets, she still couldn't shake the feeling that something was wrong. They passed Trafalgar Square, packed with people of seemingly all nationalities. Then, her heart squeezed, finally recognizing what was so off. "Where are all the fae?"

"You would care about that." Mallory sneered, then returned her attention to the window.

"Uh—well, you see, there was a recent edict that has separated the fae from human spaces." Her father shifted in his seat. "You've seen the news, all that violence. This was just enforced a couple of days ago, but it seems to be working well so far."

Freddie stared from him to the streets. Now that he'd said that, she couldn't help but notice black clad police surrounding the building and patrolling the streets with guns more intense-looking than the ones used back home. "Is no one protesting this? How come it hasn't hit the news?"

"There's no need to get upset. This is simply an experiment to help preserve the city's peace. Protesting has just been discouraged, and the news stations have been instructed not to pick it up until it becomes official."

"So, where are all the fae then?"

Her father frowned and looked out the window on his side. "I'm not sure."

"Does it even matter?" Mallory snapped.

Freddie glared at her as the car slowed to a stop in front of an elegant building—a green sign with the word "Savoy" in modern text glowed over the entrance. Her eyes widened at the sheer beauty of the building. A single night here must cost more than her parents made in a month. How could they afford this?

Ahead of them, a man in a black suit opened the door of the other town car, and Mr. Fallus stepped out. He gave them a cheery wave, then his eyes seemed to fix on Freddie. Her stomach dropped. Of course, *he* was paying. Just another way to keep her father dependent on him.

"How do you like it, ladies?" The sheen of sweat glistened on his brow through the cloud-filtered light of the sun. It made him look greasy and sinister, with the air of a used car salesman.

"It's gorgeous!" Mallory bounced in front of Freddie, nearly knocking her back into the car. "I can't believe we get to stay here."

"The best hotel in the city and owned for centuries by humans."

Doormen in crisp, black suits and top hats ushered them into the lobby. Black and white squares, laid out like a chessboard, covered the stone floors, while a blend of polished stone and dark wood covered the walls. It was both beautiful and intimidating as they were led to a set of modern couches that, despite their fine design, looked rather out of place amidst the historic style. Still, the Hotel Bethlehem, where they'd had prom, was a rundown crack house compared to this place. They sank into the soft velvet couches as Mr. Fallus and her dad went to check them in.

"I bet you've never seen anything like this slumming with your fae friends," Mallory hissed.

"Clearly you've never been to a palace in Fairy." She popped up and went to lean against one of the massive pillars lining the sitting area.

Despite the hotel's grandeur, it paled in comparison to the Winter Palace she'd been trapped in earlier that year.

Guilt clawed at her stomach as memories of that horrid place flashed in her mind. The empty blanks of Freya's eyes, just before she'd been forced to leave her behind, and now her friends… Tears pricked the corners of her eyes, but Freddie sucked in a deep breath, refusing to let them fall.

"You hear me, Wyn?"

Freddie looked up. Her dad was frowning down at her, holding out a plastic keycard. "Sorry," she muttered.

"I said, Mr. Fallus got us both junior suites facing the river. Isn't that nice?"

She looked up at the grinning man, whose beady eyes showed no sign that this was a kindly gesture. Taking the card from her dad, she squeezed it so hard the edges bit into her palm and fingers.

"Aren't you going to say thank you?" he asked.

"I didn't ask to be here."

Her dad cleared his throat. "What she means is she's more than thrilled you got her such a luxurious room."

Before Freddie could respond, Mallory bounded forward. "I'm grateful! Where's my room?"

Mr. Fallus flexed his jaw and passed her a stack of keys. "You're probably somewhere downstairs with the other interns. Why don't you go and hand these out?" He gestured to a group of well-dressed people, her age, chatting quietly near a passage that appeared to lead to the elevators.

"I have to share a room, and that fae-loving brat gets a suite?" Mallory's face had turned an unfortunate shade of red, which clashed horribly with her hair, but Mr. Fallus had turned his attention away, which seemed to have made her invisible in his eyes. Malloy's shoulders drooped as she trudged over to the interns.

Freddie looked over to the porters, but they were still checking luggage tags and shuffling out the bags. Was it appropriate to head off to her room before them? How did things even work in a place like this? Even when she'd been in luxury, visiting the Summer Palace with Pelrin, it had never been long enough to have luggage. And there had to be some sort of social difference between hotel workers and palace servants, right?

Mallory's smile pulled tight as blonde, her hair piled in a perfect coiffure, sneered back at her. Side-stepping Mallory, she held a hand out to Freddie. "Hi, I'm Anna." Her voice held a light accent that was neither American nor British—German, perhaps?

"Freddie." She shook the girl's limp hand.

A lanky boy with dark bangs that hung into his angular face nodded at her. "Rene, I'm from France." He looked like he could've stepped off a k-pop stand's social pic, but his accent was undeniably French.

"Thanks for letting me know." Freddie gave a wincing smile.

He scoffed. "Americans often get it wrong."

"Yes, so many of them are uncultured. I'm Mallory, by the way." With a not-so-light shove, Mallory stepped into the space where Freddie had been standing and held out a hand. The French boy ignored it, but his slight was barely noticed as the other three boys stepped up and introduced themselves one by one. There was Edward, from the UK, Santiago, from Spain, and Yonas from Ethiopia. While the first two gave her hand tentative shakes, Yonas hadn't even bothered to try and touch her.

It was as though she'd forgotten to shower, and the others were keeping their distance. Perhaps it was because she'd chosen to wear leggings on the nine-hour flight from LaGuardia. Mallory had chosen to wear a prim, white dress that had left her freezing on the plane and had gotten horribly wrinkled, but she still mostly looked like she belonged.

Whatever, it hardly mattered. She wasn't here to intern or make friends.

"Come along." Mr. Fallus strode over to the elevators with the bravado of someone who owned places like this.

Even the Savoy elevators were glamorous. The polished walls reflected Freddie's rumpled appearance, and she pressed herself into a corner, trying to be as small as possible as they ascended. With a gentle ding, the elevator stopped. Anna led the way, and the other interns followed her out. With a final glare, Mallory turned away and stalked down the hall. After a significantly longer wait, the elevator dinged again.

"This is us," her father said as if he'd forgotten their tense moment downstairs. Freddie shuffled off behind him and glanced over her shoulder for Mr. Fallus.

"I'm in the Gucci Suite." He gave a rich laugh and tapped his card to the keypad as the elevator closed.

There was something of relief in the air as he left. Freddie breathed out and looked both ways down the halls. They were far brighter than the usual, strangely patterned red carpets that seemed to line every hotel she'd stayed at before.

Her father let out an awkward chuckle and headed down the hall to his suite. To her dismay, hers was right next door.

"We're uh— doing dinner at six. The Savoy Grill it's supposed to be really good."

She'd heard of it before. It had at least one Michelin star. Yet, another way Mr. Fallus was holding her family in his debt. "Sure, Dad."

"And, Wyn, try to dress up a bit. This place is supposed to be nice."

"Sure." Tapping her key to the pad by the door, she stepped inside.

She'd never even heard of a hotel room with an entryway, but here she was. Three rooms lay before her in each direction: a small sitting room with a fireplace and TV, a half bath, and a luxurious bedroom. Freddie headed for the bedroom and collapsed into the amazingly scented sheets. It was enough to curl up in them for the next few hours until she had to get ready for dinner.

Getting dressed up was never something Freddie looked forward to. Her red hoodie and well-worn jeans gave her confidence in their dependability, while the silky knee-length dress made her feel as though a strong breeze would leave her naked. She scratched the back of her leg and took the last few carpeted steps into the dining room behind her father. An older man, whose pale head gleamed in the ambient lighting, stared down his nose at them.

"Can I help you find something?"

"Are we the first to arrive?" Her dad chuckled. "We're part of the party from the States, might be under Fallus?"

The man blinked, and Freddie could practically see the slow progress of the realization from his ears to his brain. "The—Oh! Yes, right this way. My apologies for keeping you waiting."

She rolled her eyes. They were not The Savoy type—why were they even trying to fit in? Following the man to a table towards the back of the restaurant where the six interns were already seated, she couldn't shake the clawing tension in the air. She'd always expected Brittain to be more welcoming of diversity than the US. After all, they'd had a longer history with international and inter-realm trade. But it seemed as though the tensions were deeper, and they'd better perfected the art of burying their prejudices.

The human patrons all laughed and talked in cheery tones over dishes that smelled amazing. Even so, it was as though she were walking across a cling wrap floor, stretched over trash—only so many people could pass before the surface broke and the garbage swallowed them up.

"Freddie, isn't it? You look so nice." Anna wiggled her fingers at Freddie, her fake smile wrinkling her nose.

"Well, I'm glad to see you're making friends," her father said before taking a seat towards the front of the table.

Before she could respond, the host beckoned to her and pulled out a chair beside Mallory. Freddie looked helplessly around at the other empty places before settling herself next to her nemesis.

"Mallory," she said in a curt greeting.

"It's—oh... yeah. Wynnifred."

"What will you be doing here in London? You're *not* part of the intern program." Rene gave her a dazzling smile that did little to disguise the disdain in his words. Was he trying to imply *she* was the spoiled rich kid?

"I—" What was she supposed to be doing? She couldn't very well tell them she was going to be spending her days at the library, researching the history of a magical fae artifact to break a curse. "I'm doing a project."

"Oh? On what?"

"Fae history. London was where some of the burnings occurred and where one of the first peace treaties was signed."

"And there is evidence of fae settlements all over the British Isles. My family went on a tour of the ruins when we were on holiday in Dublin last year," Edward said.

Freddie frowned. "I wasn't aware that Ireland was a part of Britain."

Edward opened his mouth to respond, but was cut off as Mr. Fallus's booming voice rang out across the table. "I can always count on you, Earl, to be right on time. Kinda surprised that all of the interns made it through. Teenagers." He chuckled and took his seat, placing both arms on the rests.

"Yes, it seems we've got a good group." Her father beamed at the interns, who all returned his look with fake smiles of their own. Perhaps he wished she were more like them—content in her privilege and blinded by fear, turned bigotry. Freddie sank low in her seat.

"Speaking of the interns, Earl, can you take them up to sign their international agreements? I left them at the front desk."

"Now? I thought we were doing that in the office tomorrow."

"Might as well get it over with so we're not rushing in the morning."

"Sure, Rich." Her father pulled his lips tight and got to his feet as the other interns followed suit.

"Do I need to go?" asked Edward.

"Just in case." Mr. Fallus nodded as they streamed out of the dining room, leaving Freddie alone.

She watched them go and wondered if it'd be worth going after them. Surely, standing awkwardly around while the others signed paperwork was better than God knew how many minutes in tense silence with Mr. Fallus.

"Well, I'm glad we have a little minute to chat." He leaned forward. Despite several seats between them, Freddie couldn't help feeling as though he were breathing on her. "I think I know how to save those friends of yours."

"How do—you do?"

"I've been putting a lot of thought into this. I'm not a heartless monster. People say I am, but people say a lot of things. When you're a person like me, you have connections, and I just so happen to have one that could help."

Hope surged in Freddie's chest, but she shoved it down. This was obviously a trap, and she would not be so easily caught. "Even if I did believe you were doing this out of the goodness of your heart, you don't even know what would go into helping them."

"My friend is very good. He has people all throughout Fairy. People who get stuff done."

"And the catch?"

"Do you really think that poorly of me?"

"Obviously."

"I'm a good guy. It's really a shame you don't trust me more."

"Such a shame. I wonder what you could've done to deserve it? Definitely not something as horrible as convincing my parents to move while I was trapped in Fairy."

He gave her a withering look. "That was not my idea. I said they should split the residence. That way, one of them was always in your home, just in case you returned. But they insisted it wasn't a big deal."

Uncertainty flashed through her mind. Surely her parents wouldn't...but she hardly seemed to know them anymore.

Before she could answer, Mr. Fallus laced his fingers together and leaned forward. "I just need you to send me a text the next time you meet up with your fae prince."

"What?" Freddie took a hasty, perhaps too hasty, sip of water. Of all the things she'd expect Mr. Fallus to ask, this certainly wasn't one of them. "I don't know what you're talking about."

"I don't have time to play games. I know you're close to the Prince of Summer. So next time you see him, just shoot me a message, and in return, I'll help your friends."

"Why? What are you planning to do?"

"That isn't your concern. You have at least two friends who need my help."

"Three," she muttered under her breath.

"Whatever. You need my help. Maybe it's time to stop being selfish and think of what's actually best for others."

Words failed her, and pain ripped across her heart. Maybe he was right. Every time she tried to fight against him and those like him, it ended in disaster. If she'd just passed the year with Pelrin, like he'd asked her to back at the ice castle, no one would've gotten hurt...or died. If she'd never risked everything to save him, Amanda, Raul, and Jefferson would be safe. Maybe it was time she chose the easy way, the way people told her to take. Maybe fewer people would get hurt.

"I need proof that you can actually help them."

"Fair enough. I'll get that to you tomorrow."

"And I can't text while we're here. It'll have to wait until we go home."

A cold grin spread across Mr. Fallus's face. "I've gone ahead and paid for one of those convenient international plans. You can turn your phone off airplane mode now."

He took a large swig of his water and set it down with a look of triumph. She picked up her phone with trembling fingers and with a few taps, did as he said. A text from an unknown number appeared with three words: 'Let me know'. When she looked up, Mr. Fallus was waggling his eyebrows at her. She swallowed and met his beady gaze, hoping she gave no hint of her decision.

"Don't worry about it now. I'm a patient man—for the most part."

Cold spilled through Freddie. What was she supposed to do? Sacrifice Pelrin or save the others?

CHAPTER 4
Aiden

It was close to midday when Aiden finally crept from Tatiana's room and headed to the back building of the complex in hopes of finding some food. Both Mare and Tatiana had offered to get him something while he recovered, but he was well used to being back on his feet after such a short rest. Besides, spending too much time in Tatiana's room might spark rumors about his relationship with Oberon's daughter he did not wish to answer.

Scents of rich earth rose up from the crunching leaves and twigs beneath his boots. It was fairly quiet, most of the soldiers had been sent on their missions for the day, holding posts throughout Summer and putting down the minor rebellions. Only a few stragglers remained focused on their training exercises. Sweat gleamed off their backs as the clash of their weapons reverberated off the trees. At the Winter Palace, they'd never put so much effort into their training. Perhaps the loss was a harsh reminder of their predicament. Where the greenies were content to reestablish their boots on their necks, Oberon was all too happy to feed countless brown and red fae to his deadly ambitions.

A tree bowed over him, laden with crisp, golden apples. Aiden picked one and bit into it, its juice running down his chin. Swiping at his mouth with the back of his hand, he savored the sweetness as it brought back memories of the festivals in Autumn with his parents.

He paused, waiting for the familiar anger to build in his chest as it often did when he thought of the family he'd lost, but it didn't come.

Instead, a hollow longing settled in its place, a deep sadness devoid of the bloodlust that had once been his only comfort. He pressed a hand to his chest, for a moment fearing he'd gone numb to the loss, only to remember the vision of Mare's mom standing over him and draining him of the overwhelming despair that had once consumed him. If anything, he was less numb now than he had been before, and for once his mind was clear. No longer did he seek comfort in following Oberon's orders to exact revenge. It wasn't as though the Summer King's death had brought him any sense of healing. No, now he'd gladly help the prince achieve a long and happy life if it could secure one for himself as well. Though if that help meant Wyn ended up with *him*, he wasn't so sure he could do that so gladly. A dull ache thumped in his chest, and he curled his fingers against his black leather jerkin. Perhaps they deserved each other. He'd been a fool to let her manipulate him into assisting her to risk her life to save the prince. And now they were separated, it was for the best that he put her firmly in the far back of his mind.

Reaching for the door to the mess hall, Aiden stopped when someone called his name. A dwarf, her silver beard in hundreds of dainty beaded plaits, stood behind him, an ax at her hip.

"Oberon is looking for you." She gave him a pointed look before shoving him out of the way and disappearing inside the squat building.

Aiden stumbled to the side. He'd often forgotten how strong the dwarves were. A heaviness weighed on him as he turned from the hall and headed back towards the main building. He made quick work of the apple as he climbed the stairs to Oberon's office and tossed the core out a window. The door was open, and the rebel king sat behind the desk studying a large map. Aiden crept in on cat-like feet so as not to disturb him, but partially in hopes that Oberon would forget why he'd wanted him in the first place.

"Good, you're here," Oberon said without looking up. "I need you to do something for me."

Aiden shifted uncomfortably. It didn't feel like the start of any regular mission to assist in a battle, after all Mare wasn't even there. Whatever Oberon wanted, it couldn't be good for him.

"Find a way to break the curse you placed on the Elesseans."

"But I—I don't even know if it can be broken."

"All curses can be broken. Just go back to where you got it and tell her you need an antidote."

Aiden stepped back. The idea of facing Mare's mom... alone... sent chills from his neck to the soles of his feet. And why did Oberon suddenly need to break the curse? Surely it would be harder to overcome Summer with so many of their powerful soldiers back in full force. And he couldn't imagine anyone under it who might be more valuable to him awake. Unless... Before he could ask, an annoyed sigh made him turn.

"And what is he supposed to offer her for this antidote? You know she never does anything for free." Mare stood in the doorway, the sun framing her head like a radiant crown over her black ponytail. Widening his eyes, he turned to Oberon. He'd never seen her show such blatant disrespect.

The man waved a ringed hand. "It does not concern me what the payment is. I'm sure the boy will think of something."

"It's fine, Mare. He's right. I'll figure something out." What, he wasn't sure. He didn't even have his misery to offer her. And whatever type of fae Mare's mom was, she was just like any other and would never dole out her magic without a price. At least, she was like any other fae with their free will intact.

Mare rocked her jaw back and forth. "Fine. Let's just go."

"I don't recall assigning you this mission."

"I was planning on visiting my mother anyway."

Oberon stared hard at Mare, and she returned it, her gaze unwavering. "I wasn't aware you two were so... close."

Mare huffed. "We are. My mom would do *anything* for me." She turned on her heel and headed out the door.

Aiden looked back at Oberon, his face had gone a shade paler, and his lips were pulled tight as a tripwire. Since when did Mare threaten him?

Following her out into the hall, Aiden jogged to her side. "What was that?"

"What?" Mare turned into an empty training room and wrapped her arms around her body.

"You know what. You've never spoken to him like that before."

"It was Tati's idea. She said I should use my mom to inspire her father to treat us fairly."

"Be careful, you don't know what he'll do if he's scared."

"I know, I'm still shaking, but I promised her I'd try. We can't afford to put either of us more at risk, though. Let's just do this quick. I'll figure out something to offer her, and we can go back and tell Tati this was a bad idea."

"You don't have to do this. I'm fine on my own."

"But you're not on your own."

Aiden stared at her, though she avoided his gaze. Mare's arms wrapped around her body as though warding off a chill. No doubt her threat to Oberon still ate away at her. It'd landed well, but he didn't take kindly to those who put his power into question. While Mare herself might not be at risk, he was, and Tatiana... it was hard to tell if her father truly loved her or loved possessing a living proof that his legacy wouldn't be human, at least not entirely.

"If we leave now, we can return before sundown if we hurry." He wended as a cloud of shadows engulfed Mare.

Moments later, they stood on the familiar shore of the orange beach, the glow of the sand stood out unsettlingly against the onyx sky. He led the way towards the path leading to Mare's mom's house—domain—whatever it was. Silence settled around them as they passed the odd mounds Mare had told him were home to the inhabitants of the Nightmare Plains. Yet, like before, he saw no one.

A cry rang out from a dune just off the path. Aiden stopped—a fairy with blue wings and short, frost-colored hair waved to him.

"Aiden, I've missed you."

"M-mom?"

Behind him, Mare growled and yanked him by the collar. Aiden hadn't even realized he'd taken a step to the side, nearly off the path. "I swear, you never learn. There is one rule, just one. Don't EVER step off this path. Do you understand?" Grabbing his arm, Mare dragged him forward.

"Aiden, where are you going? Come here." His mother, no—not his mother, the nightmare, beckoned to him. It was painful to ignore. Seeing her again in the Winter Palace, and watching her soul still try to protect him, was like losing her all over again. Tears pricked his eyes as she called out to him again, sand slipping beneath her feet as she ran alongside them.

Mare wrenched his arm forward. "Stop looking at it and keep going. We want to be back before dark, remember? Whatever you're seeing isn't real." Her words hit him like a stone to his chest. She was right, as much as it hurt, that creature wasn't his mother, wasn't any part of her. And it certainly didn't have his best intentions at heart.

"Aiden!" This time her voice broke, sounding more like the screech of nails on a stone tablet. He winced and turned to look at her again, but in her place, a giant ribbed worm dove through the sand as easily as though it were water.

The worm followed them until they were in the shadow of the largest mound, where Mare's mom resided. It turned abruptly away as though even the hint of the dark creature within would reach out and harm it. Mare dragged Aiden forward until they passed through the hidden entrance in the rock and into the inky blackness.

"Hello?" Mare called.

No answer.

"Are you here?" Aiden asked in a low voice. Instantly, the darkness vanished, giving way to frost-covered walls and glittering light cast by an icy chandelier.

"I thought this would be a more appropriate setting for our meeting, given the circumstances." Mare's mom descended a frozen staircase wearing a face similar to Mare's but dressed in one of Mab's gowns. The beads on it rustled like rain as she reached the bottom and held out her arms to Mare. "My little Nightmare, coming home to visit Mommy."

Mare didn't move. "We need a boon."

"No hug for your beloved mother? Aren't you relying on my protection to keep you from your *employer's* wrath?"

"How did you know about that?"

She smirked. "I know about everything, Dearheart. Now, let's discuss your friend here; he's doing so much better. My sweet morsel no longer reeks of misery. How disappointing."

"Leave him alone—"

"Mare, it's alright." Aiden took a breath, meeting Mare's mom's haunting gaze. "I need a way to break the curse you gave me."

She laughed, a dark, humorless sound which did nothing to ease his humming nerves. "Break a curse? But you wanted something *so* powerful. Why would you want to break it?"

"I—" His words failed him. His mind flicked back to his earlier questions. Who was it that Oberon wished to wake? Unless Oberon thought to use the cursebreaker as leverage. But what could be valuable enough to risk losing Summer. He shook his head. "I don't know."

Her smile grew, stretching beyond the limits of what was natural. Aiden took a step back, bumping against the prickly white wall.

"We're here at Oberon's request. He never explains himself," Mare said.

"I think you mean he's here at Oberon's request, but you, daughter, are here of your own volition."

Mare scowled. "I wasn't going to let him go alone."

"I suppose not. His heart is quite susceptible to my sweet nightmares."

Aiden cleared his throat. "Regardless of our reasons for being here, Oberon has still tasked me with obtaining the cure."

Mare's mom put one of her too-long fingers to her cheek. "And what do you propose to give me in return?"

"I have nothing. Perhaps... Perhaps you could take my misery again?" With Oberon's threat of not needing him anymore, he supposed he might have enough to satisfy her.

But she simply laughed. "I've already gorged on what you cultivated over the years. It'll take you quite some time to build up such a meal for me again."

"Let me pay the price. I'll visit you more often, once a month." Mare stepped forward; her face tight as she stared down at her mother.

"As much as I would love some mother-daughter time spent tormenting the poor fools who enter my domain, that is a price I will not accept. Believe me or not, I do not wish to make *you* miserable, Nightmare. Your place is outside these plains."

"How...caring of you, Mom." Mare's voice was devoid of her typical sharpness. She stared at her mother as though she'd suggested they streak through Winter.

"If you two have nothing of value, you can get out." The icy walls flickered as the chandelier dimmed, threatening the encompassing darkness.

Tightness closed around Aiden's throat. Oberon's order echoed in his head. There had to be something he could offer her. The tightness intensified, and black spots dotted his vision, lending holes to the flickering walls. Falling to his knees, he barely registered Mare calling his name. "Wait." His raspy voice was barely a whisper, but as the walls stopped fading, the tightness loosened.

"Thought of something else?" The pattering opals on Mare's mom's dress caught the light and gleamed a sinister green and orange.

"What about a bargain?"

Aiden couldn't remember learning much in his few years of Fairy school about bargains, but he knew they were nearly irresistible to most magic users. He'd never felt particularly drawn to them, but in the rare mentions of blue fae he'd come across, there'd never been anything about an affinity for deals.

Mare's mom approached. "What sort of bargain?"

"If I..." He took a breath. His wording needed to be perfect to ensure he'd gain the upper hand while still making it appear fair. "Oberon has given me a mission. If I succeed, the cursebreaker is mine, free of charge. However, if I should fail, I'll give you all my magic." Hopefully, she'd assume his mission was something grand, like defeating Summer or even infiltrating a town they held. She surely wouldn't guess his mission would be complete as soon as he brought the cure back to Oberon.

She laughed, though her mirth echoed of something haunted. "How sweet you try to use your tin-tongue to weave a clever bargain. And you offer me something that isn't yours to give."

"It's my magic. It may not be in my possession, but that doesn't change its mine. Do you accept?"

"My sweet, I've walked these lands long before your grandparents first unfurled their wings and took to the sky. You'd have to have been practicing bargains for at least half that long for me not to see through them."

Aiden's heart sank. "So you reject it? I have nothing more to offer." If he gave her all his magic without the protection of the bargain, it might kill him. His magic was so ingrained into his veins, even Oberon didn't dare take it all, at least not while he still used him to fight his battles.

"Let's rephrase. When you return to Autumn, Oberon will give you a *new* mission. Should you succeed, I will not come to collect my price, but should you fail, *all* of your magic becomes mine."

Aiden bit his lip. It was risky, not knowing what mission Oberon would give him. But if it was anything like the others, it would be something straightforward like fighting in a battle or destroying lode stones. All things he'd done in the past, and it wouldn't be impossible to complete.

"Don't, it's clearly a trap." Mare held out a hand as though to hold him back. When she turned to him, her dark eyes were wide with pleading, as though they too were telling him not to accept.

"I need the cursebreaker, Mare. There's not much of a choice. It's either this or give up all of my magic now."

"Mom, please, name your price, anything but that. It could kill him."

Her mother laughed and glided over to Mare in a trail of black smoke. "Anything, daughter? Even that sweet little trolling?"

Mare's face dropped, her umber skin going ashen. It was no use bargaining with a creature who knew everything. Her mother probably already knew what they would offer her before they even knew they were going to.

"What if I added that when I take your magic, I promise not to kill you?"

A shock of hope raced through him and his relief reflected in Mare's expression. Before he could agree, her face pulled into a skeptical frown. "When you say you won't kill him, does that mean you are going to leave him with barely enough magic to survive? Clinging to life in the middle of a battlefield or something horrible like that?"

The thought made Aiden recoil. Afterall, even if he didn't die, it was Mab who'd taught him there was suffering worse than death.

"Now, now dear, you will not lock me into so many terms. I gave you a generous offer, take it or get out."

Mare opened her mouth, but he cut her off. "I agree to your terms." Mare was free, and if she had the opportunity, she and Tatiana could run away together. There was no hope for him.

"Aiden," she gasped, but he refused to look at her.

Mare's mom smiled as the ice palace shattered around them, replaced by a filthy, dirt room with a cauldron bubbling in the center. With seemingly no fear of the heat, she reached into the liquid and pulled out a white spear, the opposite of the needle she'd given him to enact the curse.

"Simply break this in Elessea, and everyone will awaken." She handed it to Aiden and a shock tingled up his arm—the bargain binding him to its terms.

"Thank you," he muttered.

Mare cast him an incredulous look, but hurried towards the exit, apparently only she could see. He made to follow after her when her mother called his name.

"Good luck on your next mission."

A creeping chill spread across his spine. Whatever fate loomed before him, he hoped he was strong enough to face it.

It was dark by the time they arrived back in Autumn. Dark Fae soldiers milled about in a general current towards their respective sleeping quarters. Aiden's stomach rumbled, but from the moon's position, nearly directly overhead, it was time to meet Oberon.

Mare had been silent, though her simmering temper had been near audible. They entered the meditation hall and climbed the stairs to where Oberon's office and her room were located. Here, the wood floors were empty but for the beams of moonlight puddling on the floor. In Winter, the moon had always been ghostly pale, its light a gleaming silver. Here, the moon was gold. It spoke of something warm, but with the land filled with its second wave of conquerors and its people slain, scattered, or enslaved, the golden orb just seemed lonely.

Aiden moved towards the sliver of light that marked the door to Oberon's office, but Mare caught him by the wrist. For a long moment, they stared at one another, her hardened expression unreadable.

Finally, she locked her jaw, dropped his arm, and stalked off in the opposite direction toward her room.

His hand trembled at the closed door to Oberon's office. The bargain with Mare's mom pulsed in his mind, hissing *do not fail* over and over. What if he ran? What if he never let Oberon give him another mission? Stupid thoughts, he knew, but there had to be some shred of hope he could grasp on to. At least she wouldn't kill him, and that was all he could hope for.

"I know you're out there. Come!" Oberon's voice sounded from the other side of the door and Aiden's stomach dropped. He stepped inside, avoiding the man's gaze, and inched towards the corner of the cramped office. "Did you get it?"

"Yes." Aiden held out the white shard, not daring to say more.

Oberon took it, examining the way the light shined off the smooth surface. "Well, that's one thing you didn't fail at." Rounding the desk, he ran a finger down the case that held the crystal wand. Aiden fought back a shiver as he stared at the cursed thing. "I have another mission for you. Hopefully you'll be just as successful."

Here it was. *Freezing frosts.* He nodded, inwardly pleading Oberon would give him a simple, or at least relatively achievable task. Take back a settlement, break the curse in Elessea for whatever reason, something he could do.

Flicking open the case, Oberon withdrew the wand and tapped it against his knuckles. "My daughter told me about that interesting discovery she made in that silly book of hers. The Staff of Wind, even without its gold fae power, could be quite a valuable tool. Just imagine, I could merely wish all of Fairy to be mine. It'd be so much easier than all this pointless violence. All I need is for you to find it for me."

"How? It's been lost for centuries, countless fae have—"

"It seems the author of that book might have an idea. And won't it be nice to visit the Human Realm? Perhaps you'll see that girl you're so fond of."

Aiden's heart stopped as he tried to force the words to deny it. But no lie could claw its way out his throat and no clever doublespeak came to mind. As much as he wished to stay far away from Wyn, the thought of her hurt, or worse tore at his heart like a serrated blade. It was pain unlike he'd never known; worse than her betrayal, worse than the thoughts of never seeing her again. "Please, don't hurt her. Don't—I'll do whatever you ask."

Oberon chuckled. "Of course you will. You'll do whatever I ask regardless, or did you forget your debt?"

Aiden sank to his knees. There had to be something he could offer Oberon to ensure Wyn's safety, but there was nothing he had that the cruel human couldn't easily take. "Please," Aiden whispered.

"She was quite a thorn in my side. Lost me an entire realm, rather impressive for a human. When I first learned of your connection, I planned on having you kill her."

Aiden's head snapped up, his eyes wide. Dread, like a thousand spiders, spilled over his head and shoulders to settle in his stomach. As angry as he'd been, as angry as he *was*, with her, he'd feel that tenfold towards himself if he was made to do that to her.

"Lucky for you, she is of use to me now. What I do with her after is entirely up to you."

"I'll do *anything*."

"Good. Find me that staff before the next full moon and I'll not touch her, fail and..." he shrugged.

"But, that's only two weeks."

"Well, then you'd better get searching, because it's not only that girl's life on the line."

Aiden's eyes widened. Never had a task seemed so impossible. He opened his mouth but no sound escaped his dry lips.

"I'll be kind. You don't have to return until you complete the task. But don't be foolish and try to run if you fail. You know I'll find you." Oberon tapped the wand on the desk and looked to Aiden. "I suppose I'll spare you tonight." He waved the wand and he vanished, cursebreaker and all.

Aiden stumbled backwards out the room and slid down the wall. He buried his head in his hands, listening to the quiet hum of the insects outside. Footsteps approached, and he tensed.

"He gave you the task?" Mare loomed over him, her slight form blocking out the moonlight.

Aiden just nodded, not yet trusting himself with words.

"And what was it? Can we complete it?"

"Why are you so invested in helping me? You've never shown this kind of interest before."

Mare recoiled as though he'd slapped her. "I—you need my help. I never—"

"Dek needed your help too! We both did! But you left us to die. Why is now any different?" Anger that had balanced so tremulously in his chest overcame him. Memories of Dek staring glassy-eyed at the stars with nothing Aiden could do save him.

"I didn't know. I was scared and I'm sorry. I'm so sorry." The last sorry came out choked and she turned her face to the sky as though appealing for Dek to forgive her as well. Still, a heavy chill settled over Aiden as she spoke. He'd been alone for so long, and now when every hope had been taken from him, she wanted to act as though she cared.

"What didn't you know? That I was begging you for help? Didn't know Dek was dying? He was our *brother*."

"I didn't know Oberon had drained you of magic before we left. You were always the strongest and suddenly you weren't. I thought you were holding back."

"Holding back for what?"

"To go after the prince on your own... It sounds stupid now. But believe me, I have never been more scared than that night you didn't come home."

"Sorry, I was busy trying not to die." The scent of Wyn's blankets swirled around him as though he were there, lying on the floor with their soft fabric soothing his skin. It'd been a terrible night with an incredibly fortunate ending.

"I'm glad you didn't die. If I'd known what happened before, I'd never have suggested we go. It's my fault Dek is dead. I'm not going to let anything happen to you. But you seem intent on your imminent demise."

Aiden gave a humorless laugh. "I hardly have a choice. You probably shouldn't get too attached to me; Tatiana needs you more. Summer is getting stronger and it's only a matter of time before they come."

Mare nodded, then stopped. "What do you mean I shouldn't get too attached to you? What is Oberon making you do?"

"I'm supposed to find the Staff of Wind." He shook his head, dropping it into his hands.

"The one from Tati's book? Aiden, we both know that was barely a lead."

"As I said, I have no choice."

"Then I'll go with you, you need—"

"And Tatiana? This isn't some battle to fight, and you'll be no better than me in the Human Realm."

"I know, I just—how long do you have?"

"Until the full moon."

"Aiden, that's so soon."

"I know." He pulled his knees to his chest. Not when he'd been in countless battles, or even when Oberon had threatened his uselessness, had he felt so terrified of his own death. Perhaps now that there was a deadline associated with it, it seemed more real. But there was hardly time to drown himself in misery. Oberon had threatened Wyn, and Aiden would use what little time he had left to ensure her safety.

"Promise me you'll do your best to find it. Don't just give up." Mare took his hand in hers, her eyes glassy. "Please, Aiden. I want at least some hope that you'll come out of this alive." He shrugged, his best was all he could promise, and finding the staff would save Wyn too.

"I promise."

CHAPTER 5
Freddie

Though she'd had nothing to drink, Freddie woke with a pounding headache and crust-coated eyes. She groaned, raising a hand to block the fierce sunlight reflecting off the Thames. It was almost annoying how comfortable the bed was; deliciously warm, despite the frigid AC.

Grinding her teeth, she shoved back the blanket, and something small and rectangular hit her knee. Freddie looked down'and picked up her phone. The tiniest sliver of red on the battery bar was the only evidence of its fleeting life. She groaned again—the only thing that had drowned out the echo of Mr. Fallus's proposition was the never-ending series of chubby cat and pug videos. Guilt twinged in her stomach, quickly replaced by the numbness that always chased memories of her *former* passion for journalism. After all, it'd once been research to ensure she uncovered the perfect story, which had drained her battery.

It was for the best that she'd set such desires aside. After all, who was she to cover fae stories? Surely there were fae who could speak on these issues better than she ever could. Her desire to help was only good for getting herself and those she cared about hurt.

A text flashed on her screen. She jumped squinting at the strange gold bubble surrounding the words, "where are you?". Seconds later, another message in gold followed. "Did this work? P".

P? Pelrin? Had Pelrin gotten a cellphone? He'd always been so adverse to her "human magic" unlike... She shook the thought away and responded "Pel? Is that you?". A few moments passed before the gold bubble reappeared, followed by the text, "Yeah, it's me. Good thing this works. Just tell me where you are."

She sighed and punched back "The Savoy in London" before her phone went black. Scooting to the edge of the bed, she plugged it in. The carpet was too plush beneath her socked-feet. It was as though it too was trying to convince her to enjoy being here—living off the perks Mr. Fallus's bigotry afforded her.

It gave her some small pleasure that the bathroom was dingier than she expected. It was clearly old, and while she was certain it'd been cleaned many times, the caulk around the tub was starting to yellow. An old-fashioned iron radiator sat at the far end of the room—a gross statement on who the preferred clientele was. She rushed through a shower, twisted her curls into teddy bear buns, and tiptoed back into her room to find something to wear.

A shriek nearly escaped her lips as a handsome blond fae gently fluttered his wings and looked up at her from her bed. "Why didn't you tell me you were leaving? I was worried."

"I had about two weeks' notice, Pelrin, and you were in Fairy. Speaking of, how did you find my room?" Freddie tightened her grip around the towel and glowered at him.

Pelrin chuckled, but strode out into the hall. "Security is a lot more relaxed here than I remember."

"Really? I thought it would be tighter with all the conflict." Kicking open her suitcase, Freddie fished out a rolled pair of jeans and a t-shirt, and changed. Her red sweatshirt was balled up at the base of a chair and she snatched it up to tie around her waist.

A quick check in the mirror told her she didn't look half deranged, and that was all she could really hope for. There was no point in trying to mimic the fashionable outfits of Mallory and the other interns, nor did she feel pressured by her father's position as Mr. Fallus's yes-man to dress up more than she normally did. She adjusted a curl which stuck out at an odd angle from one of her buns. Her clothes, at least, could feel right when nothing else did.

"You look..." Pelrin grimaced, taking in her appearance. "The same, Fred." He leaned against the window sill in her small sitting room. He seemed so much more at home in the lavish setting than she did.

"Thanks, Pel. You never really told me how you found me." Or why he was here. Though the reason was likely the usual; he needed to check on her as though she were some fragile baby.

"I've been to London before, with my family. When I asked for you at the front desk, they just handed me a key."

Freddie raised a brow, no doubt he was leaving out how he mag-icked them into doing so. He'd been using much more magic as the war intensified. And it wasn't like he was great with her personal boundaries anyway. "Is everything okay? Did you find something to help Amanda and—"

"—No." His voice was low and laced with all the pain and heaviness she struggled to keep bound in her heart. "It's funny. Before you responded, I went to Jefferson's place and just sat there, waiting, like I used to. As though he'd wake any second and we'd go to the library or watch movies with you guys. It's stupid, I know, but they're my friends too." The image of Pelrin sitting alone in Jefferson's cramped mausoleum made her chest tighten.

"It's not your fault they're cursed."

"Isn't it? If I hadn't been so stupid and fallen for that troll's trick, none of you would be involved in this mess. Maybe Summer wouldn't even be on the verge of collapse. And my mother..."

He buried his head in his hands. Locks of golden hair, that had escaped his tie, spilled between his fingers. She couldn't remember a time when she and Pelrin had talked like this. Even when they were dating, it was always so light.

"I guess we're some pretty crappy friends, huh?"

Pelrin huffed a laugh and said nothing. Minutes ticked by in silence as the two of them drowned in their respective miseries. Freddie had almost forgotten about meeting Mr. Fallus and the others for lunch, when the clock tower boomed the time... eleven.

How had it grown so late? She was supposed to meet the others in Covent Garden at noon. And first she had to find the restaurant and figure out what to say to Mr. Fallus, if he even could provide her proof he had the ability to save her friends. He wouldn't; no fae-hating human like him could know anything about breaking curses. Still...

Pelrin sighed, deep and long, as he slid deeper into the chair. "At least they're safe, for now. But the islands can only hold so long like this. The Dark Fae have a stronger grip than we thought."

"And the curse?"

He shook his head. "Maybe if we knew who cast it. I thought, perhaps it was *him*, because the magic is so strong, but my uncle says it's beyond his abilities. Wherever this curse is from, it's not going to be broken by a mere spell."

Freddie chewed her lower lip. *If* Mr. Fallus could actually break the spell, and that was a big *if*, she had to tell Pelrin. If he knew Mr. Fallus was leading him into some sort of trap, perhaps it wouldn't matter. But for now, she couldn't get her remaining friend's hopes up until she knew for sure. "I have to go, Pel."

He nodded, shoving himself up from the chair. "Do you want me to walk you out?"

"No, I— They aren't too friendly to fae around here, and I don't want you to get caught up in something."

"I've noticed. It wasn't nearly this bad a few years ago. If the humans aren't careful, war might break out here too."

"Sometimes it feels like our politicians want that to happen."

"Yes, well you just keep your head down and stay out of it." His tone was sharp and the words bit into her like shards of metal.

"Sure." Freddie stepped back into the hall and Pelrin followed after her, seemingly oblivious to her hurt.

"I'll see you soon. How long are you here?"

"I should be home in a couple weeks. See you." Forcing a smile, Freddie waved and Pelrin gave her a slight bow before vanishing in a brilliant gold glow.

Her hands trembled as she stared at the spot where he'd been. But before her thoughts could overtake her, an alarm went off on her phone marking the half hour. *Crap.* Slinging her bag over her shoulder, Freddie hurried out into the empty hall. It was strange. She was used to seeing the predominantly brown fae hotel staff pushing the cleaning carts through the halls when she stayed at hotels, but here she was alone. Something pricked at the edge of her nerves, likely a hint at yet another injustice to the fae the government here quietly had put into place.

In the lobby, she followed her GPS to Henrietta Street. The walk promised to be short, and she relaxed a bit. Being on time, or even a little early, would hopefully mean she could talk to Mr. Fallus before the others arrived, and finally settle the anxiety gnawing at her insides.

It took her a few wrong turns to find the restaurant, but she finally slipped into the sunny cafe to the backdrop of the noon chimes.

Letting out a breath, Freddie scanned the tables for Mr. Fallus's melting-candle shaped form. The cafe was packed with tourists drowning out the scents of fresh bread with their sweat. Her nose wrinkled when she spotted him. Limp clumps of dark hair clung moistly to his wrinkled forehead, and his rodential eyes fixed on her.

Taking in a slow breath, Freddie made her way over. "Where's everyone else?"

"On their way. I wanted to make sure we had some time to talk. Good thing you're on time." Something in Mr. Fallus' tone made Freddie think he'd expected otherwise. He reached into his suit jacket and withdrew what appeared to be a massive fang. "Ever seen anything like this?"

"Did you steal that from the Natural History Museum?" Freddie swallowed. She could feel an intense energy radiating from the object—if it was a fang, the creature it was from must have been immensely powerful.

"Don't get smart with me, or you'll never break that curse on your friends. This is the only way to save them, and I'm willing to part with it...you know the cost."

"What do you plan on doing if I do get you a meeting with Pelrin?"

"Not a meeting. I need you to have him encounter me in secret, and the reason is none of your business. Either you save the friends you got cursed, or you leave them to rot."

"How do I know that thing would even do what you say it does?"

"Even you can sense its power, I'm sure. I'd hardly be foolish enough to risk carrying something like this around, just to fool a little girl."

Freddie ground her teeth, but said nothing. As much as she hated to admit it, she believed him. She held out a hand, but he tucked the spike back into his jacket.

"You'll get this, when you hold up your end first. I'll look out for your text." He stood, and for a moment Freddie thought he was going to leave. Her heart sank, unidentifiable emotions warring for space within her. "You have until parliament votes on what to do about their fae problem to decide."

"What do you mean?" She dug her nails into her palms and glanced around. Still, there were no fae. What was going on? Surely, the government couldn't simply disappear that many people and no one would do anything.

"What you see here is a mere test. Your father and I are serving as council and observers to the most comprehensive strategy to bring peace to our realm, and it seems to be going well so far. Two days before we leave, Parliament will vote on whether they should revert to the old ways of dealing with the fae or move forward with next steps."

"What are 'next steps'? Where is everyone? What did you do?" Several people looked up from their tables and Freddie realized she'd gotten to her feet. Swallowing hard, she sank back into her chair.

Mr. Fallus flashed her a cold smile and leaned in. "Perhaps you should've become an intern, then you'd know exactly what is happening here. But those spots are very exclusive and only for serious students, not those who try to live out storybook fantasies. Make your decision before the vote or lose your friends."

She forced down the urge to scream. The guilt from her reckless adventure was a constant bruise she didn't need anyone else prodding. And he didn't know how truly guilty she was. "That's less than two weeks."

"Generous, I know." He waved, and she turned to see the others approaching the restaurant in their professional wear.

Her heart sank as each approaching footstep further cemented her into this impossible bargain. Between her buzzing nerves, the sounds in the cafe, and the cloying scent of Mr. Fallus's cologne mingling with his sweat, she could barely breathe, let alone think.

A scream shot through the restaurant and Mr. Fallus jumped to his feet.

"Get away from me, you hag!" Mallory clutched her purse close to her chest as a girl, who looked close to their own age, took a stumbling step back. Her waist-length black hair was tangled and hid most of her face, but her worn and filthy jeans hinted at her distressed status. Did Mallory truly not even possess a crumb of compassion?

Freddie got to her feet before her rationality could hold her back. Helping this girl wasn't like helping save Pelrin... or Freya. Breathing past the pain of the memories, she shouted, "What is wrong with you? She's obviously not a thief." Freddie charged forward, but two black-uniformed policemen got to the girl first. Her gleaming eyes met Freddie's just before the men blocked her from view.

Mallory grabbed Freddie's arm, stopping her from getting closer, as one of the men shone a flashlight into the girl's face. She cried out as the other one dragged her out of the main trafficked area.

"Can you believe that little wretch snuck out here. I always thought European fae would be less aggressive."

"They are quite invasive, although I'm not sure eliminating them entirely is the right approach... " Edward's gaze followed the girl as the police half dragged her down the street.

Freddie yanked herself from Mallory's grasp, following after the girl and ignoring her classmate's grating shout. Maybe there was nothing she could do, but she had to try and do something...didn't she? Just keep it within reason. She could do that.

Rounding a corner to a shaded and less crowded sidestreet, Freddie hid in the back doorway of a shop as the police ushered the hag towards what looked like a mini metro station. The entrance was big enough to fit just one person at a time, with a hooded arch and railing leading down beyond what Freddie could see from her hiding spot.

"We're letting you off with a warning," one of the officers huffed as his companion shoved the girl forward. She glared back, but slowly descended.

"Don't let us catch you up here again." They watched her until the matted top of her head was out of sight. Freddie held her breath as the officers passed, but they barely acknowledged her presence.

When they were well gone, she peeled herself from the doorway and crept over to the railing. It led far down, into an unlit stairwell. Freddie shuddered. How could they force anyone to go down there? The little structure was devoid of signage to hint at what it might be or where it might lead. Still, an uncomfortable tightness in the back of her throat throbbed with guilt, and perhaps horror. It was dark and filthy, and surely violating several city codes, but what if… What if this was where the fae had been sent to live?

The thought was horrible. Surely it violated several rights of personage agreements signed into place when humans first accepted fae into their society. Not that such things were always followed. Still, what else could it be?

Her curiosity itched at the back of her skull. If it was where the fae had been forced, and it did violate the rights of personage, it would make one excellent story. But that wasn't her life any more; she needed to be more cautious. If she could just remember where this was, maybe she could come back with Pelrin, and… Well, maybe Pelrin couldn't help these fae, but maybe she could do more research in the library about this and stake out this hole for more evidence. Afterall, she didn't need to physically be in London to pitch her story, even a news outlet back home would jump at the chance to cover such a dark topic. Surely it would be simple enough to find more information about what lay beneath the city in the library. She didn't need to get directly involved.

Freddie took a step back, and hit something tough. "What's a human girl like you doing, snooping around a fae hole like this?" A man, or ogre rather, with gray, leathery skin and two tusks protruding from his lower lip folded his arms behind her. Sunlight caught his irises and they flashed yellow.

Crap. "I—uh." She looked around. Could she scream loud enough for those police to hear her? Would they even recognize the danger over the other shouts in the square? There had to be another way out of this. She fingered the strap of her bag.

"What's that?" The brown fae snatched it from her shoulder and shoved one of his huge fists inside. She held her breath, rooted to the alley by fear and the knowledge she had nowhere really to go.

He pulled out her passport and flipped it open. "Wynnifred Jones? Huh, well isn't this my lucky day."

"What do you mean?"

The fae didn't respond, but grabbed her arm and dragged her towards the tunnel.

Pain shot up to her elbow and she cried out. "What are you doing? Let me go!" All logic fled her body and she screamed, praying someone would hear her as she was pulled deeper into the dark.

He shoved her forward to walk on her own, blocking out the daylight from where they came with his massive form. Freddie opened her mouth to protest, but then shut it again. It was her mouth and stupid curiosity that always got her into trouble. And neither had ever helped get her out of it.

They walked deeper and deeper into the darkness, until the orange glow of artificial light gleamed up ahead. She glanced over her shoulder, but the hulking fae continued onward, so she steeled herself for whatever was up ahead. More lights appeared to illuminate the ancient stone walls. Fae or human, whoever built this tunnel was long gone. The government must've just repurposed this place; it hardly looked like they did any work to ensure it was structurally sound.

As the lights grew brighter, the tunnel widened and a cacophony of noise echoed around them. They entered a broad atrium where hundreds of fae milled about ramshackle buildings recrafted on the bones of half crumbled structures.

Freddie stopped, for a moment forgetting she was here as a captive. There were so many people down here, and the government, at least the police, *knew*. No wonder this had been kept out of the news—the sheer volume of personal rights violations was enough to keep Britain in sanctions for eternity.

The hag she'd followed earlier stepped out of the crowd and looked from Freddie to the fae behind her. "Well, you found her fast."

"She was just lurking outside of the hole." The ogre shrugged.

The girl's eyes darted down, and then back up in a mask of false confidence that Freddie had donned far too many times not to recognize it. "Good, just like I planned."

"You mean just as Mr. O planned."

More fae were gathering around the two, distracted by their raised voices. Freddie took a step back and no one seemed to notice.

"Do you think I'm an idiot? Mr. O chose me for this mission because he at least recognizes talent."

"Talent? What type of talent does it take to point someone in the same direction they're already heading?" She looked meaningfully at Freddie, then ever so slightly jerked her chin to a dark passage opposite from the one she'd entered by.

Freddie took another step back into the crowd as it pressed in around them. Voices raised into a hushed torrent of anxious whispers.

Picking her way through the fae, she caught snippets of "American diplomats", "just as bad", and "after tonight". Everything in her longed to stay and root out the truth behind what was going on here. Something rotten was brewing beneath London's streets, but satisfying her curiosity would mean getting involved. And getting involved, at least when she did it, got people hurt. It'd got Freya killed—she'd learned her lesson.

Still, at the dark opening, she looked back once more to the arguing pair. "Go," the hag mouthed.

Freddie nodded and took several cautious steps into the dark before breaking into a run. Minutes which felt like seconds passed before the sounds of shouts and herding feet came after her. *Crap.* She darted down the first twist in the ever deepening dark as fast as her legs would carry her. But the fae weren't delayed by under-developed human muscles and grew ever closer.

"She can't get away. We're so close." An angry voice rang out as she passed what appeared to be the last sconce and was forced to slow. *No no no.* The further she went, the more complete the darkness, until she was moving as fast as she could, her arms flailing wildly before her.

If there had been light, the others would have surely been easily visible. "Come out, come out." Their jeering voices made her stomach flip and a scream bob in her throat.

Thin lines of light in a rectangular form shone faint against the dark. If it was a door, by God above please let it be unlocked. The other fae were too close for her to loop back. And even if she found the strength to keep going, they would eventually catch her. She ran at it with all her might. It burst open and she lost balance flying into a bright space and a hard surface that grunted. Freddie blinked, trying to make out where she was. With a squint, she recognized books... and something else. A tall, dark-haired figure looked up from one of the shelves. She met his flame-colored gaze, her heart nearly stopping in her chest.

Aiden.

"What are you doing here?" His voice was like a soothing balm across her nerves, and she hated that it comforted her. Despite her feelings, he'd abandoned her on that mountain to die. He was no more a savior than the gang of fae behind her.

The door burst open and three figures emerged, including her kidnapper. *Crap, crap, crap.* "That human is ours." Her kidnapper stepped forward.

Aiden's expression twisted into a snarl and his familiar blue flames ignited along his arms. "Touch her, and I'll roast you where you stand."

CHAPTER 6

Aiden

Heat blazed through Aiden's body as he stared down the three strange fae. An ogre, by the looks of his gray-leather skin, and two were-cats snarled at him, then fixed their gaze on *her*.

The silence in the cramped bookshop had a near-tangible tightness to it. It prickled at the back of his neck as the flames along his arms danced in time to his thundering heart. No one moved.

The floor beneath the ogre creaked, and Aiden whipped his head around. Before the brown fae could move any closer, Aiden stepped to the side, blocking Freddie from his path.

With an awkward chuckle, the ogre held up his hands. "Let's just say we never saw you; you never saw us."

Aiden jerked his chin back to the passage they'd come from. "Go then."

"Come on, girl. You don't want to hang around a fae like him." The ogre held out his hand to her as though they hadn't just been chasing her moments ago. Was this some kind of sick joke? Or perhaps it was another one of Wyn's manipulations. He turned slowly to see her expression, but it only reflected genuine fear.

"I-I'm good here, thanks." She raised her chin in what he'd learned was her false expression of confidence. But her voice made his cursed heart stutter as though it had learned nothing from the last time they'd been together. What was she even doing here? Her home was miles and an ocean away. Unless the prince brought her here for some sort of getaway... It was just the sort of thing he would do, and the type of thing Aiden would never be able to do for her. Not while he was under Oberon's command.

Of course, he wouldn't take her on a getaway now, not after what she'd done. Why were those thoughts even in his head? It shouldn't matter what the prince did with her. If anything, her being with the prince was a good thing. He could protect her from Oberon, and it would be one less thing for him to worry about when he likely failed to find the staff. He ground his teeth, the flames on his arms intensifying in their blaze.

"You don't know who he is," the ogre said. "We're just going to hold you ransom, but there's no telling what he'll do to you."

"Ransom her?" Aiden looked from the ogre to Wyn, whose eyes had gone wide.

"Why would you think I'd want to be ransomed? And to whom? And why?"

The were cats hissed, and the ogre took a step back. "We have our orders, and that does not involve telling you anything. I'm giving you one last chance, trust me, human, that fae you're hiding behind is not your friend."

"I know." Her voice was flat. He almost wished there was some emotion to it, some hint of what her lingering feelings might be. But perhaps there were none to hide in her voice. He swallowed hard. That was fine. It was how it should be.

Regardless, he wasn't going to stand by and let these three kidnap her. "She gave you her decision. Now go."

The ogre and the two weres exchanged glances. "Don't say we didn't warn you." With a grunt, the ogre led the way back into the dark passage, the door slamming behind them.

Aiden stared at the place they'd been until their footfalls faded into the heavy quiet, then he rounded on Wyn. "What was that?"

She opened her mouth and closed it, her breathing slowly regulating. Her hands balled into fists, and she took a step back. "Why do you even care? Thank you for helping me." Her voice seemed to break on the last word. "I have to go." She looked around as though lost.

His chest tightened. "Don't you think I have a right to know since you dragged me into whatever that was?"

"I didn't drag you into anything, and I have no idea what that was. Happy?" She took off towards the stairs and he followed her.

"You led them right to me and were happy enough to let me put myself between you and them."

She whirled on the first stair to face him. "Do you really think I sought you out on purpose? How would I even begin to do that?"

Anger still buzzed in his chest, but the logic of her words seemed to deflate it somewhat. She had no power to sense his magic or wend to his location. Was it truly chance that brought them back together? Some cruel machinations of fate? "Why are you here then?"

"An unlocked door seemed like a great place to escape to when being chased by strangers." She gave him a false smile, and he gritted his teeth.

"You know that's not what I meant."

Wyn scowled at him, then glanced around the shop. "I could ask you the same thing. I never took you for a weeb."

"A what?"

"You know, into all this... stuff." She gestured at a cardboard cutout of a scantily clad cartoon woman who seemed to be bursting out of her top.

He flushed. "I'm not. I mean, I'm just looking for something."

"Something in a manga shop, that's not manga?" Her gaze drifted back to the cutout, and she raised a brow. "Perhaps I should leave you to it."

"I didn't say it wasn't—what was that word you used?" *Freezing frosts.* Why did she have to be so infuriating? "I don't have to explain myself to you."

"Right." There was something of sadness in her voice, but she turned away, heading up the stairs.

Words caught in his throat. He longed to call after her, but why, and for what? There was nothing between them anymore, and there shouldn't be. Even if she hadn't betrayed him, Oberon still wanted her dead, and the closer they were, the easier she'd be to find.

If there was any hope of saving himself, and her, he needed to focus. He stared around the shelves, searching for Tatiana's book. If he could just find another one in the series, maybe he could find some more of a hint to where the author lived... a mailing address, perhaps. The thought of finding an author in one town had seemed challenging enough until he realized just how massive a *town* London truly was. There were likely thousands of authors here. He pulled the wrinkled copy out of his jerkin and clutched it tightly to his chest.

"What are you looking for?"

Her voice seemed to make his heart beat stronger, and he looked up. The icy quip on his tongue died as he took in her softened expression. He let out a slow breath. "I am looking for more information on the author of this." He held up the book.

"Why?"

"I need to find the author."

"For..."

He remained silent. Anything he could say to her would either drag her into this mess or be a sorry excuse at a half-truth. She narrowed her gaze at him. Wyn was too smart to think his silence meant anything other than him resisting those words.

"Fine. But most authors don't just have their addresses in their books." She folded her arms across her chest as though challenging him to spill more.

It had been too much to hope that there would be that information available. But there might be other ways to find the author, especially if she was fae. "I might be able to trace her signature if I could find a signed copy."

Wyn seemed to consider his words for a moment, then dropped her hands to her sides and turned around. "Come on."

Aiden's jaw fell open, but no words came out, so he hurried after her. Was it possible her familiarity with the Human Realm could help her find this woman? Though Tatiana had no idea where to look, Wyn was cleverer. She'd survived in Fairy, uncovered Mab's tricks, fooled him, and so much more. Pressing his lips together, he followed her up to the top floor. A bored-looking man wearing a wrinkled black button-down with a cartoon man on it sat behind a desk flipping through a magazine. He didn't look up as Wyn stepped up to the counter and gestured for Aiden to join her.

There was nothing outwardly threatening about the man, and Wyn seemed more impatient than scheming. Besides, she had no motive to sabotage his mission other than her harbored resentment for him leaving her on the mountain. A dull pain pulsed in his stomach, and he refocused his gaze from her to the man behind the counter. It had only been for a little while, a momentary lapse in judgment. She would have been fine if she'd still been there when he returned, but the prince had gotten to her first. This line of thinking had played repeatedly in his mind whenever his thoughts got too caught up in her. Usually, it was before he fell asleep at night or in the wee hours just before waking.

Swallowing hard, he stepped up beside her and placed the book on the desk loud enough to signal their presence. The man didn't look up but slid the book towards himself and scoffed.

"Of course, one of the popular titles. Let me guess, this is your first manga?" He let out a snorty laugh as Wyn jerked the book back towards herself, taking his magazine along with it. He fumbled trying to grasp it and looked up. "Oh, uh you're a—I'm sorry, m'lady. Typically, we don't get girls like you in here." He smiled, revealing plaque-colored teeth.

"What's that supposed to mean?" Aiden flexed his fingers. Was this the sort of place where humans weren't welcome? Was that why those people were chasing her here?

Wyn merely rolled her eyes. "I'm not buying the book; I'm looking for the author."

"Are you two together?" The man sniffed, acting as though Wyn hadn't said anything. In the early days of the war, Aiden had been made to help Oberon interrogate the spies from the other realms. Would they have to resort to such matters with this man? He hoped not; the memories of those acts still turned his stomach.

"Not in the way you're thinking." Wyn flashed a smile at him, and the man returned it. Was it possible that she was interested in this human? Surely not. There was nothing alluring about him. His voice was nasally; he looked as though he was more fit for bed than a day at work. There was no way Wyn could find him attractive, right? Aiden stared at her, but she seemed to only have eyes for the man behind the desk.

"Excellent. Well, Ms. Hidachi is local, and so am I, by the way."

Aiden could've sworn the man's accent grew thicker as he waggled his eyebrows at Wyn. She just continued to smile. Was it possible she was falling for this man's...charms?

"So, you do have signed copies in stock, or maybe a signing coming up?" she asked.

Aiden's heart sank, and the man leaned forward. "Ah, you probably saw online that we are the place to go for that kind of thing. But alas, we are all out of signed copies. Isaka has been dealing with—" he leaned in and flicked a glance to Aiden before whispering. "—those people problems."

"What does that mean?" Aiden crossed his arms. For a human, this man's breath could rival a troll's.

The man scowled up at him. "Maybe it would be better if you waited outside, sir. It's very rude to interrupt, and I don't think *you* should be in here anyway. You're giving your people a bad reputation."

"And what is *that* supposed to mean exactly?" Wyn snapped.

He straightened. "I guess you're a tourist and wouldn't know, but fae aren't supposed to be in this part of the city for safety reasons. They can be quite violent. Perhaps I should call someone?"

Flames erupted along Aiden's arms. *He* was the problem? The discrimination against fae was never something he was blind to, but he'd never experienced it quite like this. "Do you really wish to provoke someone you think is so violent? Tell me where the author is."

The man locked his jaw. "No, I'm not telling *you* anything. The police, on the other hand, will hear all about how you just threatened me."

Wyn sighed and pinched the bridge of her nose. Did she really not care? How had she changed so much? "Look, pretend I'm not with him. Can you just tell me?"

"Oh, my poor sweet lady. My girlfriend was just like you when we first met—traumatized from a toxic relationship."

Wyn raised her brows. "*You* have a girlfriend?"

"That's it. Both of you. Out!"

"But—"

"I just—" Aiden started, but the man was already busying himself with his device. No, this was his only lead; if it was a dead end, he'd have nothing. Rows upon rows of books shrank and multiplied. The illustrations along the walls blurred together, and in the back of his mind, Oberon's threat pulsed like a dragon's heartbeat. This wasn't happening. Everything couldn't be over so soon. The air around him thinned, and something red flashed in the corner of his eye.

He looked to where Wyn had stood. Maybe she could think of something. He was desperate enough to rely on whatever she came up with. But she was gone. The shop's bell dinged, and he whirled as she passed through the door.

"Where are you going?" He jogged to catch up with her, but she didn't even look back.

"My hotel. Do you care? I'm sorry you couldn't find your author for whatever reasons. Maybe I should be glad. Who knows what Oberon is having you do to that poor woman."

He flinched. She wasn't wrong, Oberon could have very well sent him on a mission like that, it wasn't as though he never had. The blunt realization of just how much Wyn knew about him hit him like a boulder. And she'd been accepting despite that, or at least he thought she had. Now he couldn't be too sure of her motivations. Still, if he failed, as it looked as though he was going to, she was in great danger.

He opened his mouth and closed it again. "I'm not—Oberon didn't ask me to harm the author. I just have some questions for her...if I can find her."

She turned. "What types of questions?"

Aiden shook his head. The less she knew about what Oberon was having him do, the safer she'd be. No doubt, Oberon would expect him to run straight towards her with his brief breath of freedom.

Finding the staff and getting as far away from Wyn as possible was the only way to keep her from getting killed.

"Right, well, good luck with that." She waved and headed back down the street.

Panic rose in his chest. He should let her go, let her get far, far away. But what if Oberon was already on to her? She was clearly already in some sort of danger, and he shouldn't care, but curses he did. "What about those people chasing you?"

She stopped again, now several feet away. "What about them?"

"Aren't you worried they'll find you again? They only let you go because of me."

"Well, if they do, it's not like I can rely on *you* to protect me. After all, you seemed perfectly happy to let me freeze to death in Winter." She crossed her arms and stared hard at him.

Something in her gaze made him feel as small as a pixie. He'd only left her there because she'd used him to kill someone. Had she forgotten about that? A nagging voice in the back of his mind seemed to buzz the horrible, guilty thought that hadn't granted him peace since that night. For all that she'd done to him, she didn't deserve to die for it. And abandoning a human in the Winter tundra was practically a death sentence.

"I'll walk you back." At least he could continue his doomed search without being plagued by thoughts of leaving her to get kidnapped out in the open.

She scowled at him and turned back in the direction she had been walking. Flicking out her phone, she pointedly ignored her as he caught up and kept pace half a step behind her. A heavy silence wafted between them as she trailed down streets packed with people, none of whom seemed to be fae. He kept his head down. If there was truth to what that man had said back at the shop, and he wasn't supposed to be in this part of the town, he'd need to avoid drawing attention to himself as much as possible.

Aiden tried to take a deep breath but choked on the acrid smog from the cars. He glanced at Wyn, who was staring intently at her phone, likely all thoughts of helping him find the author gone from her mind. After all, why should she help him? He'd nearly let her die.

"I think I found her!"

He stumbled, nearly crashing into her.

Wyn pointed to something on the screen. "It says there's an Isaka Hidachi who teaches anime drawing in Shoreditch... wherever that is."

She held it out, and he squinted at the course information. The next class was at three pm; hope swelled in his chest. "So, how do we get there?"

"How do *we* get there?"

"Yes, I—I mean, I'll walk you back to your hotel and figure it out."

"Do you want me to come with you?"

Yes. But even if he did say he wanted her with him, it'd be far too dangerous. "I'm fine."

He couldn't help but notice the slight slump in her shoulders as she led the way down the street. Her gaze had turned back to her phone. "Here." She held up the screen. "You'll have to take the Tube, but it should be pretty straightforward."

"The what?" He frowned at the map. There was nothing familiar about it. No doubt he'd be plenty lost by the time he found the place where the author supposedly taught, and she'd be long gone.

Wyn must've sensed his overwhelming confusion. She sighed. "Let's go, but if we get into some nonsense over there, you are telling me everything."

"Yes, uh— thank you." He glanced at the shabby manga shop, but there was no turning back. It was perhaps not the worst thing to spend the day with Wyn. Only a few months ago, he would have dreamed of this, but now...but now perhaps she was his only hope.

CHAPTER 7
Freddie

They stepped out from the tube station and stared around the vibrant streets. The buildings were splashed with artwork, and the streets and sidewalks were packed with people walking or sitting outside, eating and laughing. It was in stark contrast to the turmoil so thick in her body that she was practically vibrating. They'd ridden the train in silence, though her brain kept urging her to scream and cry.

How could he leave her to die on that mountain? Was what she'd done so bad? There hadn't been time to discuss a plan with him, and he *knew* that. If she hadn't used him against Mab, she would've been killed. But perhaps to him it was a small price to pay. After all, they might be close in age now, but to him, her life span would be far fleeting—a mere blip in his existence. Why should her life matter?

The dark thoughts pressed down on her, bringing with them the heaviness of sleep. She stopped placing a hand on the wall. Her eyes searched the street, making note of five people with dyed hair. She shifted her focus to the rough texture of the wall, the worn pattern of her jeans, the feeling of her socks against her feet, the heat of the sun on her body, and continued going through her senses as her therapist taught her. She would *not* break down now, not in front of him.

"What's wrong? Why are we stopping?" Aiden was watching her; his brow crinkled with concern. Concern for his mission, not for her, she reminded herself.

She straightened. "Nothing, I was just getting my bearings." Pulling out her phone, she punched the address into her GPS and led them down a series of streets to a green-tiled storefront. A glossy door on the front read "Pilgrim's Pizza," and the heavenly scent of bread, sauce, and cheese made her stomach roar. She flinched at the side-long look Aiden gave her.

What should she care if Aiden judged her growling stomach? He'd already proved he didn't care if she lived or died. If she passed out from hunger on the street, it would be her knowledge of where they were going that would save her, and not the goodness in his heart. Not for the first time did a dark voice in the back of her mind whisper that maybe Pelrin was right, maybe there was nothing good about Aiden. Still, deep down, she didn't want to believe that.

Shifting to put a bit more distance between them, she checked her phone again and frowned up at the building. A slim man in torn jean shorts, a baggy tank top, and pink streaked hair jogged into a side door. She followed him and noted a box with a list of numbers on the side. The top one read Battery Studio, the same name as the location of the class.

"I think this is it." She pulled open the door and stepped into a narrow hall leading up to a steep staircase. Unlike the mouth-watering scents from outside, inside smelled a mix of sweat and mothballs. She wrinkled her nose as the man's footsteps faded above them, and a door closed somewhere out of sight.

"Do you think there's an elevator?" Aiden's breath hitched, and if she didn't know better, she'd think there'd been a hint of excitement in his voice.

"A lot of these old buildings don't have elevators. But it's only five floors up."

Aiden stepped past her and started up the stairs. He paused when she didn't follow. "You're not coming?"

"I—" *Can't be around you right now. Feel like my insides are shattering. Hate that I still care for you.* "I don't need to babysit you through this mission, do I?"

He drew back, almost as though she struck him. "I suppose not. Just stay here, I'll still walk you back."

She threw up her hands and started up the stairs after him. "In that case, I might as well come along. I don't know why you'd bother."

"You are obviously in danger. I'm not going to just do nothing." He turned his back to her and continued up the steps.

Freddie sniffed. "So now you care."

He paused, and for one heart-stopping moment, she thought he might respond, but he didn't and kept on upwards. By the fourth floor, she had to fight to stifle her heavy breathing. Sweat leaked down the corners of her face, and she quickly brushed it away with the back of her hand. *Why did it have to be summer?* It was as though they were coming full circle. Their first date had been her sweating and panting up a massive staircase, and here they were again. At least this time, Aiden wasn't blowing hot air on her.

When they reached the top, she couldn't help letting out a long breath and leaning against the wall.

"Are you alright?" Aiden asked.

Freddie's brow knitted together, and she nodded. "This heat doesn't bother you? There are no windows in here." There were tiny beads of sweat on his brow. While in the Winter he'd appeared underdressed, his leather armor seemed overkill for this weather.

"I've been spending a lot of time in Summer. It's not the worst."

"Ah, yes, the beautiful realm where all the people are cursed." She shouldn't be here helping him. If she were to find a cure for her friends, without betraying Pelrin, she needed to get back to her book. There had to be some clue on the staff in there, or at least some other hint at what might work.

"It's only the capital that's cursed," he muttered.

"What?" The world seemed to sharpen as she straightened to stare at him.

"The curse was enacted in Elessea; everything beyond the city is—"

"Did you have something to do with it?" She took a step closer to him as anger simmered in her chest. This whole time, if he were to blame after everything, she didn't know what she'd do.

"I...had orders." He held up his hands, but she continued to advance.

How could he? This was before she'd gotten him to kill Mab, and it had been so many more than just her friends. Pelrin *had* been right. "Then you can break it."

"No."

"But you know how to, right?"

"It wasn't my curse."

"Please, my friends are trapped. Even you can't be that heartless."

His throat bobbed, and he shook his head. Angry tears clouded her vision, and a long-suppressed sob tore its way from her chest. This. This is why so many people hated him. How could he commit such horrible acts, then move through the world as though they were nothing? She sank to the floor and buried her head in her arms, letting the tears fall freely.

A weight on her shoulder made her flinch, and she looked up to see Aiden kneeling beside her.

"I had *orders*," he said again. There was something imploring about his tone. It wasn't his fault; she knew that better than most people. Still, it was just one more thing to add to the list of things to dislike about him. Her ragged breathing slowed, and she brushed away her tears with her palms.

"Oi! Are you two finally finished?" One of the doors on the landing burst open, and the pink-haired man stepped out with a bike. Freddie ducked her head and muttered an apology while Aiden straightened. "Honestly, babes, I've got better things to do than listen to this drama." He started towards the stairs, but Aiden blocked his path.

"We're looking for Isaka Hidachi. Have you seen her recently?"

The man narrowed his eyes, looking Aiden over slowly. "I could tell from your accent you weren't from around here, but there haven't been any fae in London these past few days. Isaka got out before the movers came. She's one of the lucky ones."

Freddie pushed herself to her feet. "Movers?"

"Yeah, they're the ones that cleared out all the fae. Trust me, mate, Isaka's not coming back anytime soon." He paused, giving Aiden another scrutinizing look. "And I'd keep an eye on this one if I were you." With that, he took off, walking his bike down the stairs.

Aiden gripped his hair and pressed his back to the wall. "I have nothing. Freezing frosts. There must be another way." He flicked his gaze to Freddie, then away.

"Another way to do what?" she asked. Whatever Aiden was up to, could it have something to do with the horrible way fae were being treated? The makings of a story itched at the back of her mind. *Don't get involved. That's how people get hurt.* She clenched her fists, shoving down the longing to chase answers.

"You don't need to get involved." Aiden's usually tawny skin had gone ashen, and he flexed his hands as he paced in the narrow space.

Freddie pressed her lips together. She should leave, go back to her hotel room, and bury herself in the book that might save her friends. He didn't need or want her to stay with him. But the worry, so obviously painted across his handsome features, tugged at her heart. Sucking in a breath, she looked up at him. "If you're looking for something in the Human Realm, I can help you." Even as she said the words, her head screamed at her to take them back. This was the jerk whose temper tantrum nearly got her killed. Why was she helping him? Only her heart knew for sure, but it wasn't coughing up any answers.

He shook his head. "It's too dangerous."

"You're right."

He stopped pacing and stared at her, the pained expression on his face momentarily replaced by confusion. "I am?"

"You cursed my friends and nearly got me killed. Anything to do with you is too dangerous. But here I am, stupidly offering to help you against my better judgment." She threw up her hands and leaned against the wall. It was either this or return to Mr. Fallus's bribe-room. If the book didn't have the answers on the staff, she'd be forced to stare at the wall until her father dragged her to another painful dinner. Which hell was worse?

Aiden opened and closed his mouth several times before letting out a long breath. "If I fail this mission, I'll lose everything. And now I have no leads and no hope. I doubt there's much you can do to help me." Glum bitterness stained his voice, but he remained staring at her as though storming, or wending, away was not an option.

His words had almost seemed like a challenge. And if her lifetime of snooping had taught her anything, it was that if one lead fell through, there were plenty of others to chase down. "What information were you hoping the author could give you?"

Aiden pressed his lips together as though the truth behind them was fighting to escape.

Freddie rolled her eyes. "You'll really have no hope if you refuse to tell me anything."

He sighed. "The author is said to have some information on a magical artifact I've been tasked with tracking down."

"You're relying on a manga artist to help you find it?" She raised a brow.

A muscle popped in his jaw. "Do you truly think judging my desperation will help me?"

"Do you really think avoiding telling me what exactly you are looking for will help?"

He glared at her, and a beat of silence passed like a wall of Jello between them. "Fine. Have you heard of the Staff of Wind?"

She tensed. *Crap.* Of course, helping him was a mistake. Why would anything work out nicely for her? "Why do you need it?"

"I've been ordered to get it."

Right. He couldn't disobey. She bit her lip. "You *just* need to get it?"

"What do you mean?"

She shook her head. With his magic and her knowledge of the Human Realm and the book, maybe they had a real chance at finding that thing. A nagging sensation clawed at her stomach. Working with him to find the staff would mean using him yet again. But they were already over, and betraying Aiden wasn't nearly as bad as leaving her in Winter to freeze to death. Besides, if she let him get the staff and managed to use a wish before he returned it to Oberon, he could fulfill his mission, and she could save her friends. As though it agreed with her logic, her stomach let out a loud growl. He looked at her, brows creased.

"Let's discuss this over pizza." She headed towards the stairs, already feeling lightheaded. Perhaps it was the hunger that drove her to want to help him. But she was in it now. All she had to do was work out a plan to steal a wish.

"Pizza?" he asked.

"It's…Just trust me, you'll love it."

Several minutes later, Aiden sat across from her, staring at the images on the menu. The reserved hunger in his eyes reminded her of the first time they'd dined out. Was Oberon still letting Aiden starve in pursuit of winning the war? She swallowed down her pity. After all he'd done, he didn't deserve it.

"You shouldn't waste your money on feeding me." He pushed the menu away and looked out the window.

"If you're hungry, you should eat. And I don't want you staring at me like a weirdo while I do."

"I'm not—" He grunted and glared at her.

She smirked. "The margarita is a classic, but the pepperoni…Do you like spicy?"

He shook his head. "Whatever you choose is fine."

Scanning the menu again, she nearly jumped when the server set a water down in front of her. Why did she have to be so on edge? It was just pizza; it didn't mean she forgave him. She ordered the pepperoni—sticking with something safe would at least give her one less thing to worry about.

"You can have half," she said after the server had left.

Aiden nodded and returned to staring out the window.

She thought back to the little she'd read about the staff. "Do you know much about the Treaty of the Realms?"

He turned to her, shifting awkwardly. "I don't see how testing my knowledge of fae history is going to be helpful."

"What *I* learned about the treaty is that it was what decided where the wall that separated Fairy from the Human Realm would go. It is also the most noted time the staff was used."

"It's not impossible if you had a lead. Maybe there's something else we can find. Is it here in the Human Realm?"

He shrugged. "Fae have been searching for the Staff of Wind for centuries. It's a hopeless mission."

Freddie stiffened. "You have to find the Staff of Wind? But Oberon can't use it." Unless he planned to use the tines...

"It's not my place to question his motives." His words were clipped as though he resented the way they felt on his tongue.

"So, what does the manga artist have to do with the staff?"

"It was a stupid lead. There was a rumor that she knew more about its history, and now I have nothing."

Freddie pursed her lips. "It's funny, Autumn is the smallest realm, and somehow, it's the only place where their object of power is lost. You'd think someone would've found it by now."

Aiden looked up. "It's not just funny, it's strange. The other realms are roughly equal in size, if you include Summer's islands. But the realms can't change..."

"Unless a powerful magic changed them. Do you think the staff's magic could've shifted the borders?"

"You know about its power?"

"It's the only thing that I could find that might break the spell my friends are under." That and possibly that strange spear Mr. Fallus offered her in exchange for Pelrin. "If we found the staff, maybe it could help us both."

Something sparkled in his eyes, but he didn't respond. Before she could prod at his silence more the server returned with the pizza. It was all she could do not to snatch one of the steaming slices and swallow it whole. No doubt burning the crap out of her mouth as she did.

"So, it's bread?" Aiden lifted a piece of pepperoni and sniffed it.

"It's so much more than that." She took a slice and took a tiny bite off the crust. It was surprisingly delicious.

"And you eat it from the widest part first."

Freddie looked down. "Well, I'm weird and eat it backwards. Most people start at the tip."

He rotated it, evaluating each end before taking a bite of the crust, and nodded. "It's good."

"Try the saucy part."

Aiden continued through the crust into the pepperoni and let out a moan.

"It's good, right?" She was already half through her slice. It was delicious and slowly satisfied her ravenous hunger. He didn't respond but devoured the rest of his piece. With a gulp of water, he frowned slightly as he reached for the slice of mushroom she offered.

"Should I be concerned that it burns?"

"It's supposed to be spicy. Haven't you had spicy food before?"

He nodded slowly. "It's been a while. I guess if you were planning on poisoning me, you've had plenty of opportunities before this." She was about to protest when she noticed the hint of a smile tugging at his lips.

"I'll save the poisoning for when we fight over the staff."

His smile slipped. "There's little hope of us finding it."

"Maybe... I have a book that I might find something in. Maybe if I look for more information on the borders of Autumn, or something about the history." She placed both hands on the table. "Do *you* know anything useful about it?"

"I—" He rocked his jaw back and forth, though he seemed to be actually considering her question. "I think it was what made Autumn such a small realm."

"You mean parts of the Human Realm were once part of Autumn?"

He nodded slowly. "It's been a while since I learned about the history of the realms, and it was fairly basic.

She pulled out her phone and searched for parts of the Human Realm that were once part of Fairy. There was nothing. The top result was a link to a story in a fiction forum about the realms being one. Pursing her lips, she tried again, this time searching for areas that had ancient fae settlements.

"What are you doing?" Aiden leaned forward, but she held up a finger.

There were signs of ancient fae all over the globe, but most articles seemed to be about the British Isles. Perhaps it was because the search engine was picking up on her location, but there were a ton of tours of fae settlements around here. More than she'd seen back home or read about in other countries. Her thoughts drifted to that one intern who said they'd seen them. Maybe it was worth another conversation with him.

She tapped on the first result. It was an in-depth explanation of the "hub" of Human Realm magic located in the Kerry Ring in Ireland. It was definitely not a day trip from London, but if Aiden went on his own, she risked losing the staff. But what if she was wrong? It was a leap to think a simple Google search held the answer to a centuries-old mystery.

No, she needed to confirm her suspicions before running headlong into a wild goose chase. Especially, when she only had two weeks to find the staff or decide if she would acquiesce to Mr. Fallus. Maybe the book had more information on the Autumn Realm, and perhaps that intern knew something about the old fae settlements in the area. She would start there before she told Aiden about the Kerry Ring. It was the safest choice.

Looking up, a smile tugged at the corner of his lips, and heat crept up her cheeks that had nothing to do with the food's spice level. She couldn't fall for his charms again. She forced herself to think of Amanda, Raul, and Jefferson, their bodies still, lying as though dead, trapped in a forever-slumber until she could find some way to break the curse. That was his fault. She couldn't just swoon over him because he was cute eating pizza.

"So, did you find anything on the staff?" he asked.

Freddie blinked, the images of her friends drifting to the back of her mind. "Maybe, I need to do more research."

He clenched his hands into fists. "And how long will that take?"

And there it was, all signs of his adorable innocence were gone. "I'm doing *you* a favor. You should be grateful I'm bothering to investigate this at all."

He clenched his jaw but didn't say anything. They finished their pizza in silence, and she called a car to take her back to the hotel. The app was connected to her father's credit card and was only supposed to be used in the strictest emergencies. But since he had dragged her all the way to London, she might as well take advantage of him paying for her rides.

Aiden followed her into the car, and she froze. "What are you doing?"

"I'm coming with you." There was gruffness in his voice as though he still hadn't gotten over her snapping at him.

"I don't need a babysitter."

His gaze flicked to the driver and back. "Did you forget what happened this afternoon?"

She sighed and scooted over to allow him to sit beside her. "Fine. But you're leaving when we get to the hotel. I don't need you hovering over me while I keep researching."

"As you wish."

When they pulled up in front of The Savoy, Freddie nearly tripped over herself in her haste to exit. Aiden caught her by the arm before releasing her and turning away. Before she could take a step towards the door, he whirled back around.

"I'll be waiting here for you tomorrow morning. Either you give me an update, or we find some other place to research."

"I don't respond well to ultimatums." She put her hands on her hips. Once again, she was rooted to the spot, knowing she should leave.

He let out a slow breath and nodded. "I appreciate your assistance."

Flashing him a fake smile, she forced herself to move towards the building. "I'll see you tomorrow at eight." Though her body burned to see his expression, she kept walking. It didn't matter what he thought of her. All that mattered was that she was able to make use of his powers to find the staff and free her friends. That was it. There was no other reason she needed to spend so much time with him.

The doorman nodded to her as she passed through the grand entrance and headed up the elevator. As she hurried down the hall, she caught the flash of a housekeeper's eyes. Odd, she could've sworn the maids she'd seen earlier were human, like everyone else above ground. She clenched her fist around the key and breathed slowly through her nose. Perhaps they let a few up from their banishment to work the jobs humans refused to fill. Hopefully, in two weeks, the edict to make the fae's relocation permanent would fall through, and all those people could return to their homes. Once again, she pushed away the longing to investigate their plight for an article. That wasn't who she was anymore.

Back in her room, she collapsed onto her bed and lay there for several minutes before rolling over and fishing the book out of her suitcase. The spine cracked as she opened the weathered cover and flipped through the frail pages.

More information on each of the objects greeted her, followed by several chapters on the history of Summer. It seemed to focus on the time before they'd tried to conquer the other realms. Either that, or the author had conveniently left out their violent past. She flipped through a few more pages, finding chapters on Spring, Winter, and finally Autumn.

The first part of the chapter was on culture, but then it got into geography. Towards the end of the chapter, one paragraph caught her eye:

Few are aware of the borders prior to the separation of the Human Realm, but Autumn had the strongest foothold on the other side prior to the treaty. During the times leading up to the human takeover, there were several settlements in an area the humans called Europe. They were all decimated post-separation when humans drove out the last of the Autumn citizens.

Her breath caught. It was a strong argument; she was right. Maybe that intern could add more insights on the Kerry Ring—what had been there, the role the settlements there played in the separation, or anything on hidden ancient artifacts. If he confirmed her suspicions, it would be worth it to slip away and investigate firsthand. Her heart squeezed. Finally, she had a real lead on the staff and hope to save her friends without having to sacrifice Pelrin.

She glanced at the time on her phone—the interns should be getting back soon. Maybe she could meet them in the lobby and corner that guy and avoid another painful dinner. Getting to her feet, she tucked the book into her bag and double-checked her key, wallet, and phone. Before she could reach the door, a deafening boom shook the building, and something hot and powerful blasted her off her feet. Shards of glass scratched at her face and arms, and her head hit the wall. The room, now in ruins, blurred as she slid to the ground, and her vision went black.

CHAPTER 8
Aiden

Aiden stalked away from the hotel, frustration brewing in his chest like a nest of angry sprites. She *knew* something about the staff and was refusing to tell him. And now what was he supposed to do, wait for her like an abandoned dog?

He let out a growl under his breath, crossing the street heedless of the direction he was going. When had she become so infuriating? He'd been lovesick over her for so long, he'd failed to see just how annoying she could be. Perhaps he should've known when she kissed him that night, drunk off fae magic, and then again when he saved her from that den of vampires, she would be nothing but trouble for him. She was just a frail human sticking her nose into fae business and nearly getting herself killed over it.

Running a hand through his hair, he entered a square packed with people. It was an easy place to get lost in, and he supposed it was safer than walking through the less crowded streets. Though the human police posed little threat to him, the less attention he drew to himself, the better.

A fountain splashed playfully at the center of the plaza. He made his way over to it and sat on the edge of the basin. Humans closed in around the edges, taking pictures and tossing in coins. If he gathered enough of them, perhaps he could afford a bed for the night. Nothing as lavish as where Wyn was, but there had to be someplace he could go. Returning to Autumn without the staff was hardly an option.

He rolled up his sleeve to reach in when a loud boom shook the ground. People screamed and rushed towards him, past the fountain. Black smoke rose, filling the air with a cloying metallic stench. For a moment, he just stared, his mind too numb to process what he was seeing. Then a horrible realization hit him full on in the gut.

Wyn—the smoke was coming from the direction where he'd left her. He wended back to the hotel, not caring if anyone noticed, and his heart dropped. The building's facade was gone, and debris still rained down onto the street. Sirens blared behind him, drowning out the screams. Soot-stained and bloodied people ran and limped from the rubble. He scanned the crowd.

Wyn, Wyn, Wyn. Please be here.

But there was no sign of her. He reached out with his magic, feeling for his presence. It was faint, but blessedly still there. Following the signal, he wended

The room reminded him of one of the homes he'd destroyed in Fairy. His heart lurched as his mind dragged him back to countless battles, his flames engulfing everyone in sight. Scents of burning flesh and anguished screams clouded his senses, driving him to his knees. He shook his head and gripped a piece of glass so hard it cut into his hand but blessedly brought him back to the present.

"Wyn?" he called out and coughed as smoke crept into his lungs. Slowly, he stood and picked his way through the rubble. The front of the room was gone. Wind blew smoke to block his view of the street, giving him the false sense of a wall. Leaping over a hole in the floor that had once led into another room, his heart lurched when he saw a body, clutching a small bag, lying in a heap against a far wall. It was covered in ash and red blood, no more than a lump.

"Wyn!" He scrambled over a large bit of wall and a fallen light fixture to kneel beside her. Brushing the rubble from her scratched and burned skin, he cradled her close to his chest. "Please live." She was so still.

Outside, the sounds of the city and shouts from somewhere in the distance faded against the thundering of his heart. Removing the large bits of debris from her body, he tucked her bag beneath one arm and closed his eyes, wishing that they were far away from the building. Magic stirred in his chest, and instinctively, he pulled on it, not truly knowing what it would do. The room before him blurred, and he stumbled, nearly falling back into the fountain.

Wyn was still in his arms, her warmth pressed against him like a soothing balm. Had he just wended? But it wasn't possible to wend with another person; neither his tutelage in Summer, nor with Oberon had ever mentioned that as a possibility. Mare could travel with others, but her magic was different and mysterious. Then again, so was his own. He flexed his hand, momentarily mesmerized by his newfound ability. Wyn twitched, the slight movement snapping him back to the disastrous scene.

There were far fewer people in the square now, and those remaining stared up at the rising smoke. Sirens wailed around them, accompanied by a cacophony of shouts and screams. What in the seven realms could have caused this?

He smoothed a crease in Wyn's brow, the dust so thick his fingers drew a smudge across her forehead. "You're going to be fine." The statement was as much to her as it was to him. But at least healing magic was something he was familiar with. Drawing magic up from his chest, he pushed it to his lips and placed a gentle kiss on her brow.

For a moment, her skin glowed blue, then the burns faded, the cuts knitted themselves back together, and her body healed until her torn clothes and ash-stained skin and hair were the only signs she'd been in danger.

Her eyes fluttered open, and she stared up at him. She twisted in the direction of a passing siren, and he had to struggle not to drop her. "What?"

"Are you alright?" Aiden placed her back on her feet, but she pressed herself to him. It felt good, and he hated himself for enjoying it when she was clearly not concerned with him.

"I was just in the room and then—" Wyn looked back at him, her brown eyes searching. "What happened?"

"I'm not sure. There was an explosion, and I raced to find you." He tensed. Less than an hour ago, he'd been caught up in how infuriating she was, yet when she was in danger, he was still the moth to her flame.

"And you managed to get me out before I got hurt?" There was a tremble in her voice as she inspected the skin beneath her torn clothes.

He shook his head. "I just healed you. I didn't know—I couldn't get to you before it happened." The urge to wrap his arms around her and shield her from what she'd just been through pulled at him. Folding his arms across his chest, he pulled away from her.

"Thank you," she breathed. Shiny tears streamed from her eyes, and her shoulders shook in silent sobs.

He moved a hand to touch her shoulder, then thought better of it. Was this Oberon's doing? Had he attempted to destroy her before their bargain was even up? He wrapped his arms around himself. This couldn't be his fault—not yet. He hadn't failed. Oberon might be able to lie, but he'd lose his leverage against Aiden if he killed Wyn this soon. Her life was far more valuable than his.

Perhaps this was an attack from those people who'd attempted to kidnap her. However she'd gotten into that mess, it seemed targeted rather than an opportunistic chance. They would have had to have known she was worth a ransom. He dropped his arms and clenched his fists at his sides. Whoever it was, he'd make them regret nearly killing her, if it was the last thing he'd do.

"I need to find my dad. I need to tell him I'm ok." Wyn looked up at him. Gone was her cold demeanor, replaced by a vulnerable softness. It would've pulled him back to how they'd been before, but her fear was so palpable he knew it wasn't some sudden affection encouraging her to display this side of herself.

Nodding, he looked around the square. "Where do we go?"

"Westminster. It's about a fifteen-minute walk that way." She pointed, and they took off, gradually getting further and further away from the chaos.

People they passed gave them odd stares as they moved quickly down several blocks. For once, it seemed that it was Wyn drawing their attention. The disarray of her appearance and the smoke coming from behind them seemed to tell several stories to the passersby. His pointed ears twitched when he heard one woman whisper about them possibly being suspects of causing such a disaster. After all, who looked like they'd survived an explosion and walked away fine?

No one stopped them until they reached the final block, and the entrances to the grand building came into view. Black vested people stood around the outside, stopping those who passed them and inspecting something they handed over. Wyn slowed, her lips moving soundlessly as her gaze drifted between the nearest doors to the building.

"What are they doing?" Aiden moved closer, hoping to see what they held.

She shook her head. "Looks like they are checking IDs. Not good for us."

"Why not?"

"Did you suddenly get a Human Realm identification card?" A hint of the old sharpness floated back into her voice. He tried desperately to ignore it.

"Do you have one of these IDs?"

She nodded and snatched back her bag to dig for the contents. Rummaging through, she pulled out a small blue booklet. When she flipped it open, there was a pretty, yet dull, photo of her with some text beside it. He held out a hand to create a mirror of it for himself, but a flurry of people, clad in black, exited the building.

Wyn sucked in a breath, and he looked over the group again. This time, he recognized her father and that horrible fae-hating politician. He pulled her out of their path, but they were still close enough to listen in on their conversations.

"I need to get back there. My daughter could've been in there," her father said.

"Calm down, Earl. No one important was hurt." Oberon's brother placed a hand on Wyn's father's shoulder, and Aiden flexed his fingers.

"You don't know that. The rescue workers haven't gotten inside the room yet."

"Trust me. I just saw her at lunch, she's fine. She's probably out enjoying the city and wasn't even in there."

"I just need to check on my *things*," cried a red-haired girl behind them. Aiden scowled and hurried after Wyn as she moved alongside them.

The older men ignored the girl's cries and continued to march down the street. "You know this was part of the plan. I ensured she was out of the way before they set it off." His voice was barely audible over the clacking of the young women's heels.

"You're sure? You've heard from them?"

"Not yet, but those fae are desperate for anything that will make them feel powerful. Now, both governments can't deny the threat the fae pose."

Aiden slammed into Wyn as she stopped in front of him. The glammour flickered, but he quickly concentrated back on the spell. "What's wrong?"

"He *knew*. My dad knew this was going to happen. He knew they were framing the fae and putting unjust laws in place." She shook her head and stared blankly after the group as they headed out the door.

"I'm sorry, Wyn, I know how important that was to you," Aiden said as they watched the last of the younger people disappear.

"He *knows* what he's doing is wrong and that it's destroying people's lives. How could he?" She made to follow them down the stairs, and Aiden hurried after her. Once they were back on the street, Wyn looked around and headed back the way they came. Opposite them, one of the people who'd been with her father was getting into a shiny black car.

"Wyn, I think—"

"I don't care." Her eyes blazed with unshed tears as she turned to face him. "We have a staff to find, right?"

"Now? We don't know where to start."

"In my book, it talked about ruins from the time Autumn still had territory in the Human Realm. I have a hunch it's in Ireland, but I never got a chance to confirm." She looked down at her shoes as though half apologizing for the incomplete theory.

"No fae would have searched Human Realm ruins. They would've thought it beneath fae-kind, or something equally as haughty. We have nothing else to go on, so we might as well try. If we can find a map of the place, I might be able to wend us there."

"No need. We can take the bus." Wyn pulled her lips thin, watching her father and the others slip into a row of black cars.

"Don't you need to tell your father you're alright? I doubt he'd want you traveling after—"

"—he'll be fine. He knew about the bombing. I could've died because of his stupid crusade. Let him stew." She slung her bag over her shoulder and marched past the palace.

Aiden took one last look at the grand building, his heart racing as he followed her. Perhaps traveling together was best. Now he could protect her from Oberon or any of the other people who seeked to harm her. At least until the full moon.

CHAPTER 9
Freddie

Freddie charged towards Big Ben as though it were some sort of beacon drawing her in. Truthfully, she just needed something to guide her—some place to be headed that wasn't Westminster, and the famed clock tower was closest. There were crowds of people milling about and taking pictures as though the bombing hadn't happened. Perhaps they hadn't heard. The plume of smoke was hardly visible through the buildings.

Aiden kept pace with her, saying nothing. Something about him, seeing how little her father cared, rubbed her emotions raw. Of all the people to see her so vulnerable, and he was equally as guilty. Just another person she'd cared about, setting her up to die as though her life never meant anything to them. She swiped at the tears welling in her eyes. It didn't matter what her father or Aiden did anymore. If she could find the staff and free her friends, she could surround herself with those who genuinely cared for her and leave them behind.

Several people in bright outfits, holding stacks of brochures, called out to passersby. She paused as one called out, "Fairy Ireland." A short woman in a bright red top hat waved a brochure at an elderly couple who were backing away as though she were threatening them.

"Senior tour of Fairy Ireland! Leaving this evening, last call," she called again, wildly waving around the papers.

Freddie moved closer. "Can I see one of those?"

The woman scowled. "It's sixty-five plus, dear."

She went back to her shouting, and Freddie skirted around her, trying to catch a glimpse of the brochure. It was hard to see, but she could just make out a bus on the front. "Where does it leave from? My grandparents are back at the hotel; they might be interested."

"You want one? Fine." The woman shoved a pamphlet at her and then stalked away to the other side of the street.

"What's that?"

Freddie jerked, momentarily forgetting Aiden was there. He leaned over her shoulder, and she unfurled the brochure, angling it so that he might see. "This goes around the Kerry Ring. That's where the majority of the ruins are."

"And they will just take us there?"

She flexed her jaw and scanned the page, pinpointing the departure time and location. They only had a couple hours to make it to the train station before the next tour left. "They *might* take us there. Hopefully, we can convince them." She gave him a pointed look, and he nodded. A guilty twinge tugged at her chest, but she ignored it. Using him was nothing compared to leaving her to freeze to death. The first time she'd done it, she'd been desperate—now, she didn't care.

Digging in her bag, she pulled out her phone, and her heart sank. The screen was dark and hopelessly cracked. How were they supposed to find the station without a GPS? Several other people shouting out various tours stood at random intervals before Big Ben. She marched over to a man calling out to tourists about a double-decker city tour.

"Excuse me, can you point me in the direction of, um, London Euston Station?"

He nodded at her. "You American?"

She nodded, her heart pounding with impatience.

"I got a tour that will take you right past there. It's a hop-on-hop-off, and you'll get to see all the sights. The eye, St. James Palace—"

"—there's a train we need to catch." She tried to give the man an apologetic smile, but he frowned and looked her over as though seeing her for the first time.

"Guessing you'll be taking the bus. The station's quick walk over there. Parliament Street." He jerked his chin at the road and turned away.

For a moment, she thought to call after him and challenge him for daring to assume she couldn't afford a car based on how she looked. But then she looked down at her torn and filthy jeans and touched the matted mess that was now her hair. She couldn't blame the man for thinking that about her; bombing survivors weren't typically hailing cabs less than an hour after the explosion.

"Should we trust him?" Aiden asked and looked in the direction the man had indicated.

She shrugged. "I guess so." They took off down the street, easily finding their way to the bus stop. Aiden seemed to look everywhere but at her while they waited. That was fine, even if he was repulsed by her haphazard appearance, his opinion didn't matter. Still, she would need to find someplace to clean up if they wanted to convince the tour to accept them.

Two stories and violently red, the bus pulled up, and she dug her wallet out of her bag. At least that hadn't been destroyed in the blast. The cash she exchanged was still in there, along with her dad's black card he'd given her for emergencies. If she used it, he would be able to track the purchase, and he didn't need to know anything about where she was going. Thankfully, she'd been smart enough to get an Oyster Card at the airport and swiped it twice for herself and Aiden.

The bus driver gave her a disgusted look as she entered.

Trying not to react, she gave her a polite smile. "Do you know which stop we should get off for Euston Station?"

The bus driver scratched her chin, her nose still wrinkled as she seemed to consider the question. "Drummond Street is probably your best bet."

Freddie thanked her and selected a seat on the first floor while Aiden slid beside her. He was too close; his spring rain scent seemed to beg her senses to relax. But despite everything, he made her feel safe, and she hated him for that. Her chest tightened as she stared out the window, doing her best to forget he was beside her.

They passed buildings that alternated from sleek modern designs to older architecture that gave the city a quaint flair. The scent of smoke tingled her senses as the bus whipped past Trafalgar Square. Several people gasped and pointed at the smoke and lights coming from the emergency vehicles crowding the street leading to The Savoy. The edges of her vision blurred, and her lungs seemed to have forgotten how to breathe. She clutched the seat in front of her, turning her fingertips white with pressure.

Aiden moved his arm as though to rest it on her shoulder, then pulled it back and placed his hand on his lap. His amber gaze remained fixed on her, and she stared into his eyes, momentarily lost. God, he was handsome, but perhaps that was the most dangerous thing about him. She blinked, and the smoke and sirens were gone. The buildings resumed their stations along the street, and she let out a breath.

Throughout the bus, people talked in hushed tones about the bombing. She fought to shut them out by focusing on the city. A blue neon sign appeared up ahead with the name of a store she recognized from back in the states. Getting to her feet, she inched around Aiden towards the front of the bus.

"Is this it?"

Freddie ignored his question as the bus slowed to a stop across the street from the store, and she hopped off. Hurrying across the street, Aiden followed her inside the massive store and stared around as though it were some grand cathedral. Rows upon rows of racks filled the space with everything from toiletries to underwear, and yet an escalator led up to even more. She busied herself with picking out necessities: jeans, shirts, a comb and a bonnet, and everything else that she would need for the next few days.

"This place is incredible," he murmured as she made a beeline for the checkout. He had no idea. Not only did it have everything, but it was blessedly cheap. She still had money left for them to eat for at least a few days.

After she paid, she made her way to the bathroom to clean up. A couple of women stared at her as she washed her face and did her best to wipe the grime off from the other visible parts of her body. Changing into her new jeans and a t-shirt, she fixed her hair into two French braids, and tossed her ruined clothes in the trash.

Aiden raised his brows when she returned. "You look—I mean, I could've glamoured you."

"Then I would both feel gross from all the dirt and your magic." She gave him a wincing smile.

He swallowed, his features stiffening. "It was just a suggestion as you *clearly* needed help."

The truth of his words hit her like a blow to the gut, but she forced herself not to show the hurt. Instead, she turned and headed back to the bus stop. Minutes later, they were back riding towards the train station. When they reached, she led the way off and looked around.

There was a sign indicating the direction of the station. Her calves ached as she sped walked down the sidewalk. How much time had passed? The detour at the shop had been a necessary time-suck, but it'd been hard to tell if they'd been there for an hour or more.

Finally, they reached the station, and she let out a breath of relief when she saw the clock. They had thirty minutes before the tour left. Now she just needed to find it. A man in a blue vest, marking him as a member of the station staff and Freddie leaped out to show him the pamphlet. He brushed her off and pointed to two people in yellow vests surrounded by a crowd of old people.

"I guess this is it." She glanced up at Aiden, who squared his shoulders.

"What do we need to do?" he asked as they made their way towards the group.

"Somehow, we've got to convince them that we have tickets and there's space for us. Even though we're not elderly and way too broke for this trip."

He pressed his lips together; his gaze fixed on the crowd. "I think I can get us tickets, but I'm unsure of how to convince them we belong."

"I guess we'll figure it out."

Nodding, Aiden approached a couple who looked to be just at the age cut-off. He glanced back at Freddie before stepping in front of them. "May I see your tickets?" The air seemed to shiver around them as the man dug into the pocket of his jacket and handed them over.

"Charles! I just remember we are supposed to catch a flight to Paris in a couple of hours." The woman placed a hand on the old man's arm. For a moment, he stared at her in confusion, then slowly nodded.

"I think you're right. We'd better hurry." He gave Aiden a curt wave as they headed towards the station exit. Freddie turned back to the platform to see an elderly man, hunched over his luggage and staring at him. When he met her gaze, he quickly turned away.

Aiden tapped her on the shoulder and passed the tickets over. "Was that sufficient?"

"Do they really have a flight to Paris?" She watched the couple until they disappeared amongst the crowd.

He shrugged. "At some point in time, I suppose. I just brought the thought to the front of their minds; I can't control them. And even if I could, I wouldn't."

"Nice to see you care about some things." She made her way to the front of the crowd before he could respond. Hearing him say he cared about other things, but not her, was more than she could take. Not today, when her life had fallen to shambles so disastrously.

A woman in a yellow jacket stood in front of the crowd, her back to the empty platform. She looked unnaturally cheery, though her happiness could be exaggerated by the misery dragging Freddie down.

Sucking in a breath, Freddie approached her. "Could you check our tickets? My grandmother gave them to me. She said London was too far for her to travel in this heat."

The woman frowned. "This tour really is for seniors. Your gran shouldn't have done that."

Freddie wrung her hands and looked around. The anxiety that they truly wouldn't be able to join the tour lent itself well to her act. "We don't have any other place to stay. She said it would be fine."

The woman took the tickets and scanned them with a black box hanging from a band around her neck. "Well, they are valid. I'll go ahead and check you in, but you must keep in mind this is a senior trip. It's not designed for partying or heavy drinking. I won't tolerate guests who tarnish our brand."

"Of course not." Freddie sighed. "Thank you so much." She beckoned Aiden, who made his way through the crowd to stand beside her.

They stood to the side as a train pulled into the station. A man, similarly dressed to the woman, poked his head out of the first entrance. He chuckled. "Hello folks, I'm Liam, and Grand Tours welcomes you aboard!" Liam looked to be in his late thirties with unfortunately wispy hair and a charming accent that nearly made up for it. He grinned at his companion on the platform, who opened her mouth to speak.

"Move aside. I've been standing for the last forty-five minutes, and I need to sit." The man Freddie had caught staring at them shoved his way to the front of the group.

"I'm sorry, sir, boarding will be in just a couple of minutes, I just—"

"I have arthritis. Not all of us are as young as you, love," a woman said, following behind the man.

Their guide sighed and stepped aside. "I guess I can do introductions on the train."

Freddie allowed herself to get swept up by the crowd as they moved towards the bright red engine. It wasn't until she was halfway through the dining car that she realized Aiden was several people behind her. Stepping aside, she waited for him to catch up as the rest of the group took seats at tables or traveled beyond to their compartments.

"Abandoning me on this...long car is not going to help you," he grumbled as he finally reached her.

"And abandoning me in the middle of Winter was supposed to help?" She glanced at the tickets and stepped into the aisle. The faster they got to their compartment, the better. At least there she could be alone with her misery, or at least as alone as she was going to get with *him*.

"I didn't—I was angry," he said as they passed through the dining car.

Freddie clenched her fist and pressed her other palm against the compartment door. "You were angry, and I nearly died." Without turning back, she wrenched the door open and slammed it shut behind her, blocking Aiden out.

His shadow lingered behind the frost glass window as she sat on the bench and pulled her knees to her chest. The gentle rocking of the train was a comfort as her vision blurred from unshed tears. First Aiden, then her father, people who supposedly cared for her, had transformed into those who didn't care if she lived or died. Her friends were gone, and it was her fault. Did her mother even still love her?

A sob tore its way out of her chest, and she finally let herself fall apart.

CHAPTER 10
Aiden

Aiden drummed his fingers on the table in the dining car and stared out the window. Grassy hills and an indigo sky whipped by, so far from the city lights it almost looked like they were in Fairy. Lively chatter surrounded him, but he wished he could shut it out; shut everything out. His feelings warred within him, guilt and anger clashing like giants against his head.

Wyn had betrayed him; she had used him. He had every right to be angry with her. And it wasn't like he hadn't come back to find her. She wouldn't have died...not that she knew that. Perhaps he should tell her. Then at least she'd know he regretted how he acted and he'd tried to make it right. But she hadn't apologized either. Did she even realize how deeply she'd hurt him?

He curled his fingers, staring down at his hands, too helpless to make a difference now. It was best to leave her be after everything that had happened to her. The sound of her sobs still tore at his heart. His part in ruining her day had been minimal compared to nearly getting kidnapped, surviving that attack, and learning her father was behind it. Anger flashed in his mind, making him sit up. Her father had always been kind to him, but he'd never forgive what he'd done to Wyn.

Aiden sucked in a breath, forcing the flames threatening to break free from his skin to settle. Wyn's father should be the least of his worries. They were at least on a path for the staff, but there was no certainty, just a hunch. And what if they were wrong? What if the deadline passed and Oberon hunted them down? What if he made him...? Aiden flexed his hand desperately, shoving the worries back to the furthest corner of his mind.

"Where's your lady friend?" A gruff man eased himself into the seat opposite Aiden.

"What?" Aiden stared back at him. With most fae fearing him and many humans avoiding his fae eyes, most people didn't seek out his company. Only Wyn, and he didn't even have her anymore.

"The girl you were with. She dumped you?" He waved a hand, and a woman in a neat uniform came over to them. "I'll have a cuppa," he said before she could ask.

"And for you?" She turned to Aiden, who shook his head. She left them, and the old man frowned after her.

"Is there something you need from me?" Aiden asked. It might not be the kindest thing to say to the man, but he needed to be left alone with his misery.

"They let you enter the Human Realm with those fae manners?" He scoffed. "Name's Winston Jameson, but you're young. That's Mr. Jameson to you."

"Sorry, Mr. Jameson, but—"

"What you should be sorry about is the way you follow that girl around like a kicked pup. My wife always tells me to leave young people alone, but I'll tell you what, girls like that are nothing but trouble."

"Girls like what, exactly?" Aiden stared incredulously at the man. There were plenty of other people in the car: a couple sleeping against each other in one booth down, a group of giggling women eating snacks, and a few men playing cards at the table across from him. Mr. Jameson could join any one of them or sit alone.

"Girls that make men like us muppets." The uniformed woman set down a steaming cup of tea, and the man waved her away without so much as a thanks.

"Muppets?" Aiden looked around again, hoping the man would take the hint and leave.

"Yeah, that's right. You need to make her crazy about you, never the other way around."

"Thank you for the advice, but—"

"You hear they want us to walk all around Dublin tomorrow. As though people my age are still up for exploring. You listen to me. You take her on some fussy date but don't drop so much as a pound on it. Take her to the park or something."

"We're not exactly—"

"—It's not like she deserves you spending all that. Not until you get the upper hand, right?"

Aiden stared blankly back at him. But the man paid him no mind and sipped his tea. The sky fell to a pitch black, and the giggling women were now lumbering off towards the compartments. He yawned, partially from exhaustion, though it was nothing compared to what he endured with Oberon. Dramatizing his second yawn, he hoped that Mr. Jameson would follow the women's lead and head off to bed on his own.

"You need some coffee in you. I have my tea, helps me stay up. Oi!" He snapped his fingers, and the uniformed woman looked up from the ladies' table she was now wiping down.

"Yes, sir?"

"Get a coffee for my grandson here."

"I'm not—" Aiden began.

"—makes them move faster if they think you're a family."

The woman sighed. "Any cream or sugar, love?" Aiden opened his mouth to respond, but Mr. Jameson cut him off again.

"He's a man. He'll have it black." Again, he waved the woman away and leaned in. "That's how you Americans drink it, right? You see, I'm pretty well-traveled. My wife and I once spent an entire summer in New York." Aiden gave him a weak smile. The woman returned and set down a cup of black liquid. He'd often smelled it when their majesties had breakfast, but he'd never been permitted to taste coffee. It was a human delicacy they had smuggled and refused to share with their underlings.

He took a sip and scowled.

"Haven't you had coffee before? Or are you one of those posh types?"

"It tastes like sour dirt."

"That's how you know it's good. Now drink up."

Aiden cringed and brought the cup back to his lips. He shouldn't let this man pressure him, but where else was there to go?

The uniformed woman tapped him on the shoulder, making him jump. She held out a covered bowl and gave him a knowing smile. "Try some sugar, love." He took the bowl and took a couple spoonfuls of the white crystals. When he tried the coffee again, it was far more tolerable.

"Priss," Mr. Jameson grumbled under his breath. Aiden's mind buzzed as he slowly drained his cup. The old man had pulled out a book and was now muttering through the pages. Would he notice if Aiden got up and moved to another booth? As though triggered by the thought, the man looked up and scowled at him. "You read much history?"

"No, I can't say that I have." Aiden's shoulders sank, inwardly resigning himself to his new companion.

"Look here." Mr. Jameson turned his book to him. "It's all about where we're going. All different pre-wall fae sights. You know about those?"

Aiden shook his head.

The man grunted. "It's true what they say about that American education system, then."

For a moment, Aiden wondered if he should correct him. But it was probably better that he thought Aiden was from where Wyn lived rather than Fairy. The absence of his kind on the city streets left a strained unease throughout his body.

"You got your Knockma Wood, 'says there was once a settlement there. Probably only ruins now, but we'll see." He flipped the page, displaying a sketch of a castle designed with the curving domes and twisting spires of those in Fairy. "Ah, you'll like this one. Galway, it's an old Fairy city, but it's more of a mix now. You know what happened with all of them."

"What happened?" As much as he hated to admit it, Mr. Jameson's book was actually interesting. Perhaps the old man would let him borrow it once he finished.

"Good Lord, the burnings, the wall. Did you learn nothing in history?" The man slapped a hand to his forehead. "My wife would love you. She goes on and on about history. Boring, that's what she is, but I guess some people need it."

Aiden clenched his hands into fists. Given the chance, he'd gladly listen to any lecture about history or anything other than war and magic. Nearly half his life had been spent honing him into the perfect weapon; he had little value outside of that.

Mr. Jameson pounded a bony finger at an image of a rectangular pool. "This here's the Wormhole. Looks like it was carved, eh?"

"It wasn't?" He leaned in, studying the image, noting the sea beyond the pool and the rough waves within.

"Not that scientists and historians can tell, but what do they know? There's a legend that it was created by a powerful fae weapon." Mr. Jameson raised his brows and smiled as though waiting for Aiden to be impressed.

Aiden sat straighter. "What type of weapon? A staff, uh, maybe?"

He could've sworn he saw a look of triumph flash across the old man's face, but when he blinked, Mr. Jameson looked bewildered. "It's a legend, nobody knows the truth. Maybe a staff, maybe a sword, might even be a back scratcher for all anyone knows. We're not going there, though. Gotta take a boat to reach it."

Aiden's shoulders sagged. Yet another hunch and one that would be even more challenging to investigate. Perhaps he should focus on hiding and providing Wyn with as much protection as possible for when Oberon inevitably came for them.

The book closed with a snap, and Mr. Jameson groaned as he got to his feet. "It's late, and they are going to be herding us around all day. You shouldn't be pressuring an old man to stay up this late."

"I wasn't—"

"I'm going to bed, and you should too. Remember what I said about that girl of yours. Muppets, you hear?"

Aiden nodded, though he wasn't quite sure of what the man was saying. He watched as Mr. Jameson tottered off towards the compartment, finally leaving him alone. Leaning against the window, he closed his eyes, but sleep would not come. Despite the long day, his mind buzzed like it was charged with electricity.

The sites the man had pointed out flitted in his mind one after another. Any one of them could hold a clue to where the staff was. Especially that Wormhole—somehow, they would need to get to it.

He moved to leave the booth and tell Wyn, then froze. If she were awake, he'd be the last person she wanted to talk to, besides her father, perhaps. After all, she was only looking for the staff to help him, and he'd been cruel to her. If they were to find this thing, they couldn't always be at odds. Someone needed to take the first step and apologize.

CHAPTER 11
Freddie

Freddie stood up and looked around the empty cabin. Her hair had thankfully survived a night without a bonnet. The cabin had pull-down beds, but she had fallen asleep before she could think of using one. She wiped a hand across her face to clear away the crust of tears. Her body ached, whether it was from sleeping on the seat or from letting her heart pour out, she wasn't sure. The bench across from her was empty; it looked like Aiden hadn't used his bed either.

Where was he? Had he found some lead late last night and followed it without her? She placed a hand to her heart. As much as she wanted to yell at him again, the thought of being on this journey alone made her want to cry. There was always Pelrin... He'd probably be losing his mind once he found out about the bombing. But he was also probably busy trying to save his people in Fairy. If she asked him to join her, he might say yes out of some desperate hope she'd fall for him again, but if that left Summer vulnerable and something happened, he would never forgive her. And she would never forgive herself.

The train still rumbled along, but there was a significant amount of movement coming from outside. She eyed her bag on the floor. There was no way she was going to share a shower with a pack of old people. Digging in her bag, she pulled out some wet wipes, a water bottle, and her toothbrush and paste. The door to the cabin was still unlocked in the off-chance Aiden returned. Now, she clicked the lock and stripped down to clean up. Tugging on the same pair of jeans and inspecting herself in the faint reflection of the window, she took a breath and left the cabin.

The dining car was bustling with people chatting, moving about between tables, and eating food that made her stomach growl. Crying in the cabin had taken precedence over dinner, and she was more than ready for another meal. Clenching her fist, she looked for an empty table. Her gaze settled on an empty seat at a booth towards the back of the car. There looked like there was someone else there, but they weren't sitting up, rather slouched over, head down.

Something caught in her chest, and she approached. Dark hair covered his face and brushed the table, while his arms, hands curled into fists, served as a cushion for his head. Sliding into the seat across from him, Freddie placed a hand on his fist.

"Aiden?"

His head shot up with a gasp, eyes darting around, his muscles tensed. Blue fire flared down his arms, and she drew back.

"Aiden, it's just me." Was that comfort, or would that only serve to fuel his anger more?

Eyes settling on her, the flames died down, and his heavy breaths settled, muscles relaxing slightly. "What are you doing here?"

"In the dining car? At breakfast?" She raised a brow, her own pounding heart calming.

He swallowed and twisted from the dining car to the scenery flying by. "It's breakfast?"

"Are you alright..." Her hand reflexively moved towards him before she drew it back and squeezed it with her other hand.

"I'm fine." He rolled his shoulders and exhaled sharply. "You didn't have to wake me like that."

Her hands curled into fists. "Forgive me, Sleeping Broody. I wasn't the one who decided to sleep in the dining car."

"I wouldn't have had to sleep here if you hadn't been making so much noise over there." He clenched his jaw and turned from her.

Freddie swallowed, and the urge to cry again bubbled in her throat. Why hadn't she listened when everyone told her how awful he was? It was always the hot ones who were the biggest jerks, between him and Pelrin, perhaps giving up dating for a while was best.

"Forgive the wait, loves, can I get you coffee or tea while you get started?" A woman, dressed in the uniform of the train company, slid a menu in front of her.

"Water is fine," she muttered, her gaze flicking over the slim se-lection. The thought of the Full English Breakfast and the White Pudding turned her empty stomach; the Irish Soda Bread seemed to be the only option.

"Do you want another coffee?" the woman said to Aiden.

He nodded. "Thank you."

"Another coffee?" Freddie couldn't help wondering what exactly he'd done all night. Not that it mattered, but still...

"He and his granddad had a coffee last night." She jerked at a man hunched over his newspaper a few tables away. "A right old tosser," she said under her breath.

"Interesting." Freddie narrowed her gaze at Aiden. What on earth was he doing? There was no possible way he was simply making small talk with the strangers on the tour. She ordered the soda bread, and the woman left them.

"You just got food for yourself?" He stared after the server.

"You can order something too. I'm not your babysitter."

He grit his teeth, looking as though he might respond, but he just looked down and said nothing. Was it cruel for her not to help him?

He'd once shared how little food Oberon spared him. No doubt he was at least as hungry as she was... She shook her head. The tour was all inclusive; it wouldn't kill him to order his own food.

When the woman returned with their drinks and her food, she picked at dully as they passed a long expanse of water. It was objectively beautiful, but her mood seemed to mute the excitement she would've had if this had been under different circumstances.

Spreading some of the jam on her bread, she winced as their tour guides shouted greetings as they flounced into the room.

"'Morning, everyone! I know we had a bit of a late evening, but as a reminder, I'm Maggie, and this is my co-guide, Liam. We at Grand Tours are so happy to have you with us." The others in the car called out polite acknowledgements as the pair beamed around the room. Freddie sighed and picked off another piece of her bread and dunked it into the pool of jam she'd spilled onto her plate. "In just a few moments, we'll be pulling into Holyhead station, where you will transfer to a ferry that will take us to Dublin."

"So, you had us traveling all night, and now you want us traveling during the day too?" Aiden's apparent grandfather set down his newspaper.

"Mr. Jameson," Maggie sang. "As it says in your itinerary, we will be experiencing an exciting sea voyage and arrive at the historic city of Dublin today."

The old man harrumphed. "Sounds like a fancy way of telling us you're charging us for a ten-day trip when two of them are filled with travel. And that's not even counting the way back?"

Murmurs rushed the train car as the other seniors seemed torn between Maggie's promise of adventure and Mr. Jamison's frugal frustrations. Liam pinched the bridge of his nose while Maggie stared at them all like a hob caught at night.

"Alright, alright, that's enough. Maggie rightly said we are showing you the lovely Irish coast before taking you to the stunning capital city. It is only a three-hour journey on the ferry, and then we will be doing breakout tours. It's promised to be a fantastic day." Liam winked at a table of old women, and they burst into giggles. The others turned back to their food as all thoughts of Mr. Jameson's concerns seemed to have evaporated. The man himself had picked his newspaper back up and was muttering loudly.

Freddie looked back at Aiden, whose concentration seemed to be focused on the scene before them. Pushing the half-eaten bread to the center of the table, she leaned her head against the window and watched as more and more buildings came into view. The train slowed, and soon the others in the car were tottering off towards the docks.

"Are you going to finish that?" Aiden jerked his chin at the remaining half of the soda bread.

She wrinkled her nose; her hunger was gone, but the simmering anger in her chest flared. "You could've ordered your own food."

"I'm not—" He gritted his teeth. "Never mind."

A pang of pity shot through her, warring with the anger. She clenched her fist. "Just take it."

He didn't say anything but snatched it off the table and took a bite. They made their way out of the train and followed their group to board the ferry. Freddie made a point to find a spot on the opposite end of the boat from him, but Aiden, while giving her space, seemed to be insistent on keeping her in his line of sight.

She gripped the railing and stared out at the waves as they pulled away from the dock. Soon, they were surrounded by water. The sky was clear, and the water was an azure that glittered when the sun hit it. It reminded her of the view from the Summer Palace. If she could just shut out everything and forget her friends were in danger, forget about

Aiden, and forget her father… if she could do all of that, perhaps this ride would be peaceful. But now, she needed the ferry to move faster. The sooner they reached Ireland, the sooner she could continue her search for the staff.

Time slipped by as she watched the waves roll. Her head pounded as she stared down at the water. Was it stress? With a heave, her stomach betrayed her, and the remains of the pizza and soda bread splattered onto the front of the boat. *Crap.* She wiped her mouth with the back of her sleeve, swallowing down the sick. A hand on her shoulder made her jump. She spun, and the world spun with her as she stumbled back, and someone caught her.

"Are you alright?" Aiden's amber eyes bored into her. Her fingers curled into the rough linen as her breathing slowed. She wanted to relax, to lean into him and let him hold her until she felt better.

Swallowing down the longing, she clenched her jaw. "Why are you here?"

He helped her back to her feet, and she shook him off. "You looked like you needed help."

"Not from you." She wrapped her arms around herself and walked on wobbly legs back inside. Closing her eyes, she took a seat in one of the chairs far from the window. Her ears strained for footsteps, but none drew near—he hadn't followed. Well, good. She didn't want him near her. He needed to stop with this farce that he cared. People who were willing to let you die did not care about you. The familiar weight resettled on her chest as flashbacks of her father pulsed in her mind.

What happened to the man who'd held her in his arms after she'd come home sobbing from being bullied for being too fae-obsessed? He'd held her, stroked her hair, and told her that being herself was all that mattered. They'd laughed together on countless father-daughter dates. He'd been her refuge when, until she attended New Wall, she'd struggled to make friends. And now, somehow, he was gone. The father she'd spent her entire life loving, even when he'd picked up those disgusting anti-fae views, was *gone*.

A horn blared, and she eased herself up. How much time had passed? Her stomach gurgled, barely settled from her embarrassment earlier. A dull ache still pulsed on her brow, though she wasn't sure if it was due to the wave-caused dizziness or her dark thoughts. Probably both.

From the window, the dock didn't appear as the charming city she'd pictured. There were cargo containers stacked in garish colors along the concrete platform. Even the design of the port was far too modern and human for this to be an ancient fae city. Disappointment settled low in her gut. This was not the type of place a magical fae artifact would be hiding. It felt anything but magical.

She followed the flow of people to disembark. It wasn't until she spotted Maggie and Liam standing outside of a double-decker bus did she look around. Of course, Aiden was just a few steps out of reach. Was she some sort of magnet for him? At least, unlike her father, she didn't have a lifetime of happy memories with him to add fuel to the pain of his betrayal. Still, she'd been warned, and yet stupid enough to fall for him. He probably only wanted to be near her to get closer to Pelrin and find the staff.

The interior of the bus was spacious, and the seats were plush and dark. She hardly noticed as she sank into the second row and firmly placed her bag beside her. It seemed like the world was against Pelrin, and he was just trying to save his people. Maybe she was too hard on him. After all, he was at least trying to save her friends, unlike Aiden, who'd cursed them.

Leaning against the window, another wave of heartbreak washed over her. Pelrin had betrayed her too. Was there something about her personality that attracted guys to love and then discard her?

"What's the holdup?" A gruff voice shouted. Freddie opened her eyes to see a trail of old people and Aiden staring down at her.

"Can I help you?" She placed a hand on the bag and met his glare.

"I wish to sit beside you." Aiden's voice was strained as though he were trying to hide his own emotions.

"Well, I don't wish to sit beside *you*." She waved him along, but he didn't move. More shouts rang out behind him.

"Move the bag," he gritted out.

"No."

"Oh, for the love of all. Let the lad sit next to you." Similar exclamations increased in volume as Liam's head popped over the top of the rows of seats. She growled and pulled her bag into her lap, letting Aiden slip into the seat beside her.

"Wasn't that hard, was it, love?" A woman said as they passed. Freddie ignored the stream of old people, focusing instead on the view of the docks.

They sat in silence as the others lumbered onto the bus, and it took off. The further into the city they got, the more it looked like her vision. Gone were the industrial edifices, and in their place were ancient stone buildings and ivy-covered row houses. Even the more modern style didn't climb to half the heights of those in the city of New Wall.

The click of cameras and excited chatter of the others on the tour drowned out what she was sure their guides thought was very aesthetic, music playing over the speakers. Despite that, Aiden's breathing seemed to rise above it. Even the beating of his heart seemed terribly noisy, or perhaps she was just imagining it. God, why did he have to insist on being so close?

"Can I ask you something?" His voice startled her.

"No." She folded her arms across her chest and crossed her legs, trying to put as much space between them as possible. Aiden looked down at her, his expression tense—hurt maybe?

"If you hate me this much, why are you still helping me?" His voice was low and gentle, and she hated the wave of comfort it sent through her. She tightened her grip on her bag and turned towards the growing city. "Wyn I—"

"You, what?" She whipped her head back around. This act, like he somehow cared for her, was just like Pelrin. He broke her and now was trying to pretend as though nothing had happened between them, at least Pelrin hadn't nearly gotten her killed.

Aiden's throat bobbed. "I could help you get home if you'd rather—"

"—I can get home without your help." Looking at him hurt, and not looking at him hurt. She needed his magic to find the staff, but there had to be a less agonizing way than this.

"Then why are you still here?"

She fixed her gaze out the window again, but she could hear the way he shifted in his seat. The tension wafting off him was like a smelly blanket on a cold night. She desperately wanted to escape but feared what would happen if she did. The bus hummed along the streets as the moments ticked by. She didn't owe him an answer; she didn't owe him anything.

A nagging guilt clawed at the back of her neck. It'd been her plan that had gone wrong and forced him to kill Mab. God knows how Oberon had punished him for that. Her breath caught in her chest. Aiden didn't have to tell her about what they did to him if he failed.

She'd seen the panic in his eyes when he'd been late returning to them. Even during her brief time in Winter, they'd spoken about him as though he were an animal, slightly lower than a pet. Was it any wonder he'd turned out the way he had?

With a shaky breath, she turned back to him. He was no longer looking at her, but out the window on the opposite side of the bus. In therapy, she was told that she wasn't responsible for her trauma, but how she handled it was on her. At least her trauma, trapped in the Winter Palace, was over. Its lingering effects were manageable, especially with a clear goal ahead. But Aiden...no doubt there were several traumatic things he was dealing with. Unlike her, his free will was severely compromised.

"I have my own reasons for being here. It's not just about helping you."

He turned, considering her for a while, but before he could open his mouth, the bus slowed to a stop in front of a large white building with green shutters. A sign out front read "Hollow Oak Inn" in gold script.

"Here we are!" Maggie said over the loudspeaker. "We'll be offloading your luggage and handing out keys. Those of you who'd like to join us on a walking tour, please be back in the pub in ten minutes."

There was an assortment of grumbles as people crowded her for their keys. Swinging her bag over her shoulder, Freddie made a beeline to the bathroom. At least Aiden couldn't follow her there. Her heart pounded; she shouldn't have said anything. What if he suspected her of taking the staff from her and left her again? She was so stupid. Why did she have to open her big mouth?

Aiden was in the pub when she returned. He sat alone at a high-top where the only other people from their tour were the gaggle of grannies she'd spotted at breakfast. Edging around the room, she approached Maggie, who was clutching a small satchel perched on the table in front of her.

"Oh, hello, dear. How are you and your young man enjoying the tour?"

"It's fine. We're excited to see more of Ireland." Freddie gave her a false smile, but she didn't seem to notice.

She opened the satchel and frowned as she took out a skeleton key with a swan at the end of it and passed it to Freddie. "Your gran must really trust you, letting you go alone with him."

Shrugging, Freddie shoved the key into her back pocket. "My parents are close by."

Maggie nodded, and Freddie tried to find a spot in the pub far from both her and Aiden. Explaining to Maggie about her love life was absolutely not an possibility for this trip. But their guide was soon distracted as she looked out at the miserable turnout for their walking tour. Giving them all a weak smile, she cleared her throat.

"Well, I'm sure you're all hungry, and we have a superb treat for you. We'll be seeing the sights and stopping off at local favorites to sample the cuisine. By the end of the tour, you'll definitely be full, which is unfortunate because we have a lovely dinner planned for you back here." She laughed as though she'd made a funny joke, but even the giggling grannies were silent. "Alright then, let's head out."

They wandered the streets observing old buildings that were a mix of both the graceful lines of the fae and the sharp styles of human architecture. The half of the soda bread was long gone, and she was nearly giddy as they stopped at a coffee shop with incredible brownies, a bakery, a cheese shop, and even a cozy restaurant to try a rich stew. All the while, she kept Aiden at the corner of her vision. At least he didn't try to approach her again, he seemed just as eager to try the foods as she was, perhaps more.

An unhelpful smirk tugged at the corner of her lips as memories of their first date floated back to her. *No.* She shouldn't think about how adorable he was when trying new things. He'd been using her, or at least he'd still been the jerk who'd left her to die. A few sad looks and a year's worth of memories wouldn't erase what he'd done.

A shadow passed in front of her, forcing her to stop. Maggie dropped her satchel, and the phone of one of the women behind her clattered to the floor.

"E-eh-excuse us." Maggie fumbled with her bag while an unusually tall woman, ghostly pale, and with floating black hair down to her knees, regarded her with a cool stare.

"Are you planning on coming inside?" The woman looked at a posh boutique whose glass windows were filled with women's clothes in fae designs. If it weren't for the sickening aura rolling off the woman, she might have been interested. Now, she could barely think for the terror that was creeping through her veins. The woman let out a sigh, and her horrible demeanor shifted into something warmer and mesmerizing.

How had Freddie not noticed how incredibly beautiful this woman was? Her violet eyes glowed against the ivory of her skin. Lips perfectly stained red matched the stilettos peeking out beneath her long black dress.

"Why don't you come in and have a look?" She gestured to the store, and Freddie nodded. Why not indeed? Perhaps if she had some of the clothes that this woman sold, she could be just as beautiful. Maybe then no one would betray her ever again. Pretty people didn't get hurt; they only felt love and happiness. Her feet moved, as though in a dream, towards the entrance when a firm hand on her shoulder pulled her back.

Aiden's lips pressed close to her ear. "She's using a glammour on you. Don't give in."

Freddie blinked and shook her head. No, that couldn't be possible. Why would a woman who was so beautiful try and trick her? Aiden would trick her, though he didn't want her to be beautiful; he wanted... Freddie shook her head again, trying to remember what exactly it was that he wanted.

"Don't fall for it," he said again. The warmth of his breath against her skin sent tingles along her neck and down her back.

"And who exactly are you to interrupt the way I do business?" the woman snapped. She drew up again, and the terrifying aura she'd had before returned. Maggie let out a little yell, and Freddie turned to see her and the other women only half a step behind her.

"Perhaps you should stop using magic to lure humans into a fae shop." Aiden's gaze darkened.

"That's not—" Freddie pressed a hand to her head to block out the outside thoughts trying to compel her mind. "That's not legal." The pounding stopped abruptly, leaving the woman looking like an ordinary fae looking rather nervous.

"I didn't mean any harm by it. Business has just been a tad slow lately, and I..." she trailed off, wringing her hands. Freddie sucked in a deep breath and blinked around the street. Maggie and the other women, too, looked rather lost as the evening sun cast a golden glow against the shop windows. "How did you see through my glammour exactly? Most ordinary fae can't, nevertheless, a...changeling?"

Aiden stepped back, his body tense. Exposing just how powerful of a fae he was wouldn't help either of them now. Folding her arms across her chest, Freddie glared up at the woman.

"Did it ever occur to you that your glammour might not be as powerful as you think? Maybe you're losing your touch." She smirked.

Pressing her hand to her chest, the fae cut her gaze from Freddie to Aiden and leaned closer to him. "A changeling shouldn't have much more magic than what makes his eyes glow."

"And when was the last time you saw a changeling? Please, I could practically see through your glammour. And seeing as how the police have yet to catch on to your little business scheme, I doubt you've had much success with others." Freddie grabbed Aiden by the wrist and pulled him after the wobbling Maggie. Their guide was doing her best to lead them down a side street, while the others swayed after her.

Once they were a few blocks away, Aiden let out a heavy breath. "You didn't have to stand up to that banshee like that."

"Yes, well, someone needs to protect me."

"I—"

"—You left me to die, or did you forget?"

He recoiled as though her words had struck him. Constantly pushing him away was not going to help her find the staff any faster, and she needed his magic.

She let out a breath. "Thank you for helping to break that glammour."

Aiden straightened. "Of course. It would've been bad if she'd fully tricked you."

"Yeah, bad." God, why was it so hard to talk to him?

When they finally made it back to the inn, exhaustion weighed heavily on her. The dining room was filled with noisy conversation and rich, savory aromas. Hunger was the furthest thing from her mind. If she was going to force herself to get along with Aiden, she'd need to sleep deeply.

"I'll see you in the morning?" She paused on the first step leading to the bedrooms.

Aiden cast a longing look back at the dining room, then nodded. "Let's go."

"Let's? You can stay here if you want."

"You wish me to sleep here?" He looked back at the tables where Liam was roaring with laughter with some of the older gentlemen.

"Didn't you get a key?" She held up the one Maggie had given her earlier, and her shoulders sagged when he shook his head. Freddie scanned the room, her eyes alighting on Maggie, whose glass of amber liquid seemed to have sloshed all over her fingers. She had one hand on the arm of one of the other ladies who'd been on the walking tour with them. Freddie grabbed Aiden's arm and pulled him over to her.

"I usually don't drink much, but after today...the horrors I felt at that shop." Maggie shook her head and took a sip of her drink. She shuddered, and the older woman patted her on the hand.

"Poor dear. Those fae shouldn't be cursing people left and right. They need to do something about that."

Freddie cleared her throat loudly, and they both looked up. "Maggie, do you have a key for him?"

"No? I thought I gave it to you?" She frowned at Aiden and took another sip.

Freddie's grip tightened around the slim bit of metal. "You mean there was only one key?"

"One per family. My gran would never." She winked, and Freddie's heart dropped. Her grandmother, had she known, would never have either. Maybe the room was a double. Yes, surely the couple who'd booked this trip needed their space and had chosen a double. She gave their guide a weak smile and headed back to the stairs.

Aiden followed her as they left the noisy pub and reached the first landing. It was almost too quiet. Likely, there was some silencing spell woven into the fibers of the building, like they had at nice hotels back home. If only her school had invested in that same spell work for the dorms. She sighed as they made it to the top floor and the door furthest from the landing. Glancing back at Aiden, she turned the key and pushed open the door.

The room was small, likely too small to be rented at full price back home. There was about a foot of space that led to a tiny bathroom with a tub-shower and an extra extra-small sink. A slim chair was forced into the corner as though to prove the room could house multiple pieces of furniture. She stepped inside and slipped off her bag, Aiden nearly bumping into her from behind.

The only full-sized thing in the room was the single queen bed.

CHAPTER 12
Aiden

Even as he stared at the single bed, the room seemed to shrink. *Freezing frost.* Couldn't anything go right for them? Wyn didn't speak, and her silence made the room ever more suffocating. Her bag thumped to the floor, drawing his gaze.

There was a slim space between it and the useless chair in the corner. Perhaps he could curl up there or maybe sleep sitting upright. The thought of another night of not being able to lie flat made his muscles ache, but he was well used to it. She, on the other hand, wasn't used to making such sacrifices.

"I'll take the floor." The words came out rough and strained, not at all like he'd meant them to.

"Where? You'll be under the bed." She gestured at the nonexistent space surrounding the oversized piece of furniture. He stared at the ground. There was no easy way to make this work. Inching around the edge of the bed, he stepped into the open bathroom. The tub was small, but it was at least bigger than the space between the bed and the chair.

"I'll sleep here, then."

"The bathtub?" There was a cold skepticism in her voice, and he forced himself to keep from turning back to her. He didn't want to see the look on her face, the judgment in her eyes he'd been forced to endure throughout the day.

"You can't sleep there. There's not enough room. And what if I have to pee in the middle of the night?"

He stepped deeper into the bathroom. "You can just wake me up."

"You're exhausted. I'm not going to do that." She was so close he could feel her energy behind him. If he turned, they would be close to touching. It was everything he wanted and hated at the same time.

He exhaled through his nose, desperately trying to ground himself. "What would you have me do?"

"I don't know you could—I don't know." She stepped back, and he heard the bed creak. Finally, he turned to find her sitting on it. Her soft brown eyes looked back at him with uncertainty. How many times did he take their glow of confidence and caring for granted? He'd been so unsure, convinced she cared more for the prince than for him, and now he'd ruined everything between them for good. There was no coming back from nearly killing her.

"I'll go wait downstairs. It's fine. Take the room." What was one more restless night?

"No, don't—"

He stopped, back already to her.

"We can share. I'll stay on my side, you stay on yours."

The bed seemed to shrink around her, even if they were to share, they would be mere inches apart. His body remained rooted to the spot, unable to speak, unable to agree to her uneasy truce. Wyn rested her head on her shoulder, her eyes gleaming with an unreadable expression.

Pity? Did she pity him for not having a place to sleep? Clenching his fists, he again scanned the ground as though a larger sliver of space would reveal itself. He didn't want her pity. Though he supposed he worried she was only with him because she too had no place to go. It was almost laughable that they were together, yet both so alone.

He searched her face again, hoping for some indication of a deeper meaning to her kindness. But her expression betrayed nothing, and he was so tired. With careful steps, he picked his way over to the side closest to the door and sat. She didn't move even as the mattress dipped beneath his weight. Slowly, he removed each boot as though waiting for her to change her mind, but still she remained silent. When he made to lie down, Wyn got to her feet.

"Where are you going?"

"The bathroom." She stooped over the bag and rummaged through its contents.

He propped himself up on his elbows. "The bathtub?"

"No, just the normal nighttime stuff." Clutching a handful of toiletries, she slipped into the other room and shut the door, effectively plunging him into darkness. Aiden lay back down and listened to the sounds of her moving about the other room. The bed was far softer than anything he'd experienced since the Winter Palace. He closed his eyes, trying to force his body to relax, enjoy the small luxury, but it refused to obey. Things like this weren't meant for people like him—people who killed and left those they loved for dead.

The faucet stopped, and several heartbeats later, the door creaked open.

"Don't look," she said, poking her head out.

"Why?" He'd already rolled on his side, angling himself away from the door.

"I can't sleep in jeans." She climbed into the bed from the bottom. It moved beneath her as she crawled to the top and slipped beneath the blankets.

"What are you sleeping in then?" The stupid question left his lips before he'd fully processed the undertones.

She made a sound much like a scoff. "Not jeans."

He pressed his hands to his face and breathed in, trying desperately to banish thoughts of *her* from his mind. The space between them seemed to tremble like a film stretched far too thin. A soft rustle of fabric and the gentle dip of the mattress made him turn to where her silhouette joined him in the bed. *Not jeans.* The thought was like a curse he couldn't break, causing desire to burn in his chest for a girl he had no right to want. Maybe the tub would've been a better option.

"I forgot to turn off the bathroom light," she muttered. The blanket shifted, but before she moved fully from his side, he snapped his fingers, plunging them into darkness. "Nice trick."

She lay back down. His senses consumed themselves with the smell of her lotion, the soft inhale and exhale of her breath, even the gentle warmth of her body, so close, but not quite touching. Silence stretched between them like cobwebs, thick and tangled. The bed was so cursed small. She stretched, and her leg brushed against his before quickly pulling away. The memory of the sensation seemed to burn through the leather of his pants. There would be no sleeping like this, not with so much between them. He shut his eyes, trying to count his breaths like he had as a child, trying to sleep in the Summer Palace.

"This was a bad idea." Her words were half-whispered, as though she hoped he wouldn't hear.

"I can still go to the tub, if that would make you more comfortable." He didn't move, and she didn't respond. Tension crept between them like a third bedmate, uninvited and with no intention of leaving. He'd resigned himself to simply lying there with his eyes closed when she let out a humorless laugh.

"I'm sharing a bed with a person who tried to kill me. What am I doing?" Fabric slipped against fabric as she shook her head against the pillow.

"I didn't *try* to kill you."

"If it weren't for Pelrin, I would have died."

His fingers curled into the blankets, as something dark twisted within his chest. So now she finally saw him as the villain in her story, at odds with the perfect prince. Her savior. "So you two are—"

"—does it matter?" The harsh edge to her voice hit him harder than he'd been prepared for. She hadn't denied it—she had in the past. She'd let him believe that she chose him, but he should've known better. When she risked everything to try and save the prince, he was the weapon she chose to use against their Majesties. In the end, the prince had come out the victor like he always did.

"You aren't the only one who suffered that night." He rolled onto his side, his muscles painfully tense. This bed, with her, was a torture worse than any Mab could have invented. A sick shiver raced through his body as old pains came back to him, *almost* worse.

"I didn't nearly get you killed."

"You don't think Oberon retaliated?" Perhaps it was not Mab's style of torture, but Oberon's increased nightly drainings were surely a punishment for his vast failure. Especially now, he knew the king hardly needed them.

Wyn sucked in a breath. "He hurt you?" She hadn't bothered to ask, not that he told her any of what they'd done to him. Breathing out through his nose, he stared at the blackness of the ceiling. Maybe pulling her into all of this was a mistake—he was so good at those. "Aiden."

The sound of his name on her lips made him flinch. "Would you care if he did?" The words were cruel, but he hardly cared, not if she didn't. She'd moved on while he was trapped in the same hell.

The bed rocked as she twisted to rest on her arms, facing him. "Of course I care. I don't want you hurt."

"But you're happy enough to watch your prince try to kill me?" The words were thick and heavy in his chest. Every insecurity about the two of them bubbled up in his chest. She *knew* what he'd done, she knew everything now, and yet she still protected that monster.

"That's different."

"It's good to know you are so particular about the hand that finally slays me. Why are you here? Go back to your prince."

"That's not fair." Her voice lifted, it sounded near breaking. His heart raced when she rolled, and the fabric of her shirt brushed against his. The silence that hung between them thrived on air, leaving only scraps for him to gasp on. He'd been so blind, and she'd told him everything he'd wanted to hear. She'd fulfilled his longing to have some brightness in his bleak world until she shattered it without so much as an apology.

"I knew you would choose him in the end. Don't worry, you made the right choice." After all, Oberon was threatening her life because of him. The prince's protection would keep her safe, but for how long? At least it was better than the nothing he could offer her.

The mattress moved as she lay back down. But her breathing didn't slow to the steady rhythm of sleep, and neither did his. *Freezing frosts.* Why did the bed have to be so small? Each breath was tinged with her floral scent. It reminded him of home, of her, and everything he'd lost. He curled in on himself until the warmth of her ghosted against his back. Part of him wanted to call her name, wanted to check if she was still awake, but he couldn't trust himself to speak.

"You act as though you were the only one wronged. I don't owe you answers about who or what I choose." Her voice cut through the silence like a dagger slicing right to his heart. The worst part was that she was right. As hurt as he was, it was his choice alone that had left her stranded in Winter.

"Wyn—"

She sucked in a breath, and for a moment, he thought she was going to say something to soften the blow of her words, but she let it out. "Goodnight, Aiden."

The bed shifted as she inched further still away from him. He clenched his fists at his sides and shut his eyes. He'd ruined everything yet again. Now all that was left was to let the sweet spell of sleep take him under...but even that seemed impossible.

When dawn peeked through their tiny window, Aiden pried his eyes open. Wyn was asleep, like a maiden in a story, one hand folded across her side, and the satin of her bonnet creating a perfect halo around her face. He swallowed hard. He was no prince, and a kiss from him would hardly be welcomed. Still, the memory of her lips against his burned.

Tip-toeing into the bathroom, he hoped the scalding water of a shower would banish all his unbidden thoughts. He stood under the water until he could no longer bear its touch, then dressed. Perhaps if he could make it downstairs without waking her, they could pretend that dreaded night had never happened. He yanked open the door to find Wyn sitting upright with one leg hanging off the side of the bed. She was definitely not wearing jeans.

He stared—he knew he shouldn't—he needed to turn away. But when he was finally able to lift his gaze, he found her staring back at him with an almost equal expression of awe. Or perhaps she was horrified he was being so lecherous.

"I have to go." Without waiting for her response, he headed to the door and left, fleeing for the stairs.

In the dining room, many of their companions were already seated with steaming plates of food. The scents of coffee and fried meats made his stomach gurgle. He pressed his lips into a thin line. Was it worth risking they'd catch his glammoured money?

"Well, if it isn't the muppet boy."

Aiden flinched as Mr. Jameson slapped his back. The old man tugged him over to an empty table and gestured for him to sit. Aiden was half in his seat, trying to come up with the right excuse to leave.

"Where's your girl? Sleeping in?" Mr. Jameson looked around in a highly indiscreet manner.

Inwardly, Aiden groaned. "She's upstairs—"

"I knew it. The muppet-makers are always late risers. My wife is the same, I'm ashamed to say." He let out a hearty laugh. A slim man in a crisp apron came over to them. For a moment, Aiden thought, or perhaps hoped, he was there to tell Mr. Jameson to tone it down, but the man withdrew a notepad and donned a cheery smile.

"Can I start you off with—"

"We'll both have coffee, black, and the Irish breakfast." He waved the server off, and Aiden winced as the man's smile slipped into a scowl. "I hate time wasters. Now, you haven't made any progress, have you?"

"Progress?"

"Really now, lad—no girl's worth all this. She avoids you, and you wait around like a lovesick fool. You're falling to bits."

Aiden opened and shut his mouth. He didn't owe this man any information about him and Wyn. And what was he supposed to get in return? He scowled down at the table as the server dropped off their coffees. But perhaps the man was right; each day was a greater torment. If there was a cure, he cared not whose hand gifted it. "I don't know what else I can do." He muttered into his cup.

"You tried charming her?"

As if Wyn would fall for something so simple. He shook his head. "She's mad at me."

"And you apologized, of course?" Apparently, impervious to heat, Mr. Jameson took a swig from his steaming mug and cleared his throat.

"I—I didn't apologize exactly." Aiden curled his fingers around the handle, letting the heat burn his skin.

"You didn't—where's your dad? He never told you the number one rule of being with a woman?"

He tensed, fingertips going white as they pressed into the ceramic sides of the cup. Had his father been alive, so many things about his life would be different. What knowledge had he missed out on?

"Poor lad. I didn't mean to upset you. Lots of us don't have very present fathers. I'll give you the secret myself since looking at you has become a right pain. You need to apologize."

"But she hurt me too."

"Don't matter, you first."

"That doesn't seem very fair."

"Well, nature didn't care about fair when she made the weaker sex have to carry all the babies, but here we are. They pop 'em out and we apologize, right?" He slapped Aiden's shoulder just as the server placed two steaming plates of food before them. Aiden stabbed a sausage and shoved it in his mouth. Before fully swallowing, he choked as Wyn came down the stairs. She looked around before her eyes finally alighted on him, then turned in the opposite direction to sit on the far side of the room.

"Eat first, man up later," Mr. Jameson said as he spread yolk across his beans. "We need our strength to do hard things."

Aiden nodded and returned to his food. Occasionally, he would glance up at her picking at a sad plate of eggs and toast. The apology raced through his mind; words came to him and were quickly discarded. What could he possibly say that was strong enough to clear his conscience?

Liam strolled past their table to the center of the room and clapped his hands. "Alright, you all, today we'll be exploring the National Museum of Ireland. The bus leaves in ten minutes, but we'll give you all time to board." He winked at a woman at the table closest to him, and her husband scowled.

Mr. Jameson nudged Aiden's side. "That'll be your chance then. I'm off to the bathroom before this next death march." Nodding, Aiden rose and followed the trickle of seniors out to the bus.

Wyn sat beside him, saying nothing as they rode through the city streets. They disembarked at a grand building with a fae-style dome and sturdy stonework that spoke of human intervention. He breathed in deep, catching a whiff of Wyn's lotion, and turned. She wasn't looking at him, and something in his chest squeezed. *Just apologize.* Perhaps everything wouldn't go back to how it was, but at least he would feel better for it—he hoped.

Maggie herded their group inside, and his jaw fell agape. The ceiling was a magnificent design of architecture reminiscent of the finest lace, and an intricate mosaic covered the floor. Others pressed in around him, but they too were staring around in similar amazement. There was a hum in the air, almost like magic, but also like something else entirely. It was hard to tell if it was coming from an actual presence or an idea within himself.

The group moved forward, and Aiden fell in step beside Wyn, who was pointedly not looking at him. Having her so close, yet so disconnected from him, with only awkward words between them, was isolating.

He shifted and glanced around at the glass cases containing artifacts from Human Realm history. A guide was informing the group about them, but it was hard to concentrate with the smell of her and the almost touch of her body at his side. Everything in him wanted to reach out and touch her, but the apology was choked in his throat. How would he even begin?

Glancing to the side, he caught sight of haunting figures staring sightlessly from a row of glass cases. Wilted and brown human and fae bodies were propped up as though waiting for their group to gawk at them.

Warmth faded from his body. "What is this?"

Wyn glanced up at him, but her scowl melted in place of something more sympathetic. She pointed at a sign hanging over them. "Bog bodies. Some think they were kings, others say sacrifices. I hate how they just display them here as though they weren't once people."

He pressed his shoulder into hers, and she jerked away. "Sorry," he muttered. Was his touch even so bad now? Mr. Jameson was wrong; it was far too late for the two of them. His irrationality that had nearly gotten her killed, she'd never forgive him for that. Even if she'd been the one who'd triggered it.

They passed the bodies and entered an area filled with cases of jewelry and small cards indicating what each piece was. Aiden breathed out, noting the intricate designs and bright polish around him. He remained by Wyn's side, but his mind went blank on what to say to her. How had this been so easy before?

"In this section, you find different pieces from various ages in our history. We're starting in the medieval age. Many of these pieces represented the religious fanaticism at that time. Rest assured, while there are some quite impressive iron works, we don't house them at this location but have a separate building for those who are interested."

There were mutters throughout the crowd, but Aiden couldn't make out if it was positive or negative. Wyn drifted to a case holding an intricate wood and gold box, and he followed her.

"Back home, the museums don't separate pieces. On one field trip, a girl in my class got so iron sick she passed out. I'm glad they thought of things like that here."

"That's terrible. It's good here." What was wrong with him? He sounded as though his brain had left his body. Perhaps it was the stress of the mission, or the fact that they were no longer together, impeding his mind. Something tugged at him, like a voice calling to him in a long-forgotten language.

"Aiden?"

"Yes?" The sensation dimmed, but *freezing frost,* he sounded too eager.

"I'm sorry for last night. I don't want Pelrin to kill you—I don't want either of you hurt or dead." She moved on to the next case, staring glassy eyed at a collection of pins with emerald tips.

"Wyn." She looked up. "I'm glad he saved you."

"What?"

"I'm glad he—I didn't and don't want you to die or get hurt either. I regretted it the moment I left. I tried to find you, but with His Majesty and everything, I couldn't get to you fast enough. I—I'm sorry."

Silence settled over them as they stared at one another. His heartbeat pulsed in time to the strange call ringing inside his head and reverberating through his body. He was only vaguely aware of the group as it moved on, leaving them alone in the room.

Wyn drew a shaky breath and rubbed her arms. "I didn't mean for anyone to get hurt when I made that plan in Winter. It was just supposed to be a distraction to get Pelrin and me to safety. I was so stupid to think there wouldn't be any consequences for you. It kills me to think that you were hurt because of me. I'm so sorry, Aiden." The sound of his name on her lips sent his heart soaring. It drew him in, stoking the longing for her nearness.

But where did this leave them? Surely, too much had passed to return to how they were. In the impossible chance that they could be together, did she even want him? She hadn't denied her involvement with the prince. He clenched his fists and fixed his gaze on the pins. Did he want her?

"Maybe we can find the staff and use one of those wishes to free you from Oberon." Her words made him start, and he smiled. It was a nice thought, but even if he was free, that wouldn't stop the fae king from hunting her down, and he couldn't protect her forever. No, when they found the staff, he would have to take it back to Oberon as it was and hope that it was enough to stay his hand.

He was about to say as much, but something about the pins caught his eye and drew him in. "I think..." He beckoned to Wyn, who leaned over his shoulder. "There's something magical about them. It's— it's almost like when I was near the crown."

Wyn leaned closer. Footsteps padded behind them, and he turned. A man in a red blazer with a badge identifying him as part of the museum staff watched them intently. He moved closer to Wyn and placed a hand on her back. She looked over her shoulder and scowled back at the man.

"Do you think they are connected to the staff?" She narrowed her eyes and cocked her head to the side. "They kinda look like—"

"Lady Caoimhe's hair things were quite remarkable in her time." The man sidled up behind them, and Aiden let out a frustrated breath.

"Who was she?" Wyn stepped aside so the man had a clear view of the case.

"Ah, sad tale, that. She was a noblewoman out in County Kerry. But she fell for a fairy boy, and in those times, you know, they weren't as accepting. Though I guess it hasn't gotten much better in some places." He grumbled out the last bit and stared wistfully at the pins.

"Did something...happen to her?" The tremble in Wyn's voice seemed to mirror the man's irritation.

"For a while, no. She and her lover did a lot to help the fae being persecuted. But as with many of these tales, the mob eventually found them and..." he gestured at a charred bed frame, and Aiden stumbled back.

"And they killed her? Just for loving a fae?"

"For being a *lady* who loved a fae, most likely. Funny how history is circular. Have any questions on any of the other pieces?"

Aiden shook his head. A rush of chatter drew near as their tour group filtered into the room, and the man turned to greet them.

"What a sad story. Maybe the pins were a gift from her lover?" Wyn stepped back to his side as though they were puzzle pieces sinking back into their place.

"It was..." Aiden trailed off. There was something about that story. He'd heard it before, but he couldn't quite place where. "Was it familiar to you?"

Wyn shrugged. "There were a lot of stories like that from AP Euro."

"Maybe I heard it as a child. But—" He pressed a hand to his chest. Tatiana's book was tucked into his jerkin, and he pulled it out. On the cover was a drawing of a woman with an elaborate, jeweled hairstyle swooning before a handsome male fairy. The story was so similar, a woman in a forbidden relationship with a fae. Though perhaps it was just a coincidence...

"Having a weeb moment?" Wyn peered at the book, her lips quirked in a lopsided grin.

Aiden shook his head. "The story is similar, and the author was supposed to be an Autumn Realm historian."

"Can I see it?"

He passed the book to her and watched over her shoulder as she skimmed the pages. Her brow furrowed as she paused on one.

She pointed to the fairy. "Who is he supposed to be?"

Aiden's face heated, and he avoided her gaze. "A long-lost prince."

"Of Autumn?"

"It's just a story, it's not that I was saying the story is exactly—"

"He's holding the staff, though."

"Yes, that's part of the story. There are other books, I think, that go more in depth about him."

"Do you have them?"

"I only have the one, but we could probably find more."

"Look at the tines on the staff." She pointed at the long spindles; each topped with a small stone.

Aiden looked back at the pins. But what if they weren't hairpins? Oberon would not be pleased if the staff's magic had been all used up. "How many tines is the staff supposed to have?"

"Seven, at least, that's what it says in my book." She closed the manga and handed it back to him.

"Then at least five wishes have been spent, and we are no closer to finding that thing."

"That's not entirely true. We know that she lived in County Kerry, and the stop after next is the Kerry Ring. We might even find more clues in Blarney. It's supposed to have been central to the fae persecutions."

"Perhaps Knockma Hill, Galway, or the Wormhole might have answers." Aiden thought back to Mr. Jameson telling him about those sites. "The Wormhole sounds particularly interesting."

"It's not on the tour...." Wyn dug the pamphlet out of her bag and studied the back. "But we're going close enough If you really think it's worth it we'd just need to find a boat there and back."

Excitement bubbled in Aiden's veins. For the first time since he'd been given this cursed mission, there was hope they might actually find the staff.

CHAPTER 13
Freddie

Freddie watched the rise and fall of Aiden's chest as he lay curled on his side of the bed. His wing stubs twitched and his brow occasionally furrowed as though whatever was happening in his dreams troubled him. She balled her hands into fists, resisting the urge to smooth away the creases and ease whatever stress he was going through. No, best to let him sleep.

Sliding out of bed, she curled her toes against the thin carpet and tiptoed to the chair just visible in the pale light. Aiden's leather jerkin lay atop her own crumpled jeans. She reached inside for the manga and pulled it free. Creeping into the bathroom, she flicked on the light.

The staff had been missing for centuries, but somehow, a modern manga held clues to finding it. Perhaps that wasn't too surprising. No fae scholar she'd met would lower themselves to use Human Realm resources. But it wasn't like the history of any of the objects was common knowledge. Thoughts buzzed in her mind like angry wasps, jolting her awake at every attempt at sleep.

Perhaps there was a clue Aiden had missed somewhere in these pages. Settling herself on the toilet, she flipped open the book. The story was immediately gripping: star-crossed lovers and a battle of fae against humans to see who could dominate the island. Caoimhe was wild and defiant, while the male lead, a fairy prince called Arran, was gentle and soft. They resisted each other with such heart-wrenching passion that Freddie nearly squealed too loudly at their first kiss.

By the time she neared the end, she'd gotten so wrapped up in the story, she'd forgotten to look for clues. The longing for the next book in the series tugged at her, but she flipped the book back to the beginning, where there was a photo of a petite fairy and a short paragraph.

Isaka Hidachi started her career at the Kerry County Archaeological and Historical Society...

Freddie frowned. Where was she now? Trapped beneath London with the other fae, or somewhere...else? The thought of what might be happening to the fae made her tense. They couldn't keep them there forever. Even if she betrayed Pelrin to gain Mr. Fallus's cure, that would do nothing to save them. She tightened her grip around the book. *Don't get involved. You'll just make things worse.*

Leaning her head against the sink, she closed her eyes and tried to shut out thoughts of Freya and all the others who'd died when the Winter Palace fell. That had all been because of her recklessness. Her selfish desire to be a journalist had gotten her friends cursed, too. She wasn't some chosen one; the fae weren't some poor victims who relied on her. Speaking for them, thinking she was their savior was delusional at best.

A piercing ring cut through the silence, making her jump. There was a cry from the bedroom and a thud. She smirked at the thought of Aiden, startled by the alarm and tumbling out of bed. With a sigh, she stretched and slipped off the toilet to brush her teeth.

It was truly morning now, and time to move on to their next destination and make a plan to find out more about Caoimhe and Arran.

Aiden had hardly said two words to her during the three-hour bus ride to Blarney Castle. It'd been far too awkward to sleep beside him while he was so awake, yet her exhaustion was making her regret her early morning reading. The fresh scent of him wafted over her as he leaned back in his seat and twisted to look out the window at the ruined stone building.

"This wasn't built by fae." His voice was low and gentle, devoid of the hostility that had tinged it earlier.

She nodded, eyeing the rather boxy architecture that humans had favored during the Middle Ages. Maybe they should abandon the tour now and find the fae sights on their own, but they had a serious lack of funds. Unless she used her credit card, which would alert her father to her location, they were screwed. And she had no intention of seeing him again, at least not yet. Besides, Knockma Wood was next on their tour, and that was one of the locations he'd mentioned that might have some clues.

Tottering off the bus with the other old folks, she moved stiffly beside Aiden.

"You didn't sleep well last night?"

She jerked at the sound of Aiden's voice. His brows knit together, and she tugged up the hood of her sweatshirt over the puff of her ponytail. "I'm ok."

"Just because I can't lie doesn't mean I can't recognize one."

"Look at you, suddenly so caring." The words had come out harsher than she'd meant. They'd apologized, but the hurt was still there, though dulled. He'd come back for her; he did care, at least somewhat. And it wasn't as though she were blameless.

"It's what friends do, right?"

"Right." She'd officially friend-zoned herself. Breaking up with him was nothing like her and Pelrin. There was still something there, some spark she craved to rekindle. But he'd never agree to that now—not when they'd proved just how toxic they could be to one another.

He kept pace with her as they followed the group to the base of the castle and stopped as Maggie waved her arms to get everyone's attention.

"Good afternoon, everyone. I hope you all enjoyed that lovely drive through the country."

"Where's the bathroom? We're old and can't hold it that long." Mr. Jameson shouted. Some of the others muttered their agreement with slightly less irritation.

"It's just inside. But if you could listen just for a moment—"

Mr. Jameson brushed past her, and several others followed him, casting Maggie sheepish looks. Freddie scowled at the old man. What a jerk, just because he was old didn't give him the right to be so rude.

There were still a good fifteen people left, so Maggie tried again. "Welcome to Blarney Castle. We're going to take a tour inside, and then you're free to wander about the gardens. Then we'll hop back on the bus for a short drive to Killarney, which is a charming town where you can grab dinner and get your room assignments. Sound good?"

"Define short," someone mumbled while the rest of the group rumbled with acknowledgement.

Maggie didn't seem to have heard the snarky comment. "Excellent. Now, those of you who need to use the restroom, feel free to do so, and we'll begin our tour in twenty minutes."

Freddie turned to Aiden. "I'll see you back here?"

He shrugged, and she followed a few of the ladies to the restroom. Cluttered in the small space, she focused on her needs until a snippet of conversation snatched her attention.

"They said on the tele that some gold fairy went crazy after seeing the bombing. Interrogated the journalist and all."

"A fairy? Far too violent if you ask me, especially with all that magic. I thought London took care of that?"

Air caught in Freddie's chest. Pelrin might be able to level a city block with a single blast of his magic, but he wouldn't. Though fae were people, and people came in good and bad. And even a fraction of power in the wrong hands could be deadly. Maybe the fear of fae was somewhat justified—but coexistence wasn't as simple as she'd thought. It would take more than caring and understanding to keep everyone together and safe.

"My sister says the fae might invade. And if we have gold fae just popping up, she might not be that far off."

Her companion let out an indignant scoff. "Don't be silly. They have enough war to deal with over the border; they won't be coming here for more."

Her chest tightened as the conversation drifted further away. Of course, Pelrin would be sick with worry over her. She hadn't even thought of him coming back to find her. Letting him think she died wasn't fair, not when he had a war and their friends to worry about. What if he did something recklessly violent that proved those women right, or if he were distracted from the war... It could be all her fault. *See, this is what happens when you play savior.*

She shook her head. No, she wasn't playing savior. This was simply about righting a wrong. It wasn't her fault that her father let the hotel get blown up. She glanced up at a clock on the wall. There were still ten minutes before the tour started. Enough time to reassure Pelrin and send him on his way, if she hurried, she hoped.

Slipping out of the bathroom, she edged around a pillar and out of the entryway into the gardens. Aiden was standing at the edge of the group, his arms folded and his back to her. A twinge of guilt tugged at her heart. She *should* tell him what she was doing. He probably already suspected she wasn't doing all this for him. But he would try to stop her if he knew she was actively trying to steal the staff. No, better let him wonder. After all, they were done, and her friends needed her more than he did.

Stepping out onto the velvety lawn, Freddie glanced around to ensure she was alone. Seeing no one but tourists filtering inside, she breathed out. "Pelrin?" She kept her voice low. It didn't matter how loud she spoke his name. He'd always heard her before.

Almost instantly, a golden blur rushed at her.

"Freddie! I thought you were dead." Pelrin wrapped her in a tight hug, lifting her off the ground.

"Is that what they're saying?"

"No one could survive that. How is this possible?" There was a slight tremor to his voice, and he pulled away, his turquoise eyes shining.

She glanced around again. "Look, Pel, I'm fine. I just didn't want you to worry."

"Then why are you wandering around wherever this is alone? Let me take you back to your family, you'll be safe there."

"No, Pel. I won't be safe with them. They can't know I'm here." She gave him a hard stare, and he stepped back.

"I suppose I could take you with me. But I don't know if that's safer." His gaze drifted off, and she put a hand on his arm to pull back his attention.

"I'm fine. This tour is filled with old people. It's fully structured. You don't have to worry about anything. I promise." She reached into her bag and passed him the pamphlet. He studied it for a long moment, his shoulders relaxing.

"You have no idea how glad I am to see you. I'd come to tell you that I may have found a way to break the spell if I can get it away from Oberon."

Her breath caught in her chest. "You did? How?" Perhaps she wouldn't have to betray Aiden in her pursuit of the staff. Maybe there was some hope that things could go back to how they were.

"One of our soldiers returned with the news a couple of days ago. There's a spindle that enacted the curse; if its twin is broken, it can be released."

She couldn't help but picture the long, white spike Mr. Fallus had. But how had he got it from Oberon, unless... "And Oberon has it? What does it look like?"

Pelrin shrugged. "I'm not sure. Like a spindle, I suppose."

"Helpful." If Mr. Fallus was indeed working with Oberon, that added an entirely new layer to this nightmare.

He shrugged again. "I have to go. My uncle can't defend our people long on his own."

"I'm sorry." Freddie bit her lip, glancing back at the castle. Had ten minutes passed? It felt both too long and too short. "Be safe."

"You too." Pelrin kissed her cheek, but before she could protest, he was gone. She turned back towards the entrance to find the tour group sprawled out not too far away, with Aiden staring hard at her.

Crap. Her stomach clenched as she trooped back towards him. "Aiden—"

"You never did tell me why you are here." The stiff hostility had returned to his voice.

"It has nothing to do with him." A sickly chill crept over her body as the lie poured from her lips. It was the only way to save her friends. Now that she knew Mr. Fallus actually could break the spell on her friends, it was almost as though the universe was forcing her to choose—Pelrin, the friend who would do anything for her, or Aiden, the guy she wanted but could never be with.

CHAPTER 14
Aiden

Aiden flexed his jaw. So many words, questions, feelings all trapped in his head, and he refused to let them lose. The way she'd put her hand on the prince's arm, how he'd kissed her... But he didn't care about that, at least he shouldn't. She'd never said anything about being with the prince, though he supposed now he had his answer.

He quickened his pace to the front of the group, scouring the grounds for some distraction. Sunlight warmed the immense garden, illuminating the flowers and casting glittering reflections in the pond. It was so unlike the oppressive heat of Summer, though it was stifling nonetheless, or perhaps it was the silence between him and Wyn.

She'd wandered past, staying close to their guide, and not looking back. Why had she let him kiss her? The question burned in his gut where it had no right to be. They were friends, he'd said as much, and she agreed. It was irritating that she chose to maintain a friendship with the prince, but it shouldn't pain him like it did. And if they were more, if he had driven her away right into the prince's open arms... He clenched a fistful of hair and turned from her. It *couldn't* matter like this.

But why, then, was she helping him? Did she want the staff for herself? To help *him* win the war? That had to be it. She'd merely lied to him when she said it had nothing to do with the prince. It was what humans were best at. He chastised himself at the bigoted thought, but the simmering anger remained. What other reason could there be?

They were herded back on the bus; the useless castle faded into the distance as the countryside fanned out on either side of them. Aiden flicked a glance at Wyn, but her gaze was fixed on the window, her backpack clutched in her arms. What could she be thinking of? He gritted his teeth, forcing himself not to ask, and hating himself for wanting to.

Hours passed, or minutes that felt like hours. Chatter from the surrounding passengers made Wyn's silence all the heavier. She was as still as he was restless, staring out the window as though bewitched. He shoved a hand into his jerkin. Perhaps some reading would distract him. Something sharp sliced against his finger, and he yelped, withdrawing his hand.

"What—" Wyn looked from his face down to where silver blood bubbled up along his finger. "Are you alright?"

"Fine." He stuck his finger in his mouth. The metallic taste sent a sickening chill from his ears down to his boots. It brought back horrific images of himself lying beneath Mab's blade. Even now, the memories stole his breath and made white spots dance across his vision.

"You don't look ok." Wyn's voice was far away as though at the top of a well, and he was falling down, down, down. She grabbed his hand, her touch jolting him back to the present.

He stared, chest heaving, into her warm brown eyes. They were so different from the bright violet of Mab's. Words escaped him, so he remained, relaxing into her touch.

"Aiden, what's—"

The bus went over a large bump, and the reality of where they were and what they were doing slammed back into him. He snatched his hand back. "I'm not going to die. The prince will still have a fair fight for the staff even with my injury." He held up his now-healed finger, and she frowned.

"And what makes you think Pelrin wants the staff?" Folding her arms, she cocked her head to the side. A challenge. It hadn't been what he'd expected, though he probably should have. Some small part of him had hoped she'd deny wanting the staff for him, and for it to be true, but he knew it was foolish.

"I saw the two of you together. It didn't exactly appear as though you were enemies." He curled his fingers into a fist.

"Of course we aren't."

His heart sank. At least she wasn't leaving it up to his imagination this time.

"You know we're friends."

Aiden looked up. Friends? "Just like..." He let the words hang in the air. The final word seemed to be far too heavy to spring from his lips.

"Yeah." She hugged her bag tighter and drew away from him.

"You trust him though. You told him why you're here."

She huffed a laugh. "I told him that I was alive, so he didn't burn London to the ground looking for me. And I told him I was avoiding my dad."

"And the staff?"

"What about it?"

"I'm not so stupid as to think you've come all this way just for me. You want it for him, don't you?"

"I told you; it has nothing to do with him."

"Then what else could it be?"

"What do you think, or do your orders prevent you from doing that too?" Her voice sliced through him like a knife through soft butter.

What else indeed? He'd seen the way she fought for her own dreams; she'd never rely on magic to make them come true. What else could she want? She turned from him, back to the window.

Realization slowly sank into him as his own words echoed in his head. "Your friends?" It was barely a question. This was all about saving them, undoing the harm he'd enacted. Without the cursebreaker, there was no other way to break the spell on Elessea. But none of that would matter if he failed his mission and Oberon hunted both of them down.

She didn't turn around but nodded. Lifting a hand to touch her shoulder, he let it fall into his lap. Every touch made his skin burn for more; he didn't need to willfully stick his hands into the fire.

"I get it. A wish would help them."

"There are two." Her voice came out almost as a whisper.

He met her gaze in the reflection and swallowed. "One for me and one for you?"

"One for my friends and one for..." She turned to face him, her expression unreadable. His throat went dry. *One to win the war.* His failure would bring peace to Fairy. One life for countless others. He couldn't fault her for that. The side of her lip twitched as though attempting to smile. "Your freedom?"

"My—" The air rushed from his lungs. Oberon would be livid if Aiden used the last wish to free himself. One of them would have to kill the other, but with his freedom on the line, he would do it.

"Don't you want that?"

Of course, he wanted it. It'd been nearly the sole thing he'd longed for ever since he'd been shackled to their majesties. But fae magic seemed to always come at a cost. What would he have to give up to achieve something so precious as freedom? He opened his mouth to respond, but the bus slowed to a stop with a screech.

Maggie's voice blasted throughout the small space, shattering the moment. "Welcome, everyone, to the enchanting Knockma Wood. Legend has it, this was the site of an ancient battle between fae and humankind. In just a few moments, we'll be going on a short nature walk to see some of the curiosities that remain. Ooooo."

"What she means by that is, if you gotta pee, go now." Mr. Jameson's unmistakable voice warbled as clearly as though he were speaking into Maggie's voice-enhancer box.

Several of the old people got up and made their way to the back of the bus. He let out a breath as Wyn busied herself with the straps of her bag. Only when they found the staff would he concern himself with thoughts of freedom. They didn't even know if it had two tines left. No, it was better to spare himself the disappointment and work to fulfill his orders—everything else had to be a distant problem.

The forest that pressed in around them was magical; there was no other word to describe it. Lush moss and bushes carpeted the ground while the trees leaned into one another, creating a tangled canopy over the trail. As sunny as it was, darkness encroached around them as they hiked deeper into the woods. There was something familiar in the eerie gloom that Aiden couldn't shake.

"We'll be going along Finvara's Trail. It's said to travel through the path where the Autumn king once held court." Maggie spoke in hushed tones as though she too sensed something strange about this place.

"Speak up, woman!" Mr. Jameson shouted, making Aiden wince.

She gave them an apologetic smile and stepped closer, repeating herself in a slightly raised voice. "You may see ruins along the trail, but historians both here and in Fairy are stumped as to what they are."

"Probably because all the records were destroyed after the treaty," Wyn muttered under her breath.

He frowned. "They were?"

"Yeah, most of the books by and about fae were burned at that time. And then, when the Autumn court fell in Fairy, I'm guessing the fae records were lost?"

"I—I-uh, don't know." Perhaps if he secured his freedom, he could resume his education. The thought stung. Hope had disappointed him before; he wouldn't let that pain seep back into his heart again.

They trooped along with the group as Maggie recounted the history of the area. He only half listened, ears primed for important information, but what did he care about eighteenth-century nobility? What they were looking for was far older. The trees parted, allowing sunlight to rush onto the trail. Chatter amongst the other travelers rose, but Aiden couldn't shake the dark feeling spreading down his spine.

An open field sprawled out to one side of them, and on the other was a ruined tower, half devoured by ivy. Wyn seemed to notice at the same time he did. She paused and took a half-step towards it.

"What's that?" she asked.

Maggie looked in the opposite direction and pointed at the field. "That's the old car park. It was shut down when I was a girl due to a bad storm. They moved the whole road back a bit for safety. But it was always cool to come here and get an easy look at Castlehackett. Now, we have that little walk to see it, but there she is." She gestured at the tower, and everyone turned.

"Excellent job. I'm sure the girl was just brimming with curiosity at the old car park," Mr. Jameson said in a not-so-quiet grumble.

"Ah, well, I just wanted to give you all some context. The castle was built long before the treaty by a noble family whose line has been long dead. We don't know much about them, but we know it changed hands during the thirteenth century to the Hackett family, hence the name. Then again, in the eighteenth century to the Kirwin family, who later relocated because they said it was haunted. Ooooo."

"Haunted by the cost of installing indoor plumbing to a building that size, more likely," he huffed.

"Anyway..." Maggie turned on her heel and continued on the trail. The others followed, but Wyn didn't move.

"Wait, aren't we going in?" Her gaze was still fixed on the castle.

"In?" Maggie looked over her shoulder and followed Wyn's stare. "Oh no, it's not open to the public. The architecture is crumbling, and it wouldn't be safe to go. We'll see plenty of other sites along the tour, including the hill which is said to be the ancient home to the Autumn court."

They continued on, and Aiden made to follow along with the group when Wyn grabbed his arm. He jerked at her touch and fell back.

"I think we should go in there," she whispered.

"But we can't, it's not open."

"Don't you feel that? Something *happened* here."

He frowned up at the building and shuddered. She wasn't wrong, the air tingled with magic, but that could mean any number of things. And it wasn't as though he felt the same pull to the castle as he had when he'd been near the crown and the orb. "Maybe we should investigate the hill Maggie talked about. It is the *Autumn* Staff after all."

"I just have a gut feeling about this. Maggie said it was haunted; that has to mean something."

"There's no such thing as—"

"I know, but residual magic is real. We saw it at the Winter Palace. Just—just trust me."

He looked at the group growing smaller as they moved further away. "Even if there is residual magic in that place, centuries of history could've cultivated it. The Autumn court is from the exact time period the staff was lost."

She looked from him to the castle and back. "Don't you think if the staff were in the ruins of the old Autumn Court, someone would've found it already? Let's just check this place out, and if there's nothing, we can catch up with the others. You can just wend us to the top, right?"

He bit his lip. Wending with another person was still so new to him. What if he made a mistake and she got hurt? Still, her first point was valid. Historians and scientists had likely been all over the hill, and if they found nothing, he doubted they would either. "Fine, let's just be quick about it."

She was already several feet into the high grasses surrounding the tower by the time he'd finished his sentence. With a wave, the brush bowed, carving a path to the crumbling building. As they drew nearer, the sensation was unmistakable. Wyn was right, something had happened there, something terrible.

A wall of ivy blocked their way in. There was something sinister about the way it coiled around the base of the tower. Almost like a sleeping wyvern, harmless until it was very much not. Wyn moved to circle the building, and he followed, scanning the ivy for any breaks. Perhaps it was a mistake to let her come along. Would it not have been safer to tell her to go along with the group while he investigated alone? But this was her idea; she'd hardly have stayed behind.

Clenching and unclenching his fists, he jogged to catch up with her, then abruptly stopped. There was a hole in the ivy leading into the darkness of the tower. She took a step towards the hole, and he reached for her arm to pull her back.

"You don't know what's in there," he hissed.

"That's kinda the point, right?" She tried to shake him off, but he held firm.

Flames lit along his arms. "At least let me go first." He released her and headed for the entrance.

"How chivalrous," she muttered. The cynical praise shouldn't have thrilled him like it did. He forced himself to continue on into the darkness, rather than look for her expression. Equal parts excitement and apprehension built in his chest as he passed through the opening and stepped out into a massive circular space whose walls climbed up and up. The air seemed to shiver in the wake of their presence.

"This isn't so bad," Wyn said from behind him. He turned, the flames on his arms dissipating. "It's kinda pretty."

The ivy rustled, and he looked around. It seemed to expand and constrict as though letting out a deep breath. He swallowed hard. Pretty was not the word he'd use to describe a place like this. Wyn stepped closer to him, her eyes darting around the stone walls. Someone had marked one with bright pink paint, the letters too garbled to make out a word.

"Can you do some magic to help us find clues?"

"What kind of magic?" He looked around. There was always the option of burning this place to the ground, but that would hardly produce any hidden evidence. All the magic he'd learned was to prepare him for battle, not pick through ancient ruins.

"There isn't a spell you can use to help find something?"

He considered her question for a moment. "Do you know what we're looking for?"

She crossed her arms over her chest and turned to face him. "No, but can't you just sense things?"

"I can't do magic on something that I don't know what it is or where it is. It's not as though I can say 'clues reveal yourselves' and—" He stopped as a gust barreled towards them, carrying with it a piercing scream. The sound pressed against his skull and reverberated through his bones, bringing him to his knees. Then all went quiet.

Aiden looked to Wyn. Her eyes were wide, hands hovering just over her ears. He reached out for her hand, and she squeezed it just as the temperature plummeted. It was as cold as Winter, though the green of summer still filled the space. Shadows that had not been there before flickered along the stone as the ivy recoiled away from them. She inched closer to him until their shoulders pressed against one another.

The silence was heavy as though someone had placed a silencing spell on them. Not even bird song broke the eerie quiet. A creak, as though something were moving on a wood floor, sounded from somewhere above them. He looked up, and the world pitched.

A human woman with long pale hair and skin held an infant and was gently rocking her back and forth. She hummed a lullaby, which would have been sweet if not for the haunting echoes that followed. The adoration for the child was so strong on her face that it made his heart ache. Had his mother looked at him the same?

Something exploded behind them. He whirled, feeling Wyn grip his shoulder. Screams rang out, but there was nothing but the ruins behind them. He turned back to see the woman frantically concealing the infant in a compartment in the stone wall that hadn't been there moments before.

"Kill all humans!" The cry echoed off the stone, and he pulled Wyn closer, flames alighting on his arms. With a scream, a jet of green fae magic shot through them, hitting the woman full on. Ivy twisted along her arms and legs, dragging her down. She tried to scream, but a tendril curled around her neck and more sprouted from her open mouth. Her eyes rolled back, and she collapsed to the ground.

Wyn let out a soft cry as a high-pitched laugh came from what seemed like mere steps behind them. A man's anguished shout filled the room, followed by another scream. Aiden turned his head, but again, there was nothing behind him and only the dead woman and the ivy covering her body. The cries of the infant rang out, and a man stepped in front of them, dressed in full battle armor. A black sword hung in his right hand, covered in silver blood. Aiden recoiled from the iron weapon, but the wave of sickness didn't come. The man didn't seem to notice them either and headed to the wall. He pressed a stone, and the compartment opened, the child safe inside.

Turning to face them, the man's face was a mask of dark fury. "The hill fae will burn for what they've done this night. I swear I will cleanse this land of their blood if it's the last thing I do."

Wyn's grip tightened on him, and he pulled her even closer as the scene melted away, leaving them standing in the ruined tower.

"S-so, now we know what happened here." His breath fogged out, though goosebumps prickled his skin as the temperature slowly climbed back to normal. "It has nothing to do with the staff."

Wyn released her grip and pulled away from him. She crossed to the other side of the great space. It took him a beat before the realization hit, and he stumbled after her. Her steps slowed at the opposite wall, gaze darting around the interlocking stones. Mirroring her process, he tried to make out what she could possibly be seeing. The question bubbled in his throat, but he resisted the urge to ask.

Reaching out a hand, she pressed it against the wall. At first, nothing happened, then the ivy pulled back, revealing more and more of the stones until it stopped at one slightly smaller than the others surrounding it. Wyn followed the trail over to it and pushed the stone into the wall. With a grate of stone on stone and a huff of dust, the compartment, where the woman had placed the baby, opened. He stepped closer, and they both peered inside.

A small sheet of parchment lay in the small space, covered in ancient dirt, but incredibly intact. Wyn reached in and pulled it out. She frowned down at the script and a highly detailed sketch of a jagged rectangle at the bottom of the page.

"I can't read this. Can you?"

He stepped beside her so he could try and make out the curving letters. The characters were familiar, but the words were in no language he'd ever seen. "Let me try to manipulate this." Sending a breath of magic across the surface of the parchment, the letters rearranged themselves and formed recognizable words.

Caoimhe,

Do not let your father or anyone else see this. Keep it safe and hidden. Destroy it if you must, but this letter may hold the key to our happiness. I've heard rumors that my father's staff remains, though his body is long buried. The blue fae speak of a pool to which all lost things can be reclaimed. I go to seek it, upon this arriving safely to you. Do not fear for me, for I am its rightful holder and the only one who can reclaim it without mortal fear. Once I have it, I will not use it for war, only its intended purpose of bringing peace to our realm.

My love for you burns as bright as a dragon's flame. Hold me in your heart this night, and I will see you in the fresh dawn.

Your Love,

Arran

Wyn looked back in the compartment, feeling around the stones inside. "She lived here. They must've found the staff at some point. Do you think it's still in these ruins?" Her voice rose in excitement as she looked around the space as though expecting the staff to appear out of the nothing.

He shook his head. "I would sense it if the staff were here. It's only the restless spirits I feel."

"I feel them too. If the staff isn't here, maybe—maybe we should talk outside."

"I agree." As though responding to their decision, the ivy moved on either side of them like snakes. Flames ignited down his arms, and he placed one hand on Wyn's back. "Run."

She didn't argue and bolted ahead. Vines lashed out, whipping at her ankles. Some she dodged, while others he struck with fiery bursts before they got too close to ensnare her. The ivy seemed to give him a wide berth until he had the foolish thought to look over his shoulder. It was peeling itself off the stones and stretching towards them like a hand with far too many fingers.

He picked up his pace, sending a jet of flame ahead of Wyn, clearing her a path to the exit. She slid through the gap in the vines just as they attempted to close around her. Pain sliced across his side as a strand of ivy whipped across him. He whirled, pulling blue fire with him in a searing tornado. He pushed it towards the mass of vines, and the bone-shattering scream rang out again. Clamping his arms over his head, he raced through the opening and tumbled out onto the prickly grass.

Hands felt along his chest and face. He'd hardly noticed them until he opened his eyes to see Wyn staring down at him.

"Are you alright?" she asked breathlessly.

"Yes." He pushed himself up, and she helped him to stand. "Do you still have the parchment?"

She nodded, passing it to him. Scanning the document again, he pressed his lips together. The staff wasn't here, and the letter, of course, had no mention of where it ended up after they got a hold of it. Still, one thing stood out to him.

"This pool, where all things that are lost can be reclaimed... Do you think the staff returned there?" He held the sheet out to Wyn.

"Well, it is lost. It's more of a clue than anything else." She leaned in, her gaze trailed down the doc, then she straightened and looked back to the path.

"We'd have to figure out where that pool is. There are hundreds upon thousands of pools in both this part of the old Autumn Realm and the one in Fairy."

A small smile quirked the side of her lips, and she pointed at the sketch. "I bet there's only one pool that looks like that."

"You recognize it?" Excitement trembled in his voice, and he fought to dampen it. If it was close, if the staff was there, it was well before the deadline, he might just have a chance to save them both.

She twisted to dig in her bag and pulled out the crumpled tour pamphlet and held it out to him. The same photos of the local sites stared back at him, and he frowned, then one caught his eye. A near-perfect rectangle carved into rock at the sea's edge. "Isn't that the Wormhole?"

CHAPTER 15
Aiden

Uncertain if the rest of the group had yet made it to the top of the hill, they walked back to the bus. The excitement of the discovery fizzled across Aiden's skin as he nearly skipped beside her. Sounds of birds and insects created a melody that chased away the chill of the phantoms of the past.

Had this place truly been the home of the Autumn king? The realm had been ruled by a council when he'd invaded with Oberon. It had never occurred to him to wonder what had happened to their gold fae rulers. Though if they sent their people to brutally attack an innocent human woman and her babe so easily, perhaps they deserved their fate.

Then again, hadn't Arran been an Autumn royal? He sought to bring peace between humans and the fae. It was so strange for the father to be so different from the son, but love had been known to melt a frozen heart, or something like that.

"Well now, 'took the scenic route, did you? Wise choice coming back here." Liam's voice boomed out from the bus, snapping Aiden out of his thoughts.

"We fell behind and couldn't find the group to catch up with them, so we returned." Wyn smiled, her words so smooth he half believed them.

"They should be back soon. Poor Maggie will have worried herself to bits." He ushered them aboard, and Aiden could just make out the group coming out of the woods through the bus window. Wyn took her seat and hugged her bag to her chest.

She didn't speak to him as the bus took them back to the main road and pulled into a new town. It wasn't as though she was angry, but something about her silence set him on edge. What could she be thinking about? Was it so bad that she was stuck here with him? They were friends, yet it still felt as though she was keeping something from him. Or perhaps it was his guilt reflecting back at him for keeping secrets from her.

The bus stopped before a grand manor house, and Maggie popped up to explain its history. Compared to the tower, this place was in its infancy, though the ivy along its side gave him pause. They followed their guides off the bus and into a cozy entrance hall. A low desk sat in a corner where a slim woman waved at them.

"It's a shame we're not staying; this place is lovely." Wyn leaned around the corner, where a seating area and a dormant fireplace were tucked away.

He startled at her voice. "We're not staying?"

She frowned up at him. "We have a ferry to catch, remember?"

"Right, tomorrow, I just thought…" He trailed off. Whatever he'd meant to say was as tangled and confused as a phooka in daylight. Maggie said something, but he could hardly focus, his blood turned electric by Wyn's nearness and the complicated layers of secrets between them. The group dispersed, and Wyn held up the key and cocked her head towards where the others were dragging their luggage.

He nearly bumped into her, stopped in the doorway. For a moment, he feared it was smaller than the room in Dublin, but then she stepped forward, revealing a much more sizable space with a small sitting area, ample pathways to the bathroom, and around both sides of the single bed. At least this bed was bigger, though not by much.

She let out a long exhale, dropped her bag, and collapsed onto the sheets. "Something about running for my life always leaves me so exhausted."

He bristled. "You are speaking to me now?" She pushed herself up onto her elbows, and he realized he was still just standing in the doorway. He took several steps inside, closing the door behind him.

"I never stopped talking to you." Her expression appeared confused, but it could've been an act—she was good at that.

He ground his teeth, hating the way he couldn't simply sink into comfort beside her. She was still hiding something from him, and it killed him that she trusted him so little. "You've been silent since we returned. I figured you'd want to discuss how we're getting to the Wormhole, but it appears you already have a plan."

"I was just thinking, if that's alright with you." She fully sat up and crossed her arms. "We already knew we had to make it here for a ferry. It's on a freaking island. What's gotten into you?"

"And what was so important that you spent so much time thinking when we could've been planning. Or should I ask who?"

"I can't believe you. You're so obsessed."

He crossed the room to the window, his restless legs longing to run, fight, something other than being trapped in here with her and the horrible feelings she drew out of him. "You risk your life crossing Fairy for him, Wyn. You've never done anything like that for *me*."

"What do you want me to do? I can't straight up kill Oberon to free you."

He turned from her. This fight was pointless, he knew there was nothing she could do for him, and yet still he wanted more—more than he had any right to want. "What if there was only one wish left? Would you use it on me?" The question was soft, half murmured because part of him didn't want to hear the answer. She valued friendship above all else, and so long as he was bound to Oberon, he could hardly be a good friend or anything else.

"I suppose that would bring my choice down to the two of you." She dropped her head into her hands.

He took half a step closer. "I thought—he isn't cursed."

Her fingers curled into her hair, loosening her ponytail from its tie and allowing stray strands to seep into her fingers like shadow whisps. "Why is it up to me to decide who gets hurt?"

"What aren't you telling me? You said the staff was for your friends, not the war." Glass seemed to form over his heart as it trembled in anticipation. If she lied—if she was actively using him to enact his own downfall... The pain of the mere thought had him clawing at his chest.

"I was offered a cure for them. Mr. Fallus said all I needed to do was to bring him Pelrin, and he'd give it to me."

"And you refused?"

"I have a little over a week to decide."

He let out a breath and sank into one of the chairs. Words abandoned him. Outside, the late afternoon rays danced along the sea. Several minutes passed in the weighted silence. He leaned an arm against the small table between the two chairs. "I—"

"I need some air." Wyn slid off the bed and pulled open the door so fast his mind couldn't come up with words to stop her. He was alone with the lingering question of who she would choose.

Only a few months ago, his heart had soared when she'd told him that she wanted to be with him and not the prince. Even knowing that fate was against them at every turn, for a few hours, he'd been confident knowing that she was his. One thing the prince wanted and couldn't take from him. But now, he'd been demoted to the prince's level—friend. Never had he hated that word so much.

He lost himself in watching the scenery shift as the shadows deepened and the sun began its descent beneath the horizon. Each time a thought of her choice drifted across his mind, he'd bat it away by focusing on something outside. But as the hours passed, keeping them away grew harder and harder.

If she chose him, they could be together, if she wanted that. It was nearly impossible to deny that's what he wanted, at least. Part of him hadn't completely forgiven her for her betrayal, but a life without her in it seemed a fate worse than what already awaited him with Oberon. And he'd be furious if Wyn was the reason he no longer had such a useful weapon. Oberon had years' worth of blue fairy magic at his disposal. Aiden curled his fingers into a fist. The would-be-king could prove to be more powerful than he was. And if that was the case, Wyn wouldn't be safe, especially if she had to sacrifice the prince.

But if she chose *him*…She'd have two gold fae and an army protecting her from Oberon. It'd be selfish to ask her not to. Selfish, and if she acquiesced, suicidal. He let out a low growl. Why couldn't anything be simple for them?

It was dark, his eyelids were growing heavy despite the turmoil brewing inside of him. They both had little over a week to make the decision that would either doom or destroy, at least him. Maybe her too. His chances of getting out of this alive were slim, if any. Leaning forward in the chair, he pressed his fingers to his temples, trying to massage out the dark thoughts.

The door creaked open. He looked up to see Wyn, her shadow outlined in the frame.

"You're still here." There was little surprise in her voice that came out in a rush of breath.

"I'm not leaving." He leaned back and watched her as she closed the door. A dim light flicked on, allowing him to see her fully. Her eyes were puffy and red like dying embers. Guilt twisted in his gut. Had her tears been his fault?

She unzipped her sweatshirt and dropped it to the ground before sitting on the far side of the bed. "I know you have your orders, but I think we can both agree that Oberon having the staff wouldn't be good for anyone, right?" The words sounded as though she'd said them a hundred times before now. Her gaze was on the sheets—she knew the weight those words carried. But she wasn't wrong.

"Yes." He hesitated, the next words lingering in the air, unspoken but nearly palpable. "But I'm not doing this for him."

She looked up. "You're doing this for yourself? I thought you looked surprised when I said we should free you."

The pain of how wrong she truly was struck him like a dagger across the chest. But she deserved the truth, even if it pushed her further away and into the arms of the prince. "It's not for me. I need the staff...for you."

"Me?" Her body tensed as though she feared an attack.

He nodded. "Oberon knows about us—what we were. If I don't bring him the staff, he will..." Each word was a struggle to force from his chest as though they too didn't want her to hear them.

"Oh." The word was soft, and there was no follow-up. She shifted to press herself against the headboard and stared up at the ceiling. Minutes ticked by, and she didn't move. Perhaps telling her Oberon wanted her dead had been the wrong choice. The weight of her silence slowly pressed in on him like invisible walls. She was somewhere beyond them, out of reach, lost in her own thoughts—thoughts where he had no right to be. Still, he yearned for the way she'd once been so open with him. Even when he only half-understood what she was talking about, at least she was there, with him.

"If there is only one wish, you should use it to save your friends," he blurted out. His words cut through the air like a fury's whip. She abruptly twisted towards him and the intensity of her stare seemed to paralyze his limbs.

"You don't want me to get the cursebreaker the other way?"

Freezing frosts. She was going to make him say those hateful words out loud. It took him several seconds to draw the breath to force them to come out. "He can protect you better than I can. You may get your friends, but Oberon won't let you keep them."

"And you?"

"You shouldn't worry about me." He looked down, though his heart thundered in his ears. He didn't want to see the look on her face when she realized what her life would cost him. It would make him want to cling to life too much, cling to *her*, and lose his resolve.

"Aiden. What will Oberon do if you don't bring him the staff?"

He turned towards the window, jaw clenched.

"Aiden!" Her voice broke on his name. Why did proof of how much she cared have to hurt so much? It was all he wanted, and it was tearing him to shreds. "There has to be a way to save you both."

His head snapped back to her. "And if there's not, he's the better choice for you. You will survive with him at your side, not me. Even if there was some way I was free, Oberon would want revenge, and he is more powerful than you know. I can't—I don't have an army. All I have, would have, is me."

"And maybe that's enough. If Pelrin can defeat Oberon—"

"Do you truly believe your prince would suffer me to live?" He scoffed. "Our fate is cursed, and this is nearly a perfect design."

Kicking off her shoes, she tucked her knees beneath her chin. "N-no, there has to be another way." She hugged herself tighter and clenched his fists.

Their situation was perfectly hopeless, but still something nagged at the back of his mind. It was almost too hopeless, as though fate, or maybe someone else, was playing some cruel game with their lives. "The cursebreaker, you said Mr. Fallus offered it to you?"

She looked up, glassy-eyed. Her voice came out gravely when she spoke. "Yes, why?"

But he'd retrieved the cursebreaker for Oberon. Mare's mom had said it was the only one. His brow furrowed. "What did it look like?"

She shrugged. "A fang? A spindle? Long and white, I don't know. Does it matter?"

Aiden got to his feet and paced to the bathroom. "Maybe...maybe the staff doesn't matter."

"What are you talking about? Of course it matters, it's practically the only thing that does matter." She sat up on her knees, watching him with keen interest. Thoughts flew wildly in his brain like a pixie swarm.

"There are at most two wishes left on that staff. What difference would those make?"

"If you were free and my friends were saved?"

"The war would still endure in Fairy, and the prejudice against fae would continue to spread here as well."

"Mr. Fallus is a politician; he'll be voted out eventually," she said, but something in her tone was uncertain. "Besides, there are plenty of those who disagree with him."

"But will that endure if he's working with Oberon?"

"What? No, he's... " The realization spread across her face like honey on toast, but still she shook her head. "I knew Oberon was his brother, but how would they have even met to be working together?"

"I don't know, but Oberon had me give him that cursebreaker. If Mr. Fallus has it now, they must be working together, and that means they set us *both* up to fail."

Her expression crumpled. "So what? We just give up? Stop looking for the staff and wait for the deadline to pass and—and." She looked down at her hands, and her shoulders sank.

He leaned against the wall and stared out at the moonlight dancing along the waves. There was no way for either of them to win. No matter what choice they made, they were playing right into their enemies' hands. Even if Wyn did choose the prince, he couldn't protect her in both Fairy and the Human Realm. He was already losing one war; two would be impossible. Oberon had truly thought of everything.

Sliding to the carpet, Aiden closed his eyes. There was nothing more to say on this matter. The sheets rustled as Wyn moved off the bed and padded closer to him. He braced for her touch but let out a quiet breath when he heard her rummaging in her bag. Opening his eyes, he watched as she smoothed oil through her locs, combed and carefully twisted them along her head. Her features smoothed as her fingers moved deftly, first relaxing then narrowing in concentration as though she were reading words he could not see.

"Are you alright?" The question was stupid, of course, she wasn't alright, but her expression didn't reflect his despair.

"I think we should keep looking for the staff." She pulled out her toothbrush, the strange expression still painted across her face.

"No wish could save us."

"I don't think we need one to take down Mr. Fallus. But we could still use them for ourselves."

"You can't just kill him, with Oberon—"

"I don't need to kill him, I can just make it so no one listens to him."

"What magic could do that?"

She shook her head. "Not magic, I just need to figure out how exactly. The sooner we find the staff, the sooner we can gather more info." He scrambled to his feet as she darted into the bathroom.

His heart hammered as he replayed her words in his head. She'd been so sure there was a way out, so determined. But what could she possibly do that didn't involve magic? Mr. Fallus might be mortal, but he was backed by the strongest of fae protection; no wonder he'd gathered so much power in the Human Realm. Had he been behind the disappearance of fae in the city? It had seemed so sudden, one moment fae were on the streets and the next they were gone, and none of the mortals had seemed particularly disturbed by it. That had to indicate some type of magic at play, didn't it?

Exhaustion tugged at his mind as he crossed the room to sit on the bed. Wyn must have turned on the shower; the sound of the running water, like rain, soothed his nerves. He wanted to trust her instincts—he *did* trust her. But her recklessness at the Winter Palace still haunted him. She'd been desperate then, too, and he hadn't been the only one to suffer for it.

His head pounded, and he lay back, scrunching his eyes against the pain. When she returned, they would have to talk about her plan. Maybe he could ground her, or help her, something. But a falling sensation overtook him, dragging him under the heaviness of sleep.

Aiden opened his eyes to the dark, the ground beneath him was hard, and the only sounds were the steady drip-drip of water coming from somewhere out of sight. He blinked, eyes adjusting to the dim light of torches along the wall. Had they been there before? Pushing himself up into a sitting position, he looked around. He was alone, Wyn was gone, and he was somewhere entirely unfamiliar. Or at least it had appeared unfamiliar at first.

His stomach plummeted, and a sickening chill crept over his skin when he spied the hook hanging from the ceiling overhead. *No.* It wasn't possible. Mab was dead. He couldn't be back in the dungeon; his torture couldn't continue. Scrambling to his feet, he let out a cry as something jerked him down. It burned his wrists and ankles and smelled like... iron. Chains pulled him to his knees, and he struggled, straining every muscle, desperate to escape them.

"Now, now, boy. You didn't think I'd let you get away that easily." Oberon's dark figure stepped into a pool of torchlight—more shadow than man. Aiden stilled, mouth going dry as he stared up at him. "You always knew it would come to this."

"Please, I—I just need more time," he rasped. But there was no pity on the king's face as he withdrew the crystal wand from his sleeve.

It turned molten, illuminated by the fire, and he pointed it at Aiden, eliciting a pain like he'd never felt before. Hundreds of claws tore at his insides, tearing apart his flesh, his soul, his very being. A soundless scream poured from his lips as he crumpled forward, his cheek hitting the cold, stone floor.

But just as oblivion sought to claim him, something pulled him in. His consciousness moved from the body of the floor towards the wand, closer and closer until he was trapped in the crystal prison. *No, no, no.* It wasn't supposed to be like this. Oberon draining his magic was supposed to kill him, not trap him.

He screamed and tried to bang on the iridescent wall of his prison. But with no mouth and no hands, the effort was futile. Oberon turned, and the scene shifted. An icy sensation flooded his consciousness as Aiden recognized the familiar house Oberon approached. *No!* He wanted to scream, he needed to do something, he couldn't just watch. Struggling against the crystal, he stared out in horror as the door swung open and Wyn turned to face him.

Her smile dropped as she beheld Oberon standing before her. *Please, no!* The words refused to come out as the king raised the wand, and blue flame gathered at its tip. *NOOOOOOOO!*

"Aiden!" Something hard slammed into his chest and he wheezed.

"No, no, no." The words dribbled from his lips like water. There wasn't enough air wherever he was. He was drowning or suffocating, he wasn't sure. Something warm pressed against his face.

"Open your eyes." The voice came from far away and was painfully familiar. He didn't want to open his eyes to a world where she wasn't, where it had been *his* magic that had caused her destruction. "Aiden, please. You're ok."

He took a painful gulp of air and opened his eyes. His chest tightened, and he lifted a hand to stroke her cheek. "Wyn?"

She placed a hand over his and squeezed. "What happened? You were shouting and convulsing."

Taking several ragged breaths, he tried to sit up, but something was stopping him. *Chains.* No, it was Wyn. She was straddling him, her free hand pinning down his arm. He swallowed hard, and she seemed to realize the awkwardness of her stance and quickly slid off him with a muttered apology.

She moved to pull her hand away, but he caught her fingers within his own. He *needed* to feel her, know she was real, alive, safe. His other hand curled into the sheets, grounding him in the truth of his surroundings. But if this was so real, why did panic still burn in his throat?

"I—I didn't want to do it. I—" The words scraped against his aching throat. "Please."

"I'm here. I'm not going anywhere. You haven't done anything. We're ok." She laced her fingers through his and pressed her lips to them.

Fear still coiled around his ribs as he sharply exhaled. Shakily, he lifted his free hand, hovering it above her shoulder. She leaned in, and the warmth of her seared away the icy dread paralyzing his body. A twist tumbled forward to brush against his chest. She was so close—real, alive, safe. The words pounded a rhythm in his head, stirring his heart into a frenzy. How was he supposed to keep her this way? The nightmare might as well have been a premonition.

"Breathe." Wyn inhaled slowly and exhaled through her mouth. She did it again and again as he attempted to sync to her rhythm. Their entwined hands rose and fell on her chest as the fear waned and he relaxed against the pillows. "You're safe. *We're* safe. Don't let your mind convince you the shadows are more powerful than they are."

He frowned. Her words, at least the last ones, didn't sound like her own. His breath hitched, and she sank down beside him, not letting go of his hand. When he lifted his gaze to her face, she gave him a half smile. "My therapist tells me things like that. I thought it might help."

The corner of his lips twitched. "It did," he rasped. Biting back pain, he forced himself up. It was as though he'd been hit by a charging minotaur, his stiff muscles protesting his every movement.

"Do you feel better?" Her gaze searching as though she feared he'd shatter at any moment. *Freezing frost.* What must she think of him, crying like a babe in the middle of the night? But there was no judgment in her gaze, only concern. He should be grateful that anyone cared this much about him. Still, the shadow of the nightmare clung to his back. Oberon could easily make that horrible vision true, and there was nothing he could do to stop it.

"What time is it?" He muttered. Time. Time was a grounding thing; it kept one in the present, and he desperately needed to be here and not several days into the future.

"A bit past seven. I don't want to rush you, but we have a plane to catch."

His brow furrowed. "Plane?"

Taking his hand, she gently pulled him off the bed, a bright smile spreading across her face. "Trust me, you're going to love it."

CHAPTER 16
Freddie

The sky had just begun to pinken when they arrived at the empty field. Well, empty, save for the stout man standing beside a small plane. In the dawn light, she could make out several scratches along the white body, but beyond that, it seemed in good condition, she hoped.

Velvety grass bent beneath her sneakers, so unlike the crunchy summer blades back home. She glanced at Aiden who moved stiffly by her side. His eyes seemed darker as though the shadows of the nightmare still clung to them. With a half step to the side, she bumped his shoulder, and his gaze snapped down to her. Whatever had plagued him must have been truly horrific, but hopefully the plane would provide enough of a distraction to give him some peace. At least for now.

"Freddie, I was this close to leavin' without you." The man, Mr. Kelly, grinned as he patted the door to the small plane.

"Sorry, I didn't think we were that late." She jogged the last few steps across the field. When she'd met the man at the coffee shop and convinced him to give them a ride to Ines Mor, she couldn't help but think how excited Aiden would be to see the craft. The choice between him and Pelrin still nagged at the back of her mind, but there was hope, no matter how slim, that she wouldn't have to make it. But they needed to find the staff first, then she could worry about the rest.

"I'm only winding you up. But we do have to get a move on. I promised I'd be back in time for breakfast." He grinned and pulled open the small door, but his smile dropped. "Hey, what are you doing?"

Aiden was reaching out towards the propeller. His hand pulled back at the man's shout. "Sorry. I just—never mind."

"What is he; fresh over the wall?" Mr. Kelly shook his head and gestured towards the inside of the plane.

Freddie shrugged. "We don't see a lot of small planes back in the states. Maybe you could give us a tour?" When she was small, her parents had taken her to the Air and Space Museum in DC. It had been painfully dull, but now she'd give almost anything to have back the people they were in place of the monsters they'd become. She rubbed at her chest and followed after the man as he led them to the front of the plane.

The shadows seemed to have been chased away from Aiden's eyes which now gleamed with keen interest as he watched the man gesture at the nose.

"These smaller planes are pretty different from those commercial ones. Much more light weight, no bathrooms, louder, bumpier. But you don't need to worry, I've gone back and forth more times than I can count and we've been fine. As long as you have good weather and fuel there's nothing to worry about. You into planes?" He gestured at Aiden who nodded as though the man were showing off a treasure trove of jewels.

"This here is a Duchess N6627x. It'll be a bit cramped, but it's a short trip."

"And this is like a ferry?" Aiden rounded to the back of the plane and out of view. Freddie smirked as the pilot shot her a concerned look.

"A ferry in the air of sorts." He let out an uncomfortable laugh.

"You mean this craft flies?"

Freddie skipped around to catch up with Aiden as he was dragging his fingertips along the tail. "I told you, you would like it."

"You never told me humans had the power of flight."

She couldn't help the smile creeping over her face at the way he danced around the plane. He'd been the same when she'd lured him on a second date with the promise of showing him her car. But those days were behind them now. Her expression dropped, and she leaned back against the body of the aircraft. "I figured you knew about planes."

"These are common?"

"The bigger ones definitely are," she replied.

"How did you all get here? There hasn't been a border in the Isles for decades." Mr. Kelly opened the back door.

"We—uh, took a ferry from France." Freddie scrambled inside the tight space behind the seats.

"Right. Well, we have to get going. You can sit up front with me if you want to see how to fly it." The man waggled his brows at Aiden, whose eager look would put a begging puppy to shame.

"Yes—If that's ok with you." He looked to Freddie. She smiled and gestured for him to go. Apprehension brewed in her chest as she wondered if letting the awestruck fae be a co-pilot was a good idea, but he was buckled in and nearly bouncing out of his seat by the time she'd thought to change her mind.

Within minutes, the plane's engine was sputtering loudly, and they were speeding across the field. Aiden gripped the door handle as the plane tilted up and they left the ground behind. Leaning forward over the seats, she couldn't help but mirror the broad grin spreading across Aiden's face.

"It's been so long since I've flown," he breathed. She squeezed his shoulder and peered out at the rolling waves beneath them.

Mr. Kelly snapped his fingers. "Attention, please, copilot."

Aiden straightened and followed along with the man as he described each button and gear. All too quickly, Freddie found herself swallowing to clear her ears as they descended. Something heavy settled in her chest as the tires bumped against the runway. Was it disappointment or perhaps dread at what was to come?

They stopped, and Freddie hopped to the ground. The island was beautiful, and so unlike any island she'd ever visited. Soft grass rippled out for miles to trail up a low ridge of hills. Mr. Kelly led them towards a white house just off the runway.

"You two alright getting back? My family's here and I told you I can't take you."

Freddie nodded. "We can just use the ferry. Thank you for the ride here."

"Yes, thank you. Your um, plane, is magnificent." Aiden looked back at the aircraft, his lips pulled tight and fingers twitching at his sides.

The man chuckled. "You should go for your pilot's license if you like it that much. There are planes you can probably rent and fly all the time if you choose."

For a moment, excitement flashed across Aiden's face, and he opened his mouth. But then his expression fell, and darkness ghosted across his features. "Perhaps," he said, sadness tainting the hope that had once shone in his words.

Freddie bit her lip. She wanted to say something to comfort him, but her idea on how to take down Mr. Fallus was just that. It'd give him little comfort that there was hope they'd make it out of this. Still, she had to believe. Digging in her bag, she pulled out the wrinkled tour pamphlet. "Do you know where the Wormhole is?" She pointed to the image.

Mr. Kelly leaned over to look and nodded. "The Serpent's Lair it's also called. About a twenty-minute walk that way. There are signs in the village."

Freddie turned in the direction he pointed. "Thank you!"

"Just take care not to get too close. The tides are not forgiving, and you wouldn't be the first the sea monster's claimed."

Aiden frowned. "There's a sea monster in there?"

"It's a legend, but the tides are risky. The best view is from above." He waved them off.

Freddie led the way down a road lined by a low wall towards a small village. It didn't take them long to find the signs and crowds of tourists following the well-trodden path.

"We should wait until there are fewer people," Aiden said. He was so close, the warmth of his breath tickled the side of her face and sent a tingle of joy down her spine

"That probably won't be until nightfall. It won't be safe."

Aiden shrugged. "So be it."

They found a small cafe where Freddie shelled out some of her limited cash on breakfast for them. It was blessedly less expensive than many of the DC restaurants. Still, without the senior tour, they would have just enough for the ferry back and maybe two other meals. Their server told them about a few sights along the island, and they passed the remainder of the day wandering from place to place: an old church, a fort, and the ruins of an ancient fae town.

By the time the sun was a mere sliver on the horizon, they found themselves alone, staring off a cliff at the near pitch-black wormhole. Flickering blue light burst from the flames along Aiden's arms. Illuminating where they stood and little else beyond.

"I guess we have to go down there," she said, fighting the tremor in her voice.

He let out a huff of a laugh. "You mean, I have to go down there."

"You don't have to do everything alone I—"

"You *could* go in my place, and I can stay safely here and hope you survive long enough to bring back the staff."

"Aiden, I just meant that you don't have to keep sacrificing yourself."

"That's not what this is. My fae blood gives me an advantage over you. I'm stronger, can hold my breath longer, and heal faster. If anything were to go wrong, I can survive while you..."

"Oh." Her voice softened, and she squinted into the darkness, but the moonlight bouncing off the choppy surface was the only indication the pool was still there. "I hate it, but you're right."

He smirked.

"But I'm at least going to the edge with you."

For a moment, it looked as though he were going to respond. Then, with a sigh, he led the way down. When they were at the edge, she peered in. The tide was high, only a couple of inches from the lip of the carved pool.

"It's still rising, I'll go back up."

"Fair enough." Aiden kicked off his shoes. "Wise choice."

"Be careful." Her voice was barely above a whisper.

Aiden tuned and grasped her hand in his, giving it a squeeze. "You too." Stepping to the edge of the pool, he sucked a breath and waved back to her. Before she could say anything else, he jumped. The dark waters closed over his head, and soon he was gone, vanishing beneath the surface.

CHAPTER 17
Aiden

Aiden resurfaced for a moment as rough waves battered against his body. Taking a deep breath, he dove just as a wave pushed him down. For a moment, everything was black, the waves too violent for him to focus, and panic took hold of his heart. Wyn was standing on the rocks staring back at him as though all her hope was somehow within his reach. Concentrating on her, he pushed magic into his arms, allowing the flames to come alive beneath the water—their magic seemingly unperturbed by the opposite element.

He swam deeper, the cold digging into his bones, causing sharp pains in his limbs. Only darkness surrounded him. His eyes burned from the strain, and he shut them for some relief. Before opening them again, a siren song called out from somewhere below. Aiden opened his eyes again, but the sound cut off.

Something was haunting about the melody. It could be a siren seeing a struggling fae in the water and getting a kick out of trying to drown him, but something told him it was more than that. If he didn't make up his mind soon, he'd run out of air.

Trusting his instincts, Aiden shut his eyes and pushed himself down, down towards the voice. Something scaly brushed against his leg, causing him to jerk and nearly lose what little air he had. Re-centering himself, he pushed deeper, trying to ignore the creeping sensation that some*thing* was swimming alongside him. Gradually, the voice grew clearer.

Hello, young fairy, I know what you've sought.

Six hundred years it has been lost, and now shall be found, but at what cost?

Your answer is here, worry not.

Another cursed riddle, but it wasn't hard to decipher that whoever, or whatever, was singing knew about the staff and knew where it was. He longed to ask for more information, but opening his mouth would be foolish. A giggle darted past his ear as if it sensed his thoughts. Then the voice began singing again.

In Kirwan's quiet, forgotten lair
A season's treasure for the heir
While human greed takes fearsome forms
A fairy will rise with the power of storms
Noble is the quest for those most true
Fate rests with those with wings of blue

Wings of blue? He had blue wings...once. But the rest of the song was just nonsense. How was that supposed to help him find the staff? Fury burned inside him, and the flames on his arms grew brighter. The giggle zipped past again. Aiden turned, but the tightness in his chest was growing too painful to ignore.

He needed air.

Kicking upward, his body shot towards the surface, just before he broke through to the moonlit sky above, another wave pounded down on him. Aiden struggled out of the grasp of the current and tried again to reach the top. Again, another wave slammed him down, knocking his back against the rough wall. Air escaped his lips, and white spots flashed behind his eyelids. The strength to try and reach the surface again faded, and cold seeped in.

Everything was quiet, there was an unending nothingness around him, but he was no longer in any pain. If this was death, he was grateful it had come at the hands of the waves rather than Oberon's wand. Still, Wyn was depending on him; he needed to find his way back. Yet there was nothing in all directions.

Something red, like a scarf drifting on a breeze, moved towards him. As it grew closer, the colors shifted, and it took on the form of a bird, an owl. A gnarled tree appeared, and the owl landed, growing and elongating into the form of a woman. Aiden stared at the lady who seemed to haunt his worst moments but said nothing.

"So, you are finally on the right path." She smiled; the first time he could remember her doing so.

"I am?" Speaking took more effort than he thought it might. Perhaps the dead had no more need for words.

"You are no longer seeking revenge, and you are willing to accept your enemy's aid in exchange for peace."

"I'm not able to do much of anything now." The thought of the prince being Wyn's only hope still turned his insides sour. He hadn't done nearly enough to try and convince her to seek refuge with him, but hopefully she would see it was her only option. With him dead, perhaps that would loosen Oberon's hold over her.

"You aren't dead, though you might be soon. That is up to you."

"I'm not dead? But how—"

"You are under my protection, for now. And I will return you to where you were when we are done here."

"If you return me to where I was, I likely won't survive long."

She gave him a withering smile. "Some advice, if I may. No new path is carved without sacrifice. To get what you truly desire, you must be willing to give up everything."

"You mean give Wyn the staff and hope the prince can wipe all the dark fae, including me, out of existence?"

"You must interpret my words as you see fit. But you will only live once you've sacrificed all."

"Haven't I sacrificed enough? My life is barely mine."

"It is not up to me to decide what is fair. I merely wish to help you. Now, heed what I've said and choose life."

"Wait! Will you at least tell me what this riddle means?"

A wave pounded into Aiden, and he landed hard on a rocky surface. Coughing up seawater, he looked around. Pale light gleamed on the waves as they crashed into the rectangular pool. He pressed his back against the damp wall of the cliff. Taking a moment to catch his breath, he wended, not bothering to stand. As he materialized, something slammed into him, knocking him onto his back. Another wave?

"God! Aiden, I thought you drowned. I saw you go under, but you didn't come back up, and it's been hours. I thought you were—" Wyn sobbed into his chest, and he rubbed small circles around her back. They lay like that for a long while, far past when her sobs subsided and peace fell over them.

Eventually, the cold set in, and Wyn shivered against him. Pushing himself upright, Aiden dug his fingers into the grass, then waved a hand to bring forth a campfire. She leaned against him as they stared into the flames. He didn't know how long they sat for, but eventually light blossomed over the horizon.

"So, the staff wasn't down there?"

Aiden breathed out. "There was a clue. It was just a song that I couldn't decipher."

"What was it?"

Aiden recited the song, and she frowned.

"Kirwan's forgotten lair. I bet we could find something with the name Kirwan in it. Let's get back to the village, and we can ask around."

"Do you think we can find it in a week?"

"We have more than anyone has had in centuries. There's hope, right?"

"Yes, there's hope."

CHAPTER 18
Freddie

When the fire simmered down to nothing and the hill was washed in pale, lavender light, Freddie let out a breath. It was too easy to fall into the temporary comfort. Aiden's shoulder had become her pillow while his head was bowed in a light doze. They only had six days until everything went to crap. As much as she wanted to forget their impending deadline, ignoring it would only guarantee things would get worse.

She stretched her legs out, wincing at the ache of stiffness. He stirred, and she straightened. They needed to head back, who knew how long it would take them to find whoever Kirwan was and seek out their forgotten lair.

A burble of chatter sounded behind them, and she jerked, immediately regretting it as pain shot through her body. Aiden snapped awake and twisted to a group of people, not too far in the distance. If the first tourists were already on the move, then they needed to be too.

"We have to go." The raspy quality of her voice startled her into further alertness. She glanced side long at Aiden, though he hardly seemed to notice as he pushed himself to his feet and held out a hand to help her up. Clearing her throat, she stood smoothing her hair, hoping she didn't look as much of a wreck as she felt.

They trooped past the tourists towards the village, where they returned to the cafe where they'd grabbed snacks the previous day.

Scents of coffee and freshly baked pastries sent dizzying waves across her vision. They still had a few dollars, just enough to buy tickets back to the mainland and perhaps something small to eat. Still, she craved a real breakfast.

Her back itched as though the credit card in her wallet could hear her stomach growling and was determined to remind her it was there. No, the alert it would send to her father's phone wasn't worth it, at least not yet, and especially if Mr. Fallus was close. If Oberon caught wind that she was hunting the staff with Aiden, she doubted she'd be able to stop him from interfering with her using the remaining wishes for her desires.

"Excuse me, can I get a few things to go?" She leaned over the counter towards a dark-haired fairy girl who danced over to take her order. Pouring herself a to-go cup of water, she waited for the fairy girl to return with the pastries and Aiden's coffee.

"Enjoy," the fae said, waving.

Freddie took a step away from the counter and pivoted. "You wouldn't happen to know anything about a Kirwan, would you?"

She frowned. "You mean Kirwan's Lane in Galway? Most people call it the Latin Quarter. 'You looking for a place to eat over there?"

"It's a place, like a—a destination?" Freddie's heart lifted as relief and elation chased away the dread she'd hardly realized she was harboring. Could it be that, for once, something wasn't hard for them?

"Did you think it would be too crowded during tourist season? There's plenty of spots you can go without a reservation if that's what you're worried about. But if you don't have ferry tickets, it might be a bit of a wait to get over there."

Freddie's heart raced. Her adventure in Winter had been enough puzzling through cryptic fae mysteries to last her a lifetime. It was nothing short of a blessing that Kirwan's forgotten lair would be so easy to find. "Can you tell us when the next boat leaves?"

The fairy smiled brightly and glanced at a clock on the wall. "You'll want to hurry. It leaves in thirty minutes. Probably boarding already, but you need—"

"—thank you!" Freddie waved to her and skipped towards Aiden. Dragging him outside, the crease in his brow smooth as she recounted the news of Kirwan's Lane.

He grinned. "We might actually find this thing."

Thankfully, the walk to the docks was far less taxing than the hike to the pool. Still, Freddie's legs ached by the time they got there, though it may have been the overexertion from the day before. There was a trickle of people making their way aboard. If they tried to buy tickets before they got on, the ferry might leave them behind.

Her heart pounded as they fell in line behind the last few people.

Aiden frowned down at her. "Are you alright?"

"Fine. I think we have enough, but..." She swallowed, looking at the ticketing agent scanning each person's ticket as they passed.

"But?"

"Well, we don't exactly have tickets, and I don't think we have time to buy them. I should've planned better, but without my phone, I'm a little lost."

He seemed to consider her words as they inched closer to the agent. Five people were ahead of them, then four, three... Aiden leaned close. "I have an idea, but we need to move quickly."

"If it gets us on the boat, I'll take it," she breathed.

The agent scanned the tickets of the couple in front of them, just as a huge splash sprayed them all with water. Aiden pulled her forward, passed the crouching people. A prickling sensation skittered across her skin, but she didn't look back until they were several yards away. The agent was looking back at them, frowning. Freddie's breath hitched as they opened their mouths as though to call after them. But as the prickling intensified, the agent seemed to shrug and turn away.

"What was that?" she asked.

Aiden shook his head as the prickling faded. "It was just a distraction."

"And you just relied on them not looking up as we booked it onto the boat?" She let out a breath as they boarded, and no one seemed to notice as they made their way to the upper deck.

"I glammoured us to look like the people who just went through. I figured they wouldn't notice."

"That was brilliant."

A row of seats looked out over the sea. Freddie sank into the nearest one, and Aiden took the one beside her. Just as the boat pulled away, a wave of exhaustion hit, and she leaned against his shoulder. He let out a slow breath, the ever-present stiffness in his body relaxing slightly beneath her. Before long, sleep overtook her.

It seemed as though mere seconds had passed by the time a loud horn woke her. To her dismay, they found themselves an hour away from their destination, forcing them to have to sneak aboard a bus to finally arrive in Galway. The sun was high overhead, and hunger gnawed at her stomach as they disembarked in a not-so-picturesque industrial landscape. But it didn't matter; they were so close. They just needed to find Kirwan's Lane, the Latin Quarter, and before long, the staff would be theirs.

Galway was as loud and bright as the countryside had been quiet and peaceful. Its quaint design and myriad of both humans and fae moving about the packed streets reminded her of a much larger version of Easton.

Freddie half skipped through the roads, getting lost twice before finally finding their way to Kirwan's Lane. Colorful buildings lined tight streets far too small and congested for cars to pass. People were taking pictures, eating outside, and shopping at the myriad of stores that lined their path while tiny flags fluttered in the breeze above.

"This isn't exactly what I expected." She scanned the shop names looking for something advertising tacos, or margaritas, or even mofongo, but there were no such signs in sight.

Aiden too looked around. "It looks...almost like a city in Fairy might."

Nodding, her fingers itched for her phone to look up why this place was called "Latin" when there seemed to be no Latino influences, perhaps the name dated back to the original language itself. Curiosity burned inside her, but she couldn't afford to waste time and energy chasing distracting thoughts.

She leaned into Aiden. "Do you sense anything?"

He stiffened and shook his head. "I think we have to get closer. Maybe we should investigate these buildings?"

A year ago, window shopping in Europe with a hot fae at her side would've been a dream. Now, it was tainted by the ticking clock of their impending demise. Still, they were so close, she could practically taste it. Maybe they could find the staff; there would be two wishes: Aiden could be free, and somehow she would convince Pelrin to set aside his vengeance, and they could work together to defeat both Oberon and Mr. Fallus. If even a little bit of that came true, it would at least give her some hope.

Letting out a breath, she led the way into the first shop. They wandered about, pretending to look at finely crafted pieces of pottery. Every so often, she would look to Aiden, who would shake his head. They moved on to the next store and the next, until the sun cast the street in a golden light, and the lack of food made her dizzy.

She stumbled, half tripping into Aiden's back. He whirled and caught her.

"You're not alright." It wasn't a question. His amber eyes seemed to bore into her, shoving away any pretense.

"I—maybe we should take a break." Though even as she said it, the disappointment in finding nothing ate away at her. They should be searching until they found *something*. If she'd been fae, her stamina would've lasted her far longer.

Aiden placed a hand on hers. "We should eat, it's getting late too."

"Well, we did save money by not buying the tickets for the ferry, but it's not going to last us for the rest of the week." She pulled out her wallet and recounted the last fifty Euros. "I don't even know where we're going to sleep tonight." Tucking the money back into her wallet, she let out a choked laugh. Aiden skipped meals all the time, and he didn't complain—she could too.

As if to counter her reasoning, a breeze wafted over the mouthwatering scent of something fried, and she groaned.

He turned in its direction. "Let's go. We can figure everything else out later."

Fifteen euros later, they were carrying a box loaded with fries and a large piece of fried fish. She popped a fry into her mouth and winced as it burned her tongue. Offering the box to Aiden, her lip twitched as he inspected his fry before taking a bite. His expression softened into bliss as he reached for another.

"It's good, right?"

He nodded and followed her to lean against a stone wall and devour the rest of the food. When they'd finished, unease resettled in her gut. With only thirty-five Euros remaining and no place to stay the night, there was no chance of them being able to make it five more days here. She clenched her jaw, watching the people pass as though one of them held the answer to their trouble.

Pushing herself off from the wall, Freddie took a breath and looked around. "Let's see if we can find a cheap hostel for the night. We'll just have to take it one day at a time."

"Are we truly so low on funds?" Aiden's brow creased.

She forced a smile. No use troubling him with anything more on top of their impending doom. "Let's just worry about that when we find someplace. Now, we just need to find a free computer." Her heart pounded, and she took several more steadying breaths. Even trapped in the ice palace with Pelrin, she'd at least had a place to stay. With no access to the internet, no place to sleep, and no bathroom, a chilling sense of vulnerability cloaked her shoulders.

She pretended to ignore it as she approached a fairy selling candied nuts and asked about the computer.

"There's a library not far that way," she said and pointed down the street. Freddie thanked her, and they took off, her vision tunneled for signs pointing them to where they were headed. At least there she could also do more research into possible locations of the staff, and perhaps plot her takedown of Mr. Fallus too.

The whisper of books greeted them as they passed through the doors. If only they could spend the night there...

She headed straight to the bathroom to clean up, leaving Aiden alone in the manga section. As she'd left, he was reaching for a book that looked suspiciously like the next one in their series. Shoving back the temptation to join him, she forced herself to focus.

After cleaning herself the best she could, she fixed her braids and stared back at her reflection in the mirror. *Five more days.* And that was including finding a way to show the public what a hypocritical creep Mr. Fallus was. It wasn't as though she had a huge following on social media, and even if she did, she had no way of posting about him. And it wasn't like she knew anyone with a big social following here, even if she could compile a story, and was willing to give it up.

She mulled over her favorite liberal influencers—they always told stories about the different cases of anti-fae discrimination across the country. A few had even spoken about how deplorable Mr. Fallus was, though even as she thought back to when she'd broken the story about her classmates last year, none of them had reached out to her even after picking up the story. Perhaps she would have to be the one to make contact first.

With a breath, she returned to Aiden. With any luck, she'd be able to send out a few emails before they left and get a solid lead in the next couple of days. Her thoughts jerked from her list of liberal influencers when a family of three walked through the library doors. A fairy girl, no older than three, clung to the hands of a human couple, both wearing false wings.

Freddie caught Aiden staring, his jaw agape, and hurried to his side.

The woman caught his stare and frowned. "Can we help you with something?"

"Your wings..." He pointed, and Freddie nudged his side. Typically, she was all for staring at those who were inviting attention, but not when a kid was involved.

The woman pulled the girl in front of her. "We wear these to signify to our *daughter*, and others, that we are safe."

Freddie opened her mouth to commend the couple on opening up their home, but the words faded when she caught sight of the look of fury on Aiden's face. "False wings will do nothing to teach her how to fly. Do you even mist them?"

"Mist?" The man frowned, his gaze drifting down to the child's dull wings—a stark contrast to the glittery wonders on Pelrin's back.

"If the veins calcify, she'll never lift off." He spoke as though there was something stuck in his throat.

The child gripped her mother's leg. "How we raise our daughter is none of your business. What do you know about wing care anyway?"

Flames sprang up on his arms, his expression darkening. Freddie tugged on his wrist, dragging him towards the opposite side of the library. "Sorry, he's just invested in fae health. Definitely look into misting, though."

The woman gave her a wincing smile before ushering her family towards the children's section. Freddie let out a breath when they were out of sight, and Aiden's flames died. Sinking into a computer chair, she guided him into the one beside her.

"They are going to ground her permanently," he hissed.

She pressed her lips together. "Maybe you got through to them." With his chances at flight stolen from him, it was little wonder he wanted to spare the girl from the same fate. The humans who opened up their homes to fae war orphans had always seemed like such selfless people. She bit her lip; it was her desire for a byline that had gotten Freya killed. Hopefully, the influencers she reached out to would be more focused on ruining Mr. Fallus than hollow altruism.

She sent out several messages while Aiden stared back at where the family had been in silence.

Finally, he turned. "What are you doing?"

"I just need to send out some emails. We have to take down Mr. Fallus, right?"

His brow furrowed. "What are *emails*? Will they hurt you?" His voice was gravely as though laced with pain.

Freddie clenched her fists, his own mirroring hers. "The people I'm sending these messages to talk about fae advocacy. If anyone wants to help ruin his reputation, it'll be them. I'll be fine."

He nodded, though she could tell by the slight wrinkle in his brow he didn't fully understand. But that was fine, if Aiden could stand against Oberon, then she could, would have to, handle Mr. Fallus.

The sun cast sleepy orange light on the walls by the time she'd pressed send on her last email. "I'm still not too sure where we'll stay tonight." She tried to find a hostel again, only to come up with the same discouraging results.

Aiden straightened, his expression still tense. "If we can find a wood, I could make a bower. It won't have a bathroom or a true bed, but it's a place to sleep." Aiden didn't look at her, his features were tight as he spoke. It wasn't as though she was highly concerned with sleeping in the woods; she'd been camping before. Still, there was something gut-wrenchingly terrifying about having nowhere indoors to go. But what choice did they have?

They asked the librarians about the way to the nearest wooded walking trails and made their way out of the city. Her chest tightened as the noise of cars and people faded away to the hum of insects and the calls of numerous birds.

With Aiden by her side, she could almost pretend the walk was pleasant, just the two of them enjoying each other's company. But it wasn't like that for them anymore, nor was there time to mend what their heated emotions had broken. It would have to be friends for now and hope there was some future to look forward to.

By the time they found their way to a wooded area, it was dark. Exhaustion weighed heavily on her shoulders, and she'd all but forgotten that their destination was hardly a soft bed for her to curl up into.

Aiden led her a ways off the path and into the brush. She clung tight to his arms to keep from falling over the numerous roots, stones, and sharp branches that were determined to keep them out. Blue light glowed along his arms, and the sounds of rustling leaves surrounded them. A bright floral aroma filled the air as a burst of blue exploded before them, settling into glittering stars among the leaves.

By their light, she could just make out a tent of vines and soft, spongy plants. A canopy of fragrant flowers hung overhead, lending their sweet scent to the lavender plants that grew around the circumference of the inside. She ducked into the opening to find the ground carpeted with velvety leaves and soft moss.

"Aiden, this is beautiful." Tucking her bag into one corner, Freddie rested on her side, finding herself surprisingly warm.

Aiden followed after her, lying on the opposite side of their bower and closing the entrance behind him. "My mother used to make these for me when I was a child. A lot of fairies make them in Spring." His voice hitched, and he rolled onto his back. The glittering light of his magic reflected back in his eyes.

The urge to touch his shoulder, move closer, anything to be with him, nagged at Freddie's mind, but she couldn't give in, not when so much was on the line for them. An entire day of searching without finding anything related to the staff was to be expected. They had at least something to look into and were one small step closer to defeating Mr. Fallus.

She let out a shaky breath. This was *not* a failure—they'd come further than most who searched for the staff, she was sure of it. But if that was true, why then did she feel so hopeless?

CHAPTER 19
Aiden

Aiden gritted his teeth and stared harder at the small text on the page. No matter how many books on the history of this place he read, how many maps he studied, it all proved useless when they searched the streets. He'd thought finding the insight about Kirwan's Lane might get them closer, but the staff proved as elusive as ever.

Glancing over his shoulder, he looked at Wyn as she stared, features tight, at the computer. While he hardly understood what she was trying to do to Mr. Fallus. If Oberon was on his side, any effort Wyn made to destroy the man was dangerous. He pushed back in his chair and made his way over to her. "Any news?"

She shook her head. "So far, I've only gotten two responses. One person called me a fake, and the other person wrote me a long note about how I need to focus on what was going on in Britain, where fae are *actually* suffering rather than on American politicians whose anti-fae beliefs are fringe. Part of me wants to respond, but it's just so frustrating. Can't they see how it's all connected?"

"Do you think they'll help you?" He knelt beside her, trying to make sense of the message.

"No." She sat back. "Most of these people care more about views than the truth. It's better to cover a trending story than break something new and risk it not catching on."

"I don't...Must we beg them for aid?"

"We could always try and post thirst traps to build up a following, but besides not having a phone, something tells me our ultimate message might get lost." She dropped her head to her hands. His fingers twitched towards her, but he resisted. There was no point in getting attached and making things worse.

"Should I know what a thirst trap is?" The words were meant to be teasing, but he had a hard time scraping up enough joviality to shove into them.

Wyn just shook her head.

No staff, no help from Wyn's contacts, only Oberon and Fallus working together and four days of relative safety left. The air thinned as he desperately tried to suck in more. Even if by some miracle they did find the staff, what could they possibly wish for to fix all of this? And what if there were no wishes left?

He let out a shaky breath and blinked hard. The library lights were far too harsh as they stabbed into his skull.

Abruptly, he turned towards the door. "Can we leave?"

"Hmm?" Wyn looked up at him, her brow slightly furrowed. "Is everything—"

"—I need some air." He massaged his temples, trying desperately to shove back thoughts of their inevitable doom. The soft pressure of her fingers on his arm made him flinch. Her brow was still wrinkled in concern but she didn't argue as she followed him to the exit.

Outside, the air smelled of earth and petrichor. Sleek cars passed through the streets, and people, dressed in what appeared to be brightly colored bags, shuffled past. Wyn pulled up the hood of her sweatshirt and shivered. His heart sank, leaving had been selfish. She'd get cold in this, and what if it led to her getting sick? A speck of rationality reminded him that it didn't matter if she got ill if Oberon decided to kill them both in the next four days.

"Back to Kirwan's?" Her smile was too tense to be genuine. He wanted to retreat into the warmth at the sight of it. Her stomach grumbled, not for the first time that morning. He'd been trying to pretend not to notice, and not to show how much it killed him that she was starving herself for him.

"Let's get something to eat first."

Her smile dropped. "We don't have much cash left."

"Just take care of yourself. I've survived on less before."

Fingers curling around the strap of her bag, Aiden followed her stare in the direction he'd become all too familiar with. This time, when they entered the tight alleyway, he pressed himself as close to the stone wall as possible, straining his senses for any glimmer of magic. Today, he couldn't fail; he *had* to find something.

They passed several cafes, but Wyn didn't express the slightest interest in any of them. The tremble in her shoulders intensified the more they walked and the more the maddening rain dripped down upon them. At least in Fairy, there had been something to fight, the battles, no matter how futile to his personal survival, made him feel like he was at least doing something. This wandering and waiting was akin to a torture Mab would invent.

Hours passed, and Wyn remained silent with her head down. He missed her teasing, her laugh, and he even missed fighting with her. The silence was more proof that he was doing something wrong. She paused to lean against a building with a long awning and hugged herself in the temporary dry.

Cold. Wet. Hungry. And it was all his fault. If he'd told her sooner not to feed him, or perhaps if he'd never agreed to a second date with her, they could have been living separate lives, and she would be somewhere safe and fed right now.

"This is ridiculous. We can't keep going on like this." He slicked back his wet hair with his hands, lacing them over his head.

"What choice do we have? It's here somewhere." Her words were soft, measured, exhausted—the defeat in her tone only served to add kindling to his frustration.

"Is it? We've seen no hints, no clues, and it's been nearly three days. Even your contacts won't help us."

"And the alternative is what, exactly?" A spark of anger seemed to chase away some of the pressing fatigue in her expression. "If we fail, we die. So, we keep trying until that happens. If you have another plan that helps us out of this mess faster, I'm wide open to it." Despite the passion in her words, her voice was still low, just audible over the rain.

Aiden's chest heaved as he racked his brain for a response. She was right. If they weren't actively trying to find the staff, then they were just killing time before Oberon hunted them down. Sliding his hands down to his neck, he turned to face the street. There had to be something more they could do.

"You'd think a girl your age would know better—this blasted rain is agony on my knees." Mr. Jameson's familiar rumble made Aiden straighten. His gaze fixed on a shuffling group clad in the same bags that so many of the other people on the street were wearing. Beside him, Wyn pushed herself slightly off the wall, her eyes wide.

The group moved closer as Wyn pressed against his side. A thrill shot through him as the heat of her seared him through his wet clothes. As though their silence was a shout, Mr. Jameson turned. He pulled off his glasses, hiked up the bag, and rubbed them on his pants before replacing them on his nose. "Well, if it isn't my own flesh and blood!"

"Please, Mr. Jameson. We'll be at the hotel in just a moment, no need to be so dramatic." Maggie sounded as though her travels had been just as exhausting as his and Wyn's.

"Dramatic? I'm not the one who lost the two young ones. But there they are, right as rain, you see?" Mr. Jameson pointed.

Maggie turned and screamed. She rushed over to them and swept up Wyn in a one-armed hug. "Oh, thank goodness, I was so worried. Liam stayed behind. I'll have to give him a call. What happened? You two disappeared, and we couldn't delay, and the emergency contact must've been a wrong number because they hadn't a clue what I was talking about." She pressed a hand to Wyn's cheek. "Oh dear, you're freezing. You got lost, didn't you?"

Wyn nodded. "We just stepped out for a coffee and got distracted. Everyone was gone, so we went to the next place we could remember to try and catch up." He pressed his lips together, marveling at her smooth lie.

"Well, let's get you to your room." Maggie ushered them forward, and they followed the group a short way into the lobby of a hotel they'd visited the day before. Again, he reached out for any hint of the staff's magic, but there was nothing. Still, as he followed Wyn up the stairs, a sense of relief flooded through him.

They entered the room, and while small, it didn't feel as tight as the one they shared that first night. It was lit with warm, dim lamps against the wall, and the only furniture, aside from the large bed, was a built-in desk and chair opposite it. Wyn ripped open her bag and pulled out her shirts. Neatly placing them on the ledge by the window, she stripped off her jeans and sweatshirt to do the same.

"I—I'm going to shower. Sorry," she muttered and hurried into the bathroom. He stared after her, his mind half memorizing the phantom curves of her body and the other half bewildered by their luck. At least they would have some comfort before they perished. He let out a dark chuckle and shivered.

Soft patters followed by the rush of water sounded from beyond the bathroom door. Perhaps Wyn was right to get out of her wet clothes so quickly. His face heated, and he shook the thoughts from his mind.

Pacing the small space, he hesitated, then moved to place his own wet clothes on the desk. With a wave of his hand, a ripple of warm air moved throughout the room, and both of their clothes fluttered and settled back down, now fully dry. He sank into the chair, staring blankly out at the misty landscape. For better or worse, this would all be over soon, and it seemed there was nothing he could do to divert fate. The door to the bathroom creaked open, and he jumped. Wyn returned, dressed in a fluffy white robe.

"Oh. I suppose you could always do that, too." Her cheeks pinkened, though it was likely from the warmth of the shower. "The shower is still really nice, though." She made her way to the other side of the bed and sat with a sigh.

He didn't need much convincing. Leaping up, he sped to the bathroom and locked himself inside. The scalding water pounded onto his body, burning away his fears. If he were to die, he could at least savor these last moments of life. By the time he left the shower, he'd become almost numb to the idea of Oberon finding him. If not for Wyn, he might even welcome the fae king's ambition to finally put an end to his suffering. But it was for Wyn that he still fought for the chance at a future.

When he returned to the bedroom, she was asleep. He sat at the edge of the bed watching her chest rise and fall with each of her heavy breaths. Had his bower been so uncomfortable? He dug his fingers into the blankets. It wasn't as though he had much of an opportunity to practice that sort of magic, but he'd found it nice. At least, it'd been nice to share the space with her.

As though reading his thoughts, she stirred and rolled towards him. Aiden jerked back, tumbling off the edge. "Freezing frosts!"

"A-Aiden?" Wyn frowned down at him. "Are you—"

"—fine. Sorry." He scrambled to his feet, refusing to let his eyes meet hers. Since when had he been so clumsy?

She reached out and grabbed his hand. He flinched and stared at the place where heat radiated from where their skin connected. For a long moment, neither moved. It was as though the orb's icy blast had frozen him in place, yet somehow, he blazed.

Slowly, his gaze trailed up from her hand, along the fluffy sleeve to her bare neck, her chin, and finally to her full lips. The memory of their softness against his own consumed him as he moved closer. Lemon-scented soap wafted off her skin as he knelt before her.

She shifted, putting mere inches between them. All doubt, all fear at what a horrible idea it was to be so close to her, lay muffled as though the rain was somehow able to drown it out. He leaned in, the air between them almost visibly fleeing the ever-shrinking space. So close he could almost taste—

A sharp knock at the door made him jerk, and he got to his feet. Wyn pulled back and twisted away from him. His shoulders sagged, and he let out a breath.

"I've got your meal vouchers!" Maggie's voice came out in a singsong from the other side.

With a groan, he got to his feet and crossed the room to open the door. The moment had been thoroughly killed. Perhaps for the best. Maggie shoved two strips of paper at him, and he blinked, turning them over. "There are a few choices on the back. And it covers a full three courses. Is there anything else I can get you two?" The pity in her expression was sickening, but Aiden forced his features to remain neutral as he shook his head and thanked her.

When he turned back around, Wyn was sitting up on the bed, the hopeful gleam in her gaze restored. She held out a hand for the vouchers, and he passed one to her.

"There's an Italian place on here. You like Italian, right?" she asked.

He frowned. "I do?"

"Shrimp scampi?" The corner of her lip twitched, and the memory of their horribly awkward first date flashed in his mind. He'd tried so hard that night, as though some part of him had already felt for her what he now did.

He waited for her to dress, and together they headed back out to the restaurant. A nagging sensation clawed at his back, reminding him that they *should* be searching for the staff. But they'd hardly have any hope of finding it starved and exhausted. Wyn might have been more awake, but by the way she clung to his arm, as though for balance, he could tell she was still hungry.

The Italian restaurant was one they'd passed several times during their searches but had been unable to fully explore the inside. His own stomach betrayed him by growling a greeting as they entered. The tables were clothed in white and red checked linens, and what looked like iron tools hung along the walls and ceilings, but they must have been replicas, as he felt none of the sickness.

Wyn's nose wrinkled as she studied the menu. "They certainly have a lot of choices."

"Is that a bad thing?" He frowned down at his, homing in on the pizzas. Perhaps he would go for one of those instead of the dish he'd had on their first date.

She shrugged. "We'll see, I guess."

Their server came, and Aiden blurted out his desire for the seafood pizza before the man could greet them. Wyn raised her brows before giving her own hesitant order.

"Are you alright?" Her expression seemed torn between amusement and concern.

He shook his head. "I'm hungry."

"And worried we still haven't found the staff?" she asked. He nodded. "Yeah, I just need to clear my head. Maybe we can look for it tonight. We could check the other floors in the hotel."

"We still have four more days. I just want something to make it feel like this isn't just one big failure."

"We're not failing. We've come further than most people, and…It would probably be best if we found it tonight." She didn't meet his eyes as she prodded the table with her fork.

"Ideally, perhaps. But that hasn't been our luck."

"The tour also goes back to London in the morning. So, if we don't find it, we're back to no place to stay and no food."

Aiden's fingers clenched into a fist. Of course, their blessing would be ripped away as soon as it was gifted to them. Did they stay up all night searching in hopes of finding the staff and getting a ride back to the city, or did they enjoy their last night of comfort before they would have to return to the hard life?

The server returned with two glasses of water balanced in one hand and a salad in the other. He made to rest the salad on the table, but his hand slipped and the dish spilled into Aiden's front. With a gasp, he pushed himself back as bits of lettuce and cubed bread fell to the floor. From an uncomfortable itch against his chest, he could tell some of it had gotten into his shirt as well.

"I am so sorry sir. Your dry cleaning is on us. There's a bathroom back there, I—I'll be right back with the manager. Don't worry. Sorry!" The man waved one hand frantically, while gesturing at the back of the restaurant.

Aiden gave him a wincing smile. He reminded him of some of the hobs that had once skittered around the Winter Palace, always in constant fear of their Majesties and the members of their court. "I am unharmed. I'll just clean up a bit." He nodded to Wyn, who was easing the water glasses out of the panicked man's other hand. She pulled her lips in an awkward shrug as he headed off to the bathroom.

He made his way to the back of the restaurant and pushed the door open. It closed behind him, cutting off the sound from the noisy dining room beyond.

Alone. Aiden took a deep breath and examined his reflection as he undid the straps of the jerkin. An amber-eyed boy stared back at him, sleep-deprived and anxious. Was that how Wyn saw him too? Something throbbed at the back of his mind. If he could just focus on his breathing, he could get through the rest of the day and just enjoy the time he had left.

Still, the impending doom throbbed in the back of his mind. Shaking out the remaining particles of food, Aiden headed towards the door but paused as the throbbing grew fainter. He stepped back, and it intensified. Heart leaping into his chest, he moved closer to the sink. It grew stronger and stronger, reminding him of the pulse he'd felt near the crown and the orb, yet somehow weaker, as though this object were clinging onto its last remnants of magic.

He stopped at the lip of the sink, but saw nothing, though the pulse continued. The door inched forward, but a wave of his hand closed it on whoever was on the other side and firmly locked them out. Aiden felt along the surface of the sink and off to either side. Each time he stepped away from it, the pulse would fade. Growling, Aiden fidgeted with the taps. How was it possible that he was so close and yet the staff continued to elude him?

Pacing the length of the bathroom, he focused on the pull and ebb of the staff's magic. It was the sink, it had to be. Was it possible the staff could've been re-carved into the sink? He grasped the edge of it again, then peered beneath it. He nearly laughed at himself when there was nothing, but he froze. A metal pipe came out from the wall to feed into the sink basin beside him, but this one seemed propped up by a wooden stick. He'd thought it'd been part of the sink, but was it possible?

Grasping a hand around the sink base, Aiden pulled, and it came free. Almost reverently, he lifted a staff as long as his arm with one curving tine that ended in a tiny green gem. The wood throbbed like a heartbeat beneath his fingers. This was it. He was certain. Centuries of fae had been searching, but none of them had thought to look in a Human Realm bathroom. Yet here it was.

Aiden hurried out of the bathroom, nearly bowling over the old man who'd been tugging at the door handle. Forcing himself to slow, he took his seat before Wyn.

"Aiden, what is that?" Though from the tremor in her voice, she'd already guessed.

"It was in there, the whole time."

"You mean—"

He nodded.

"The Staff of Wind was in a dingy bathroom, and you two kids somehow found it." Mr. Jameson pulled out the chair beside Aiden and plunked down. "I knew I'd do well putting my trust in you."

CHAPTER 20
Freddie

Freddie stared down at the old man, eyes narrowed. Elation at finding the staff, anger over another person nosing into their quest, and fear over what she might have to do next flooded through her, cutting off all words. Aiden's grip shifted as he moved closer.

"Now don't you go getting upset. I've had over seventy years of practice being sneaky, and no one suspects an old man." Mr. Jameson lifted two fingers and flagged down the server. "A coffee, black. And no, I don't want to hear all your chatter." The man looked affronted but said nothing as he strode back towards where Freddie assumed the kitchen was located.

"Now that *we* have the staff, what do you plan to do next?" Aiden asked. Freddie kicked her leg out in a nervous twitch and hit his. Aiden jerked and flashed her a look, but she shook her head.

"Ah, well, that's up to you. I'd initially planned to ask nicely for a wish, assuming there were enough to go around, but it appears as though there is only one left."

She and Aiden exchanged looks again. It was just as bad as she feared. One wish to wake her friends and condemn Aiden? A wish to free Aiden and condemn Pelrin? And Oberon would still hunt them down either way. What wish could possibly get them out of this mess?

Her chest tightened. Using force to keep an old man away from the staff wasn't ideal either. And by the cold smile spreading across his wrinkled face, he was counting on them not being willing to hurt him in the pursuit of their own desires.

Inching closer to Aiden, Freddie touched the smooth, dark wood of the staff. It seemed to crackle with magic, and the gem on the remaining tine winked in the artificial light. "Sorry, we aren't going to just give this to you."

Mr. Jameson scoffed. "Are you trying to sort out your pitiful love life? A decent therapist will help with that. I have much larger things at stake."

"And if we refuse?" Aiden's eyes flashed as he leaned closer to the old man.

"I'd rather not have to tell the authorities a violent fae robbed me."

"Are you really trying to rely on prejudice to get your way?" Freddie curled her fingers into fists to keep them from hurling something at the man. Were the other people in London so despicable? Was this how they were able to relocate the fae without creating an international riot?

"I'll do just about anything I have to for that wish." He licked his lips; eyes fixed on the staff.

Aiden leaned closer. "Why? What is your desperate wish?"

Mr. Jameson shook his head. "I need it for my wife, not that it's any of your business."

Something twisted in Freddie's gut, and she looked over to see Aiden's features soften. They were all just trying to protect the people they loved; it didn't matter the cost.

"I know well the pain of loss," Aiden said. He sucked in a breath. "But magic cannot bring back those who have passed."

"God, no! What's wrong with you? She's not dead, she's in London. They have all the fae in lockdown. She was caught doing the shopping, and they took her away. I need to get her back."

"Why do you need the staff for that?" Freddie asked.

"You think if I asked nicely for my wife, they'd let her go? 'Course not. Those police think they're doing people like me a service, and that we'll somehow get over it. No, I'm not going to get her out without a miracle, like the staff.

"If I could free your wife, would you forgo your efforts towards the staff?" Aiden laid it across his lap just as the server returned and plopped down Mr. Jameson's coffee.

"And the others? It's an ongoing problem if you haven't noticed. We won't be able to live freely until things are back to how they should be."

Freddie nodded. "We are already working on changing things. But even with a wish, you can't just force people into believing as you do. The public needs to be swayed."

"So, I should just trust you and give up saving the woman I vowed to protect?"

Freddie opened her mouth to respond but stopped when Aiden straightened beside her. "I'll help you save her," he said. She frowned over at him, but he didn't meet her gaze; instead, he focused on Mr. Jameson.

"I appreciate the willingness, but they're supposed to be voting on deporting them in just a few more days. I can't move to Fairy, not at my age. Especially not with a war going on. And the news is just now starting to talk about it." He harrumphed and sipped his coffee.

"Is the news is covering the deportations? I didn't see anything before we left." The spot on her leg where her phone usually was burned. Without it, she was so disconnected from the rest of the world.

"Well, it was so new. They'd only been gone for a couple days. It wasn't until some kids on the socials started spreading the word that anyone took up this story. Now it's all FAF this and FAF that. No one is actually doing anything to help."

"FAF?" Hadn't that one condescending response included that? She hadn't paid too much attention past their initial no. But if there was a movement she could tap into, maybe there was a different way to position her emails.

"Free all fae. It's what the young people are chanting in the streets. Not doing anyone much good though."

"If people are starting to take notice, the officials will hear them," Freddie said.

Mr. Jameson let out a dry 'ha'. "Hear them, maybe, but it won't change their minds. They believe they are acting on what's good for us, rather than what we want."

She glared at the old man as the server returned with their food. "Protests work."

"Maybe they did back when people cared more about the cause than their posts. They just want these issues to continue so people can donate and line their pockets. What was the last positive change you've seen in fae relations?"

She grit her teeth. The anti-fae politicians like Mr. Fallus were so obviously bad, she couldn't bring herself to believe that there were no people genuinely trying to do the right thing. But even as she thought through all of the people she'd reached out to, not a single one had made a tangible difference in the lives of those they claimed to speak for. Should they even be speaking *for* them? Fae leaders, like Pelrin, scarcely knew they existed. What did they know about what the fae wanted or needed?

But the two sides in Fairy were equally muddled. As terrible as Oberon was, Pelrin's family had been nearly just as cruel, if not worse. Was it just the state of things that there were only bad guys, and no one was good? The thought haunted her throughout the meal and into her dreams that night. If there was no powerful force to help them, maybe magic was the only way to save their fracturing world.

Freddie slept deeply on the bus on the way back to Dublin. Images of a flood coming and destroying the world kept her from finding rest. Aiden nudged her, and she jerked upright with a gasp.

"Wyn, I—"

Freddie shook her head. "Sorry. I'm just on edge."

"Me too." He rubbed his hands against his pants and scowled as Mr. Jameson twisted to stare at them.

A shout from somewhere beyond the bus pulled her attention to the outside. Dublin looked just as charming as it had before, but there was something different about the people walking the street. So many more of them were fae—or at least they had wings. The cheap wire and stretchy fabric contraptions strapped to the backs of the humans reminded her of the parents of the little girl they'd seen in the library. Those with actual wings were few and far between.

One person turned, revealing a large, painted "FAF". "I think it's a sign of protest."

"It says online that wearing wings is a symbol that you are a safe person for marginalized fae," a woman, a couple seated in front of them, said loudly.

"Looks more threatening than inviting if you ask me." Another woman muttered. Voices on the bus rose as everyone peered out the windows. Some people were on their phones, and Freddie caught snippets of videos.

Is colonial guilt fueling fae activism? And *Inter-realm intervention is warranted...*

The train ride back to London seemed to take far too long, and Mr. Jameson didn't let them out of his sight the entire way. When they finally separated from the tour, back in the city, he scowled at them.

"Now what?"

Freddie glanced at Aiden. "I know an entrance to where the fae are. Let's start there."

"We may be able to help them escape at least," Aiden said.

They made their way back towards the hotel, Freddie's chest tightening as they drew near. From the square where she'd seen the entrance, the hotel wasn't visible. Still, knowing the place where she'd almost lost her life sent a cool sheen of sweat to prickle against her forehead. By the time they were only a block away, she was panting.

Aiden rubbed a soothing circle on her back, and she smiled up at him gratefully. Angry chants punctuated the air, making her frown.

"What's that?" She strained her ears, just able to make out the shouts of 'Free all fae'.

Mr. Jameson didn't appear to be too comfortable as they drew nearer, but for once, the old man refrained from complaining. Rounding the corner to the square, she found it packed with false-winged protesters waving signs and chanting.

Skimming the signs, her gaze settled on one: "Humans stop talking over fae voices." The woman holding the sign was yelling, "Stop letting human journalists tell fae stories. Let fae talk about fae!"

Freddie swallowed. Her fears about her own passions, spoken aloud, sent pangs of guilt into her gut. More and more people crowded the square, bumping and jostling them in a sea of bodies. Instinctively, she reached out for Aiden's hand and gripped it tightly. She cried out, startled by Mr. Jameson clinging to her other arm.

Someone let out a bone-chilling scream, and it was echoed by more screams from somewhere much deeper in the crowd. The jostling grew fearsome, and she almost lost her hold on Aiden. Elbows and torsos slammed into her, and she cringed, struggling to maintain her footing. He wrapped an arm around her waist, and Mr. Jameson clamped down on her arm so tightly she was sure it would bruise.

By some miracle, they made their way to the edge of the crowd just as an explosion sounded from behind them. The scent of gasoline tainted the air, and smoke pricked her lungs. *Not again.* She surged forward, panic gripping her heart. Unsure of where she was going, she ran alongside others who were fleeing amongst angry shouts. Sirens blared as more explosions went off.

"This way!" Someone grabbed the front of her shirt and pulled it along. Freddie's breath came in tight bursts, making her vision far too blurry to make out the figure pulling them along. Racing down a side street where the crowd substantially thinned, they opened the door to a posh townhouse and tumbled inside, gasping.

"Thank you." Freddie sank to her knees, forcing back a sob. Since when has the pro-fae movement become so violent? She'd been to protests on campus, but they'd been far smaller and less angry.

"I knew you couldn't be dead. You're always chasing a lead. Now you can share it with me." Freddie looked up at the familiar voice and swallowed.

Mallory leaned over her, a triumphant smile alighting her face.

CHAPTER 21
Freddie

A cold, sick feeling spread from her chest down to her toes as Freddie glared at Mallory. She scrunched her hands into fists, her heart still pounding from the mad dash. How cruel of the universe to show her just how violent the pro-fae movement she'd always trusted could be, only to have the worst anti-fae creep save her.

Aiden reached out a hand to help her up. "Are you hurt?"

"No," she muttered, not taking her eyes off Mallory.

Mr. Jameson shuffled forward. "Well, my back is killing me. Where is this place? Who are you?"

Mallory cut her gaze from Freddie to the old man and gave him a wincing smile. "I'm Mallory Sheppard, and who are you? Wynifred's babysitter?"

"It's Freddie," Freddie snapped.

"Who cares! Where are we? How is this supposed to be helping me get my wife back?"

"Your wife?" Mallory took a step towards him. What appeared to be sympathy creasing her brow—it didn't fit her face.

"She was rushed off with all the others, and these two are supposed to help me before Parliament votes on that ridiculous deportation edict."

Mallory opened her mouth, then shut it again. She then gestured for them to follow her into a small sitting room. "Here, have a seat. I don't know how much Wynifred and her flavor of the week are going to be able to help you."

Aiden bristled and looked at Freddie as Mr. Jameson plopped himself into the nearest chair. She shook her head ever so slightly, wishing she could slap the smug grin off the girl's face, but she wasn't smiling. Instead, she watched Mr. Jameson as though he might fall apart at any moment.

"It's alright, Mal, you wouldn't care for his wife anyways. She's fae." Freddie rounded to the far side of the room, where a stiff, lavender couch sat at the edge of a sage-patterned carpet.

Mallory wrinkled her nose. "Is she dangerous?"

Freddie scoffed, but it was Mr. Jameson who responded in a gruff voice. "'Course not. Do you think all the fae would be gone if they were only rounding up the dangerous ones?"

She at least had the decency to duck her head. "It may be a tad extreme."

"Mal, I thought this was your dream come true!" Freddie crossed her arms and took a seat, but Aiden remained standing behind her, staff clutched in one hand.

"I just wanted to feel safe. This is the Human Realm, and humans should have a right here to not be in constant magical danger—not that you would know anything about that."

Freddie huffed. "I'll take that as a compliment."

"You've always thought you were so much better than everyone else just because your fae *pets* fawn all over you."

"Pets?" Aiden leaned forward, his burning amber gaze fixed on Mallory.

"I—I just meant she dates a lot of fae and pretends like it's some sort of activism. No offense." She shifted uncomfortably, and Freddie scowled.

"I've dated *one* other fae. Aiden and I have been together for almost a year, not that it's any of your business." The rest of her argument died as the gravity of her words hit her. They weren't together anymore.

Mallory didn't seem to notice her stumble and continued on. "Wasn't your whole thing to prove those people kidnapping our classmates weren't fae? But guess what—they were. And remember that time a fae kidnapped you? Not to mention that bombing was done by fae." Her voice trembled when she mentioned the bombing, but it wasn't like she'd been there.

Freddie swallowed hard. Just because some fae were bad didn't mean all were, not that Mallory could see the nuance. "At least I told the truth and *tried* to help people. What have you done?"

"I've tried to help people too, *human* people. It's not as though I'm desperately trying to fluff up my own ego like you and all the other liberals by profiting off of fae gullibility."

"I'm not profiting off of anyone." Freddie's breath hitched, and she pressed a hand to her chest, shoving back images of Freya and the collapsing palace. That had been her fault. If she hadn't been so desperate to prove herself, maybe they all would have lived. *Or maybe Mab would've sent them to their deaths on the battlefield.* The rational side of her brain slowly pulled her back into the present.

Mallory held up her phone. "Look. This is the FAF website where all the libs are buying those wings."

She turned the screen so Freddie could see, and Aiden too peered over her shoulder.

"Wow, they're so expensive. But you see, all proceeds go to the FAF movement."

Mallory tapped the about page where four humans and a were girl grinned from a photo. "There's only one fae founder."

"It's kinda the point to get humans to support fae rights." But Freddie's heart sank. The false wings themselves had been giant red flags that the organization at best was ignorant about what fae refugees needed, and at worst...

Mallory switched tabs, showing a video of a raging party that moved soundlessly from a social post. The were girl's face appeared in frame confidently looking at the camera. The caption read FAF rave. "They are throwing parties with that wing money. And according to the British assessor's office, the house is brand new."

Freddie pinched the bridge of her nose. "What exactly do you want?"

Mallory scoffed. "I simply wanted to show you proof that your good cause was going in the wrong direction."

"I almost died because of anti-fae people like you, Molly. These people may be corrupt, but the cause isn't wrong."

The redhead shifted uncomfortably and drew back. "I know. I didn't want to believe it, but I know what *he* did to you."

Freddie sat up straighter. "You know, about Mr. Fallus?"

Mallory nodded. "I overheard him and your dad arguing about how they'd set the fae up to bomb the hotel. That's how I got fired."

"Fired?" It was as though the floor had fallen out from beneath her. Freddie stared back at Mallory in shock.

"I was looking for evidence, and I got caught. There's not much to write a story on."

"I might be able to help with that." If Mallory was angry enough to help take down Mr. Fallus, she was not in a position to refuse help. "Mr. Fallus, being Oberon's brother *and* setting up the bombing, would be a pretty big story. He's actively working with the worst kind of fae to gain power over humans."

"Oberon's brother? That's not—"

"Oscar is a changeling. I bet we can find records of that since they aren't that common. A kidnapping report or news article from that time. It's just that the deportation vote is tomorrow, there won't be time to break the story and reverse it if we cover it, but I reached out to some journalists."

Mallory pulled her lips tight. "What did they say?"

"May I?" Freddie held her hands out for Mallory's phone, and she passed it over. Her fingers flew across the screen, praying for a response. There were a few more responses directing her to look into FAF. Her heart lifted when she saw one, a smaller creator who mostly focused on pop culture, mentioned he was interested. It was better than nothing. His ten thousand subscribers were significantly more than what she had.

Mallory peered over her shoulder. "These are all libs. We can get this posted on Chattable and *really* get the word out."

Freddie's stomach tightened at the thought of the conservative outlets dominating a story she'd put together. They would probably twist it in some way to make the refugees out to be the bad guys. She shook her head. "It'll just get lost under all that junk and probably do more harm than good."

"I worked there, I know all the right tactics and people, to make this go viral. If we write it up now and upload the couple of docs that I have, it'll be all over by tomorrow morning."

Freddie pressed her lips together. "And the fae it would hurt once the narrative is twisted? It would probably only speed up the deportation process."

"This isn't your average article, Freddie. I can control the narrative, I can interfere with the algorithm, and reach out to the creators."

"And I'm supposed to trust you to stop all of these fae from getting deported?"

"You can trust me to bring down that turd, Mr. Fallus. He's a traitor to everything we believe in, and I'm willing to bet all the creators will see it that way. No one is going to trust Parliament with him interfering. The vote will be delayed at least, and it will give you more than enough time to compile a story to sway people, if that's what you really want. I just want him to eat dirt for making conservatives look bad."

"And firing you?"

"And giving you a suite while banishing me to room with some weirdo."

Freddie looked back at Aiden, who was frowning at them both. "Let me know what I can do to assist."

Mr. Jameson's only response was the soft huff of air coming from his open mouth. His chest rose and fell—deep in slumber.

She didn't like the idea of having to trust Mallory with her story, but what choice did she have? None of her journalists were picking it up. They were either duped or in league with those corrupt FAF people. Finally, she nodded. "Alright, let's do this."

CHAPTER 22
Aiden

Aiden's head pounded as dawn light finally peeped through the drawn curtains. Sharp pains shot along his back as he stretched and pulled himself to his feet. Mr. Jameson's loud snores had made finding his own deep sleep difficult, though they seemed to have died down. Although he hardly trusted his desire for the staff, he was glad the old man had been spared from a night on the hard floor. It was hardly the first time Aiden had slept in such conditions; however, his body had grown far too used to the comfort of the hotel beds and having Wyn by his side.

He tensed, eyes searching the room for her form, ears primed for the sound of her breathing. Almost instantly, he spotted her on the opposite side of the couch, curled around the other girl's computer. Mallory, apparently, had been too good for the floor and was sprawled along the length of the long seat. Scowling, Aiden made his way around to kneel beside Wyn.

Soft puffs of coils had escaped her two braids to frame her face like little clouds. Though deep in slumber, her brow was furrowed, and her fingers twitched as though her mind was still working on the article. It'd been late by the time they'd finished, and he hardly remembered falling asleep. With one day left to figure out what to do with their wish and return the staff to Oberon, there was little time to indulge in the luxury of rest.

With a heavy breath, he placed a hand on Wyn's arm. She cringed in on herself but didn't wake. He hesitated; they'd been through so much, she clearly needed sleep. His heart longed to give her just a few more minutes, but every second seemed as though it was counting down to their ultimate deadline.

Leaning close to her ear, he gently rocked her shoulder. "Wyn."

She gasped and shot up. Looking back at him with wide eyes, her lips moved soundlessly before she turned and opened the computer. Her fingers flew across the keys, and the screen changed. Short blurbs of nonsense text appeared in row after row. Her brow creased further as she scrolled down, then stopped.

"You've got to be kidding me!" Her shout sent Mallory flailing, nearly falling off the couch, and Mr. Jameson let out a snort.

"What's wrong with you?" the red-haired girl groaned. Aiden turned to narrow his gaze at her, then peered back over Wyn's shoulder. She was pointing at a line of text bolded at the side of the screen: **US Senator's Fae Secret**.

Turning the computer towards Mallory, she pointed at the line of text. The girl leaned in and tapped once on the keyboard. Her eyebrows rose. "Wow, that was fast."

"Fast? The story is completely twisted. It's painted as if Mr. Fallus is a secret fae lover working to bring down the Human Realm from within. No one is going to want to vote against the fae deportation now."

Mallory shrugged. "Serves him right for firing me."

"Not everything is about you! Hundreds, maybe even thousands of people, are going to be hurled into an active war zone. Doesn't that mean anything to you?" Wyn got to her feet, and Aiden moved to her side.

"'Don't know much about her, but I doubt it it does," Mr. Jameson grumbled.

Mallory glowered. "Do you really think fae and humans mixing is what's safe for everyone? I bet he could wipe out the entire square with hardly any effort."

Aiden smirked. It was the first time she'd shown any indication that he was even there, not that he'd wanted to involve himself with someone like her. "That's right, I could."

Shrinking back, she looked fearfully at Wyn. "See! They can't lie either."

"Just because he's able to do that doesn't mean he will. There are plenty of humans who are capable of mass killing, but they don't."

"Weapons can be controlled, magic cannot." Her voice was soft, and she still didn't look at him. He clenched his fists. As much as watching Wyn tear the hateful girl down was enjoyable, they needed to move on. Regardless of the impact on fae, they'd gotten the outcome they needed. Mr. Fallus's reputation was tarnished. There had to be another way to free Mr. Jameson's wife and the other fae that didn't involve a wish.

"Interesting, so you *are* for gun control?" Wyn crossed her arms, and Mallory shook her head.

"Not as long as there isn't control over magic. Humans need a way to defend themselves."

"You're such a hypocrite!"

Aiden grabbed her arm as she moved closer to Mallory. He doubted she would strike her, but they needed to *go*.

"As lovely as it is to watch you roast this piglet, we need a new plan. The vote is this afternoon." Mr. Jameson shuffled over to them.

"What did you call m—"

Wyn held up a hand. "Shut up, Mal." In one swift motion, she shook Aiden off, then leaned over to scoop up her bag and march towards the door. Casting a last glare at Mallory, he hurried after Wyn, Mr. Jameson on his heels.

"Do you have a plan, love?" the old man asked when they were back on the street. The air almost smelled like a battlefield; smoke made his throat itch, and he could almost taste the slight coppery tinge of blood. Whatever had happened at the protest, at least a few people were harmed, if not worse.

"We need to go to where the fae are being held. If we can't get them out legally, then we'll do it by force."

"Doesn't sound too safe." Mr. Jameson puffed behind them.

A shock of cold washed over Aiden as he stared at Wyn. "He's right. There's so many ways for this to go wrong, especially without a plan."

She whirled. "Then you think of something. We're out of time."

"I know, I—" But the words he was going to say left his mind as he stared out at the square. It was blocked off with cars flashing bright, colorful lights. Black uniformed guards patrolled all sides. One of them looked up to meet Aiden's gaze, and the man's eyes widened. Hurriedly, Aiden ducked his head, but it was already too late as he approached, and several others followed.

Stepping in front of Wyn, he reached for his magic just as a wave of nausea hit him. *Freezing frosts.* The lead guard held up a baton—it must have had iron somewhere in its core. Aiden pressed his palm to his forehead, and Wyn turned from the guard to him.

"They have iron?" The fear and dread were painfully obvious on her face. He longed to say something comforting, tell her that he could protect her, but all he could manage to do was nod.

"You're fae. Do you have a permit to be up here?" The man said as the other circled them.

Wyn pressed close to his side, her warmth giving him a slight boost of strength. "My father is a US diplomat, we're here with him." Her voice trembled, but the words were clear and definite.

The guard let out a humorless laugh. "The only US diplomats we have here are rumored to be working with fae terrorists. You all will need to come with us."

She gripped his arm, and Aiden sucked in a breath as the guards pressed in and marched them past the barriers.

His chest tightened as they descended into the dimly lit tunnel and were passed through several beeping archways, each with more iron-armed guards. With a great push of magic, he cast his strongest glammour around the staff, the effort of which nearly drove him to collapse as they passed through the final arch and were shoved past a metal gate.

"Don't worry, we'll be back for you soon enough." The guard chuckled, and he and his fellows turned and disappeared back the way they came. Aiden sank to his knees, letting the glammour drop. Little by little, his strength returned, though not in full force. The distant iron weapons still sent ripples of sickness towards him, dampening his power. He was no stronger than the average fairy, and without magic, they were trapped.

"Are you alright?" Wyn knelt by his side, helping him to his feet.

"I'll live." His attempt at a smile did nothing to smooth the crease in his brow. Movement flickered in the corner of his vision, and he straightened.

To his surprise, Mr. Jameson stepped forward. "Who's out there?" His voice shook harder than Wyn's, but still, he took another step towards a large shadow moving along the wall.

"I didn't expect anyone to have evaded them for this long." A large fae with gray leathery skin rounded the corner, the amber artificial lights illuminating his yellow stare. Two others followed behind him, half obscured in his shadow. "Are you alright? We don't have much, but—" His eyes widened as Mr. Jameson stumbled back.

Wyn stiffened, her fingers digging into Aiden's arm. "I wouldn't think that you'd care about our well-being."

He studied the ogre as recognition spread across his face. Grinding his teeth, he pulled her behind him, but his power was still weak. Was he strong enough to take on a fully grown ogre in this state? Perhaps if he'd not spent so much trying to disguise the staff.

"Y—you're that politician's daughter. I thought you'd be uh—"

"What?" Wyn hissed. Aiden shot her a look, but she seemed to ignore him.

"Hey, we tried to keep you out before the bombing, but you wanted to run off with Dr. Murder over there." The ogre held up his hands, and one of his companions stepped out from his shadow.

Dark, scraggly hair that was braided so that it hung just above the ground, her face the blue color of suffocation, a hag tilted her head to the side. "I think I saw her going back to her room just before it happened."

"You? That was you?" A snarl tore from Aiden as rage, hot and electric, raced through his body. It didn't matter that he was weak. It didn't matter that they were trapped; he would gladly rip these fae to shreds. But something held him back. He turned to find Wyn holding him tight.

"The bombing wasn't our idea. We had this benefactor who said it could secure our freedom if we showed how much more violent humans were if fae weren't around." The hag stumbled over her words as though there was something behind them, trying to shove them out.

"And you believed killing innocents would help?" Aiden shook Wyn off, but she only grabbed onto his other arm.

"You're one to talk. How many innocent fae have you slaughtered?" the ogre spat. Aiden drew back, the fire in his chest dampening. "The humans won't keep us down here forever. Who knows what they'll do next?"

"The plan is to send you back to Fairy." Wyn's voice was flat, as though her fury had also faded.

"I haven't the faintest idea what they'll do about us...and frankly, that worries me." Mr. Jameson.

"J-johnny? Is that you?" The ogre's other companion peeked from behind his massive form. A petite fairy, with straight, dark hair, took several steps forward and then raced towards Mr. Jameson.

"Alice!" He wrapped her in his arms, burying his face in their embrace. "I told you I'd find you."

"You shouldn't have come. It's too dangerous." Her voice wavered as though on the verge of tears. Something about her was familiar, but Aiden couldn't quite place it.

"I followed the signs in your book. All that research, and we found it." The old man pulled back, his face stretched in unfamiliar joy.

"You *found* it? How? All that research—I knew it was close but...how?" She still clung to his shoulders, shock and disbelief painting her face.

"I had some help." He looked to Aiden, who flinched, grip tightening on the staff. The woman turned to him, her mouth slightly ajar as she stared at the artifact. "Oh, don't look so tense, boy. I know I can be a grumpy old sod, but you try staying posh when your girl is spirited off to God knows where."

Aiden didn't reply, and the corner of the woman's mouth twitched, though her gaze was still fixed on the staff. "May I?" She held out her hands, but the "no" was already forming on Aiden's lips before the sounds of footsteps cut them off.

His chest tightened as he whirled to face the gate. Again, he pulled the slight bit of magic he'd regained into disguising the staff, just as the iron sickness intensified. A soft cry sounded behind him as Alice fell. Mr. Jameson just barely caught her before she hit the ground. Aiden sagged against Wyn, and she wrapped an arm around him. *Freezing frosts.* He should be protecting her, not the other way around.

The guard from earlier, followed by at least ten others, marched up to the gate. "You lot didn't get very far, but good to see you made friends. Thank you for making our jobs so much easier for us." He pressed something on his chest, and the door swung open, and they swarmed in.

Wyn pulled Aiden tighter to her as the guards made to herd them out. "Where are you taking us?"

"Back to where you came from, don't bother resisting. You don't belong here." They were pushed through the gate and forced back down the long tunnel.

"No, the vote couldn't have happened yet. We still have time, we—"

The man laughed. "Do you think they were actually going to vote on something like this? It was decided a while ago to ship you people out, and now we have the infrastructure to do it. Makes you think twice about attaching yourself to these...*creatures*, doesn't it?"

Wyn didn't reply, though her breaths grew heavy. They moved back through the tunnel and the arches, but rather than stepping outside, the humans directed them into the back of some large vehicle.

When the door enclosed them in darkness, Aiden sank to the floor, releasing the staff once again from his glammour. Wyn half-dragged him over to the wall, and he leaned against it, resting his head on her shoulder and focusing on his breathing.

"Can't you use the staff to save us?" The fairy's weak voice was barely above a whisper. In the darkness, movement sounded from the others as they settled into various places throughout their new prison.

Aiden pressed his lips together. Bringing the staff to Oberon, wishless, was as good as signing his and Wyn's death warrants. But if she used the wish to save herself, it would at least buy her some time before the king found a way around it. Perhaps even enough time for the prince to provide more lasting protection. The question remained: would she value her own life over those of her friends?

She leaned her head against his, and he breathed in the scent of her. Despite everything, he savored the moment as though they were truly at peace. He was far too exhausted to be afraid and far too weak to form a protest. His arm straining against the slight weight, he passed the staff to Wyn. She sucked in a breath and accepted it.

Now it was up to her to determine their fate.

CHAPTER 23
Freddie

"I need to think." Freddie's heart raced as her fingers tightened around the staff. It would hardly be worth saving her friends now that she couldn't even save herself. But then what wish could get them out of this mess, and help her friends, and save Aiden?

He lay against her, his breathing slowing to a steady rhythm. Was there still iron in this place? It was far too dark to see, and there was no point in moving around to explore.

"Did I hear right? You have the power to save us?" The ogre's voice was strained as though speaking softly was painfully difficult for him.

She pulled her knees to her chest. "Maybe. I just—I need to think, please."

"His magic's depleted, huh? Never thought I'd be relying on the Dark Fae dog to save my life." He huffed, and the truck's metal interior groaned as he sat back.

Her jaw tightened as a flash of fury shot through her. "Keep talking like that, and I'll ensure *you* don't make it out of here regardless."

"Please, Glarg. Don't take away our hope." Alice's soft voice was no more than a weak groan. There likely was iron somewhere in there then. She sounded no stronger than a rain-drenched moth.

"It's not him you need to worry about. They've got the magic. All they need to do is quit being so damned selfish and share it." Mr. Jameson huffed, but before Freddie could respond, the doors flew open and bright light flooded in. Another wave of people crowded into the back. She pulled Aiden closer to her, but he hardly stirred.

Sniffles and quiet sobs punctuated the silence as the others pressed in around her. There were far too many bodies in the small space. Did they mean for them to suffocate before dumping them on the other side of the border? The truck jerked as the engine rumbled to life.

Her stomach tightened as they took off. What if they weren't taking them over the border? There'd been a long history of people, both fae and humans, doing horrible things to those they didn't like. Her heartbeat so hard she feared it might leave her chest. *Relax, breathe.* She leaned her head against the metal wall and closed her eyes, breathing in through her nose and out through her mouth.

Eventually, her mind calmed, and the staff remained a comfort in her hands. No matter how bad things got, at least she would have a way out...from this. Hours must have passed as they continued to move—the vote was likely over. Finally, the truck slowed, and the panic slammed back into her.

"Please, please, please." Alice's sobs joined the others, growing in volume and intensity.

Aiden lifted his head, his breath catching. "Where are we?"

"We're still in the truck, I don't know where they're taking us. The border is so far away." Freddie cringed at her own sob building in the back of her throat. No, she had a way out; she couldn't break down. There had to be a good wish.

He straightened, his hand finding hers. "Have you...tried to free us?"

Freddie laced her fingers between Aiden's and flexed her hand. "No." There was nothing else to wish for. Her friends still had a chance if she were somehow able to get free and steal the cursebreaker from Mr. Fallus. With the media rising against him, he might not be able to do anything to harm Pelrin. And there had to be a way to protect Aiden.

She bit her lip. Oberon was formidable, but maybe if the curse was broken, Pelrin had a shot against him. After all, he wouldn't have to worry about the people in his capital and would likely have more soldiers. With two objects of power, Oberon couldn't possibly be stronger.

The truck stopped, and she held her breath waiting for something to happen. Minutes ticked by, and the sounds of the trapped fae rose and fell like waves. Their terror filled the air with a metallic tingle that prickled along her skin.

Wishes needed to be clear and specific, or they could have horrendous consequences. But she could hardly focus. How was she supposed to come up with something like that? It wasn't as though it could be as simple as wish that fae and humans would just get along, or that she and all the others would be safe. How was she supposed to define get along? For all she knew, the fae and human leaders could agree that deporting all the fae back to Fairy was the right choice. And Oberon and Mr. Fallus were aligned, who's to say that Oberon couldn't convince his followers to fall in line with Mr. Fallus? And if she wished they were all safe, she needed to specify from what. Keeping them safe from the humans might leave them vulnerable to the fae.

There had to be a way for them to get help. If only FAF weren't so corrupt, they might be actually useful. But even if she wished for that, they would have no way of finding them now. She didn't even know where they were. If only there were a way to...

An idea sparked to life, and she sat up. "I think I've got it."

"The wish?"

"Yes..." Her mind moved through the possibilities. It wasn't perfect, but it was at least something.

"Can you tell me? You must be careful, we don't know how the staff might interpret it." Aiden's whisper sent goosebumps down her neck, but she was far too focused on the wish to comprehend his words. Now, how did the thing work?

"Alice," she called. There was no point in keeping her voice down now. Once she knew how, she could easily make the wish before anyone could attempt to take it from her. If Mr. Jameson was right about his wife's knowledge of fae history, she'd know better than anyone. "How does it work?"

"What? The staff? You mean it still has wishes?"

"Yes. Just one though. I need to know how to make it." She considered the phrasing; it had to be exact. Perhaps she could wish that the progressive influencers would finally pick up her story, but she would still have no way of communicating with them.

The sobs quieted slightly as the engine started up and they rumbled onwards.

"From what I've read, it must be something for the benefit of both human and fae kind. To activate it, you must remove one of the tines, but I know little more than that." Her words were muffled by the hints of chatter spreading throughout their prison. If she could just figure this out, help would be with them soon.

Freddie fumbled her fingers along the staff to find the remaining tine. The wish would most definitely rely on fae and humans working together. With a deep breath, she pinched the bit of metal between her fingers. Spreading the news out about their capture was the key. If the FAF protest had taught her anything, it was that there were people out there who were willing to help. She just needed to tell them how.

"I wish that everyone in this truck could communicate beyond the barriers with both humans and fae, so we can call for help and escape."

With a snap, the tine fell into her hand. For a moment, nothing happened, then a breeze raced through the back of the truck, and everything fell silent. Something cool and stiff pressed against the palm of her hand, and she looked down. It was a phone—a real phone—fully charged and unlocked.

Her breath as she swiped through the screen to find all of her apps, just the way she'd left them, as though this phone had always been hers. She opened a social media one and her eyes widened at the speed everything loaded. This was far better than her old phone. Had the wish made it so that she could call for help literally? But who did she know who would come? Certainly not her father.

Voices rose throughout the truck; it seemed as though she wasn't the only one with a device. Scattered conversations, choked by sobs of joy, filled the space. The glow of the cell light illuminated the darkness, and she could just make out hundreds of people.

"What is this thing?" Aiden's voice made her jump. He held out his own device, still on the home page.

"A phone. You can use it to contact people." She took his and hesitated before tapping in her old number. The new phone rang, and relief washed over her as she saved the contacts on both devices. "Now, if anything happens, we can always contact each other."

He took the device back and tapped his finger against various buttons. Leaning over, she shot him a text. His face broke into a smile as he tapped the message and read the "hi" on the screen. He made to reply, but a shout made them both look up.

"We're near that nature park in France, Mum!" A child's voice rang out. Another wave of voices erupted at that, and Freddie's fingers flew to her GPS. Why hadn't she thought of that before? Around the truck, several others made calls, but that would hardly spread the word fast enough.

Almost instinctively, she opened one of her social apps. She might not have a ton of followers, but if she could get the attention of just some news outlets and bigger accounts, maybe she could get some visibility. And if they all did it. She leapt to her feet, almost falling if not for Aiden steadying her.

"Listen please," she shouted, but few paid attention.

"Silence!" Glarg shouted, and the truck quieted.

"Thank you." Freddie took a deep breath. "I need you all to post our location, share your stories, share that we need help, and tag as many accounts as you can. The more eyes we can get on this, the better. Please, I know you want to speak to your friends and families, but there is a chance we can get out of this if we all work together."

"She's right. The more attention, the better. Glarg's booming voice made her wince. Could their captors hear? She waited several seconds, her body stiff and primed for any change in motion, but there was none.

Quiet settled among the fae as people began sharing their stories. The words from the protest came back to her. Humans needed to stop talking over fae voices. Well, she didn't need to rob them of their stories, but she could tell her own, and link it to Mr. Fallus's viral corruption. Sitting back down, she pressed herself against Aiden as he watched her type.

"Can I help?" he asked. She glanced down at his phone. There wasn't time to teach him the ins and outs of social media. "Not on this, but if you can think of a way we can get out of here and steal the cursebreaker from Mr. Fallus?"

He laced his fingers together and dropped his head down. "Forgive me, Wyn. I know I've failed you, but I'll do my best to make it up."

Leaning against him, she kissed his shoulder. "I know you didn't have a choice."

She tagged all the news outlets she could think of, including those back home, her school, and even the one liberal influencer who'd been kind enough to respond to her. She tapped his profile and spotted the headline of his most recent article. *Are US Politicians Influencing Anti-fae Sentiments in Great Britain?* At least it was better than the trash that the conservative outlets were putting out that completely threw fae under the bus.

Before she could tap in to read the story, the truck slowed to a stop. Several people let out cries of alarm as the doors flew open and black clad soldiers started yanking people out of the back. Freddie rose and stowed her phone in her pocket. Some...any assistance would be greatly appreciated. Wasn't that wish supposed to help them escape?

She stumbled out of the flatbed and into a dark, wooded clearing. The other fae soon filled the space, and the soldiers pressed in. Glarg roared and charged at the nearest one. Freddie's heart lifted. If he could break through, maybe they could all follow.

But just as her hope peaked, a blue burst of lightning shot through the air and struck the ogre straight in the chest. He hit the ground with a trembling boom and didn't rise.

"Anyone else want to try running?" One of the guards shouted. Shouts and cries ripped through the air.

Freddie stared hard at Glarg. "He can't be..."

"Dead," Aiden finished. "Just stay close, I'll protect you." He didn't sound fully confident, and it was the hesitation that made her legs feel as though they were becoming liquid. Somehow, she made jerky movements to join the others as the soldiers herded them into a poorly crafted pen. Her heartbeat pounded in her ears, drowning out all other sounds. She whirled as something screeched and looked up to see a spotlight shining down on them from above.

"Get some sleep, beasts," A woman's voice blared out from a microphone, and Freddie tensed. "It's about a two-hour hike to the border in the morning, and we wouldn't want to lose anyone on the trail." Her final words sounded like a threat.

Curling into Aiden, Freddie took a seat on the grass along with the other fae. She passed the now-useless staff back to Aiden. So much for the wish; they needed a miracle to save them now.

CHAPTER 24
Aiden

The staff no longer felt as it had—its pulsing power gone, no greater than a wooden stick. Even with all the wishes spent, it should still feel like something. Both the crown and the orb had no additional magic, but they still called to him. Something was wrong.

He looked at Wyn. Her head was bowed, but she was tapping furiously at the screen of her phone hidden beneath her sweatshirt. Around them, some of the other fae had assumed similar positions. The human guards stood with their backs to them along the perimeter, though it was unclear how many watched them from beyond the spotlight.

There had to be more they could do to get out of this. The impact of the iron weapons was less strong out in the open, he could feel some of his magic coming back. Without having to cloak the staff, perhaps with a little rest he would be able to wend them both to safety. That is, until Oberon hunted them down. His time was up at midnight, and it was already dark.

"Has anyone seen the messages yet?" He spoke low, leaning close to her so that anyone who saw them might simply think they were huddling together for warmth.

"Yes, I'm reposting but—" she paused and tapped again on her screen. His own phone pressed against his chest on the inside of his jerkin. He longed to explore its capabilities if only to help her efforts, but the magic in this world was a wonder beyond his comprehension. The hope that he might one day learn more seemed smaller and smaller by the moment. "Do you see this?" She tilted the screen to him, and he leaned in to read.

French Officials Look Into UK Sanctioned Kidnappings

"Kidnappings?" He frowned.

"This deportation law isn't legal in France. The government is pressing charges, which means someone high up knows where we are." There was excitement in her voice that made his heart ache.

"If they know where we are, why haven't they come?"

She shook her head. "We're pretty deep in the woods. Maybe they just need more time."

He let out a doubtful sigh, but didn't press the issue. Arguing at this point would be cruel. More time was an impossible luxury without more wishes. How could they hope to capture more of it? Oberon's words played again in his head, "Find me that staff before the next full moon..." Well, he'd found it, but did that mean his compulsion had ended? He felt no strong urge to return to Autumn, and the moon was already rivaling the spotlight with its brightness. Perhaps he need never return to the false king. At least not willingly. The thought was laughable; there was nowhere safe that he or Wyn could hide.

And she wanted to save her friends. He couldn't help with that either, not without first getting them out. Mr. Fallus might be distracted enough not to be protecting the cursebreaker as he should, but first, Aiden would need to get close enough to steal it. They all just needed outside help, and while the humans might, *might*, be coming to their rescue, who did he know?

Thoughts of Mare crept into his mind. He was about to shove them away, then froze. With the right bargain, Mare's mom could easily take the cursebreaker back from Mr. Fallus. Looking down, his breath caught. Surely, she'd do it for the staff. It might be useless to them, without the wishes, but to a creature like her, the staff should have plenty of magic to feed on.

"I have an idea on how to get the cursebreaker back," he murmured in Wyn's ear.

Her head shot up. "How?"

"There's someone in back in Fairy. If I can enlist their help, we might be able to trade the staff for their aid."

Her brow creased. "But what about your bargain?"

"Oberon only said I must find the staff for him by the full moon. And on his orders, I did find it." He grinned, gesturing at the staff.

"There you are, thinking like a fairy. How can I help?"

"Just stay here. I'll be back soon, then we can escape before they do anything more."

"But how are you going to get out?"

"I—I think I may have just enough strength to wend. If I can get out, I'll come back for you before sunup."

She squeezed his hand and his pulse raged against his wrist. "Be safe."

"You too." He held up the phone. "Call me if you need me."

She let out a soft chuckle. Pulling at the core of his magic, he focused, much more than he ever had, and wended.

The cool bite of Autumn tickled his cheeks as he stumbled to the forest floor just outside the meditation center. His head pounded as he dragged himself to his feet and crept towards the tiered building. All was quiet; likely all of Oberon's soldiers were pursuing acts of warfare or sleeping. Moving silently through the underbrush, he turned over the half-formed plan in his head.

Mare was probably in Tatiana's room on the top floor. If only he had wings, creeping like this would be so much easier. He eased open the door and tiptoed past the rooms packed with sleeping soldiers. Each creak of the stairs on his way up sent petrifying pangs of panic through his heart.

He passed Oberon's office, and the air seemed to thin. Forcing himself onward, he hurried past, making little effort to mask his movements. He just needed to get away, and fast. Finally, he made it to the top floor, but before he could make his way to Tatiana's room at the end of the hall, something in the darkness shifted.

"Who—Aiden?" Tatiana's voice called out to him as she stepped into a patch of moonlight from a nearby window.

"I—yes. I need to find Mare. Is she here?"

"Yes, but—"

He took several strides down the hall to stand in front of her. "—please, Tatiana. It's important."

A door opened, and Mare's slim silhouette stood out from the warm glow of firelight. "Tati, what—You're back! Did—did everything go ok? Did you find it?"

"I did," he breathed and held out the staff.

Tatiana clapped her hands together. "That's wonderful."

"What's wrong?" Mare reached for him, but he stepped back.

"I can't give it to him."

"You *can*." Folding her arms over her chest. "I won't lose you, too."

"Giving him the staff won't necessarily save my life..."

He could just barely see her glower. She beckoned to him. "Let's talk about this in here. Why would you just throw away your mission?"

Tatiana led him back to her room. "Why is your life in danger? My father—"

Mare shook her head and shut the door behind her. "Tati, please—"

"No! You two have been keeping secrets from me since I returned. Why won't you trust me?"

"It's not about trust, it's just—"

"Then tell me."

Mare and Aiden exchanged looks. This was not the derailment he needed. There was only so much time Wyn would be safe. And before Oberon would start looking for him.

"I can explain, but first I need Mare's help."

"My help?" Mare's brow creased, and Tatiana folded her arms.

"Oberon has threatened my life and—a human girl's as well." He hesitated. Revealing this was all to save Wyn wouldn't go over well.

"Why would I care about saving a human girl? Why would you?" Mare's lip curled in disgust.

"He's really that terrible, isn't he?" Tatiana let out a long breath, her head turned as though meeting their eyes would cement the truth.

Aiden's features softened. "He's still your father." The words were stilted. Defending Oberon pained something deep within him.

Mare jabbed his ribs. "Are you serious? You've suffered more than any of us. Tati, I'm sorry, but you *know* they were awful. The only good thing they did was send you away so you didn't have to see this stuff firsthand."

Aiden swallowed hard, and Tatiana nodded. "Who is the human we're supposed to be helping?"

He shifted and rubbed the back of his neck. "She's—uh. The girl who visited the palace last winter."

Tatiana whipped around. "The one who murdered my mother? Why, of all people—"

"—I have similar questions," Mare hissed.

Aiden rocked his jaw back and forth.

"Don't tell me you fell for the prince's human?" Mare let out a harsh laugh.

"It's more complicated than that. She's not with the prince."

"Is that what she told you to seduce you into sparing her life?" Mare folded her arms.

"She *used* you, Aiden. Why are you protecting her?" Tatiana clung to Mare's arm, and he clenched his jaw. Everything they said was correct—a couple of weeks earlier, he would have agreed. But not now. Not when she needed him to succeed.

"I—she was just trying to survive. Things are complicated between us, but I can't let her die. Please, Mare, I need your help." Aiden fought the desperation creeping up the back of his throat. Tatiana hugged herself, and Mare wrapped an arm around her shoulders. The intimate gesture tugged at his heart—what he wouldn't give to hold Wyn that way. Just one more time.

Mare sighed, her expression tight. "What do you need?"

"A trade with your mother."

She pinched the bridge of her nose. "You want to protect her that badly?"

"Please, Mare. I need you to guide us."

Tatiana sucked in a shaky breath, and Mare ran a finger down her cheek, making Aiden turn away—the pain in his heart clawing at his chest.

"Fine. But I'm only going to help find a way to keep *you* alive. And you'd better hope she's not up to something, because if she is, I'll feed her to a nightmare."

"Thank you." Hope filled his lungs.

"When do we leave?"

"Now...If you can."

Mare shot him a glare, then kissed Tatiana on her brow. "Let's go before I change my mind."

CHAPTER 25
Freddie

Freddie pulled her knees to her chin and ducked her head down. Cold air burrowed past the thin layers of her clothes, making her shiver. At least it was summer, but that thought gave her little comfort as summer there was far from the sweltering stuffiness of DC. Around her, groups of fae huddled together, their backs to the cold. If anyone slept that night, it would be a miracle...or a symptom of hyperthermia. Why hadn't she thought to ask Aiden to magick something warm for her before he left? Would you have had enough power to do it?

"Hey." A figure moved towards her and sank down at her side. She hardly looked up, her body drawn to the warmth of another person. "You'll freeze if you sit out here alone." The hag scooched closer to her, the rough tangles of her hair cloaking her body like Freddie's sweatshirt.

"You're not sitting with..." She looked around at the clusters of fae, trying to spot a familiar face. Surely the hag must know these people better than she did.

"Glarg was my best friend. We grew up together and both came to London to study. His parents are going to be devastated when they find out." Her voice broke, and she buried her face in her knees.

Freddie reached out a hesitant hand to touch the girl's shoulder. "I'm so sorry. Do you—do you want to talk about it?"

She shook her head, and silence settled over them. At least she was slightly warmer. Looking around again, Freddie bit her lip, wondering how Mr. Jameson must be faring. Hopefully, his wife was able to use some smidge of magic to keep him comfortable in all of this. If only the staff had worked the way it was supposed to.

Closing her eyes, she tried to force her mind to block out the sounds of barely concealed panic and find some semblance of sleep. Despite her body being beyond exhausted, she was failing miserably. Somewhere in the distance, a dog barked. She scrunched her eyes tighter, it was almost as though her eyeballs were cold too.

Beside her, the hag stirred as more dogs joined in with the first. Freddie lifted her head. It was one thing to have to shut out the sounds of a chorus of dogs in the city or in the suburbs. But out in the middle of nowhere, France? Surely that wasn't normal.

"Everybody up!" Shouts rang out from the soldiers as they stampeded into the gated area, swinging the iron batons. The fae rose clumsily in awkward clumps—many stiff from the cold and struggling to find their footing. Sobs and cries joined the shouts as the soldiers corralled them back to the gates.

Freddie stayed close to the hag as they were forced into the trees. The barking grew louder, and then a new set of shouts rang out. Hesitating, Freddie turned and yelped as someone nearly shoved her to the ground. Soldiers on either side of them were forcing the group to practically run deeper and deeper into the trees. Inconsistent light from flashlights guided their way. Every so often, there was a piercing scream followed by a "keep moving" from a soldier.

She didn't want to think of what the screams meant. Had someone succumbed to the same fate as Glarg, or had they simply fallen only to be trampled by the stampeding feet? Swallowing hard, Freddie tried to focus on just staying upright and moving along with the group. How was Aiden supposed to find her like this? She brought a hand to the ring hanging around her neck and prayed he would find her soon.

"What's going on? Why are we running?" a breathless voice said from somewhere nearby.

"I thought we weren't leaving until morning?"

"Are we being chased?"

Questions rippled through the group as they continued to make their way through the forest. She had questions of her own, but there was no one nearby who would be willing to give her answers. More shouts and screams tore at her mind as terror seared away all other thoughts. Ahead, the trees thinned as the forest opened up into a clearing.

"Get them past the border!" a soldier cried, but they were cut off by a cacophony of barking and screams.

Someone shouted in French.

Freddie wrapped her arms around her head and turned at the unexpected cry. Bright light flooded the space, and whistles pierced the night along with screams and a mix of garbled languages. People pushed past her, but now she could move out of the way of the rough shoves and moving forms.

"We can't get out!"

"I'm not going in with them!"

The scent of the forest pines mingling with the various body odors from the surrounding fae was far too sharp. Her footsteps wavered as rocks and twigs sprouted in her path, determined to trip her. She stumbled sideways and something hit her hip, then the world fell away.

"Wyn, Wyn!"

Freddie blinked up at an ink black sky, but something was illuminating it. A warm hand pressed against her cheek, and she leaned into it.

"Please, please, say something," a voice, Aiden's voice, said. It took her far too long to register his face staring at her with a fierce intensity.

A girl, not much older than herself, leaned over his shoulder and frowned. "If she's not dead, she's definitely dumb."

"I'm not dumb," Freddie snapped and drew back.

"Well, isn't she poised?" Dressed in all black with a braid that hung down to her waist, the other girl smirked. She looked familiar, and Freddie's heart sank when she realized this was the same girl who'd taken her from Summer to Oberon's palace. Her mouth opened and shut, and she shot a meaningful look at Aiden who shook his head.

"Mare, stop. Be nice," he hissed.

"What? She was stumbling around like a newborn kitten. What am I supposed to say? Good try walking, you'll get 'em next time?"

The last vestiges of fear melted away, and Freddie glowered. "Who are you? And what is this place?" She took a step and noted the unnatural orange sand that seemed to give light to the world around them. Gentle waves lapped against the shore on one side, and odd-shaped rocks rose up from beyond the dunes on the other. It was neither hot nor cold, and there was no vegetation, not so much as a speck of moss on a pebble. If they were in Fairy, it was part of no realm she'd ever heard of.

Aiden wrapped an arm around her shoulder. "It's alright, Mare's *not* going to hurt you. She's—"

"—actually, I haven't made up my mind about that. Let's just get this over with before I do."

"Get what over with, exactly. I thought you were going to get help, not whatever *she* is."

Mare scoffed, and Aiden pinched the bridge of his nose. "Look, Wyn, Mare is going to take us to visit her mom, who is a very powerful fae, and the one who gave me the cursebreaker."

"She didn't just *give* it to you," Mare snapped.

Freddie's mouth went dry. She'd seen the self-sacrificial ways that Aiden tended to bargain. There was no telling what magical debt he'd incurred to get such a powerful artifact. "What's that supposed to mean?"

Aiden shrank back. "I—well you see—"

"He gambled all his magic on his ability to complete Oberon's quest and find that cursed staff." Mare folded her arms across her chest.

Freddie opened and closed her mouth several times before the words came. "Wouldn't losing *all* of your magic kill you?"

"He's been pretty cavalier with his life since you melted our home." The girl hissed, revealing her pointed teeth.

The world seemed to spin; it was nothing but one terror after another. But Aiden had found the staff—he had completed his mission. Unless there was more to it. "Aiden—"

"—the longer we spend arguing, the more time Oberon has to find us. If we're going to have any hope of getting the cursebreaker, we need to move now." Aiden started towards an area of flat stones, and Freddie looked to Mare, who nodded.

"I'm only going to say this once. So, you *both* better listen up." Aiden paused and looked back at them, then Mare continued. "This is the path. Do not stray from it, no matter what you see or hear. I'll take the lead. Aiden, you should know better than anyone how this place likes to mess with people." She pushed past him, and Freddie flexed her fingers and headed out after her, Aiden bringing up the rear.

The scenery shifted as they drew further from the beach. Stone mounds marked the landscape but cast no shadows. Freddie remained focused on the path, looking down every few seconds to ensure she was still on track. She'd read plenty of stories where small mistakes, like straying merely a foot from the intended trail, had gotten humans irreparably cursed or worse.

Something whispered her name. She looked up, then immediately refixed her gaze on the path.

"Wyn dear, it's Mommy." Freddie rolled her eyes. That didn't even work with her actual mother; she certainly wasn't falling for such a thing in this realm's version. It seemed to comprehend the eyeroll and changed tone. "Wyn, please. I need your help."

Nice try. Her mom would probably roast herself alive before *asking* for her help with anything. Demanding was more her style. Freddie continued on, focused on the path ahead.

"Hey, Fred, it's me!" Now Raul was sliding down the sand. A dull ache tugged at her heart to see him so alive, so awake. She wanted to stop, get closer, but a small voice at the back of her mind told her it wasn't real. "Come here, the others are just over this hill." He gestured, but she shook her head. *Not real, not real.*

Forcing herself to turn away, she caught sight of Aiden nodding at nothing.

"Nona?" he cried out. Another pang shot through her at the memory of the blue fairy they'd seen in Spring. She might have been helping the queen to trap them, but she'd been important to Aiden—the only remaining member of his family.

"That's not really her." She grasped Aiden's hand but he pulled free. The not-Raul snarled, then shifted form. A scream nearly tore its way from her throat, but the sound was muted in that strange place. Freya, but not the girl or vampire she'd known, stood there covered in cracks and with a large chunk missing from her forehead.

"You let me die," not-Freya said.

Freddie shook her head. It'd been an accident. Freya had tried to help more people than she could and...

"Come with me and suffer for what you did!"

"I—I can't. There's so much more I need to do."

"More lives to be ruined? It's more than just a bunch of teenagers relying on you now."

Freddie paused. The creature was right. There were a bunch of people relying on her to save them, more even than just in the UK, if that bigotry spread. Who was she to carry such responsibility? Shouldn't there be some adult to guide her, or even do this instead? Her parents and Mr. Fallus were hardly sage examples to look up to, but there had to be someone.

The dead girl cried and thrust out a pale hand.

Freddie looked down again; her feet were firmly planted on the path. No, her recklessness may have gotten them into that situation, but it was Oberon's cruelty that had ripped Freya from her life in the first place. The blame wasn't solely on her. Freddie straightened and looked up at the not-Freya. "I'm sorry I couldn't save her, but that doesn't mean I'm going to throw my life away."

"Fine! I'll take just this one instead." Freya dove into the sand, and Freddie stumbled back a step and looked around. Beside her, Mare's expression was of barely contained fury while black tendrils of hair flicked against her dark skin, but Aiden was gone. No, he was running into the sand.

"Every. Single. Time." Mare took a deep breath and rounded on Freddie. "You stay here; he just needs something to snap him out of it." She stepped off the path, leaving Freddie to frantically search her pockets. All she had was the phone. If she threw it and missed, she might never have a device like it again. Tapping his name on the screen, she nearly dropped it when his ringtone blared from across the sand.

Aiden, so startled by the noise, tripped over his feet and fell face-first into the sand.

"Ha! I don't know how you did that, but maybe you're not as use-less as you look." Mare gave her a crooked smile. But before she could reply, something massive and flesh-colored rose up behind Aiden. He cried out, frantically scrambling to his feet. "Stay here, human!" Mare rushed forward, and Freddie bounced on the balls of her feet. Shadows shot out from Mare as she knocked the worm aside just in time for Aiden to dodge its jaws.

He got to his feet and shot a jet of blue flame where the monster had been, but it only burned a glassy puddle into the sand. The crea-ture exploded upward a few feet away, catching Mare off balance and sending her tumbling down the dune. Aiden shot out more flames, and the beast let out a roar that shook the ground.

Freddie dropped to her knees and fumbled with the phone. There had to be something she could do to distract the creature. She tapped aimlessly on the phone, her gaze continuously drawn to the two fae battling the giant creature. Sound blared out again from her phone, and the creature bristled, lengthening and stiffening. It let out a pierc-ing wail as a wall of Aiden's fire hit it just before it could dive beneath the sand.

Music...or maybe just sound, seemed to impact it. Typing into the search bar, she pulled up a playlist of brain rot songs and hit play. Aiden and Mare hardly made it a few steps before the creature burst out of the ground in front of them. Freddie snarled as an ad for a screen protector played. Every second she waited for the skip button seemed to take a year. Finally, it appeared, and the music started.

"—doo doo doo doo doo doo doo!" She cranked up the volume to the highest decibel and stared out at the battle. The ground rumbled and shook so violently, both Aiden and Mare fell to their knees. Sand sprayed out from the ground as the worm burst fully free from the ground and arched over the path. Freddie screamed and covered her head to protect it from the raining sand. Several seconds passed as the massive body sailed over her and landed on the other side with a quaking thud. The worm dove deep into the sand and vanished.

Aiden helped Mare to stand, and they raced back to her, coughing and gagging as they struggled onward. Freddie shut off the music and stowed the phone back in her pocket.

Mare got her breath back first. "What was that?"

"My best friend worked at a daycare over the summer. All the kids loved that song." Freddie wanted to give her a half smile, but the thought of Amanda chased away any of the joy she'd felt over the defeat of the worm.

Aiden let out a breath. "Whatever that noise was, it saved us."

"Yes, well, no thanks to you." Mare looked at her and shook her head.

Freddie was about to respond when a large black rock cast a massive shadow over them. Something about it set her skin on edge. "What is that?"

Mare held out a hand in mock presentation. "This is my mom's house."

CHAPTER 26
Aiden

The familiar shadows cast by the rock of Mare's mom's home loomed over Aiden, stripping him bare. Embarrassment stung his cheeks. It was Wyn and Mare who should rely on him for protection; he shouldn't be the cause of their peril. There was just something about this realm, as though it was designed to break him. The other two were staring at the rock too, Wyn in awe, while Mare's expression seemed to reflect her irritation.

Mare took the lead into the small opening, and they passed through into the darkness. A tightness gripped Aiden's chest as he tried to imagine what form her mother would take this time. What if she was Wyn's mom again? How would Wyn react to that? Or perhaps she would resemble someone of significance to Wyn. He should've warned her about the woman. At least it was safe here, well, safer.

The irony ate at him as he peered around in the darkness. "Hello?"

No answer.

"Mom?" Mare called.

The interior of the room came alive with a blaze of light. It bounced off elaborate white and gold surfaces, making Aiden cover his eyes.

"Hello, children! Mare, dear, you spoil me by visiting so often." Mare's mom's sultry voice rang out, and Aiden squinted to make out her form.

"I haven't done it on purpose, but I've had to of late," Mare grumbled. Her mother made soft tutting noises.

"That is an *interesting* glammour," Wyn said. Aiden looked from her to Mare's mom. She was almost too thin with vibrant blonde hair and a pinched face. He'd only seen the woman she resembled a few times, but Mr. Fallus's wife's near inhuman appearance was unmistakable.

"Do you like it?" the woman cooed.

Wyn smirked. "If you're going for disturbing, you nailed it."

Mare's mom smiled, revealing her rows of sharp teeth. "Thank you, sweetie. Mare, I do so love meeting your friends."

"*She* is not my friend." Mare folded her arms, but her expression wasn't nearly as sour as it had been. If she could at least tolerate Wyn long enough to secure her mother's help, that was all he needed.

"And Aiden, so good to have you back. Did you come to bring me my magic in person?"

"My mission was a success." Aiden drew back, his grip tightening on the staff. Oberon had said nothing about handing the staff over once he found it and brought it back. "I—I returned to Autumn."

"That you did. Clever boy. Now what brings you here now?"

Mare let out a low snarl. "Stop asking questions when you already know the answers."

Her mother cocked her head as though unsure of what she was talking about, and Mare huffed.

"I came to make a trade, to help her." Aiden gestured at Wyn who frowned back at him. "I'm offering you the staff."

"He means he wants another cursebreaker, like the one you gave him before." Wyn shot a glare so fierce at him he lowered his gaze. A desperate part of him had hoped that the vague phrasing would grant

Wyn this one last chance at protection, but he knew she would hardly sacrifice a chance at saving her friends to save herself.

Another gleeful smile broadened Mare's mom's lips. "There is only one cursebreaker. Just like there is only one staff."

Aiden licked his lips. "Are you able to take it back?"

She shrugged, a motion that looked odd on the woman's overly put together form. "I probably could."

Aiden cast Wyn one last silent plea to save herself, but she shook her head. He loved her nobility, but now he prayed it wouldn't get her killed. Taking a deep breath, Aiden held out the staff. "I offer this staff in exchange for your help in retrieving the cursebreaker."

"Hmmm." She pursed her lips and sauntered up to Aiden. With the tip of her black coated finger, she pressed it to the staff. Darkness blossomed from the spot she touched, and Aiden shook the staff as though it would rid it of the dark magic that was creeping through it. "I don't know if this is worth my time."

Aiden gritted his teeth. "It's one of the most powerful objects in the Seven Realms. The wishes might be gone, but the magic is not."

Mare's mom giggled and held up the now blackened staff. "This has no more magic than an old stick." Her grip tightened, and the staff crumbled to dust before them.

"No!" Aiden sank to his knees before the black pile. Dread and despair tore at his heart. Everything, *everything,* they'd worked for was gone. There was nothing to trade and nothing to even bring back to Oberon in hopes he'd be merciful.

"You should thank me. Think of all the headaches I've saved you. Can you imagine trying to use that thing?"

"Mother, you don't know what you cost us. Oberon—"

Mare's mom held up a finger, effectively silencing her daughter. "If Oberon tried to gobble up any magic from that thing, he would've accused you of giving him a fake. I doubt he'd be very happy about that."

"It's not a fake, we used a wish." Wyn's voice was far too calm as though she were on the verge of unleashing a terrible anger he'd never seen before. Turning from her barely concealed fury and the challenging grin on Mare's mom's face, Aiden stepped partially in front of Wyn. If Mare's mom was willing to break the staff, what else would she do?

"Oh, I know it's not a fake. I can still sense the memory of its magic. Surely, it didn't feel the same as the others to you?"

Aiden stiffened. "It was a little different. But how is that possible?"

"Ahh, well, someone drained it of all its power. Drank it up like a soda, right, hun?" She winked at Wyn, who drew back against him. Mare's mom scoffed. "Oh, it's not that serious. There's plenty of magic in this world. One less little artifact won't matter."

"Mom, how do *you* know what happened? Who could be powerful enough to do that?" Mare knelt to examine the ash. It was dark with a slight green glitter, but her mom was right, there'd been no tingle of magic after they'd used the wish, and especially not now. It reminded him uncomfortably of Oberon's wand. Could it be powerful enough to steal the magic from the staff? But Oberon wouldn't have sent him to retrieve it if the magic was gone. Would he?

"Oh no, sweetie, you're close, but Oberon has never tasted power like this. It requires more magic than he possesses to contain one of the four objects of power.

Aiden jerked at the invasion of his thoughts, but kept his discomfort to himself. "Then who?"

"It was you, wasn't it?" Wyn said. Her tense expression had softened as she looked Mare's mom over. "No one else would know as much about this."

"I like her, Mare. She's smart." The white and gold entry was dissolved into a circular stone room. It had an enormous four-poster bed, and the walls were hung with elaborate tapestries of humans and fae acting in harmony. Something felt eerily familiar about it, but he couldn't quite figure out why. She sank into one of the couches and her body-hugging dress faded into a mantle of green, yellow, and blue wool. "You're right. It made me what I am today." She held up her arms in a half-hearted manner.

"Why? You're already so powerful." Mare said to her mom.

But the woman shook her head. "I wasn't always. There was a time when I was as helpless as you." She pointed at Wyn, whose eyes widened.

She stepped from behind Aiden over to one of the tapestries and pulled it back, revealing a small alcove. Gasping, she spun around. "Caoimhe?"

Mare's mom's expression softened. Her hair darkened, and her features shifted into a pale reflection of Mare. "Fae and humans don't have happy endings. Arran was burned, and in my grief, I wished for enough power to not only wipe out his killers but everyone who supported them."

Aiden's chest tightened. Mr. Jameson and Alice, he and Wyn, none of them were destined for a peaceful end. Why did it have to be so unfair?

"Who's Caoimhe? And how do you know all of this?" Mare looked from Wyn to her mother, her black eyes flashing.

"Mare, dear, didn't you ever wonder who your father was?"

"I always assumed he was some poor soul you took a fancy to...and ate."

"Don't be so crass. The nightmares eat people; I merely drain energy. Besides, I truly loved your father."

Mare scoffed.

"And I love you too, dear. Believe it or not."

"You tried to eat *me*." Mare stepped towards her mother. If she'd tried to eat her in the past, she was giving the woman another opportunity to do so now.

"No, I never tried to eat you, but I did let you stay with Mab and Oberon when they dared to kidnap you. Living out there gave you a far better life than here. And I am not quite ready to leave my domain."

"What do you mean, kidnap?"

"Do you honestly think I gave away my last gift from Arran? When Oberon bargained with me for the wand, he took you as well. And it is because of you that he is still breathing."

"But you can leave here, right?" Aiden asked. She'd left easily enough to steal his magic. Surely living anywhere else in Fairy would be preferable to this place.

"Yes, and no. I can leave, but I start aging just like your precious king. I would have to constantly consume magic to sustain myself."

"But you consumed my despair, not my magic." Aiden's brow furrowed as he tried to think back to when she'd appeared before him.

"There is a good amount of magic in strong emotions. Your despair was a good snack and allowed me to see that my daughter was safely moved to Autumn."

"You let her *feed* on you?" Wyn touched his shoulder, and he flinched.

"He was about to let her have all of his magic to protect you," Mare snapped.

Wyn scowled. "I don't need saving."

"But—" Aiden began, but she cut him off.

"—I need to save my friends, and now the staff is useless."

"So, you'd ask him to sacrifice himself for your friends?" The outrage in Mare's voice pierced Aiden's heart. Even if he chose not to risk himself, Oberon would still end him. At least he could do some good to make up for all the evil he'd done.

Wyn crossed the room to Mare. Both girls stood unnervingly close to her mother and each other.

"I'd never ask him to sacrifice himself. I'm more than capable of making my own bargains."

Before Aiden could jump in, Mare's mom, no Caoimhe, quirked her lips. "I doubt there's anything a little human could offer me."

Mare folded her arms. "If you love me so much, why not help us for free?"

"Ha! Help someone who isn't even your friend without a price? What kind of fae do you take me for?"

"One with a human soul," Wyn grumbled.

"I gave up many things when I took in the staff's magic. My kindness was a small price to pay for vengeance."

Wyn shifted a step back. "And did you get it?"

She shrugged. "I carved a bloody path across the realms. The seasonal rulers had to band together to lock me in this prison. But it seems they've all fallen, except Spring."

Aiden tensed at the mention of his home realm. He'd avoided speaking of it in hopes Oberon would set his sights anywhere else. If one place could be saved, he'd prayed it was what remained of his innocent memories.

She sneered. "Now, if there's nothing you have to offer, you can leave. Though, Mare, *you* are always welcome to stay."

"No, thank you," Mare spat.

"What if we could offer you another of the objects?" Wyn put a finger to her lips.

Aiden frowned. They didn't have any of the other objects of power. The prince still had both the crown and the orb. Unless she meant…his mother's ring? He swallowed hard. There had to be something else.

"Go on?"

"If I can convince the Summer Prince to give you one, will you get us the cursebreaker?"

Aiden's chest squeezed. The prince would never willingly turn over one of the only things keeping his realm from falling just to save her friends, even if he did care for her.

But Mare's mom's smile grew feral, and she got to her feet. "Oh, you deliciously crafty girl. Agreed. One object for one cursebreaker."

"Then it's a deal." Wyn held out her hand, and Mare's mom shook it, dark tendrils of shadow sparked along their joined hands.

Part of him was grateful she hadn't thrown away the last thing he had of his mother, but if she failed, the prince could turn on her. Then there would be no one to save her from Oberon's wrath.

CHAPTER 27
Freddie

Freddie sucked in a breath. Now she was truly betraying Pelrin for her friends. Was this so much better than a bargain with Mr. Fallus?

A nagging sensation in the back of her head told her to tell him the truth. They were his friends, too. But if it put his people in danger, was it worth the risk, or would it give him an advantage? Now was not the time to overthink this; it was done.

Caoimhe's hand left hers as the threads of a plan knit together in her mind. She clenched her teeth until her jaw ached. It wasn't a solid plan. Just like her quest to free Pelrin from Oberon. What if more people got hurt because of her? No, this time there were lives to lose, not just one prince to save. If she freed her friends, all of Elessea would be free too. Surely that was worth it.

"Just how do you expect to convince the prince to give up one of his precious objects?" Mare plopped down onto one of her mom's plush sofas and looked to Freddie while Aiden still stood pressed against the far wall. His face was contorted as though his mind were in agony. He wouldn't sacrifice himself for her again, but...

"I need your help."

"No," Mare said.

While at the same time Aiden replied, "Anything." Mare glared at him and folded her arms over her chest. Freddie swallowed, praying the risk to his safety was minimal.

"If you guys pretend to have captured me, Pelrin will come to my rescue. Then you can trade my life for the orb." Freddie pressed her lips together. It was far more likely that Pelrin would be willing to part with the orb than the crown. "Mare, can you lie?"

She smirked. "With pleasure."

Aiden ran his fingers through his hair. "I don't like this. What if something goes wrong? What if he isn't willing to part with them?

"You'll just have to make him believe you'd really kill me if you don't get what you want."

"I can't. I can't hurt you just so he'll think we're serious."

"I'll do it," Mare said, her black eyes glinting.

"See, Mare's on board." Freddie held out her hand towards Mare, and Aiden groaned. The idea of putting her safety in the hands of a fae who seemed more than eager to do her harm made her a bit nervous. But if Amanda's and everyone's lives were on the line, she was willing to risk it.

"Mare, if you hurt her..."

Caoimhe tsked and Aiden fell silent, a fist trembling at his side. "It sounds like you kids have some work to do. And because I'm feeling generous, I'll make things easier for you." She waved a hand, and a warm breeze wafted over Freddie.

They stood on a wide, elegant balcony overlooking the ocean. It was beautiful, but why were they here? She turned, and her breath caught. Rubble and debris littered the ground behind them amongst the shattered glass of an opulent building. Several uniformed fairies lay among the ruins, unmoving.

"What—" Freddie took a step towards the fae, but Aiden grabbed her arm.

"They are just sleeping. It looks like she sent us to Elessea. The prince couldn't get everyone to safety."

Sunlight just peeked over the horizon, casting a blush glow over the space. Freddie curled her fingers against Aiden's arm, resisting the urge to try and wake them. But if her plan went well, they'd be up soon enough.

"I suppose you want me to spirit your girlfriend off after we do this?" Mare asked, nudging one of the fairies with her boot.

"Yes, we still need to get the cursebreaker. And we're just friends."

Aiden's words send a dull ache through Freddie's chest. It was better than enemies. It was too late to reclaim what they had. Best case scenario, they would both survive, and Aiden would still be under Oberon's control.

"Sure. Don't worry. I won't let her go. As soon as you have the orb, we'll be out of here." How was it that Mare, the fae who seemed to be still on the fence about killing her or not, was more ready to do this than Aiden?

"There's so much that could go wrong. We could lose everything." He looked imploringly at Freddie, but she couldn't stand to meet his gaze and turned away.

"If we don't try, we've already lost. It's my fault my friends are cursed."

"No," he said. "I enacted it."

"So noble. Now let's get this over with." Mare flexed her fingers, and the shadows in her hand solidified into a dagger. Grabbing Freddie's wrist, she pulled her to her chest and wrapped her weapon arm around Freddie's neck.

Freddie coughed. "You could've at least warned me."

"Watch it, Mare." The flames on Aiden's arms blazed.

"Let's just do this." Freddie took a deep breath and screamed. "Pelrin, help!"

Gold light filled the sky, blinding her. Mare pulled her back, and the light condensed into a singular form. Pelrin's red uniform was brilliant against the sunrise. He landed on the balcony, golden wings outstretched, and tendrils of his braided back hair clung to his face. "Freddie, are you alright?"

"Pelrin!" The false desperation in her voice sent guilty twinges through her stomach.

His expression turned murderous when he spotted Aiden. "You." He stalked forward.

"Fight and she dies." Mare tightened her grip, and Freddie winced. *Easy.*

"What do you want?" Pelrin turned slowly from Aiden to face Mare, his teeth gritted.

"A trade. The orb for her life."

Pelrin clutched at the large pearl hanging from his neck. "You can't even use it."

"No, but without it, neither can you."

"Do you think I need it to crush you?" he snarled, still glaring at Aiden.

Aiden grinned. "You've yet to defeat me without it."

"You're like a hydra, you just keep popping back up."

"If I were you, I'd stop flirting with him and worry more about her. Or perhaps you don't love her as much as you seemed to at the Winter Palace." Mare stroked the side of Freddie's face, and she whimpered. Something warm trickled down her neck. Aiden shot Mare a look that Freddie feared might give them away.

"How about I end both of you instead?" Pelrin launched a jet of flame, narrowly missing Aiden as he dropped and rolled out of the way. "I almost thought your master killed you, it's been so long since I've been able to roast your worthless hide."

"You wish." Aiden launched a torrent of blue flame at Pelrin, and Freddie had to suppress a sigh.

"We really should have expected this," Mare sighed and loosened her hold. Freddie sagged. She'd hoped Pelrin would care more about saving her than defeating Aiden, but it appeared she was wrong.

More blue flame barreled past, and Mare dragged her into the doorway of the ruin. Pelrin leapt into the air and fired a shot at Aiden that grazed his shoulder.

"My money is on Aiden taking the win, but loverboy's getting in some significant damage." Mare leaned against the doorway.

"Aren't you worried Aiden might get hurt?"

"Your prince is a gold fae while Aiden's a—" She stopped, the words dying on her lips.

"I know what he is."

"He told you?"

"Are you surprised?"

"He really does trust you. Hurt him, and I will end you."

Freddie nodded. "I won't."

Mare huffed out a breath, her eyes trained on the battle before them. Pelrin and Aiden seemed to be evenly matched. While Pelrin didn't have the crown, it appeared he wasn't using the orb either. Still, his wings allowed him to dip and dodge out of range of Aiden's attacks. But Aiden was making good use of the rubble around them, jumping off larger pieces and hurling dust into Pelrin's eyes when he got too close.

The ground shook as Aiden leapt out of the way of Pelrin's fireball, letting it explode away part of the railing. He returned the shot with a flaming tendril that seared across Pelrin's wing, causing him to cry out. Freddie lurched forward, but Mare gripped her arm. The plan had been faulty, she knew, but she foolishly hadn't thought of one of them actually killing the other.

Pelrin dropped down a few feet, leaning heavily on his left side to fly. A cold grin twisted Aiden's face as he moved closer, letting loose another jet of flame. Pelrin whirled out of the way and alighted on the flat surface of the balcony, his back to them. Tucking his wings against his back, he raised a hand, igniting a warped ball of red fire. He shoved it forward, and it spanned out in front of him like a shield. Aiden raised an arm, blocking Pelrin's blast with his own fiery wall.

The wall of red faltered, and Aiden took advantage by putting more force behind his own. Pelrin lashed out with a red-hot vine that curled under Aiden's boot and made him lose his footing. He fell hard on his rear, the blue flames vanishing as he flailed to gain balance. But Pelrin was too fast. Shooting a jet of fire at Aiden's arm, he laughed as Aiden fell again and scrambled back.

Freddie leapt to her feet and raced towards him—Mare on her heels. The air seemed to thin, and her heart fluttered like an angry pixie's wings as Aiden caught her eye and shook his head.

With one quick motion, Pelrin shot out a hand and closed it around his wrist. Frost crystals blossomed from where their hands met, and Aiden cried out. Pelrin's smile was nearly manic as he pushed the crystals further down Aiden's arm.

"You will never touch her again," he snarled.

Freddie opened her mouth, but Mare's "no" cut her off. In a streak of shadow, Mare was gone from her side. Pelrin let out a strangled yell as her darkness hit him square in the chest, knocking him flat on the ground. Before he could right himself, she wrapped an arm around Aiden and dragged him off the balcony towards the sea.

Racing to the edge, Freddie stared down at the waves crashing against the rocks; no sign of them. She trembled and looked back just as Pelrin limped to her side.

"It's alright, you're safe now." He pulled her close, and she let out a sob. Now what? How was she supposed to save everyone? Pelrin kissed the top of her head and let her cry. "We do need to get out of here. I can take you to our stronghold for now."

Freddie frowned as she touched the empty gold chain at his chest. "The orb, it's gone."

He touched where the pearl had lain. "At least we still have the crown. What's important is that I get you to safety. Then you can tell me what happened."

Freddie nodded, realizing she'd have to come up with a lie to placate him. Mare must have taken it when she hit Pelrin. Perhaps they would still try and get the cursebreaker. At least there was hope.

CHAPTER 28
Freddie

"I thought you said you were being safe." Pelrin helped Freddie down a cluster of rocks and onto the sandy beach. His damaged wing was tinged with black, reminding her of Aiden's blue stubs.

She held out a hand, letting it hover over his wingtip. "Will it—"

"—heal. Yes, wing injuries heal slower, but it's just a singe."

"Good." She let out a breath. How severe did the injury have to be to become permanent? Perhaps she didn't want to know.

He rounded on her. "Just tell me how they found you."

She shrugged. "How was I supposed to know Oberon would find me in Ireland with a bunch of old people? It wasn't like we had a friendly chat before they decided to use me as a hostage."

"Right. Sorry. It's just that it was too close. I could've lost you."

She swallowed. He shouldn't have to worry over her like this. But staying put would only keep her safe from Oberon for so long. Amanda, Raul, and Jefferson needed her, and even he had to admit idling wouldn't help.

Water lapped up against the shore, and sand crept into her sneakers. Freddie ignored the complaints bubbling in the back of her throat. She had bigger things to worry about. Would Aiden truly use the orb to bargain for the cursebreaker? Or perhaps he'd use it to secure safety and freedom for himself. Was she selfish for wanting to free her friends when he was still indebted to Oberon?

She winced as they clambered around a particularly large outcropping of porous rock to face the ocean. The early morning sun was blinding as it glinted off the waves, but the soothing sounds were an enchanting lullaby.

"There! It's still here!" Pelrin scrambled down the side of the rock and raced across the sand to a rowboat butting against a few sharp rocks at the water's edge.

"What's that?"

"I left a boat here when I would run away from the palace as a kid."

"You're still a kid." She smirked. By fae standards, Pelrin's nineteen years were very young, but she would be long gone by the time he hit a respectable fairy age.

"Says the human."

Freddie peered into the boat. It was old, covered in moss and riddled with holes and barnacles. Drowning would be a certainty if they even made it past the rocks. She looked to Pelrin and raised a brow. Smiling, he waved a hand over the craft. The moss and barnacles fell away, and the wood smoothed over all the holes. It looked as good as new. She squinted side to side; it didn't appear to be glammoured either.

"It's safe now?"

"I'm not entirely useless with magic." He turned from her, jaw clenched, as he guided the boat off the rocks and into the water.

"Pel, you know I didn't mean it that way."

He shook his head. "My uncle has just been on me about not practicing like I should. I'm still not that great, but this is one spell I've practiced. If I were stronger, maybe that curse..."

"No. You weren't even there. This isn't your fault." *It was mine.* She bit her lip, letting the cold water distract her from her thoughts. If Oberon hadn't taken over, none of this would be happening. Neither of them was fully to blame.

He got into the boat, then held out a hand to help her in. "It's my fault I wasn't there. I fell for their trap. If I'd been better at magic, maybe I wouldn't have had to rely on you to save me."

Their craft shot forward, skimming across the waves and rounding the coast. The beach receded into steep cliffs, blocking the land from view. Only a few trees sticking out along the tops gave any indication that there was greenery up there.

Freddie concentrated on the scenery as it slipped by, trying to block out the foreboding pounding of her heart. It seemed to ask *what now* with every beat. Here she was in Fairy, with Pelrin, and no cursebreaker, no way to save her friends. Aiden was out there injured, with Oberon hunting him and Mare as his only ally. If she went home, she'd have to face her parents, who had thought they'd said their final goodbyes to her. They'd probably never let her leave the house if she showed up again.

"Fred?"

She jerked at the sound of Pelrin's voice. He didn't look at her but instead stared listlessly out at the sea. "Yeah?"

"I don't know how to keep you safe anymore. I—I keep failing, and all I want is for things to go back to how they were." He sucked in a shaky breath.

"Wha—are you alright?" The sudden outburst of emotions was more than she'd ever seen from him. Even as a bear, Pelrin hadn't seemed as vulnerable. But now it was as though he were on the verge of breaking. She placed a hand on his shoulder, and he sighed at her touch.

"I haven't slept in days, and I barely eat anymore. All I do is fight, and worry, and now I'm returning a failure again."

"You're not a failure. I'm safe, *you* saved me." If there'd been any other way, she'd gladly have spared him from this misery, but now she was responsible for it.

"And I lost the orb in the process. My uncle is going to be livid. With my mother gone, he wants me to ensure the safety of our people. I know it's my duty, but I don't think I'm ready."

"You're doing great, Pelrin. It's just new. You're just finding the leadership style that works for you."

"Tell that to my uncle. He says we don't have time for me to figure it out. And he's right. Oberon's forces grow closer to defeating us every day. I was starting to think that it was too good to be true that that dog hadn't shown up in a while. Now I realize it was because he was hunting you. It was me. I probably led him right to you."

"Don't blame yourself. You had nothing to do with it." At least that part wasn't a lie.

"You don't know that."

"My dad's been all over the news; he probably gave me away."

Pelrin just nodded. "I wish my mother were awake. She'd know how to handle this."

Freddie pressed her lips together and stared off at a thin cloud curling up in the distance. If Pelrin hadn't been hunting leads with her, he would've never gotten captured by Mab in the first place. And now he was beating himself up over her trick to get the orb.

It was almost laughable that a year ago, her biggest problem was trying to figure out a way to get Pelrin to stop barging into her room. Pulling her knees to her chest, Freddie concentrated on the horizon.

As it grew closer, she frowned. The thin cloud grew broader and darker and smelled of smoke. Pelrin turned at the scent, and his eyes went wide.

"No, no, no!" He stood and fluttered his golden wings. With a grunt of pain, he folded them again and stared out at the plume of smoke. The boat sped up, faster and faster, towards the dark smudge.

Freddie dug her fingers into the sides and squinted as wind whipped past her face. "What is that?"

He didn't respond, though she feared she knew the answer. The pungent odor grew stronger as they neared the shoreline. Shouts and screams were just audible over the sounds of the wind and sea. Freddie struggled to peer over the side.

Flames licked the sides of most of the buildings in the seaside town. A fairy zipped past them, a goblin hot on her heels. Pelrin hurled a fireball at the goblin, who crashed into the waves. The fairy gave them a curt nod and zipped off back towards the battle.

"Stay close." Pelrin took several awkward strides across the boat and wrapped Freddie in both arms, shielding her from attack. Their craft plunged onward, directly into the fray.

Colors and lights flashed around them as the various fae and their magics collided with one another. It'd be beautiful, save for the occasional spray of silver or red blood, the metallic smoky odor, and agonized shrieks in all directions.

Freddie huddled beneath Pelrin as they drew near a goblin who'd just clubbed a feathered fae back to the ground. He roared his victory, and Pelrin cursed under his breath. With a pained grunt, he gripped her tight and leapt into the air. They hovered for several minutes as the boat crashed straight into the goblin sending him plummeting down.

Pelrin let out another pained groan as they dropped several feet. He dodged a warring pair of fae and continued their descent in short bursts. It was all she could do to not let out a scream each time they dropped. No doubt Pelrin didn't need any more pressure.

Finally, they landed, and he pulled her into a mostly deserted alley. People fled in all directions as Oberon's forces seemed to be trying to cause as much havoc as possible. They weren't attacking fighters as one might expect, but anything and everyone; smashing wagons and windows as they carved a path of destruction throughout the city.

"This must've been part of Oberon's plan. He used his dog to lure me from the city so he could launch a surprise attack. My people are dying, and it's all my fault."

"No, Pelrin, it's mine. You shouldn't have come to my aid; they are your priority." Guilt clawed like a feral cat up Freddie's stomach. Oberon must've anticipated Pelrin leaving somehow. Why else attack now?

A blast of heat cut their conversation short, followed by the shrieks of several goblins as they fled a fiery blast. Howls from several werewolves sounded throughout the city.

"Stay here and out of sight. I'll come back for you." Pelrin rose from his crouch and stepped onto the main street. He disappeared down a crossroad, but a torrent of flame indicated he hadn't gone far. Freddie waited, crouched in the alley. Eventually, she pulled her knees to her chest and tried to block out the violence surrounding her.

Several minutes or maybe hours passed when she jerked and shot her head up at someone tugging at her hair. She batted at her head only to hear an "ooff" as a pixie doubled over backwards before her.

"Watch it, human!" The curly red head glared at her as she straightened.

"Ginny?" Freddie took in the tattered appearance of her old friend. The Barbie-sized pixie was Pelrin's favorite messenger, and not completely useless in a fight. Something fragile in Freddie's chest trembled as she struggled to find other words to greet her, but none came.

"His Highness sent me to get you. He's in the town square assessing the damages."

Sounds of the battle had faded, but now sobs and moans hung in the air. Freddie moved her stiff limbs and got slowly to her feet before hurrying after the tiny creature. They moved past injured people lying against debris and buildings. Some were being tended to by equally ragged-looking fae. She pulled out her phone and panned the camera over the scene. Those in the Human Realm needed to see the horror the fae were escaping from.

Several soldiers in red uniforms fanned out along the perimeter of the town square. They moved aside to let them pass. Pelrin stood by a damaged fountain beside an older blond man Freddie took to be his uncle. She'd probably met him during her trip to Elessea back when she and Pelrin had been dating. It was hard to remember him now—she'd been so concerned with his parents.

Fury painted Pelrin's uncle's expression, but Freddie tried to find solace in Pelrin's. He looked pained as he turned, revealing a prisoner. A hag, far older than the girl she'd met in London, spat at the prince's feet.

"I'll never tell you what you wish to know, only what you *should* know," she cackled.

"And what is that?" Pelrin snarled. Freddie placed a hand on his shoulder, but he didn't relax.

"You haven't noticed? The sleepers you saved are missing. You have until dawn tomorrow to get them back."

"What?" Freddie moved closer to the young woman, and she bared her teeth. Pelrin yanked Freddie back just in time to avoid her acid blue spit.

Her eyes flicked to Freddie, and her smile went manic. "That's right, little human. His majesty sends his regards from Elessea. Meet him there by dawn, and you may get your precious friends back; don't, and your friends and all the sleepers will die."

A soldier raced up to them, panting, and Pelrin stepped forward, eyes wide. "I'm sorry Your Highness; the queen and the others. They're gone."

Freddie's heart sank as one word repeated itself over and over in her head.

Gone.

CHAPTER 29
Aiden

Pain lanced through Aiden's arm as he curled in on it. Warm sand shifted beneath him, but he took little notice of his surroundings. Every heartbeat seemed to drive a knife deeper into his arm. The cursed prince had gotten too good, and that trick with the orb...

Aiden's eyes flew wide, and he looked around. Mare sat hunched on the orange sand, tossing pebbles into the still black water. She raised an eyebrow when she met his gaze.

"So, you're conscious."

"How long did you let me lie there?" Aiden stifled a yelp as he tried to right himself, still cradling his arm.

"Not long, you've only been like that for an hour or two...maybe more." She shrugged and faced him. The orb was clutched in one of her fists, her black painted fingertips showing in stark contrast against its white surface.

"And Wyn? Where—"

"—she's with the prince. You did say he'd keep her safe, so I figured I'd better get you to safety."

"You mean you just left her?"

"It was either that or rely on the prince's kind nature to win him over and protect all three of us. But seeing as he was actively in the process of killing you, I had to make a choice." She grinned, showing off her pointed teeth.

Slumping, he stared at the tiny granules, trying to make sense of how he'd gotten there. They were supposed to come back together; the Nightmare Plains were the only safe place from Oberon. At least maybe for him, perhaps Mare was right and the prince would protect Wyn. Still, they couldn't stay down here forever, and she'd do anything to find a way to save her friends. That alone could put her in Oberon's path.

He bit his lip. If they stuck with the original plan, got the curse-breaker, and saved Wyn's friends, at least she wouldn't do anything foolish in pursuit of saving them. Then there was nothing Oberon could hold over her, and she could survive under the prince's protection.

"Hello?"

"What?" Aiden looked up to see a clearly annoyed Mare standing over him.

"What's the plan with the orb? Are we still giving it to my mom? I doubt Oberon would take it in place of the staff, but it's something."

"We're staying with the same plan."

"But she's gone, and *you* need protection."

"You said it yourself, Oberon won't spare me just because we've brought him the orb. We might as well save some innocent lives while we can."

Mare scoffed, and he gave her a pleading look, praying she cared more for him than she hated Wyn. Reaching out a hand, she hauled him to his feet. It took a few moments for him to catch his breath. His arm pulsed in agony at her touch, and he cradled it until it subsided.

"Wait." Mare held up her finger. "Mom, I know you can hear me. Why not meet us here rather than force us to trek all the way to the center of this hellscape?"

"Oh, and deny the nightmares their favorite game?" Mare's mom's voice seemed to come from all directions, but Aiden saw no one.

"Aiden is injured, and I don't have the energy to haul him out of a nightmare's mouth."

He scowled at her, but she flipped her braid over her shoulder and took a step towards the path.

"You're no fun, little hellion." The air before her rippled, and her mother stepped out of the scenery looking as what he assumed was her original form. "Did you get it?"

Mare held out the orb, and her mother squealed.

"Good job. But there's one of you missing. Am I to assume that your price has changed?"

"No," Aiden said. "We still need the cursebreaker...Please."

She gave him a pitying smile, her eyes settling on his arm. "Your little nemesis took your love again? Well, I suppose a daring rescue is one way of winning her back. And what do you get out of this, Mare dear?"

"I just want to keep him from getting killed."

"A challenge, I'm sure."

"Rather than discuss my mortality, could we plan how we're getting the cursebreaker back?"

Mare's mom scowled and snatched up the orb. Shadows fell across its pearly surface, and it darkened until it was completely black. The woman's grip tightened around the orb, and it crumbled to dust at her feet.

"With the power of half the seasonal realms, this place is hardly the prison it once was." She chuckled. "Still, let's get going since this will eventually wear off too."

"Mom, do you have a plan?" Mare reached for her mother just as the woman strode from her grip to stand between the two of them.

"I'm sure we'll figure something out." She swept a hand before her, and shadows engulfed them. Aiden gasped as pressure built up, making his chest and ears ache. Just before he feared his ears would pop, the shadows faded, and they were standing beneath a glowing streetlight. Pain shot up his wrist to his shoulder, and he doubled over, gasping. Someone gripped his shoulders, keeping him from tumbling into the pavement.

"Can't you do something about this?" Mare's voice was frantic, a stark contrast to the bored hum her mother let out.

"Did the orb bite him? Poor lamb."

The woman grabbed his arm in one fist and jerked it upward. Aiden screamed as white hot pain exploded across his vision, then turned to blackness when she dropped him to the pavement.

"Better?"

He panted, the concrete biting into his side, but only a dull ache remained in his joints. Along where the dormant flames rested, thread-like tendrils spanned out from where the prince had grabbed him. He nodded and slowly got to his feet.

"It won't fully heal, but I've taken as much of the curse within the vestiges of the orb's magic that now rest in me. So, we have even less time now. Come along." She strode down the street, not bothering to check if they were following.

A car rumbled past, and pale buildings rose up around them—their windows still lit despite the late hour. The last time he'd been here, Wyn's father and that horrible human had been discussing how they'd nearly killed her. Flames licked up along his shoulders. Perhaps he should roast Mr. Fallus alive once they secured the cursebreaker. After all, Oberon had never commanded him not to.

Mare's mom lifted her skirts as she strode towards the entrance, leaving Mare and Aiden to hurry behind her.

A black uniformed guard took a bold stance in front of a metal gate. "Sorry, ma'am, no visitors at this hour."

She waved a hand, and he collapsed into a heap.

"Is—is he alright?" Mare stared down at the man.

"What do you care?"

"I mean, I don't want us to deal with the humans coming after us because of this."

"He'll be fine. Just a little taste of the sleeping curse."

"You mean we'll need another cursebreaker to wake him?" Aiden ran a hand through his hair. Wyn would never forgive him if his actions led to the Human Realm becoming even more anti-fae.

"The sun will be sufficient."

Mare hefted the man into the guards' station and followed her mother inside the building.

Aiden had hoped it'd be empty, but several people stopped and stared as the three of them walked into the main atrium. A tall man in a suit stood open-mouthed as the phone by his ear clattered to the ground.

"Mi-might I h-help you all?" A plump middle-aged woman said as she looked up from a circular desk.

"We're here to see, curses, what was its name again? It was something crass." Mare's mom leaned against the desk and tapped a black-tipped finger to her chin.

"Dick—I—I mean Richard F—Falluss?" The woman stuttered.

"Ah, yes, that's the one. Can you help us find him?" Mare's mom gave her a wicked smile, and Mare slapped her forehead so loud that it echoed off the walls. If the situation hadn't been so dire, Aiden was half inclined to think the entire thing funny.

"So, it's true! He really is a fae. Wait until I tell my Arthur, he didn't believe me, but I was right."

"We are in a bit of a hurry, my dear."

"Right, well, I won't be sticking my nose into fae business. I have a family to look after. You'll want the last office on the third floor. And don't tell him I sent ya."

Mare's mom pushed back from the desk to glide towards the stairs. Hurriedly thanking the woman, Aiden followed after her.

The path leading to Mr. Fallus's office was sparse; all the doors in the polished, stone hall looked exactly the same. Between his and Mare's fighting gear, and her mother's medieval gown, they earned the stares of each person they passed. Though with each floor, they encountered fewer and fewer people.

"I think this is it." Aiden pointed down the long hall. Mare's mom didn't slow as she strode up to the office door and hauled it open. Inside was chaos.

People in suits ran about, talking in harsh whispers and tapping erratically on their computers. A small group of teens huddled in the corner, whispering to one another. And at the center of the chaos were two men shouting, their voices drowning out all other sounds.

"My daughter is still missing. We have to find her." Wyn's father stabbed his brown finger into Mr. Fallus's chest.

The other man batted it away. "She was meddling. You know we can't afford that kind of liability. Not when the media has turned against us."

"I did all this to make a better world for *her*!"

"Stop being so selfish. There's more than your own brat to be concerned about."

Wyn's dad swung his fist and slammed it into the side of Mr. Fallus' jaw. The other man grunted and then lunged. A dark-skinned boy, standing with the teens, whipped out his phone, and the others followed suit while the older people screamed and scrambled desperately out of the way.

Aiden caught one of the young people muttering, "At least this internship taught us what not to do."

"Can you imagine if someone recorded this? I'm sure any news outlet would pay millions." Mare's mom sighed loudly and lifted her hem as she moved out of the path of a charging office chair. Several people pulled out their phones, working to get closer to the fight, but still out of harm's way. Aiden tried to copy them, but his screen remained dark, and he was unsure of what button to press.

"You ungrateful bastard, your kind isn't much better than the fae. And to think I was willing to give you a chance. No good deed goes unpunished." Mr. Fallus flipped a desk towards Wyn's dad, who fell backwards, his legs crushed beneath it. He cried out, and Aiden moved to help, but Mare's mom caught his arm.

"My daughter was right," the man panted. "You're nothing but a bigoted *dick*." His pain-twisted face grew ashen as he leaned back on his elbows.

"He's going to die!" Aiden struggled to free himself from the woman's grasp. He doubted Wyn would want him idling while her father was in danger, no matter how angry she was at the man.

Silence washed over the room, save for the sounds of Mr. Fallus's enraged grunts as he pressed down on the table, crushing Wyn's father.

"My, my, isn't this embarrassing?" Mare's mom stepped towards him and clapped her hands together.

"He—he attacked me. I had to defend myself. Ask these people, they'll tell you." Mr. Fallus gestured at the frozen people around the room.

"I suppose. After all, we could always replay the video, or should I say, videos. And from so many angles, too, there's plenty of evidence to proclaim your innocence."

Mr. Fallus licked the sweat from his upper lip and pulled back from the desk. "I've seen what you people can do, addling minds, manipulating truths. You can erase the footage, right?"

"Do you have something to offer me in exchange?"

Aiden's chest tightened. She wouldn't truly betray them for a better offer, would she? They'd already paid. His gaze drifted back to Wyn's father, who, while frozen, was bleeding from where the desk pressed into his legs. There was so much blood. How would he tell Wyn? If he could ever get close to her again.

"I can offer you and your family protection. None of the police will go after them. Pure immunity, how's that sound?"

"Like something someone with my power doesn't need."

Mr. Fallus's lips went thin, and he looked around the office. "Money? A government job? His job?" He gestured at Wyn's father.

Mare's mom let out a soft laugh. "Do I strike you as someone who has any use for your petty mortal offerings?"

"Th—then what do you want?"

"I'm so glad you asked. Your brother gave you something that once belonged to me. I want it back."

"Oscar? He hasn't given me anything but a headache."

"Try again."

"No, you can't know about that."

"Oh, but I do. So, what's it going to be? Will you hand it over, or become even more infamous?"

"You don't understand. He'd be livid with me if I gave it up. He's really powerful in Fairy, you should know that." Mr. Fallus was sweating heavily now, his thin hair looked painted on.

"But he's so far away, while *I* am right here."

A smile tugged at the corner of Aiden's lips. Had Mare's mom planned this? It was pure genius.

"So, if I give you the cursebreaker, you'll make all this go away?"

"Why not?" She flashed a cheshire grin.

"You can't double-cross me because you're fae. You're bound to your bargains."

"Sure."

"Stay here." He turned and shuffled back into his office, then returned with a black spike. With trembling hands, he held it out to Mare's mom, and she examined it closely.

"I'm glad you didn't try and cheat. I would've known if you gave me that fake in your drawer. Can you imagine what I might do to someone who tried that?"

Mr. Fallus's sallow skin gleamed beneath the fluorescent lights, rivulets of sweat soaked into his collar and giving off a musty stench. He held up a finger and waddled back through the door and brought out a long white spike. This time, Aiden could feel the magic pulsing off it. *Foolish man.* Mr. Fallus held it out to Mare's mom and gave her a sheepish grin.

"Thank you, precious." She tossed the fake to the floor and tucked the true cursebreaker into the folds of her gown. "You know, I once knew a few men like you. Men who'd prefer if fae were nonexistent. It was simply awful, fae were actually burned at the stake. I'm sure you wouldn't do something like that, though. Come, dears."

Mr. Fallus didn't respond but worried his hands before him, shaking like a drenched ifrit.

Mare and Aiden crossed the still-frozen room to her mom.

"You." Mr. Fallus pointed at him, and Aiden glared back, flames alighting down his arms.

"Peace, sweetheart. There's no need to punish him further, after all, he doesn't know who I am."

"Wh-what do you mean? Who are you?"

Mare's mom sauntered towards the door, with Aiden and Mare on her heels. "I am just a human who's ingested so much fae magic that the humanity inside me died. But, I suppose I did retain one useful trait."

"And what's that?" Mr. Fallus eyed Aiden as they reached the door.

Mare's mom turned to face him, a cold smile on her face. "I can lie." With a wave of her hand, the room came alive again. Gasps and shouts rang out as people rushed to move the desk off the now-unconscious body of Wyn's father. "Good luck."

Darkness clouded around them, and the pressure returned. When it faded, Aiden stood beside Mare in the stone room with the hearth. He rubbed his head as the pain from their journey faded. Mare's mom held out the cursebreaker.

"Thank you." He tucked it into his jerkin and rocked back on his heel.

"Of course, happy to help those who keep me so well fed. But might I recommend you hurry with whatever you're planning?"

"Why?" Mare rounded on her mother, and Aiden shot her a perplexed look.

"Well, Oberon's plans might make your shiny new cursebreaker pretty useful in a few hours."

"Wyn." Aiden hurried towards the door, but Mare placed a hand on his.

"Let's just go. We don't have time to parse through her riddles."

"Good luck." She wiggled her fingers, and the world plunged into shadow.

CHAPTER 30
Aiden

The salty breeze of the Summer capital filled Aiden's lungs. A sharp tingle reminded him of the air just before a battle. It was too quiet, but it was to be expected with the curse. Still…

Aiden slipped behind one of the large pillars lining the front of the Elessean palace. Among them were lit sconces, but by the line of lavender at the horizon, they wouldn't need their light much longer. Of course, Mare's mom would drop them right at Oberon's doorstep with little indication of how much time they had to succeed.

He pressed his back to the stone as two trolls passed, each dragging a pair of unconscious fairies like dolls. They passed through an arch leading deeper into the interior. What did Oberon plan on doing with them? Whatever it was, it couldn't be good. Hopefully, Wyn was far away from this place, but something told him this danger would be too grave for her to resist.

When the walkway was empty, he let out a breath. Looking up and down the path, he followed the trolls.

Mare grabbed his arm. "What do you think you're doing?"

"Your mom said we only have a few hours."

"We don't even know what Oberon is planning. Barging in like this would be suicide, especially for you."

Aiden looked at his boots, silently hating her for being right.

"We need to find Tatiana, she's the only one who can fill us in."

"Wouldn't she be in Autumn?"

"Not if Oberon is cleaning up this place."

Aiden gritted his teeth and looked out at the waves reflecting the growing sunlight on their dark surface. Reaching out with his magic, he felt for Tatiana. Mare was right; she was close.

"This way," he hissed, then fell back. Two more brown fae soldiers passed each with a limp body slung over a shoulder.

"This doesn't feel right," one of the soldiers said.

"Don't tell me you're going soft on the greenies." The other let out a snort.

"No, I just mean burning these people alive. I can't see how this helps."

Aiden's jaw clenched so hard it made his headache. This had to be a trap, likely for the prince or Wyn or both. *Freezing Frosts.*

"They're practically dead."

"What if there's a cure?"

"If they all wake up, they are just going to attack us. They wouldn't hesitate to do the same if we were asleep."

"It just feels so *wrong*. Shouldn't we be better than them?"

"Now you're sounding philosophical. Just do as you're told."

The soldier ducked his head, and they passed, dragging the bodies behind them. Aiden let out a breath and stepped out from his hiding spot.

"How many others do you think are doubting Oberon's motives?" Mare stared after the soldiers.

Aiden shrugged. "Does it matter?"

"If Tati saw what her father was doing to these people. She wouldn't be ok with it."

"And she's ok with everything now?"

"Well, no. But she hasn't tried to stop her father either. Maybe if she stood up to him—"

"He'd kill her too? Oberon didn't give a fluttering flake when his wife died. Tatiana's right to stay out of it. The best you two can hope for is survival."

"And you too!"

Aiden didn't say anything. There was almost no chance he would make it out of this alive, but at least there was hope for Wyn. Threads of a plan knit together in his mind. He stepped out from behind the pillar and headed towards the courtyard.

"Wait! Where are you going?" Mare hurried after him.

"I need to find Oberon. If this is a trap for Wyn, maybe I can delay him long enough for her to escape."

"You're going to sacrifice yourself for *her*? Again?"

"In a heartbeat."

"How is she supposed to escape anyway?"

"I'm counting on the prince to be somewhat prepared."

Mare's eyes narrowed. "You are relying on the prince...are you feeling alright?"

"Do you have a better plan?"

She muttered something unintelligible under her breath, then followed him through the palace. Another set of soldiers led them to the entrance of a large courtyard. Aiden bit the inside of his cheek at the sight of soldiers dumping bodies into a pile like bales of hay.

Beyond the bodies, Oberon talked in animated whispers to one of his werewolf generals. Did he yet know of his brother's betrayal?

"Let's go find Tati. She has to be close. If we reveal ourselves now, he'll kill us both."

"You think Oberon would kill you?" Aiden looked to Mare. She'd always been so confident in her position, no doubt because of her powerful mother. But now, her expression was dark and her brows were knit together.

"I don't want to lose you, Aiden. He's already said he's willing to do away with you, and there's nothing we could do to stop it."

"What is finding Tatiana going to do other than add another witness to my execution?"

"Execution?"

They both jumped and spun around. Shadows flared in a grim aura around Mare's hands. Tatiana held up her arms, eyes wide behind her glasses. She was dressed similar to Wyn in jeans and a loose t-shirt—hers read "Moon Crystal Power". Letting out a breath, Mare's shadows faded, and the bone-chilling fear eased from his body.

"Why are you guys sneaking around?"

Mare gestured at the courtyard. "—do you not see all those bodies? What do you think is going to happen?"

Tatiana looked over Mare's shoulder and frowned. "My father said he was going to free them of the curse."

"And you think he's had a sudden change of heart?"

Tatiana pulled her lips tight, her expression darkening in contemplation. A ripple in the air made them pause and turn back towards the bodies. The prince, with Wyn at his side, appeared in the circle of soldiers. Aiden's heart lurched, and he had to grip the wall to keep himself from running towards her. She looked whole and only slightly more rumpled than the last time he'd seen her.

Tatiana's eyes narrowed in at the couple and she crossed her arms over her chest. "What are *they* doing here?"

"She's not what you think." Aiden reached a hand out, blocking Tatiana's path from Wyn.

She frowned down at his arm then looked to Mare. "I hate this. She killed my mother. Why do we have to help her?"

"Would you rather let all those people die?" Mare scowled and Tatiana shrank back.

"Sorry. It's still hard. Some part of me always wanted to believe my parents were just doing what's best."

Mare cupped her cheek and brushed away a tear. "I get it. My mom's no maiden either."

Aiden's chest tightened at the tenderness between them. What he wouldn't give to have such a moment with Wyn, one last time.

A stomping of boots made them look up. Four soldiers carrying a richly dressed gold fae on a stretcher passed. Aiden's lip curled as he recognized the Summer queen's perfect beauty. Honey-colored hair curled around a petite face with delicate features.

When they reached the courtyard, the prince ran to her, leaving Wyn alone with Oberon. Aiden clenched his fists. How could he be so foolish?

"What do you want?" The prince shouted. Oberon crossed slowly towards him, while Wyn inched closer to the bodies.

"Surrender all your forces to me, here, and I will wake them. You will all be my subjects and we'll live in peace with no more of the green fae lording over the brown. Oberon held out his hands, and the soldiers around him cheered.

"You're lying!" Wyn abandoned the pile and marched towards Oberon. Aiden lurched forward, but strong arms grasped around him. He looked back at Mare, who'd let go of Tatiana and was now holding him fast.

"Don't you dare," she snarled.

Oberon laughed down at her.

"He can't, he's fae." the prince said. He flexed his fingers and took a step towards Oberon.

"No." Wyn stood between the two of them, and Aiden struggled again.

"Listen to your prince, girl. Everyone knows fairies can't lie." Oberon shoved Wyn aside, sending her sprawling on the ground. Throwing all of his weight forward, Aiden broke free, but before he could run to Wyn, Tatiana rushed past.

"She's right, he *is* lying." Tatiana stepped into the courtyard, and the laughter of the soldiers died down. "My father is not a fairy. He's lied to me, and he's probably lied to you all."

"Darling, what are you doing?" Oberon's words were stilted, his face hard as he turned his fierce stare to his daughter.

"You lied to me about how you and Mother treated my friends. You lied about being a green fae, I have no magic, none, and I would if you were a fairy. And you're lying now about waking these people."

"He can't break the curse." Wyn pushed herself to her feet, her fists clenched at her side. "He doesn't have the cursebreaker." The prince drew back from Oberon, whose face was now twisted into a beast-like scowl.

"It's just words. Where is your proof?" Oberon's chest heaved as Aiden moved closer with Mare at his heels.

Wyn launched herself at Oberon, and he cried out and threw her to the ground. She grunted, her face contorted in pain. Aiden raced out into the courtyard but froze as the man turned to look back at his soldiers, a red streak of blood trickling down his cheek.

"It's red," the prince said. "How is that possible?"

Oberon growled, and the air around them grew warmer. Aiden sensed the familiar tingles of his magic brushing past him and pooling towards Oberon. Chest rising and falling at an unnatural rate, Oberon dropped to all fours amidst the cries of his soldiers. He glowed as though someone had lit a fire within him, and Aiden watched as his body stretched and thrashed, growing larger and larger with each movement. The magic around him shimmered when he'd grown to roughly the same size and shape as a large boulder. And for a moment, everything was deathly quiet.

Bat-like wings snapped open from either side of the former fae king, and a deformed head resembling a cross between a goat and a lizard shot up and let loose a ground-shaking roar. The soldiers screamed and ran away from the beast.

Mare nudged Aiden hard in the chest. "Now, wake them now. It'll give them their best chance."

He blinked several times, then reached into his jerkin and snapped the cursebreaker. The pulse from so much magic releasing knocked everyone back to the ground, including the beast that had been Oberon. Aiden lay on his stomach watching as the fairy queen began to stir. Others in the pile of bodies moved slow at first, then faster as they scrambled out from under one another.

"Mother!" The prince was the first back on his feet as he rushed to the queen's side. He helped her to sit, and she brushed a hand against his cheek. Around them, others were getting back to their feet and stumbling over to one another. Aiden got back up and started back towards Wyn when the queen's scream shattered the air, and the Oberon beast let out another roar.

Both gold fae leapt into the air as Wyn and Tatiana raced to opposite sides of the courtyard. A blast of light hit the creature, and Aiden shielded his eyes. He needed to find Wyn. Somehow, he had to get her to safety.

"I have to go find Tatiana," Mare said at the same time he confessed his own plan. They held each other's gaze for one long moment, then nodded just as molten goo shot from Oberon's mouth.

Mare ran off towards Tatiana, but Wyn was no longer with her. He finally spotted her running towards another human with long black hair. They embraced as two others, a were and a vampire drew near. He ran to intercept them—they'd come too far to be cut down by red fae now.

"Stay back." Aiden wended into the path facing the two fae. Flames alight along his arms, he raised his hands ready to fight. The vampire took a step forward, then doubled over and cried out. Dawn was just barely turning the sky from indigo to a pale lavender.

"Jefferson!" The girl who'd been hugging Wyn pushed past him to wrap her arms around the vampire. "You need to get out of here."

"Jefferson?" Aiden now took in the familiar appearance and the flames along his arms burned brighter. This was the creature responsible for Dek's death.

"We don't have time to fight. Aiden, we need to get Jefferson out of the sun." Wyn placed a hand on his arm. He looked from her to the vampire.

"You know this—"

A crash sounded from overhead as flames sent the beast hurtling into one side of the palace. Its tail whipped around and flung the prince into a wall as it fell.

"Let's get inside." Wyn ushered the group towards the palace and Jefferson slumped into the shade of a pillar.

Aiden glared at him, half wishing he could shove the vampire back into the sunlight. "Do you know these, these, people?"

Wyn gave him a wincing smile. "These are my friends. Amanda, Raul, and Jefferson, you seem to know. And guys, if we make it through this, this is Aiden, he's my—person, friend."

"Person-friend?" The dark-haired girl who must've been Amanda raised a brow.

Jefferson pinched the bridge of his nose. "You're not serious."

"Welp, 'nice to meet you, Aiden'. Any ideas on how to get out of here?" Amanda asked as another boom sounded from the fight above.

The werewolf stepped towards him and held out a hand. Aiden stared at it for a moment before shoving the were out of the way as a piece of ceiling came plunging down where he'd been standing.

"Uh, thanks, man," he said, and Aiden nodded, helping him up.

"Well, the border isn't close, but maybe if we can find the basement, we can hide out there..." The vampire straightened, moving deeper into the palace as the daylight intensified.

The queen shot up a blinding barrier, making them all wince as she blocked another of the beast's attacks. Aiden thought back to the passages where the brown fae would traverse to serve the palace royals. Perhaps, if he could get Wyn and her friends in there, they could wait until the fight was over. Though, perhaps he could leave the vampire out to roast for what he'd done to Dek.

"Follow me." Aiden led the way back down the hall, ignoring Jefferson's pained grunts as the pre-dawn light licked his skin. The others were silent, with Wyn at his side. He wanted to pull her aside, ask her what a person-friend was, kiss her...but there wasn't time. Glancing down, he met her gaze, a weak smile passing between them. Maybe, somehow, later...

They reached a dining chamber, and Aiden shut the door behind them and wrenched back a curtain in the wall, revealing the barely visible outline of a door. Pushing it open, he shot several fairy lights down a flight of stairs that led to a narrow passage.

"Go, you should be safe in there." He pointed, and her friends hurried into the darkness.

Wyn stood at the top of the stairs and held out a hand. "You're coming with us."

"I can't. I have to make sure Mare is alright."

"Please, Aiden, just put yourself first, for once."

He bowed his head. "You know my life is not my own."

"I—"

A scream sounded from the direction of the courtyard.

"Go! I'll find you later." Aiden wended, praying Wyn would stay where he left her. He arrived back in the courtyard just in time to see the queen recoil a ribbon of light and the right arm of the beast on the ground. One of its claws had speared a fairy who now lay still, covered in silver blood.

It thrashed in the air, letting out spouts of its molten goo. Aiden cast a barrier around himself as he crossed the now abandoned open space. Bodies still littered the courtyard, but these would never wake—casualties of the royals' battle with Oberon. Green, red, and brown fae alike lay scattered in red and silver smeared heaps. The familiar stench of blood and burnt flesh choked his senses as he reached the side where Mare had been heading.

He spotted her and Tatiana huddled under a bit of fallen roof, Mare's shadowy barrier holding their make-shift shelter together. Relief shone in her expression when she saw him. Another scream rang out, and Aiden turned in time to see a jet of goo hitting the queen and sending her body tumbling to the ground—the prince darting after her.

Mare's barrier dissolved and she pulled Tatiana out to meet Aiden. "Where do we go? Is there anywhere safe?"

"There are tunnels under the palace. I can—" but he stopped as the creature dove towards them. Instinctively, Aiden wended to the other side of the courtyard, expecting them to follow. He looked back at the spot where he'd been.

"No!" Mare cried out. The creature's remaining foreclaw was wrapped around Tatiana, pulling her into the air.

Mare jumped, and her fingers just brushed Tatiana's leg as the girl was pulled away, and the beast flew further and further away from the palace. The courtyard fell silent as Oberon's form disappeared into the cloudless sky.

An agonized cry pierced the quiet. The prince knelt over his mother's body but slowly rose to his feet and rounded on him. Of all the times Aiden had faced him in battle, never had he seen the fairy's face so contorted in hatred. Aiden wended to Mare's side and tugged at her arm. Whatever came, he would not leave her behind—they needed to go.

The prince let out an intense jet of flame. Aiden winced as the heat just barely kissed him, but it was too late. The world faded, and he and Mare left the prince alone with his grief.

CHAPTER 31
Freddie

It was too dark to be so hot. Sweat clung to the back of Freddie's neck, and the smell of it, combined with Raul's and Amanda's, made the small passage almost unbearable. Still, the four of them waited in silence. Aiden *would* come back for them unless he couldn't.

Freddie's heart clenched, and she tried to push the dreadful thought from her mind. The thunderous sounds from the battle had long since died down, and they were still here. How long were they supposed to wait? The anxiety, which had started as a mere itch at the back of her mind, had grown into a full-blown burn. She had to get out.

"I'm going up." She moved to leave, but Jefferson's icy hand clamped around her arm.

"You can't. What if *he* won?" The vampire's wide eyes glowed red in the reflection from Aiden's fairy lights. At least wherever he was, he was still alive if his magic was lasting.

"If Oberon won, don't you think we'd hear him crashing about the palace? We can't just stay down here." Her reasoning came out more confident than she felt. There were many reasons Oberon might not be crashing around; losing to Pelrin was merely one of them.

"Didn't Aiden say he was coming back?"

"He can't if Pelrin won."

"Fine. But you can't go alone."

"Jefferson, no." Amanda grasped hold of her boyfriend's arm, and his expression softened when he turned to her.

"I know. If it's still daylight, I'll burn. Raul, can you—"

"I've barely been uncursed for an hour, and I'm already getting dragged into a life-ending adventure," Raul grumbled and shuffled forward.

"In fairness, it's probably been over an hour," Freddie said.

"Who knows down here?" He threw up his hands and marched up the stairs. Freddie followed behind him and stopped when he paused at the door. "It's quiet. Let's go."

They eased the door open and stepped into the empty dining room. Freddie looked out the large window facing the ocean. Sunlight streamed through, and by its rough position, it was sometime in the late afternoon. Tip-toeing through the bright space, they paused at the next door.

"I hear people, but no fighting." Raul leaned against the door.

"Can you tell what kinds of people?"

He gave her an exasperated look. "The kind that have voices and footsteps."

"Sorry, that was dumb. Let's risk it."

The hall was deserted, but the faint sounds of talking trickled from the direction of the courtyard. Her muscles tensed as she forced herself towards the noise. A fairy flitted past them in the hall, seemingly intent on getting to wherever she was headed. The tension in Freddie's shoulders eased. No fairy would be flying so unbothered if Oberon had won. Of course, she could be misinterpreting the green fae's intent.

As they neared the courtyard, the more people they passed, all of them were green fae. A flurry of commotion greeted them by the time they reached it. People darted about removing bodies, having hurried communications with one another, and at the center, Pelrin stood with his uncle by his side. The two of them were speaking intently with one another, though even from her distance, Freddie could still make out the pain marring his handsome features.

She drew close to Raul as they moved through the fae, occasionally garnering a disapproving glance, but little else. It reminded her of the first time she'd visited the Summer Palace—they hadn't been too welcoming of a human back then either. When they were only a few feet from Pelrin, he looked up and his expression flooded with relief. Breaking away from his uncle, he rushed to Freddie and scooped her up into his arms.

"I was so worried, I thought I might have lost you too." Damp tears tingled against her neck as she breathed in Pelrin's tropical breeze scent. She'd feared for her friend, but the familiar trepidation held her back from running her hands against the back of his head and soothing him. If she led him on, gave him the wrong idea now, when he was on the brink of reclaiming his realm, that distraction could cost him everything.

"We're alright, Pel. Raul, Amanda, Jefferson, we all made it."

He pulled back and looked up at Raul and grinned, reaching out for his friend.

"What are *they* doing here? It won't be a good look for you to be seen with a human and that which resembles our enemy." Pelrin's uncle strode between his nephew and Raul, casting the latter a look of utter disgust.

"They are my friends, Uncle."

"We'll find you new friends. Now, let's get them back where they came from before too many people notice."

"I don't need *new* friends."

"Trust me, Pelrin, you are still young. Let me guide you on the path to rule."

Anger pulsed through Freddie as she looked between the two fae. She had not gone through everything she had in the Human Realm just to face it again here. "So, you are guiding him into repeating the same cycle that landed you all in this mess in the first place?"

The older fae jerked, looking down at her as though he hadn't expected her to be capable of speech. "What did you just say to me?"

"Oberon only gained the power he did because green and gold fae permitted treating the others like dirt. If you think that doing that again is going to help anything, you're just asking for another war."

"Don't be ridiculous. I'm not going to explain myself to a child—a *human* child at that."

"She's right, and the power of the crown is *mine*. We won't go back to how things were. All fae and humans are to be treated with respect under my rule."

"Then it will be a short one. There is a hierarchy for a reason; it's the natural order."

"Is that a threat, Uncle?" A ball of flame ignited in Pelrin's hand, and his uncle took a step back. Others in the courtyard had now stopped what they were doing to stare at them as well. "If all types of fae can get along fine in the Human Realm, they will learn the same here." He spoke loudly and clearly enough so that all in the courtyard could hear. Soft mutters followed his announcement, but no one appeared unduly hostile.

His uncle merely bowed his head. "As you wish. I just hope you won't be dragged into another of these wars before this one ends. Don't expect me to aid you."

The flames vanished from Pelrin's hand, and he shook his uncle's shoulder. "Thank you, but I can look after myself. You'll see, it might take some time, but the people will learn to get along with one another. Freddie's right, it's the only way forward."

Freddie smiled up at Pelrin as his uncle stepped back for him to throw an arm around Raul.

"But my uncle was right in one thing. You all need to go home. We're not stable enough to protect you and the realm."

"That's fine with me. My mother might curse me anew, but I still want to see her," Raul said. They all laughed.

Raul and Freddie went back to find Jefferson and Amanda. When evening rolled around, the two joined them, and they returned to the courtyard to say goodbye to Pelrin. Freddie rubbed a hand against the phone in her pocket. As soon as she got home, she would call Aiden. Hopefully, he wasn't hurt, though she hadn't built up the courage to ask Pelrin.

"I'll check on you guys, but it won't be as frequent as before." He hugged Jefferson and Raul in turn while Amanda leaned her head against Freddie's shoulder.

"We'll miss you, Pel." Raul stepped back beside Amanda.

"Bye, Pelrin." Freddie gave him a final hug, and he tossed wing powder on them all, whisking them back to their homes.

Freddie blinked as she took in the dark shapes of her room. At least this time, everything was in the same place as she left it. A cold chill washed down her back as she recalled how her parents had up and moved when she'd been trapped in Winter. This time, she hadn't been gone as long.

Something moved from downstairs, and she crossed over to her door. Had her father returned home? Was her mother there, worrying? Would they ever let her leave again if she revealed herself now? She pursed her lips. With the scholarship and the internship with the Inquirer, she *might* be able to support herself through school. That independence with the promise of a career had been everything she'd wanted, but something about that life felt hollow. Regardless, it was better than being trapped with her parents. Maybe one day she'd forgive them, but that day hadn't come.

Downstairs, something moved again, and Freddie took a breath. She would have to face them eventually; it might as well be now. Then she could head back to school and figure out her next steps.

Scanning the room, she spotted her keys on her dresser. She packed everything she could. Traveling with Aiden had taught her just how little she truly needed—this time, there wouldn't be a powerful fae to back her up. Swinging the bag over her shoulder, she shoved her keys in her pocket and headed towards the door as it burst open.

"Wyn?" Her mother's silhouette stood frozen in the doorway.

"I was just leaving." She took a step forward, but her mother blocked her path and wrapped her in a tight hug.

"I thought—Don't go. You can't."

"I can. After everything, I don't even know why you'd want me here. Don't you have to worry about what the Fallus' want you to do?"

"Those people aren't our friends. Not any more."

"Did the bomb change your mind, because you should know, Dad was in on it."

"What? He—When I heard about that, I was frantic, we thought you were dead, but that wasn't them. The news said it was fae terrorists." Freddie wanted to argue, but her mom had yet to release her. "Mr. Fallus is the reason your father is in the hospital. He's too injured to make it back from Britain. I was going to see him, but I wanted to stay here in case you returned."

Freddie shook her off. She'd never wanted her father seriously injured. "What happened?"

"It's been everywhere. They repealed those acts in Britain. France has been extremely vocal about the need for change, and your father stood up to his boss when he tried to keep pushing for that horrible legislation, and Richard attacked him. He flipped a desk onto him, and they had the police and paramedics over there."

"And Mr. Fallus was arrested?"

"He was." She bit her lip, and Freddie leaned into the silence waiting for her mother to say more. After several long moments, she sighed. "They let him out, even though the video is all over social media, it was deemed an accident. There's just no justice these days."

"Not if you're not willing to fight for it," Freddie muttered. "Dad really stood up to Mr. Fallus over anti-fae legislation?"

"He did. For you, sweetie." She moved to hug Freddie again, but Freddie stepped out of her grasp.

"I—I can't be like that again with you."

"What do you mean? I've missed you."

"Mom, you and Dad nearly got me killed with your bigotry. You forced me to travel with that creep because *he* wanted me there, and you moved when I was kidnapped because that racist Dick told you to! Do you really think a recent change of heart would make me forget all of that?"

"Oh honey, I'm so sorry. Remember the Bible teaches forgiveness."

"But it doesn't tell you to forget. You've hurt me every time I've forgiven you and it's just gotten worse. Maybe I'll be able to forgive you some day, but definitely not now. I have to go." She pushed through the door and raced towards the stairs, her mother close behind her.

"Where are you going?"

"To school. It should be starting soon." Freddie charged towards the front door, but her mother grabbed hold of her. They stared at one another for a long moment—her mother's expression conflicted.

Finally, she let out a breath. "Stay here, just for a minute." She darted into the kitchen and shuffled around. Freddie seriously considered leaving, but curiosity rooted her to the spot.

"Here." Her mother handed her a large, open envelope stuffed full with papers. "It's your school information and some cash, it should help."

Freddie took the envelope slowly. "Thanks…"

"I love you, Wyn."

Nodding, Freddie turned and left.

It felt strange to drive again after so long relying on magic to travel any significant distance. But with her phone in her cup holder, and the wind blowing in through the open window, the familiar feeling of the girl she'd been at New Wall crept back into her skin.

When the house was out of sight, she tried dialing Aiden. It rang for a long time, but no one answered. She let out a shaky breath. He was fine, maybe he didn't know how to answer, or he was sleeping. If Pelrin or Oberon had captured him, she'd surely know about it, right?

By the time she pulled into her school parking lot, her body buzzed with nerves. So many 'what-ifs' bombarded her mind, suffocating her senses. She made her way to the admin building to pick up her key. It was annoyingly painful to go through the motions of normalcy when her world felt anything but.

Opening the room, she looked between a neatly made-up side and her own sparse walls and naked bed—at least whoever her roommate was, wasn't here. Collapsing onto her bed, Freddie checked for missed calls and messages. The only message was from her mom, telling her that she'd keep the credit card active so long as she was responsible with the spending.

After a much-needed nap, she wandered the upper school halls, trying to identify the rooms for her classes. She'd start school in two days, but it hardly felt real. There were few people on campus, but the majority were crowded around the dorms. No longer did some ominous mystery or magical threat loom over the campus, but it was far too peaceful to be her life.

She walked past a room where it sounded as though someone was making a lot of copies of something and towards an open door at the end of the hall. Freddie turned, she tried the handle and found it was unlocked. When she pushed it open, she nearly yelped, spotting two people staring back at her.

The office was somewhat familiar. The giant tree-like structure and the unending bookshelves would be out of place anywhere but Dr. Rhydel's office.

"Sorry, professor." Freddie ducked her head and made to turn.

"Freddie Jones. I'd hoped I would be seeing you this year, though with your adventures, nothing is guaranteed." The petite woman's expression broke into a smile. "You were in London last. Working with the deportees?"

"How did you know?"

She gestured at the girl beside her, and Freddie narrowed her eyes. *Mallory.*

"Miss Shepherd has quite the exposé on this Richard Fallus, but as I mentioned, it needs more facts and less speculation."

Mallory scowled. "There's only so much I can find."

"Why not take a page out of Miss Jones's book and do a little investigative journalism?"

Freddie smirked at the bone-white rage just barely concealed in Mallory's expression.

"The people who posted he was a fae got sued for defamation. It seems that it might not have been completely accurate." The professor raised an eyebrow.

"You're joking." Freddie laughed, the sound feeling strange as it left her throat—how long had it been?

"You just want me to take a leftist approach to journalism like all the other sellouts." Mallory sniffed and shot Freddie a dark look.

Professor Rhydel sighed. "I find the truth is neither left nor right politically, but somewhere in the middle. Despite your biases, and those of those you'll eventually work for, are going to impact it. In this class, we'll be focusing on staying as centrist as possible regardless of political leanings." She looked from Mallory to Freddie with her sharp green eyes.

Freddie's jaw tightened, and she thought back to the protesters with their false wings. What would they do to keep the conflict going so they could make more profit? Still, it wasn't as terrible as actively kidnapping people and trying to cart them over the border. "I think I know what you mean. Not everyone has entirely altruistic motives, and I've seen firsthand how devastating that can be."

Mallory scoffed. "At least people don't die when I cover stories."

Anger flared in Freddie's chest, but the professor held up a hand. "There's no need for anyone to risk their lives in my class."

Freddie bit her lip. Could she really go back to a life as a regular student? An entire year of sitting in class and doing assignments while Pelrin was hunting Oberon, people in Fairy were displaced, and others like Mr. Fallus still thrived, felt wrong.

There had to be more she could do. "Professor, is it possible for me to do a practicum this year?"

"What are you thinking?"

"This isn't over. Just because Dick Fallus got booted from the UK doesn't mean there aren't others like him who won't try to do the same. Fae lives here, and in Fairy are still at risk, and no one is telling their stories."

"That's because no one cares." Mallory crossed her arms.

"Or because no one has the guts to cross the border and actually show what's going on over there."

"Ms. Jones, it's not that there aren't brave journalists, but human technology only goes so far. Any person risking their lives in Fairy would have to do it without cameras or anything that might keep an audience engaged." Professor Rhydel gave her a soft smile.

Her heart pounded. Maybe this was part of her wish, too. After all, what good was an interrealm phone if she couldn't use it to bring understanding between humans and fae? "What if I could go to Fairy and get footage?"

"Do you have some ability you haven't told us about?" Professor Rhydel peered down her nose, and Freddie shifted. Telling her professor about the phone might not have been so bad if not for Mallory's hungry gaze fixed on her.

"I—I have an idea of how to cover these stories. If it works, then I pass; if it doesn't, I'll come back. Would that be alright?"

"I'm sorry, Ms. Jones. I can't imagine your parents would even sign off on something like this."

"Please, I've been to Fairy several times over the past year and have come back unscathed. I *know* how to handle myself."

Mallory scoffed. "Unscathed might be an exaggeration."

The professor shook her head. "As fascinating as that is, I'm afraid I can't let you go unaccompanied to Fairy. It's far too dangerous, and you're still a minor."

Freddie opened her mouth, then shut it again. Her parents would, of course, be against it. Even with her mom's guilt-driven indulgences, she would never get permission, unless... "What's today's date?"

"September third. Don't they have calendars in Fairy?" Mallory smiled as though she was a cat gifted cream.

"Perhaps you can give me one for my birthday because I'm officially eighteen, so I'm no longer a minor. That means I can go, right?"

Professor Rydell sighed. "I can't officially sanction it, but I won't tell you what methods to use to investigate for your practicum."

Freddie's heart lifted, but Mallory scowled. "So, she gets to lounge around Fairy and submit one story, while I have to go to class, submit multiple assignments, *and* work on mine?"

"You do realize that Fairy is an active warzone, Mal?"

The professor held up a hand. "Please, Ms. Jones, don't make me reconsider."

"Thank you, thank you!" Freddie grinned, her mind racing through all the angles she would take. She just needed to make a plan, then she could drive across the border before the next day. With a wave to Professor Rhydel, she started to the door, and Mallory followed after.

The closer she drew to her dorm, the stranger it seemed that Mallory was still following. It didn't seem like she had anything to say to her, but perhaps they were in the same building again. When Mallory stopped a few feet behind her as Freddie made to open the door, she turned.

"Can I help you with something, Murphy?"

A muscle twitched in Mallory's jaw. "You can move out of the way so I can get into my room."

"Your room?" Freddie closed her eyes. Would God really be that cruel?

"Yes, my—don't tell me."

"At least I'll be in Fairy most of the time," Freddie said and opened the door. She threw her bag on the empty mattress and sat down.

Mallory, still scowling, stomped over to her desk. "What exactly are you looking for in Fairy?"

Pulling her lips tight, Freddie withdrew a fresh notebook and pen from her bag. Where would she start? "I suppose I can try and do some interviews with soldiers and refugees. And since Summer is actively searching for Oberon, it might be interesting to cover that."

"You're going to get pictures of Oberon? How?"

The phone in her back pocket pressed against her, lending its satisfactory comfort. "Shouldn't you be focused on your story? How are you planning on investigating Mr. Fallus?"

Mallory opened and closed her mouth several times as though grasping for a thought floating in the air like a fish searching for food. "I'm going to... I'm going to look into that changeling story. It must've been on the news. Maybe I can even talk to Oscar Fallus. There has to be someone who knows about what happened."

"That's not a bad starting point, actually. You know, his actual brother is in Fairy, maybe you should pop over." Freddie gave her a sarcastic smile, but Mallory looked thoughtful.

"Do you know him, or who took him? If he's still alive, someone must have raised him."

She opened her mouth and closed it again. Mallory was right; someone had to have created that evil within Oberon. But who? And who would want him in the first place?

"I—" Freddie started, but a knock at the door made them both freeze. It sounded again, and Mallory crossed the room to crack it open.

"I'm looking for Wyn?" There was uncertainty in the familiar voice and Freddie froze. Emotions warred in her chest, joy and fear all paralyzing her vocal cords.

"Oh, it's you again." Mallory's lips curled into a sneer as she cocked her head at the door. "There's a fae here to see you."

Her roommate's words seemed to break the spell holding her. Freddie stumbled off the bed and scrambled to her feet as she pushed Mallory out of the doorway to stare up at their visitor.

"Hi, Aiden."

CHAPTER 32
Freddie

Freddie half-smiled at Aiden and found herself floundering on the edge of a very dangerous feeling. Nothing good could come of falling completely for him. Everything that could be was impossible, and yet here he was, at her door yet again, and she didn't want him to go.

"Why is he here? Didn't you guys get shipped off with the other fr—fae?" Mallory's voice snapped Freddie back to the present.

"I left." Aiden tore his gaze from Freddie to glare at Mallory.

She drew back. "I don't feel safe having him in our room." Her voice was quiet with a soft tremor to it.

Freddie sighed. There was no use digging more into her story. Mallory could figure out Mr. Fallus's past on her own; Freddie had her own stories to cover. She might as well leave now. "Do you want to come to my car? I was going there anyway." Her fingers twitched to reach for his hand, but she stayed them. *Get a grip.*

She paused just before the door. "Mallory, what's your number in case I need to send you some info?"

"Phones don't work over there. You should know—"

"—just tell me." Freddie shot her an exasperated look and pulled out the enchanted phone. Mallory gave her the digits, and she saved them into her contacts, texting her a simple period so that she had hers as well.

"I'd say good luck, but something tells me *I'll* be doing the heavy lifting on this one." Mallory gave her a smug smile, and Freddie resisted the urge to fire back and instead headed out of the room.

Aiden followed her, so close she could smell his fresh rain scent. The silence between them was loud, filled with pounding heartbeats and short breaths. By the time they made it to her car, Freddie's face was burning, so hot that she was sure he couldn't help but notice.

"Might I ask where we—you are going?" Aiden flexed his fingers at his side, and she noticed a patch on his wrist where several thread-like lines spread up and down his arm.

She reached for his wrist, and he moved so she might take it. "I'm going back to Fairy."

"It's dangerous." He stared down at their hands, both their gazes transfixed on the strange scar.

"Does it hurt?"

"Not as much as it did. But you know I can't protect you there, and the prince..."

She stepped closer, their bodies almost touching. "He won't be happy, but he can't keep wasting wing powder on sending me home. I have a story to cover, and I won't let anyone stop me."

He let out a shaky breath. "I'll try my best."

"You shouldn't risk yourself for me." She shook her head, but she didn't want to send him away. It was selfish to want to drag him along, dangerous even. But her heart seemed to forget logic. Her head tilted up, and she couldn't tear her eyes away from his lips.

He seemed to ask her an unspoken question, and she nodded. The memory of his last kiss blazed throughout her body. Leaning in, the scent of rain and peonies washed over her. She breathed him in, and he cupped her face, pulling her closer until their lips met and she melted into him.

The first time, she'd been barely lucid, fumbling about his lips trying to find what felt right. This time, it'd been everything she'd longed for. The passionate familiarity in the taste of him sent chills through her chest, and she clung ever tighter to him.

When they finally broke apart, there was a gentle ache in her lips that reflected the one in her heart. What were they doing? A future was impossible. Aiden searched her face, and Freddie pushed aside the encroaching dark thoughts. What *was* possible was now. They were together now and had an hour-long car ride to just be.

"S—so should we get in?" She fumbled with her keys, and he rounded to the other side.

They sat side by side for a long moment. He broke the silence first with trembling words. "I missed you."

"I missed you, too. When you didn't return I—I worried."

"I'm fine. Mare's fine. I just couldn't return without risking—and I knew you'd be safe...with him." He bowed his head, flexing his fingers on his lip.

She reached for his hand, her own curling into it. "I still don't want him."

"You want the impossible." His laugh was devoid of humor, seemingly on the verge of sadness.

"I know. But it's what I want. You, safe, and maybe here. If—if you want." She started the car, anything to not look at him. It wasn't fair to ask him to leave everything he knew for her.

"You would host me? I'd be a burden, I know nothing of the Human Realm, but I would learn."

Freddie pulled out of the parking lot and headed to the road. "I think you'd be fine. We'd figure things out together."

He smiled. "As much as I hate resting hopes on the prince. Perhaps, if he kills Oberon, that future might come to be. At least until he finds us together."

"At least it's hope."

She squeezed his hand and savored the feel of his presence. It took a while until they managed to start up a conversation again. Aiden told her about how they stole back the cursebreaker. She laughed out loud when he told her how Mare's mom scared the crap out of Mr. Fallus, but sobered when he described what happened to her father. She shouldn't care, but deep down, she did. Maybe he, like her mother, would have a change of heart, and she could forgive him with time. Things would never be like they were, but maybe they could find a way to make a familial relationship work.

They continued chatting about their imagined life in the Human Realm; the things they'd do to get by, and the places they'd travel to. But the closer they drew to the border, the harder it was to push away the impossibility of their happiness. Whether it was Oberon or Pelrin, neither would let them live in peace.

Warning signs flashed from the sides of the road as they drew near. Freddie ignored them. If she were taking her car, she'd need to go through an official checkpoint. The hard part wouldn't be going into Fairy but coming back.

A lone light cast a pool of light upon a dirt road blocked by a barrier no more intimidating than the ones blocking paid lots in the city. A tiny gate house stood at one side, a ways off, just outside the light from the lamp was a full-sized cabin. The windows were alight, making it appear cozy against the darkness.

Freddie pulled up to the gatehouse and cast a glance over at Aiden. He raised his brows but said nothing as a short man in an orange vest opened the door.

"You folks lost?" His words held a slight twang, but his tired face looked friendly enough.

"We'd like to cross."

"Cross? You know there's that war going on, right?" He rocked back on his heels.

"I know. I'm a journalist covering it."

"Aren't you a bit young to be a journalist?"

Freddie shrugged, hoping he didn't ask for any paperwork to prove it.

"I don't even think any of the checkpoints have had journalists cross, not ones that have made it back."

"Well, I'll be the first then." Freddie forced her lips into a smile. There had been journalists who had crossed into Fairy when the war first broke out. But the man was right, most hadn't made it back alive.

"Well, can't say I didn't warn ya. The seasons change tomorrow night. It'll be a long journey back if you don't intend to spend a year over there." He sighed and stamped her passport. She tucked the battered booklet into her bag, letting out a relieved breath.

"I know what I'm doing." Freddie tightened her grip on the steering wheel as the gate rose.

"Good luck, I'll have my eye out for your story."

"Thanks!" She pulled forward, and soon the guardhouse and the light were out of view. People actually cared about what was going on, at least some of them. Perhaps the problem was that they were so far removed with so little information that it was easy to pretend it wasn't happening. Well, that would change soon.

Her stomach turned in knots as the gauge on her gas tank grew lower, and she had to navigate around a road of increasing disrepair. Several times, she'd had to stop in order to let Aiden blast a tree out of the way or smooth the path. She unzipped her sweatshirt as the warmth of Summer washed over her. Finally, there was only a quarter tank left, and she pulled to the side of the road. It might not be enough to make it back to the border, but it would be enough to make it to the nearest gas station if Pelrin were able to magic it back to the Human Realm.

She let out a breath and got out, Aiden following her. Moonlight shimmered on the ocean just beyond an open field. She could just spy it between the spires and domes of Elessea.

She looked to Aiden, and he laced his fingers in hers. "Should we make camp here?"

"I'll be able to get you closer to the city at night. It might be dangerous to approach on your own in the daylight."

"I don't think Pelrin would—"

"—but green fae who don't know you might. I can get you into the city at least."

"After I'm there, what are you going to do?"

"Mare and I have a mission of our own we need to take care of. If you show me how to use this device, I'll be able to check in." He grinned and held up his phone. She leaned over, walking him through how to answer a call and text. His fingers flew across the screen, opening and closing apps and typing her nonsense messages. Finally, the tension eased back in, and silence weighed down on them.

"The ring will still protect you. Keep in on." He didn't look at her, his eyes fixed on the horizon.

"Will it protect you? Maybe you should take it."

He shook his head. "I wouldn't be able to live with myself if something happened and I could've prevented it. Please."

She slipped off the chain and put the ring on her finger, pocketing the gold strand just in case.

"Be safe."

He didn't respond, but they both left the car and stood side by side in the ankle-high grass. Freddie slung her bag onto one shoulder, and Aiden led her across the field, his magic tingling along her body. With each passing second, she feared the sound of a shout or some indication that they'd been found. Finally, they made it to the city.

Tiptoeing through the deserted streets, she took in the ramshackle apartments which likely belonged to the brown fae. It seemed now, everyone who'd been cursed was at the palace, as it was the only place glowing with light. At least Pelrin was taking care of them, she hoped.

The pungent aroma of the sea greeted them, and Aiden pulled her against the palace wall as a fae with glittering wings passed, holding a light that reminded her of a snowdrop.

"I can't go further," he whispered. "Will you be alright from here?"

She nodded and placed a brief kiss on his lips. Smiling, he gripped her ring hand.

"Don't forget me."

"Never."

With one last kiss, he pulled away and slipped back the way they'd come.

Freddie took a shuddering breath and stepped out before the guard. "Excuse me." He turned abruptly, his green eyes blazing. "I'm Freddie Jones, I need to speak to Pelrin—uh, Prince Pelrin."

The guard drew closer. "What business do you have with the *king*?" He took another step towards her. "You're human?"

King. *Crap.* That was right. How was Pelrin doing with an entire realm on his shoulders? "I'm a friend of his. I'm sure you heard that a few of us were hit with that curse, too."

"Weren't you all sent home?" He lowered his lamp, allowing his curious expression to come fully into view. Apparently, humans were hardly a threat to Pelrin's guards.

"I came back."

His expression hardened. "Why? And how?"

"Well, the border is still open until tomorrow, and I need to tell him something that I can't just tell anyone. Can you take me to him or not?" She pulled her passport from her bag and showed the guard her stamp.

"The general won't like it."

"Then don't tell him."

The guard looked up at the palace. "I suppose. The new king is fond of blending the ranks." He led her up the steps. A few other guards eyed them suspiciously as they passed through a grand atrium and down the familiar breezy corridors.

As they passed the courtyard, still in shambles from the battle just a few days ago, anxiety grabbed hold of Freddie's heart. What if Pelrin was unavailable, and she'd have to meet with his uncle? He'd never let her stay; he wouldn't even hear her out.

But as they approached a door at the end of the hall, the unmistakable sound of Pelrin's voice permeated the night's quiet. She flicked a glance up at the guard, but he barely acknowledged her presence. They stopped before the door, and he knocked twice. Freddie sucked in a breath, bracing herself for the argument ahead.

It opened, and Pelrin looked up from leaning over a map spread across a long table. "Yes, what—" His jaw fell open when he saw her.

"Hey, Pel."

"Fred, what are you doing here?"

"I came to see you." Freddie stepped deeper into the room, and Pelrin straightened and crossed over to her. He gripped her shoulders, his turquoise eyes roving across her face as though reading words on a page.

"Leave us." He waved at the guard, who bowed and stepped back out of the room. "How is this possible?"

"Before you try and send me away, I know it's risky that I'm here, and I don't expect you to spend all your time protecting me."

Pelrin's brow furrowed. "Go on."

"I'm covering a story. I have permission, and people know what I'm doing." Her heart pounded, knowing her permission was relative.

"And you're expecting me to be fine with this?"

"If you're not, I can find someplace else to stay."

"Where?" Pelrin waved a hand over the map. It was one of the six fairy realms, with the four seasonal ones in the center.

"I'll find somewhere." It was an empty threat. There wasn't anywhere else for her to go.

"And if I send you back?"

"I'll return and not tell you. And if Oberon's in Autumn, he'll have an easy time finding me."

He sighed and leaned back over the map. "We've lost track of him. If he's in Autumn, it's nowhere my spies have looked. Luckily, his forces have halted in exchange for peaceful surrender. They're citizens of Summer now."

"That's really *kind* of you. What prompted that?"

"Are you saying I'm not kind?"

"It's not a common way to end a war."

"Yeah, well, I'm trying something new. My uncle isn't a fan, but it's working so far. Oberon is the only loose end."

Freddie joined him and stared down at the intricate drawings of mountains, rivers, and cities. "So does that mean I can stay?"

He sighed. "For now. But if things turn violent, you go right home, understand?"

"Fine."

"No, Fred, promise me."

She rolled her eyes. "I promise."

"Great." He crossed to the door just as a pounding knock sounded from the other side. Pelrin opened it to be greeted with four guards with a prisoner chained in iron and a bag covering their head between them. Stumbling back, Pelrin scowled. "What is this?"

"We figured we'd take him to you first," one of the guards said.

"There *is* a dungeon. Did no one tell you?" Pelrin eyed the iron, and Freddie's stare widened, realizing that the soldiers were all brown fae. Had any of them once served Oberon? It seemed too soon to assign them such critical roles.

He continued to back away, and she couldn't help but wonder if he was recalling the iron crown Mab had forced on him. The prisoner was reacting to the iron as well. They were slumped over, their legs trembling. If not for the well-armored guards holding them upright, she wouldn't be surprised if they'd collapse.

"This isn't just any intruder." The guard removed the cloth from the prisoner's head, and the blood in Freddie's veins turned to ice as she let out a soft yelp.

From between the Summer guards, Aiden's golden gaze met hers.

GLOSSARY

Fairy - The land separated from the Human Realm by invisible borders accessible in specific locations in the Human Realm. Fairy is the homeland of the green, brown, and gold fae.

The Dark Fae Army (Dark Fae) - These rebel forces led by Mab and Oberon who've crowned themselves Queen and King of the brown fae. They seek to overthrow the gold fae rulers of the Seasonal Realms.

The Seasonal Realms - Summer, Winter, Autumn, and Spring are the four Seasonal Realms that make up Fairy.

The Sea Realm - The Sea Realm encompasses all of the magic of the oceans. It expands between Fairy and the Human Realm.

The Air Realm - Similar to the Sea Realm, the Air Realm encompasses everything in the sky. It is also said to be home to dragons.

The Human Realm - This is home to the humans and red fae. It borders Fairy and polices the crossing locations.

Blue Fae - The mythical and most powerful of all the fae. They are marked by their blue wings and have been known to grant the wishes of humans.

Gold Fae - Rulers of Fairy, the gold fae are incredibly powerful. They are marked by their gold wings.

Green Fae - These are magic-using natives of Fairy. Some examples include genies, fairies, and leprechauns.

Brown Fae - Non-magic-using natives of Fairy. Some examples include dwarves, goblins, and fauns.

Red Fae - These are closely related to humans but are supernatural in nature. Some examples include vampires, werewolves, and banshees.

Sundiva – A type of green fae who have immense power over fire. They have large feathered wings and are rumored to have lava instead of blood.

Drekavac – Derived from Slavic mythology, these brown fae are humanoid with disproportionally large, bald heads and are thought to be the souls of dead children.

Undine - These green fae are derived from the writings of Paracelsus. Also known as water nymphs, undines call the Sea Realm home.

Mare – Derived from Germanic folklore, this green fae is traditionally a creature who rides on people's chests and brings them nightmares.

Anansi – These rare red fae live in Fairy. They are half spider and half human and are said to feed on "flesh".

Satyr – A bipedal green fae with the torso of a human and the lower half of a goat. They also have large ram's horns and pointed ears. Satyrs can use their magic flute to compel people to follow them.

Faun – These are brown fae, similar to satyrs, but with much smaller horns and no magical abilities.

Minotaur – Inspired by Greek mythology, these brown fae have the head of a bull and the body of a human.

Garuda – Inspired by Hindu mythology these brown fae are native to the Air Realm and have a mix of human and eagle features.

Naga – Inspired by Hindu mythology, these brown fae have the tale of a snake and the torso and head of a human.

Marid – Inspired by Islamic mythology, these green fae are humanoid with blue skin and power over water.

Anubis – Inspired by the Egyptian god, these rare red fae have the heads of jackals and the bodies of humans. They give off an energy preventing people from lying in their presence.

Wili- Inspired by Russian folklore, these red fae are veiled, graceful women. They are spirits with a reputation for dragging philandering men to watery graves.

Ifrits - Inspired by Islamic folklore, these green fae have power over fire, though often not as powerful as sundivas.

Thank You

Ifyou enjoyed this story, please leave a review on Goodreads or your favorite retailer!

About Ann Dayleview

Hey all! Thank you so much for reading the third book in the Tales of Fairy series, A Tale of Storms. I spent two years crafting this story as I navigated immigration challenges in my personal life and welcomed a new member of my family!

A little bit about me. In addition to being a fantasy author, I'm a mom, a baker, and someone in desperate need of a nap. Based in the Philadelphia area, when I have a rare second of free time, I love to listen to my favorite audiobooks or even delve into a chunky romantasy novel. I especially love finding a new favorite read by a little-known indie author.

I am a huge advocate of diversity in all forms. It's something I cover in many of my TikTok videos where I talk about how to incorporate diversity in fantasy that goes beyond just skin color. Follow along my journey as I explore fantasy writing by signing up for my newsletter or following me on social media.

Newsletter:

TikTok: @anndayleview2

Instagram: @anndayleview

Twitter: @anndayleview

If you loved A Tale of Storms, stay tuned to my social media as the final installment will be launching soon.